No PEACE
with the
DAWN

A NOVEL OF THE GREAT WAR

Lynn - Thanks so much
for reading our book - we
hope you enjoy it.

All Best,

PEACE

No

with the

DAWN

A NOVEL OF THE GREAT WAR

E.B. WHEELER *and*
JEFFERY BATEMAN

BONNEVILLE BOOKS

An Imprint of Cedar Fort, Inc.
Springville, Utah

ISBN 13: 978-1-4621-1900-4

Published by Bonneville Books, an imprint of Cedar Fort, Inc., 2373 W. 700 S., Springville, UT 84663
Distributed by Cedar Fort, Inc., www.cedarfort.com

LIBRARY OF CONGRESS CATALOGING-IN-PUBLICATION DATA

Names: Wheeler, E. B., 1978- author. | Bateman, Jeffery S., author.
Title: No peace with the dawn : a novel of the Great War / E.B. Wheeler and Jeffrey Bateman.
Description: Springville, Utah : Bonneville Books, an imprint of Cedar Fort, Inc., [2016] | Includes bibliographical references and index.
Identifiers: LCCN 2016029742 (print) | LCCN 2016037445 (ebook) | ISBN 9781462119004 (perfect bound : alk. paper) | ISBN 9781462126828 (epub, pdf, mobi)
Subjects: LCSH: World War, 1914-1918--Fiction. | GSAFD: Historical fiction. | War stories. | Love stories.
Classification: LCC PS3623.H42955 N6 2016 (print) | LCC PS3623.H42955 (ebook) | DDC 813/.6--dc23
LC record available at https://lccn.loc.gov/2016029742

Cover design by Michelle May Ledezma
Cover design © 2016 by Cedar Fort, Inc.
Edited and typeset by Jessica Romrell

Printed in the United States of America

10 9 8 7 6 5 4 3 2 1

Printed on acid-free paper

To the thousands of young Americans who willingly "did their bit," turning the tide in the Great War to achieve peace in Europe. It is our sincere hope that this work brings their story to life in some small way. They deserve to be remembered.

I

Students are invited to a one-night-only performance by the Gwent Royal Welsh Singers, six o'clock at the Student Chapel, sponsored by the M.I.A. In addition to a rousing selection of contemporary tunes, classics, and Welsh folk songs, the singers, survivors of the sinking of the RMS Lusitania, *will tell of their harrowing adventure on the high seas, a story of tragedy, treachery, sadness, and hope. Not to be missed!*

—*The A.C. Student Life*

Reed Lewis paced along the ridge of the steep roof of his fraternity house like a tightrope walker. He held his Latin book out in one hand.

"Cum vincunt, tum pācem . . ." He stopped. "Gosh darn it." He flipped the book open, squinting in the fading sunlight. The wind ruffled his short blond hair and snatched the pages from his fingers. He shivered at the chill and turned back to his page. "Spērant. 'While they are winning, they are hoping for peace.' Huh. Where's the sense in that?"

He repeated the Latin phrase several times before his gaze wandered to the valley stretching in front of him. The Bear River glinted in the dusk light as it meandered through farmland toward the Wellsville Mountains. Reed visualized some of the yearling horses he'd seen in the canyon back home last summer and how much fun it would be breaking them come spring. The adventure was all out there, but his chance to make his family proud was here in Logan at the Utah Agricultural College.

Bert Lyman poked his head out the attic window behind Reed. He had to turn to fit his wide shoulders through.

"Reed! What are you doing out there?"

"Just trying to stay awake, my friend. I dozed off twice at my desk."

Bert glanced at the edge of the roof. "If you trip, you'll roll off and break your neck."

"That's the idea—the excitement helps me focus."

Bert chuckled and shook his head. "Don't expect me to cry at your funeral. Why aren't you dressed? The M.I.A. concert starts in less than thirty minutes!"

A gust of wind shoved Reed. He staggered and caught his balance. "Can't you see I'm engaging in a rare bout of studiousness? Besides, I don't feel like being preached at."

"You looked like you were engaging yourself in a good daydream. Come on, Alonzo's gonna pick us up soon, and it'll be inspiring to hear those Royal Welsh Singers."

"Welsh Singers? Say, didn't I see their obituary in the paper?" Reed clambered through the window. "I thought they went down with the *Lusitania* after their last tour."

"They did." Bert grinned.

"Okay, you've got my attention."

Reed quickly buttoned his white shirt and tied his tie, glad for his vest and jacket to hide his less-than-enthusiastic ironing job. He ran his fingers through his blond hair in an attempt to corral it under his driving cap. Their friend and fraternity brother, Alonzo Jensen, was never late.

"Let's go!" Bert called.

Reed ran outside for the short, but cold, ride up to the main building of the Utah Agricultural College. Bert elbowed Reed, who was sitting next to him in the back seat of the open Model T, then nodded toward Alonzo. "This is one nice Ford. Where'd ya get it?"

Alonzo sighed. "You know very well my sister, Clara, fixed it up and lets me borrow it to tow you lunkheads around. How many times are you going to ask me that?"

"I reckon until it stops sounding so funny." Bert guffawed.

"Say, when do I get to meet your sister?" Reed rested his arms on the bench seat in front of him. "Bert tells me she's cute."

"Never," Alonzo said.

Bert and Reed laughed.

Alonzo parked in the grassy field behind the main building. Its square stone towers rose like a castle guarding the farmland below. A crowd of students in suits and dresses filed into the south wing, and

Reed and his fraternity brothers joined them. Inside, students packed the aisles of the two-story chapel. Reed bumped into a redheaded girl from his French class. He grinned and winked at her. She giggled and turned to whisper to her friend. Reed followed Bert and Alonzo up the stairs to the curving wooden balcony. They had to pack together to fit in one pew, but Reed was glad for it given that his hands were still icy from the ride.

Reed kept his arms tightly folded, both to ward off the chill and to keep "the message" at bay a little. He knew very well why the Mutual Improvement Association sponsored events like this. He was prepared to enjoy the music, but he could do without their attempts at an inspiring message. *More than eleven hundred innocent men, women, and children died when that German submarine sank the* Lusitania. *Let them try to explain that.*

The four members of the choir and their pianist walked out onto the raised platform at the front of the chapel. All five men wore white from head to toe. Reed closed his eyes to suppress an eye roll. But then they began singing.

The rich tonal quality of their voices, the power they generated, the depth of feeling. Reed had never heard anything like these Welshmen. They carried him away to stand on the cold Welsh coastline, the town of Newport to his back, the Irish Sea wind in his face, salt air in his lungs.

They sang traditional folk songs such as "Eileen Alannah," interspersed with modern tunes and adaptations of classics. Reed particularly liked their rendition of "Blue Danube." It was the first time he had ever heard a non-instrumental version of Strauss's famous waltz.

The group's baritone, Ben Jones, explained that the Welsh tune "Men of Harlech" was, in fact, the slow march of the Welsh Guards, just now on the Western Front of the Great War facing the Germans. He sang:

> *Men of Harlech, march to glory,*
> *Victory is hov'ring o'er ye,*
> *Bright-eyed freedom stands before ye,*
> *Hear ye not her call?*

By the end of the song Reed's throat felt tight. He glanced at Bert to see if he was reacting in some way, but Bert had his eyes locked on the Welsh singers, perfectly still except for the old pocket watch he turned over in one hand. Reed tried to look at Alonzo on the other side of Bert, but Bert's big frame blocked a discreet peek. He sat back and let the music take him where it might. The choir sang the soldier's chorus from Faust by Gounod:

> *Glo-ry and love to the men of old*
> *Their sons may copy their virtues bold*
> *Cou-rage in heart and a sword in hand*
> *Rea-dy to fight or rea-dy to die for Fa-ther-land*
> *Or rea-dy to fight or rea-dy to die for Fa-ther-land*
> *Or rea-dy to die or rea-dy to die or rea-dy to die for Fa-ther-land*

Reed wondered about this stirring song. A Frenchman wrote it about a German folk character. Did both sides find meaning in this song? Did they sing it before they went "over the top?"

Welsh Singer Risca Williams stepped up to the front to tell the story of the sinking of *RMS Lusitania* while his compatriots sang softly in the background.

"We were just off the coast of Ireland, near Queenstown, when the alarm sounded and the crew went to general quarters. Like many passengers, we ran to the rails to see what was amiss. There we saw crewmen with glasses looking out over the calm water, and we followed suit with naked eyes." Reed leaned forward as Williams continued.

"Aye, and sure enough, we saw a ripple coming at us fast. We didn't need to be told what it was. A crewman murmured, 'Jesus and Mary save us,' as he ran for a deck phone." Williams stepped closer, hands out in front, bending toward the audience.

"The torpedo took her amidships, below the waterline. There was an explosion, but it was muffled, distant. Other passengers said maybe it would be all right. But she started to list right away, and us boys, well, we grew up in a seafaring town. We knew she was doomed. We put life jackets on and tried to help others toward the lifeboats. We quickly talked it over and decided our best chance was to get clear of the ship by swimming as fast as we could—or else we'd get sucked down with

4

her when she sank." Williams mimicked the action of donning a life preserver and swimming strokes.

"Seven of us boys, strong swimmers all, jumped off the ship at the lowest point we could get to, then swam for our very lives. The ship, she went up on one end and sank straight down, so quiet that those of us still swimming never heard her go. She was just gone, as were three of our number." He hung his head in remembrance, his hands crossed at his waist.

"Now we were four, clinging to the outside of an overturned raft. We could not turn it over, and the cold, it was soon beyond endurance. Fingers that could no longer hold onto the raft, teeth chattering uncontrollably, breath coming in ragged, exhausted gasps—so cold one felt physical pain from it, an ache unceasing, sapping life away." He held himself with arms folded tight, his body stiff, as if back in the channel's frigid waters.

"We determined to sing a hymn together, one last verse with our brothers, then to slip quietly into God's embrace, together in death as we had been in life."

And the choir sang.

> *Abide with me! Fast falls the eventide:*
> *The darkness deepens; Lord, with me abide.*
> *When other helpers fail and comforts flee,*
> *Help of the helpless, oh abide with me.*

"And out of that very darkness came our salvation. The crew of a destroyer heard our song and crept toward us, calling out. We were rescued, along with a handful of others, while one thousand, one hundred and ninety five souls were not. Why us, you may ask? Why did the Lord spare us? Perhaps to bring you this message of hope, as simple as this hymn we give you as a benediction. *Nos da*, my friends: good night."

After a lengthy standing ovation, the three friends turned to leave without a word. Reed caught glimpses of Bert's and Alonzo's faces. Both were red-eyed and melancholy. So was Reed's. They waited in silence for the chapel to empty ahead of them, then slowly marched out, as if in a funeral procession.

Back in the brisk November air, Bert shook himself, looked at the other two, patted his stomach, and announced, "I think an ice cream is in order. Let's drop by the Bluebird."

"It's November, Bert! We're already cold," Alonzo complained.

"Yes, I know," Bert said, "but I think it will cure what ails us right now, don't you, Reed?"

"Indeed, my friend, especially with you buying," Reed said, managing a smile.

"Why not, boys? Let's go." Bert grabbed both men around the shoulders, propelling them toward Alonzo's car.

Sitting on stools along the Bluebird's white marble counter, all three men ate their ice cream slowly, relishing it, though they shivered from another ride in the Model T.

Bert drew his finger along a black vein in the cold marble as he spoke. "What did you think of the concert?"

Alonzo spoke first. "Well, it was—powerful. And beautiful, too. The Welsh. It's like they have been sad forever, you know? You can feel it in their music, even when they sing in their native tongue. It's in their soul."

Bert nodded. "Yes. But for me, it's the sense that they were truly with God in their greatest moment of need. When I hear the testimony of others, I always wonder at how they were tested, you know? These Christian men transcended their great moment of peril. I hope I would do the same. They are a worthy example, don't you think, Reed?"

"They were certainly brave," Reed said. "What struck me as the concert went on is that we, meaning America, sit here and do nothing while the world goes insane. We go to concerts and eat ice cream while young men like us fight and die for their freedom." He shoved his empty bowl away. "It bothers me, that's all."

"Surely you don't think that adding another combatant to a world at war would help the movement toward peace, do you?" Alonzo asked.

"I don't know," Reed said. "I try to leave all that deep thinking to you. I just know that killing nearly twelve hundred civilians is wrong under any circumstances."

"So, if it came down to it, you would be willing to fight to stop the war?" Alonzo asked.

"Yes," Bert and Reed answered together.

II

*The Psychology of War: An address from the War Department
Summer Instruction Camp*

*Understanding the mind in relation to battle is the most
important part of your instruction in the Art of War. We need
men who are loyal, who obey their officers, and above all, who
are disciplined. Discipline overcomes fear and confusion and
wins the day in the face of attack.*
*The morale and steadfastness of the soldier in victory and
defeat also depends upon the patriotism and spirit of the
nation. The brave mothers of this country must raise a nation
of men willing to do their duty, and not a nation of cowards.
I am not advocating militarism, but a spirit of self-reliance
and preparedness that will preserve our peace and ensure victory when war is thrust upon us. If we are not prepared, we
will pay a terrible cost in suffering, humiliation, blood, and
treasure.*

—The Logan Republican

The Western Front. Reed traced his finger over the map on the wall
of the library, touching the cold tacks stuck across Belgium and
France like a line of stitches on a wound that never healed. Captain
Santschi, the professor of military science, updated it every day.

"We're going to that camp, aren't we?" Bert nodded toward the
Preparedness Movement poster next to the map. It showed a U.S.
soldier, rifle at the ready, captioned, "Are you trained to defend your
country?"

Reed knew he had tipped Bert off, gazing at the poster too long, but
he was drawn to it. The soldier wore the same uniform they did for the

college's mandatory drills, but he was actually doing something about the war. He was part of the action, not just playing soldier at the A.C.

"Just tell me if we're going, will you?" Bert said. "I have a feeling it's something we ought to do, but we have to raise the money. Rail fare, ten dollars for uniforms, seventeen dollars and fifty cents for food."

"Captain Santschi said we can wear our drill uniforms issued here for camp, plus the college will pay train fare for eight students."

"Ah ha! I got you." Bert laughed. "You've already planned all this out!"

"Not all of it, my friend. We both have to explain to our fathers how we're going to miss four weeks of work on our farms this summer, while not getting paid." Reed grinned. "You tell your father first and let me know how it goes."

"You can see for yourself. He's coming into town this week. I'll blame you and let you smooth talk him."

Picturing Bert's massive, demanding father, Reed demurred. "Ah, funny coincidence, Bert, but I think I have an appointment the rest of this week!"

Bert chuckled. "How are you going to tell your father?"

"Very quickly and over the telephone. Let's go sign up first so they can't say no!"

Reed took a deep breath and lifted the fraternity house phone to ring for Gerti, the operator who managed his parents' party line switchboard. She chatted about local gossip until he urged her to send the double ring code that would cue his parents to answer the phone. He tried to keep conversations with home short. He knew for certain Gerti would be listening in, and there was no telling how many others on the party line would also be listening. As quickly as he could, he explained his plans to his father.

"You're leaving school to join the army?" His father's disappointment stabbed him through the telephone wires.

"No, Sir. I'm not enlisting. There's no commitment whatsoever. The camp, they're calling it a Preparedness Movement camp. Theodore

Roosevelt and some other men figure it's only a matter of time before the U.S. has to defend itself, no matter what President Wilson says, and right now the German army outnumbers ours twenty to one. The camp will help us be ready. It's privately funded, though. That's why me and Bert have to pay our own way."

"If you're not getting paid while you're down there, you'll have trouble saving enough for next year's tuition, won't you?" his father asked.

"Yes, Sir. I've thought about that. I'll work double shifts at the mill when I get home to pay for next year's schooling. I know education is important. I'm not giving up on it. I just want to help my country too."

His father sighed deeply. "Look, son, there's something I want you to remember. I'm grateful every day your grandfather came to this country. And the men on your mother's side of the family, the Crams, they've served this nation with honor, back to the revolution. So when you wear that uniform, even for this camp, you stand tall—and you remember where you came from. You give the Lord and your country your best every day. That's all I ask."

"I will, Sir. Every day. Love to you and Mother." Reed said, his voice shaking.

Alonzo saw Reed and Bert off at the Oregon Short Line Railroad depot downtown. Reed and Bert wore their old khaki drill uniforms, a contrast to Alonzo's crisp, pressed suit. The train's distant rumble announced its approach, and their conversation lulled into an awkward silence.

"Well, Alonzo," Reed said, "I sure hate to break up the three musketeers for a month. But I know you've got a lot going on taking care of your family and the farm. Sure wish you could come."

Alonzo looked at his shoes. "Reed, you know there's more to it than that. I can't support militarization. It will only lead to war frenzy and destroy our hopes for peace."

"I understand your concerns." Reed hoped others would as well, if it came to war. Already some people branded the peace movement as cowardice, even treachery. "But the way I see it, the rest of the world won't respect us and our hopes for peace unless we can show them that we are strong enough to defend ourselves." The train whistle blew, and people pushed past them to board the train. "I value your friendship, so I'm happy to part as good friends who disagree."

"Indeed." Alonzo smiled. "Safe travels, gentlemen."

Bert just nodded and socked Alonzo on the shoulder before he boarded.

Reed spotted another uniform on the train. "Say, Bert, isn't that Moses Cowley?"

"I think so, but I don't know him well. He's hardly ever at the fraternity house."

Reed nodded. Cowley was a "big man" on campus. He was the two-time winner of the Hendrick's Medal for best student oration, Vice President of the Associated Student Body, and business manager of the campus newspaper, *Student Life.*

"Good afternoon, Moses." Reed plopped down across from him and stretched out his legs as Bert found a seat. "Are you headed to the training camp too?"

"I am. I didn't know anyone else from the A.C. was attending."

"Just us. I'd have thought you'd want to rest this summer, though," Reed said.

"Rest? I don't see how anyone can rest when our national preparedness is so low. Hopefully by taking the steps as civilian volunteers to be ready, we'll send Congress and President Wilson the message that they need to do their part to prepare the army. Why are *you* here?"

"Us? Well, Bert here, he heard that Monterey has thousands of lovely girls just pining for the chance to dance with a soldier at an outdoor park on a nice summer's eve. As for me? I just don't think Bert can handle all that attention without my guidance and supervision," Reed said, straight-faced.

"Joke if you will, but I hope the two of you take representing the A.C. seriously," Moses huffed. "I, for one, intend on achieving the highest results possible at this training camp and becoming its top graduate."

Reed had little idea what they would be doing, and none at all regarding results they could expect to receive, but his competitive spirit stirred at the challenge. "Ah, but I already told Captain Santschi that Ol' Bert here and I would be taking top honors. Sorry, Moses."

"Yes, sorry, Moses," Bert parroted, stifling a chuckle.

Moses looked at them and raised one eyebrow. "We'll see about that soon enough."

Reed dozed off, leaning his head against the warm train window. Neither the novel in his lap nor the brown desert scenery flashing by could keep his attention. As he drifted in and out of sleep, he heard snatches of Bert's conversation with Moses.

"Why did you fellows really decide to come?" Moses asked.

"Ah, you know Reed. He's always looking for the next adventure. And I just felt like it was the right thing to do. I suppose it's our duty."

"To our nation?"

"Sure, but I was thinking more of our families and our faith. Utah's still the odd man out in this country. We can show everyone that we're as loyal as the rest of them. And we ought to be able to protect our own, if it comes down to it."

"That's true." Moses's voice grew wistful. "And I want to make my family—my father—proud."

Reed nodded to himself. Cowley might be a bit stuffy, but he wasn't a bad guy.

They arrived at the Southern Pacific Railroad Depot in Monterey, then transferred to a horse-drawn carriage for the trip to their training area. The black canvas sides of the carriage were rolled up, revealing a breathtaking view of Monterey Bay and the Pacific Coast. The endless blue ocean rolled in to crash and foam against the rocky shore. The cries of seagulls rising above the murmur of the surf reminded Reed of Utah, but the salt-scented air was much fresher than the stale, almost sulfurous odor of the Great Salt Lake.

"Have you men been to Monterey before?" Moses asked.

"Heck, no." Bert leaned out to watch the waves below. "I've never seen the ocean before, either. It's so beautiful here!"

"Nor have I," Reed said. "Fact is, my only trip out of Utah was north up into Idaho. Have you been to California, Moses?"

"Yes. I took a steamer from here to Hawaii for my mission. One of my younger brothers, Sam, is in Hawaii now, and Matthew is in New Zealand. I worry about what will happen to them if this war keeps spreading." He stared out across the ocean, then glanced down. "You see the name on this carriage? Del Monte Hotel? It's the nicest resort on the West Coast. That's where they're taking us."

"What?" Reed asked. "Why would we go to a resort?"

"We'll be training on the grounds of the hotel, not staying in it."

They pulled up outside the hotel and jumped off the wagon. The hotel was a sight to behold. It reminded Reed of the main college building at the A.C., with its nearly symmetrical layout framed by towers, but it was adorned with a veranda and Victorian lattice work.

The view reached all the way past the town of Monterey and out over the gentle curve of the bay to the ocean. Green, well-groomed grounds stretched in either direction as far as the eye could see. The parking lot was lined with an array of new cars, including a few the men had never seen before.

"What kind of car is that?" Bert asked, pointing to a sleek green convertible.

"That's a Rolls Royce," Moses said. "You can tell by the RR on the front trim and the lady with arms outstretched on the hood."

"Darned if I don't feel like a hobo standing here," Reed said.

As they gawked at the cars, a U.S. Army private marched up to them and stopped at attention. "Gentlemen, if you are here for summer camp, please follow me." With that, he performed an about face and marched off down one of the groomed paths leading into the woods. All three men followed, their feet crunching on the packed gravel trail.

They arrived at the camp, neat rows of musty smelling canvas tents lining both sides of a central pathway. They signed in, received their tent assignments, and then milled around the common area waiting to see what would happen next. As they mixed with the rich boys coming up from San Francisco, Reed and his friends stood out like scruffy mustangs at a thoroughbred show. The California boys had brand new uniforms, many of them crisp and tailored. Reed straightened his A.C. military drill uniform, which time and abuse had rendered faded and tired-looking.

"Look at those fancies," Bert said under his breath to Reed. "We're not exactly on equal footing here."

"We'll just have to show them we're up to snuff."

"Hey there, Utah boys," one of the fancies said. "Get those uniforms down at the surplus?"

Another snickered. "Well, having to pay for two or three wives, heck, who could blame them? How many do you have, Utah?" He gave Reed a challenging stare.

Reed was about to ask him what his sisters looked like, but his father's admonition stopped him cold. "Come now, boys, surely you know Utah left polygamy behind many years ago. Perhaps it's time for some new insults?"

Bert stepped up next to him, arms folded.

The arrival of the camp commandant, Captain George C. Marshall, saved the fancies from thinking of a reply. The trainers, mostly non-commissioned officers, quickly herded the men into a rough-looking formation facing Captain Marshall.

"They call him 'Dynamite,'" the fancy behind Reed whispered to his neighbor. Studying Captain Marshall's stern expression, Reed wondered what he'd gotten himself into.

"Gentlemen," Marshall began. "On behalf of the United States Army, I welcome you to this second year of military training here at the Presidio of Monterey. I know you men are all volunteers. You have come from colleges all over the western half of the country to learn military skills. You are here, in my estimation, to learn the difficult task of leading others, for presumably you plan to serve as officers should your nation call you forth. Well, by golly, men who can lead other men is exactly what I aim to make out of you during the next four weeks. Sergeants! Take charge of your platoons. Let's start with an easy ten mile road march!"

So began the nonstop grind of physical fitness training, shooting, drilling, and road marches that totaled over one hundred miles per week.

One clear morning, they marched up a steep hill carrying heavy packs. Reed and Bert admired the distant views of the ocean.

"This sure beats working on the farm," Bert said, panting a little. "The weather and the views are a lot more pleasant."

"Smells better too," Reed said with a laugh.

The fancies pushed on with grimaces, sweat dampening their faces. A few stopped, hands on their knees, gasping for breath until the sergeant prodded them back into motion.

"City boys," Moses mumbled.

Reed nodded, feeling sorry for the California men. All three farm boys had spent weeks every summer on the range and in the surrounding mountains, rounding up horses or cattle, hunting, and camping. Bert even skied up Logan Canyon every winter to check on his family's summer cabin, and Reed had made the cold, breathtaking trip with him. This training was tough, but it was the kind of tough they were used to.

"You have to admire them for not giving up," Bert said quietly. "Maybe part of the reason we're supposed to be here is so we can learn to respect each other and work together. If we do have to fight a war, we won't get very far if we're still fighting each other."

"It might not be easy to convince them," Reed said in a low tone. Utah and the rest of the Western states got along about as well as a pair of hungry mountain lions in a one-room shack.

During the second week, their crusty platoon sergeant pulled Reed, Bert, and Moses aside. "You three are now squad leaders. That means you are each responsible for twelve men through the rest of their time here. If they don't measure up, it's your fault. Get to it."

"Yes, Sergeant," all three said.

"So what do we do?" Bert asked no one in particular.

"We lead. That's what we do," Reed answered.

They took their squads through all of the field training exercises, kept them all moving during road marches, and helped others who floundered. Reed's California boys struggled on the marches and at the range, but he never said a sarcastic word to them. He wanted their respect. As much as Reed would have liked to compete with Moses, he was just too busy taking care of his squad to give it a second thought.

"We're going to do something different today and let you boys play baseball," Captain Marshall said one morning.

Reed perked up, and a lot of the other boys did the same.

Captain Marshall smiled as the sergeants handed out gas masks. "You're going to need these, though. You'll be playing with simulated battlefield gas on the diamond. We're going to keep your training hard and realistic, as close to combat conditions as possible."

Reed and Bert exchanged an uncertain glance as the sergeants showed them how to don their gas masks.

During the game, clouds of yellow-green gas drifted around the field. Reed, waiting his turn on the sidelines, could see through the gas, but the players acted lost. Men swung the bat at nothing. When some- one did manage to hit the ball, usually by sheer luck, the outfielders ran blindly around the field, crashing into each other. Bert struck out for the first time that Reed had ever seen.

Reed was appalled. "Bert, what happened out there?"

"Gee whiz," Bert said, his voice muffled. "The centerpiece of this mask, it creates a blind spot. The ball just disappears! I can't imagine trying to fight in one of these things."

Bert went off to cheer up the men in his squad, who slouched on the ground in dejection.

When Reed's turn came, he understood what Bert meant. He couldn't stop tilting his head this way and that, trying to get a clear view. When the other team smacked the ball right at him, he missed the catch. He tore his mask off in frustration and scrambled after the ball. His teammates wouldn't be able to see to catch it, so he ran with it, reaching first base before the disoriented player to score an out. His team members cheered.

"You're a casualty now, squad leader," his sergeant called. "Chlorine gas will damage your eyes and your lungs. You breath in enough of it, and it mixes with the water in your body to form hydrochloric acid. You want to drown in acid?"

Reed shook his head, his grin gone.

"Maybe you think this isn't serious because the gas isn't real. Well, tomorrow you're taking your men into the chemical room for war exercises. We use actual, diluted gas in that room. You'll be responsible for making sure none of your men are exposed. That includes leading by example."

"Yes, Sir," Reed said, his tone subdued. He imagined his father shaking his head in disappointment.

He woke up the next day determined to take the exercises more seriously. This wasn't a game. He watched each man closely on their way into the chemical room. The fancy who'd made the polygamy comment walked past. Reed stopped him.

"Soldier, I can see condensation on your eye pieces. You don't have a good seal on that mask."

Reed adjusted the mask on the man's face, tightening the lower straps and loosening the upper to get a better fit and seal.

"Thanks, Utah. You boys are all right in my book. Sorry I was a buffoon when we met."

"Don't worry about it, Buffoon." Reed smiled, slapping him on the shoulder.

The last night of camp, the men were packing their things to leave for home in the morning. Captain Marshall suddenly appeared in the tent opening. "You three men, where exactly are you from?"

"Utah, Sir. The Agricultural College in Logan," Moses answered.

"Ah, farm boys. That's what I figured. All three of you did well. I'd be honored to serve with any of you. Cadet Lewis, is it? Step outside with me, will you?"

Reed followed Marshall outside the tent. "Here, Cadet. I think you'll be able to use this at some point." Marshall placed a U.S. officer's insignia in the palm of Reed's hand. Marshall turned around sharply and strode off without another word.

Reed watched him walk away, then looked down at the insignia, turning the U.S. letters back and forth to catch the dimming sunlight. *I want to get out there and serve, but not without a war to serve in. I join now, then what? Months or years of sitting around, waiting? I need to be doing something. When is the country going to wake up to the fact that there's a war going on all around us?*

III

September 1916
Logan, Utah

The war in Europe rages on, but with fall semester starting up this week, the question on everyone's mind is, will we field a football team we can all be proud of? Enlistment for athletes begins today, Coach Watson Commanding!
— *The A.C. Student Life*

Clara wrinkled her nose at the dust from the Model T rattling along in front of her. It was newer than hers, but she doubted the boys driving it had spent as much time as she had fine-tuning the engine. After working with the steam engines on the farm, fixing up the old Ford was easy, and she was willing to bet that her Tin Lizzie was a match for any other car on the road.

It was easy enough to find out. Clara shifted to high gear and the car jumped forward, overtaking the boys. They gawked at her as she rattled by. She waved. They whooped and laughed, and one blew her a kiss. The cloud of dust from her car enveloped them.

She eased back to low gear as she entered Logan. The twin spires of the LDS temple dominated the town, but the buildings of the Utah Agricultural College stood above it in the foothills, stark and isolated on the treeless bench. She wondered if that had been a deliberate choice.

Clara spotted a familiar figure walking toward the college.

"Trudi!" she called, slowing down and waving her friend over.

Trudi carefully stepped across the muddy sidewalk, looking pristine as always. The wind had whipped Clara's hat into the back seat and tousled her short blond hair into a mess. *Well, not everyone can be Trudi.*

"Hop in," Clara said. "I'll give you a ride."

Trudi eyed the car warily. "Have you been making improvements on it again?"

"Of course," Clara said. "Come on, give my Lizzie a chance."

"All right."

Trudi climbed in, holding her hat. A skein of yarn peeked out from her handbag.

"Taking your knitting to class?" Clara asked. "That's German efficiency for you."

"My mother is from Germany, but the rest of us are Swiss," Trudi said, the faint lilt of her accent a little more pronounced than usual. She put on an offended expression, but Clara saw the laugh in her eyes.

Clara shot forward into the traffic on Main Street, a mix of horse-drawn wagons and automobiles. A horn squawked behind them. Trudi clutched her handbag more tightly.

Clara looked back and laughed. The boys had caught up with them. "Hold on!"

"What—"

Trudi yelped as the car lurched forward. "I don't think you're supposed to go this fast!" she called over the wind as Clara pulled the throttle on the steering column down and swerved around a pair of pedestrians.

"Can't let them beat us!" Clara shouted back.

She swerved onto the steep road that led up to campus. The other car screeched around the turn. Students making the long trudge up the hill stopped to gawk.

"Watch this!" Clara slowed enough to turn the car around and put it in reverse.

The boys' car whizzed past them.

"Are you crazy?" Trudi asked. Clara gave her a look, and Trudi added, "They're going to beat us."

Clara laughed. "I thought you didn't approve of my racing."

"Well," Trudi said sheepishly, "if we're going to race, we ought to win."

"Don't worry. Those boys don't know what they're doing." Clara grinned and half-turned to steer by watching out the back window.

The boys' car slowed and came to a stop.

"Going uphill, these cars do better in reverse," Clara said.

She waved to the boys again as she passed, and they laughed in appreciation. Some of the watching crowd whistled and cheered. Trudi released the side of the car and straightened her hat.

Clara slowed to turn the car around again. The engine stuttered. Clara gripped the metal steering wheel. The timing was off. The engine caught again then died. The car paused then rolled back down past the astonished boys.

"Clara!" Trudi yelled.

"It's the timing coils. Useless Ford!"

She slammed on the brakes, but they skidded and the car kept rolling. Another car turned up the hill toward them. The driver's face froze in an expression of alarm when he saw Clara careening toward him. Trudi gasped. Clara swerved and smashed into a clump of bushes near the bottom of the hill. Branches screeched along the side of the car and snapped. Clara groaned and looked over at Trudi.

"Are you all right?" she asked.

Trudi nodded. "What now?"

"We have to move the car, and quickly. I don't want to get kicked out of school before it even starts."

Trudi looked doubtful, but she hopped out to help. Clara put the car in neutral, and they climbed through the grasping branches to push, but the car was stuck.

Clara wiped her forehead and muttered something unladylike that earned her a reproachful look from Trudi. A small crowd had gathered to stare at them, but no one yet came forward to help.

"Clara!"

For a moment the figure striding toward them looked like her father. Her whole body went rigid, braced for the whipping and the tongue-lashing. *What's wrong with you? Aren't you even trying? Why can't you do better?* She wanted to run—or even better, drive—fast and far, putting him behind her forever.

But her father was gone. Only his harsh words remained to play in her mind like a phonograph recording. It was Alonzo coming to her rescue. Her brother never raised a hand against anyone. She would have to endure his exasperation, but he never let her down. The crowd parted for the tall, sturdy figure that had been the hero of the high school football fields.

"Are you hurt?" he asked both girls.

They shook their heads, and he loosened his tie as he studied the car. Under his direction, a few other boys came forward, and together they pushed it back to the side of the road. Clara exhaled and wondered how much damage she had done to the car.

"Now, what kind of crazy stunt is this?" Alonzo asked in a low voice.

"It was an accident!" Clara said.

"Clara's quick thinking saved us from a much more serious one," Trudi added, drawing Alonzo's wrathful gaze away from Clara.

His expression softened when he focused on Trudi, and he straightened his mussed brown hair. Clara raised an eyebrow. *So that's how it is? Poor 'Lonzo.* Since their father died, Alonzo usually stayed quiet in the background. Trudi hardly seemed to notice he was there, and when he was in one of his mad, stubborn moods, he wasn't likely to make the best impression. He'd say something foolish.

"I thought you had enough sense not to encourage my sister in her shenanigans."

Clara nodded to herself. *Something like that.*

"I'm not." Trudi gave Clara a look that warned her the race through Logan would be a conversation for another time. "I'm telling you, her engine malfunctioned, and she was quick-thinking enough to stop the car without causing injury to anyone. You ought to be grateful she's so clever."

Alonzo glanced at the car for a moment. "I knew that thing was unsafe. It's my responsibility to watch after you, Clara. I should have—"

"I can fix it," Clara said. "I have more timing coils in the back."

"You should sell it. I can take you to campus in the buggy."

"No."

Alonzo sighed and shook his head. Before he could continue the argument, a couple of his friends joined them. Bert Lyman towered over the other two. She nodded politely to him, and he returned a wide, friendly smile.

The other man, a handsome blond with the tanned face of a farm boy, grinned at Clara. His military drill uniform showed off a trim figure with broad shoulders.

"That was some nice driving, Miss . . . ?"

Alonzo gave him a dark look. "Reed Lewis, this is my sister, Clara Jensen, and our friend Trudi Kessler."

"Miss Jensen, Miss Kessler, it's a pleasure to meet you both." Reed gave Trudi a polite nod, but his gaze quickly returned to Clara.

"And you, Mr. Lewis," Clara said, responding to his bright smile with one of her own.

"I hope we'll be seeing you around campus. Are you planning on joining a sorority? Or maybe the home economics club?"

"I want to join the French club. I'm not studying home economics."

"You're not?" Alonzo asked. "Then what classes did you enroll in?"

"They wouldn't let me take mechanics or engineering, so I'm going to study general science."

"You're just trying to be contrary." Alonzo shook his head.

"It's not as if I'm doing anything improper."

Reed grinned his approval. "Don't worry, Alonzo. There are a few other brave females that will keep her company in the sciences. I daresay she knows what she's doing."

Alonzo rolled his eyes, and Clara gave Reed a grateful smile.

"I'd best be getting along," Reed said. "Miss Kessler, Miss Jensen, welcome to campus."

The crowd that had gathered to watch dispersed. As Reed sauntered off, Bert tipped his hat to the ladies and followed.

"All right," Alonzo said, "Clara, fix your car and get it parked somewhere. You'd better move fast so you're not late."

He strode off up the hill.

Trudi shook her head at Clara. "Well, no one can say you don't know how to make a first impression."

Clara laughed and squinted up at the stone building crowning the hill above her, backlit by the morning sun. *Welcome to campus.* She was here to make her mark.

IV

An intra-campus debate competition will be held tonight to welcome students back to the A.C. and showcase our college's clubs and activities. Sigma Chi promises blood will be spilled, and Der Deutsche Verien threatens to sing Deutschland Uber Alles *if they win. This is an event you won't want to miss.*

—*The A.C. Student Life*

Clara tucked a strand of blond hair behind her ear and closed her eyes for a moment. *Don't let your nerves show.* She pushed open the door to the college chapel where they were hosting the debate contest between the student organizations. The cloying heat of the crowded room washed over her. Sweat trickled under the collar of her blouse, and she dabbed discreetly at her throat with a handkerchief.

She recognized a few faces, including Alonzo's handsome friend Reed. There were women in the audience, but the only other female competitor represented the Sorosis sorority. The only reason Clara had this opportunity was because none of the men in the French club had been interested in the debate. Most students thought women weren't up to the challenge of matching wits with men. All the more important, then, to show everyone that she could keep up. Clara jotted her name on the competitors list with a flourish and took her seat.

Professor Hendricks, the public speaking chairman, called the group to order and named the first pairing, giving them their topic, "Resolved: That the United States should abandon the Monroe Doctrine." The professor flipped a coin to determine which of the two men would take the affirmative and which the negative and allowed them a few minutes to prepare.

Clara considered what she would argue in their positions. Abandoning the Monroe Doctrine meant giving up U.S. neutrality and

23

nearly guaranteed that they would send soldiers to Europe. It would be fairly easy to argue against that idea. Clara hated to think of American boys shipped off to a foreign war. The argument for the position rested more on the moral imperative to aid America's allies and stop German imperialism. The debaters took their places at the podiums and presented arguments that followed Clara's thinking. She smiled and settled back in her chair.

Several other pairs debated settling labor union disputes, increasing military preparedness without abandoning the peace movement, and the nationwide prohibition of alcohol.

Professor Hendricks called the next pairing, "Miss Clara Jensen for the French club and Mr. Reed Lewis for Sigma Chi. Resolved: That women in the United States should be given the vote nationwide by an amendment to the Constitution."

Clara's knees trembled a little, but she stood smoothly and joined Reed for the coin toss.

"Heads or tails?" the professor asked.

"Heads," Reed said quickly.

Clara glared at him, and he grinned back. She focused on the dime in the professor's hand. *Please let it be tails. I can't argue the negative.* He tossed the coin in the air. It flashed silver in the light from the window and landed showing Liberty's head.

"Mr. Lewis for the affirmative. Miss Jensen for the negative."

The crowd broke out in murmurs of interest. Clara glided back to her seat, lost in shock. Confound Reed Lewis and the coin toss. How could she debate against women voting? She knew the arguments well enough. Women were too ignorant to vote and ought to be content with the protection of wiser men. They would be corrupted by politics and abandon their families. They didn't contribute to national defense and therefore didn't deserve full citizenship. Clara refused to argue for any of those stances, but she had to make a good showing. Nearly the whole college was watching.

She sat up straight, dimly aware of the whispers from the balcony above and of her opponent's gaze. She looked up once and met his eye. He gave her a brilliant smile, but Clara only nodded curtly. He wouldn't use his charm on a male opponent, so she wouldn't give him the satisfaction of trying it on her. She wasn't here to flirt. She was here to win.

The moderator announced the start of the debate. Clara still didn't know what she was going to say as she walked to the podium with a blur of faces watching her. The room quieted. The person arguing the affirmative went first. Reed turned his electric smile on the audience for a moment before donning a serious expression.

"Ladies and gentleman, here in Utah our women enjoy equal opportunity to express their high morals through voting, and we have seen its benefits in social programs that better the lives of men, women, and children. Many of those who oppose women's suffrage do so out of ignorance or self-interest, such as alcohol manufacturers or those who employ children to work long hours in factories. Giving women the vote nationwide through a constitutional amendment would override these self interests in favor of the moral right."

Clara smiled as she recognized a weakness in Reed's argument. She faced the audience and rested her hands on the podium to deliver her response.

"A constitutional amendment to give women the vote would fail to achieve one of the most important goals of the suffrage movement: to recognize women as equal and contributing citizens of this country. If we give women the vote on the basis of moral superiority, we fail to recognize them as people and see them instead as symbols. We also supply men with an excuse to avoid rising to their own moral potential." Clara paused to let her argument sink in, then pressed on to the point she had to convince the judges of, even if she didn't believe it herself.

"For this reason, it would be better to let women win the right to vote on a state-by-state basis, a process which has already begun, especially in the Western states where the contributions of women—not just as guardians of home and family, but as members of society— has already been recognized. Women's suffrage shouldn't be decided by a handful of politicians hoping to win votes, but by common consensus in recognition of women's natural rights as human beings."

A few members of the audience nodded, but most looked skeptical. Reed raised an eyebrow at Clara, but the rules didn't allow him to respond to her directly. He plunged ahead with his rebuttal, directed to the audience.

"The important contributions of women to politics cannot wait on the whims of individual states. My friends, we create an unequal situation and rob our country of strength by allowing some women in our great country to vote while others are denied this right. The only solution is a constitutional amendment allowing universal suffrage."

Clara stopped herself from nodding her agreement. She had to convince the judges Reed was wrong. "Forcing suffrage on states not yet ready to adopt it is overreaching and may cause resentment and possibly even violence, as we have seen with universal male suffrage in some parts of our country. This would undermine the benefits gained thus far by the women's suffrage movement. The right to vote should be extended to all, but it should be done peacefully, led by example in the states where women have been successfully enfranchised. An amendment granting women the vote would be a grave political and social mistake."

Clara felt disloyal making the argument, and even worse because she wasn't sure it was strong enough to win.

Reed, arguing for the affirmative, had the final say. He held the sides of the podium and leaned forward.

"We cannot let fear stop us from doing what we know is right. This nation needs the voices of its women joined with those of men to achieve our full potential. A constitutional amendment in favor of women's suffrage would bring the full benefits of women's inherent goodness and moral sensibilities to our country."

The audience clapped, and the judges, after a few moments of deliberation, declared the winner of the match: Reed Lewis for the affirmative.

Reed turned his grin on Clara and gave her a wink. Clara held her polite smile, but she gritted her teeth in frustration. Losing was bad enough without being condescended to.

She took her seat, her back ramrod straight as the other debates continued. The woman from Sorosis was eliminated in the next round. Reed moved on to win the debate contest, arguing in the negative against a man from the Cosmos club for, "Resolved: That the United States should end its pursuit of Pancho Villa and its involvement in the politics of Mexico."

Clara kept her plastered-on smile, but didn't meet anyone's eye as they congratulated her on her attempt. She didn't want congratulations for trying. For failing. All she had done was give that strutting rooster Reed Lewis a chance to show off and make her look second-rate in front of the school. He made his way toward her through the crowd. She headed for the door as quickly as she could without making it obvious that she was fleeing.

She'd parked near the main building. Footsteps came up behind her as she put the key in and adjusted the timing stalk on the steering shaft. She hopped out of the cab to crank the engine and found Reed smiling at her.

"You made a great argument in there, Miss Jensen," he said.

"Thank you," Clara said stiffly. "As did you."

He shrugged nonchalantly, as if it was a given that he had. "Say, I wondered if you'd like to join me for some ice cream."

She stared at him incredulously for a moment. "No, thank you, Mr. Lewis."

"You're not sore that I won, are you? It was nothing personal. You were a tough opponent."

Clara flushed. Of course it was childish to be upset by her loss, but Reed didn't understand what it was like to have to prove yourself. To have to do better than your best at everything just to have people consider taking you seriously.

"I'm not taking it personally," Clara said.

"Then why won't you go out with me?"

"Because I don't like you."

"Don't like me?" He wrinkled his forehead in confusion, then his eyes brightened with amused determination. "Well, I can fix that."

Clara almost slapped the confidence off his face. *So much for women's inherent goodness and moral sensibilities.* "Not likely, Mr. Lewis. I think you like yourself well enough for both for us."

"Come, now. You wouldn't make me celebrate alone, would you?"

"I'm sure you have a flock of admirers who would love to join you for ice cream."

He laughed. "Maybe. But I don't want a flock of admirers." He leaned closer, so that the spicy scent of his cologne wrapped around her. "Just one."

He winked again, and Clara glowered. "I would say I'm sorry to disappoint you, Mr. Lewis, but then I would be lying."

"I like a challenge, Miss Jensen. And I always win."

"So do I," Clara said.

"Almost," Reed amended, and before Clara really could smack him, he added, "Are you waiting for your brother to start your car? I can do that for you."

Clara pushed past him, grabbed the crank, and gave a vicious upward jerk, kicking the engine to life. She climbed in, slammed the door, and scooted behind the wheel.

Reed folded his arms and grinned and she drove away. She almost thought the look he gave her was admiration, but that made no sense. She wouldn't waste time worrying about it. She wouldn't give Reed Lewis the satisfaction.

V

*Seen just this last Saturday afternoon: "Kaiser" Havertz,
beloved campus bell ringer and erstwhile baseball umpire,
arguing with the second baseman, goose-stepping in a circle,
planting his boots firmly in American soil, giving "the salute,"
ordering the player to make his get-away.*

　　　　　　　　　　　　　　　—The A.C. Student Life

As baseball diamonds went, the field behind the main building
wasn't bad, especially since the backstop fence had to be taken
down after each game to allow for other activities on the quad, military drill in particular. Patches of alfalfa added color and drama—the
latter associated with wild things ground balls did when skipping off
the clumps and sensational falls by young men running at full speed
without looking down.

Reed stood by the backstop, hands in his pockets, watching Sigma
Chi's boys play a "friendly" with the Washakie Shoshone team. Alonzo
walked toward them from the steps of the main building, Clara on his
arm. Reed perked up and met her eyes. Alonzo suddenly seemed to
struggle to walk in a straight line, like Clara was pulling him away. Reed
grimaced. *Looks like I've got a real challenge on my hands.* But he couldn't
forget the way Clara's eyes lit up when she smiled, and he liked a woman
who didn't back down from a challenge.

"Alonzo, here to root for the home team?" Reed called. "Oh, and
good afternoon, Miss Jensen, lovely to see you again." He tipped his
driving cap toward her.

Alonzo started to speak, but flinched, like he was pinched or
something.

"I'm sure, Mr. Lewis." Clara said. "Tell me, shouldn't you be out on the field dominating the proceedings or something like that?" Clara kept her eyes on the diamond as she spoke.

Reed bent forward to peer at her around her brother. "Well, Miss Jensen, to be frank, there wasn't much time for baseball, growing up on a farm. You see, we—"

"Are you saying you're not good at baseball?" Clara raised an eyebrow.

Reed straightened. "Of course I'm good. I'm just here to support our team today. They've already got Ol' Bert. He can really smack that ball."

Alonzo plunged in, cutting off Clara's reply. "I saw the advertisement for this game. It said 'friendly' but promised bets, punches, and a few drops of blood. It looks rather serious to me, don't you think, Reed?"

"That Indian pitcher looks serious enough. Did he just throw a curveball?" Reed asked.

"Believe so," Alonzo said. "I've met him. Joseph Sorrell. He races horses, so Bert knows him from the track."

At the inning, the teams switched places. George James came up to bat for the Washakie and hit a hard grounder off a 1–2 pitch. It skipped on the edge of an alfalfa clump and smacked John, the second baseman, right between the eyes. Base hit. John toppled over backwardlike a domino and the other men carried him off.

"Oh, dear! I'm going to see if I can help." Clara gathered her skirt and raced toward the crumpled figure on the sideline.

"There she goes." Alonzo smiled. "Always trying to rescue someone."

"I doubt she'd rescue me, Alonzo. I don't think your sister cares much for me," Reed said.

"Did you really wink at her when you won the debate?" Alonzo glared at Reed, arms folded.

"Well, I may have. It's just natural for me to flirt a little. I didn't mean offense; you have to believe that. I'm quite, well, I'm . . ."

"Oh, no! Are you telling me you're fond of my sister? Good gosh, man. Have you read *The Taming of the Shrew*? I mean, she's a great girl, but so headstrong. Did you see us walk over here? She'd pull me around like an eight-week-old puppy if I let her. Do you want to be pulled around like a puppy?"

"What I'd like is for you to help me, maybe tell me when I say or do something she wouldn't like. Perhaps we can lift this cold blanket she drops on me whenever we meet."

Alonzo shook his head. "Very well. In the interest of friendship and harmony. But I've warned you against romance. I don't think you can keep up with her."

Bert jogged over to the field side of the backstop and pressed his face against the fence fabric. "Hey, Gents. We need a fill-in at second base. We don't have spares so one of you needs to play."

Alonzo spoke first. "I don't care much for baseball, Bert. Looks like you're up, Reed!"

"Ah, but Bert, this is my only suit besides my drill uniform."

"Reed, now is the time for all good men"—Bert grinned—"to come to the aid of their fraternity! Now get in here!"

Reed trudged around the fence and took his place after Bert in the batting order. He glanced around and saw Clara gently dabbing at John's swollen face. *That kind of attention might almost make it worth it to take a ball to the face.* Reed shook his head. He'd find a better way to win her over.

Joseph pitched Bert a fastball on the first pitch, which was a mistake. Bert whipped the bat in an even arc, driving the ball well out over second base. A triple.

As Reed walked to the plate, he saw that Clara had rejoined Alonzo behind the backstop. *Great. Two outs, runner on third, and I have never hit a curve ball in my life.* He nodded toward them and smiled slightly but suppressed an urge to wink at Clara.

"Good day, Mr. Havertz. You're looking rather Teutonic today," Reed said, grinning at the umpire.

"Yes, Mr. Lewis. But flattery iz not going to help hit that Indian's pitches," Havertz replied.

Joseph stood calmly, waiting for Reed and Mr. Havertz to get ready. Short and powerfully built, Joseph sported a worn baseball jersey in place of his work shirt. Otherwise he had on everyday clothes like Reed. He wore no hat, and his squinting eyes made him look intimidating, fierce.

Reed took his place. The pitch came. *Fastball, just like Bert's!* He swung mightily, but it was a curveball that spun off at the last second, leaving Reed swatting at air. The energy caused him to spin off the plate and almost fall over. He glanced backward. Clara had her eyes forward, away from him, but her lips twitched with the effort not to smile.

"Pleased to entertain you, Miss Jensen," he called as he resumed his place in the batter's box.

Joseph nodded at a signal from his catcher and launched another curveball, fooling Reed for a second time. Reed reached so far out that he spun himself to the ground, scuffing his knee and tearing his trousers.

He couldn't help but look back. Clara held a gloved hand over her face to smother her laughter. There was no sound, but her eyes danced. He liked that a lot, even at his expense.

The third pitch was another curveball, but Joseph threw it too far to the right. When it curved left it was still in the strike zone. Reed decided to go out in a blaze of glory and took another strong swing, just connecting enough for a nice line drive over the first baseman's head, bringing Bert home.

As Reed tossed the bat down, he stopped, just for a second, wiggled his eyebrows at Clara, then trotted off for first base. Out of the corner of his eye, he saw Clara sock Alonzo on the arm.

"Ouch," Alonzo griped, just on the edge of Reed's hearing. "What was that for?"

"Making friends with such a cad."

"He seems to be charming you, Clara, not bad for a cad," he said, moving out of her punching range.

"I don't know what you're talking about 'Lonzo. He's perfectly dreadful."

"Dreadfully good at baseball, did you say?" Reed called from first base. Clara's cheeks reddened and she pretended to focus on the other players.

Notwithstanding Reed's heroics, the Washakie Shoshone won the game. Bert nodded toward Joseph at the end of the ninth inning. "Come with me, Reed. I want you to meet this Indian. Besides, I owe him five smackers for beating us."

Bert and Reed walked to the plate, where Joseph's teammates pounded him on the back.

"Joseph, here's your money," Bert said when the Washakie team dispersed. "Good game. Hey, meet my friend Reed Lewis. Reed's a farm boy too, from Sanpete way."

"Pleased to meet you, Mr. Lewis, I'm Joseph Sorrell."

"Pleasure is all mine, Mr. Sorrell. I hear you know Bert from the track. You race those Indian ponies?"

"Haha," Bert interrupted, "people think that, but the Shoshone have been racing horses for a lot of years. They got stock from French racing stallions, some Morgans, what else, Joseph?"

"Well, we got some quarter horse stock, pony stock too. We use some of the stock for ranching so they got to be tough."

"Huh. I didn't know that," Reed said. "I grew up rounding up and breaking horses on our rangeland for ranch work, but we never did any racing."

"I got me a mare, I call her Buckskin Nelly. You come see her at the Cache County Fair, Mr. Lewis, she ain't never been beat. Might make a dollar or two off that horse," Joseph said, winking.

"I believe I'll do that. Say, Mr. Sorrell, where'd you learn to play baseball like that?" Reed asked.

"Washakie Day School. Supposed to make us Injuns all civilized an' such." Joseph smiled. "Hope to see you at the fair, Mr. Lewis."

"Hope so too. Day to you," Reed said, as he walked with Bert toward Alonzo and Clara. Trudi had joined them as well.

"Ah, Miss Kessler. A smiling face, how nice." Reed tipped his cap.

"Hello, Mr. Lewis. Sorry I missed all the excitement," Trudi said.

"There was some of that for sure." Reed laughed. "Say," he said, looking toward where Clara and Alonzo were standing, "any chance you could patch up the knee in my trousers?"

Clara's eyes narrowed. "You want Alonzo to mend your trousers?"

"What? No. I was asking—I was wondering if . . ."

Alonzo frantically shook his head in the background.

Reed swallowed and plunged ahead, like a man who knew his saddle was slipping and wasn't sure what he was going to land on. "Well, if you wouldn't mind, perhaps you could? Uh, please?"

"Oh, of course! My mistake! I assumed you were asking your fraternity brother rather than his little sister, whom you barely know. I should have assumed you meant me because, I am, in fact, a woman, and therefore I'm at your beck and call. Why not, Mr. Lewis? Perhaps you have some socks in need of darning as well? Are your collars pressed and white? Your boots blackened and polished?"

Trudi gave Clara a chastising look. "I don't mind, Mr. Lewis. I'd be happy to help."

"Oh no you don't, Trudi. You have more than enough to do as it is!" Clara stormed off, snatching Trudi by the arm to take her along like she was picking up an umbrella.

Reed stood looking after her, hat in hand.

Alonzo approached him. "Remember what you asked me to do, earlier? Well, that was one, right there. Don't do that."

"Yes, Alonzo. But it would be good to get your advice before I need it. Seems a bit late now."

"I'll try to read your mind next time."

Reed smiled at him. "She is lovely when she's angry, though, don't you think?"

Alonzo laughed. "Hopeless, Mr. Lewis. Truly hopeless."

VI

Friends show their love in times of trouble, not happiness
—Euripides

About six hours into his ride, Joseph wished he had brought the buggy rather than riding his gelding, Major. For one thing, pony-ing Buckskin Nelly was a pain in the neck. She liked Major well enough, but she wasn't much good for anything but racing, and she yanked on her lead rope or bit poor Major pretty much the whole ride. And, much as Joseph hated to admit it, his rear end was getting pretty sore on the long ride from Washakie to Logan, longer since he had decided to take the scenic route through the canyon. But Joseph knew he couldn't show up in a buggy and give those white men more reason to poke fun at him. *They won't be laughin' so much when they see Buckskin Nelly run.*

At least it was a dang pretty ride through Sardine Canyon. Late September, the first blush of fall color in the trees, still green but kissed with gold and red, hinting of what was to come. The only thing Joseph could see moving were cattle up in high country pasture and red tail hawks circling silently for prey.

It gave him time to think in peace, and he liked that. Life on his uncle's allotment was good, but there was rarely time to think. Hard work. That was life on the allotment. But Joseph loved it. It gave him purpose, meaning. Besides, the Shoshone tradition of horse breeding and racing had opened a whole new world for him. Today, it was taking him to the Cache County Fair to race Buckskin Nelly at a quarter mile, and, hopefully, to win some much needed purse money. *Yes. Coming to Uncle's allotment from the reservation was good. Very good.*

As he passed Wellsville at the bottom of Sardine Canyon, Joseph glanced at the twin spires of the Logan Temple in the distance. Many Shoshone worked on that temple, his uncle among them, right alongside

35

the people of Cache Valley. Yet he felt like a stranger, as if the Shoshone had never lived there at all. They were pushed to the margins, a people without a place.

About a mile from the fairgrounds, Joseph climbed off Major and walked the horses, letting his legs stretch out and sensation return to his tired rear. Once his muscles were loose again, he mounted up and rode the rest of the way into the stable area. When he saw everyone look at him, he jumped off Major all fresh and relaxed, like he hadn't spent the last eight hours in the saddle.

Someone called out, "Say, you just ride over from Washakie?"

"That I did. What of it?" Joseph said, smiling.

"Well, it's just a long ride, that's all." The stranger shrugged and strode off.

As Joseph turned the corner, he spied Bert leaning against the Dutch door on a stall, thumbs in the straps of his overalls, watching him with a grin.

"Well, Joseph," Bert said, "come to take my money again?"

"Ah, Bert, so good to see you, and yes, I hope to take your money," Joseph smiled back.

"We'll see. By the by, how'd you pull off looking so fresh jumpin' off that horse when you rode up. I know your bum has to be killing you."

"You know that all us Indians are warriors and horsemen, right? We can sit in a saddle all day and ride bareback at a full gallop while shooting a whole quiver of arrows."

Bert gave a deep, booming laugh. "Okay. That's really interesting. So, how'd you do it?"

Joseph grinned. "I jumped off a ways back and walked until I got the kinks out, then rode in all hero-like."

"Nicely done." Bert chuckled. "I'm camped over by the canal. Come camp there too if you like. We'll make us some stew, tell some tall tales."

Joseph hesitated. The local farm boys usually weren't all that friendly to the Shoshone, but Bert seemed to be on good terms with everyone.

"Sure, that sounds fine," Joseph said.

Bert grinned. "Come on over once you get your horses settled."

Joseph laid his bedroll and ranch saddle next to where Bert had set up a pup tent and a fire pit along the canal bisecting the fairgrounds. It was a nice spot, with the late afternoon sun filtering through the poplars and cottonwood along the canal. It was also within sight of his horses' stalls, which Joseph liked. The two men sat and talked as the savory scent of Bert's beef stew and the smoke from the crackling little fire drifted around them.

"How are things up in Washakie?" Bert asked.

"Pretty good. I like it better than the reservation."

"Haven't you always lived there?"

"No, I came to my uncle's allotment when I was ten," Joseph said. "I was born on Fort Hall reservation in Idaho."

"Mind if I ask why you left? I mean, are your parents . . . do they live on the reservation?"

Joseph didn't talk to white folks much, but there was something about Bert's open, honest face that made him feel comfortable. "Yes, I mean, no, I don't mind. They live there. I was sent to help my uncle farm because he has no sons, and also so I could go to Washakie Day School to learn to read and write."

"What was that you said about an allotment?" Bert asked.

"My uncle and his family were granted a farm allotment in Washakie from the LDS Church. They joined the Church, and they became citizens of the U.S. since they stayed off reservation."

"And you? Are you a citizen? Did you join the Church?"

"I'm a member of the Church. Baptized at twelve. But I'm not a citizen. I'd like to be, but I'm stuck now, sort of between two worlds. Not really Shoshone, not really American." Joseph shrugged off the sting of the truth and leaned back. "What about you? Have you always lived in this valley?"

"Me? Oh, yeah. Why heck, my family's been here for a few generations." He took out a pocket watch and rubbed the worn brass lid with his thumb. "We run a dairy farm north of here, out near Richmond, and grow mostly alfalfa and feed corn. I'm up at the A.C. getting smart on agricultural sciences and all so we can run our farm better. 'Course," he said with a wide grin, "we raise a few fast quarter horses here and there."

"We'll see." Joseph smiled then cleared his throat. "The Mormons I've met weren't much for racing though. At least making money off it."

"Well, my family does our best to honor Heavenly Father every day, 'cept perhaps on race day; we may falter a little on race day." Bert laughed.

Joseph chuckled too. "Not too many Mormons laugh about their faith either."

"Well, Joseph, the way I figure it, I live my life as best I can, trying to honor the Lord in all things, trying to treat all men like I believe the Savior would. I feel that if I do those things, the Lord may cut me some slack on racing, long as I don't do it on a Sunday."

"Fair enough," Joseph replied, smiling. "Good thing tomorrow is Saturday."

Bert nodded and caught Joseph's gaze as he glanced at the pocket watch Bert was still fidgeting with. "A family heirloom. My great-grandfather carried it over from England when he joined the Church. His family never spoke to him again, and this was all he had left of them. I always wonder if I'm brave enough to live up to that legacy, you know?"

"Yeah, I think I do," Joseph said, thinking about his own warrior ancestors and what they might think of him now. He hoped none of them had fought against Bert's people, at least.

Both men woke the next morning to a cheery Reed Lewis whistling bird songs while he stoked their fire up enough to cook on.

"What gives, Reed? What brings you down here so early?" Bert asked.

"I've come to make you breakfast," Reed said. "I've got big things in store for you today, my friend, mostly making me some money. I'm still a little behind after paying for that camp last summer." He glanced at Joseph. "Say, it's Mr. Sorrell isn't it? We met at the baseball game."

"Yes. Call me Joseph."

"Pleased to. And I'm Reed. Glad I brought extra grub! Where's that cast iron pan, Bert?"

Reed cooked the whole meal in the one pan. Eggs, bacon, and hashed potatoes. He had two forks stuck in a jacket pocket, and Joseph produced one from his bedroll. The three men all ate right from the pan, a silent ritual all of them knew well.

Joseph pulled out his supply of flat bread and shared it around. Reed took a bite, nodded, and said with a wink "This Navajo flat bread?"

Joseph rolled his eyes. "Not if my aunt made it it ain't." All three men laughed.

Reed spent the rest of the morning puttering around the stables, talking with horse owners and looking over the horses—seeing who looked frisky for the morning races and which horses might be lame or too squirrely to run well on a crowded track. The other men did the same while readying their own horses for the races.

Reed stopped by Bert's stall. "So, what do you think for the quarter mile?"

"Well, I'd go with Buckskin Nelly to win, my horse, Two-bits, to place," Bert said.

"You don't think you can beat Joseph?" Reed asked.

"Not at a quarter mile. Look at the haunches on that mare. On a dry track like this, she'll be out a half-length before the rest of the field gets started. She's never lost as far as I know."

Reed spotted Clara with Alonzo and Trudi.

"I gotta go."

Bert shook his head. "You don't know when to quit."

"Nope!"

Reed snuck up behind Clara, Alonzo, and Trudi as they talked to race entrants just like Reed had.

"I'll give you good odds that my horse will beat Two-Bits," the skinny young man said to Alonzo. "Look at Bert. He's not built like a jockey."

"I've seen him ride," Clara said. "He's good, and so is Two-Bits."

The young man smirked at Alonzo. "Well, we know ladies just judge a horse based on how pretty its coat looks. They don't know much about the muscle beneath it."

Clara's eyes glinted, and Reed bit back a smile. She was even prettier when she was mad at someone else.

"I'll take your bet." She pulled a fistful of crumpled bills from her handbag.

The skinny young man reached for her money, but Alonzo glared at him and pushed Clara's outstretched bills aside, turning her away from the stalls.

Clara glared at him. "You wouldn't say anything against a bet if I were a man."

"Yes, I would," Alonzo said.

Trudi's eyes widened. "Clara! You're not serious." She lowered her voice. "That's illegal."

"It's only a few dollars, and we have to stand by our friends against smirking little pipsqueaks like that one. Just pretend you didn't see anything."

"Oh, Clara." Trudi shook her head, looking disappointed, and walked off toward the home economics displays.

"Betting on horses, Miss Jensen?" Reed asked.

Clara gave a start and reddened. "And if I am?"

"Well, if you are, Clara . . . may I call you Clara?" Reed said.

"I believe you just did, *Mr. Lewis.*"

"Your friend is right, you know. Betting on horse races is illegal in Utah. You could be arrested, thrown to the mercy of the court, disgraced," he teased.

"Oh, that's half the fun."

Reed considering proposing on the spot, but Alonzo—or Clara—might sock him.

"Well, if you insist on betting, take my advice." Reed made a pretense of checking for eavesdroppers and leaned in to whisper. She smelled like wild strawberries. Heavenly. "For the quarter mile, bet on Buckskin Nelly to win."

"You would bet against your friend?" Her look made him feel like a filthy traitor.

"Well, he told me Buckskin Nelly is faster."

Clara stepped away. "Thank you, Mr. Lewis. I'm sure that's worthy advice. I'll keep it in mind."

The horses gathered on the opposite side of the half-mile track in a portable wooden starting gate, riders and handlers struggling to line them up for the start of the race.

Reed managed to sit with Alonzo and Clara. He knew his father disapproved of gambling, but he hadn't been able to resist exchanging a couple of friendly bets with some of his fraternity brothers, who insisted Bert would beat "that Indian pony." Despite his excitement, Reed concentrated on looking disinterested, even a little bored.

Clara made no such pretense. She was tense as a spring, tapping her foot and sitting rigidly upright. Reed guessed she'd managed to place a bet after all. He couldn't imagine anything stopping her once she'd decided to do something. As long as she'd taken his advice, she had nothing to lose.

The bell rang, and the horses were off. They hit the first turn in just seconds, bunching up and shifting dramatically as if the whole bunch of them were one creature. Clara leaned into Reed's shoulder, just like the jockeys were leaning left into the corner. Her whole body rocked back and forth like she was urging her horse forward—she shouted, "Go, go, go!" as she squashed the ticket in her hand and bounced up and down in her seat. Reed grinned and watched her from the corner of his eye, almost forgetting about the race entirely.

As the horses turned for the home stretch, the cream-colored buckskin mare surged out of the crowd, her massive haunches built for short track speed. Joseph crouched well up on her back, knees tucked high by the racing stirrups, his torso forward, his head along Nelly's neck. Reed could see his lips move. He was talking to his mare. No whip was necessary. Reed tightened his grip on his ticket, praying the buckskin had more in her. Yes! Joseph was still holding her back as she pulled out of the crowd, until the turn was complete and she was clear—Joseph gave her her head and she accelerated to full speed, pale golden skin over rippling muscles, strides overlapping front to back, head pumping in a hard rhythm, her nostrils flaring open and closed. She won by three lengths.

The race for second was much closer. Bert was just nosed out by the skinny "pipsqueak" jockey.

Reed looked at Clara, expecting gratitude, ideally a kiss on the cheek, for his warning. Instead, she sat there ashen, staring at the ground.

"Clara, what's wrong?" Reed asked.

Clara balled up her fists and smacked them down on her skirt. "How could I be so foolish? 'Lonzo, why on earth didn't you stop me?"

"Why, I'd no more be able to persuade you to fly to the moon than—"

"Well, what kind of big brother are you anyway!"

"Clara, I take it you bet on Two-Bits after all?" Reed asked, backing up a little.

"Obviously! I thought Bert was just being modest about that other horse being faster, and I wanted to show that little . . ." She gritted her teeth and glowered toward the pipsqueak jockey.

"Your loyalty does you credit," Reed said, "but I would never mislead you. Why, Buckskin Nelly has never lost a race—it's just that most folks around here don't know that so they bet on the bigger horses . . ."

Clara shook her head and shredded her race program into tiny white flakes.

"Say, I'll tell you what," Reed said. "How about I take you and Alonzo and Trudi to dinner back in town?"

"So you can rub my face in it the whole time? Oh, really. I must decline, Mr. Lewis. You can just go . . . Errrrrr." She stormed off.

Alonzo gave Reed a sympathetic nod and followed her.

As Bert and Joseph were packing up their camp, three men in filthy overalls and worn hats formed a semicircle around Joseph.

"Hey, Injun," one of them called, "we lost money on that race 'cause o' you."

Joseph turned to face them, his left leg forward for balance, and so he could get to the boot knife he carried there if he knelt down quickly.

"Sorry to hear that," Joseph said to no one in particular, careful to keep his eyes distant, off theirs.

"No you ain't," the first man replied, "but you about to be."

Bert, who had been packing his tent, stood up to his full height at this. At nearly six feet, he was taller than any of the other men by three inches, and outweighed them by forty pounds, none of it fat. They sized him up, then looked at each other.

Bert stepped over next to Joseph. "We don't need no trouble here. Why don't you boys head on home now."

"I don't think it's any of your dang business, Mister. I'm talkin' to that Injun."

"Welp, I'm not much of a talker, *Mister*, so let's try this. I'm going to pick you up and throw you over that canal. If I can throw you over it, you gents gotta leave, okay?"

Bert grabbed the bib of the man's overalls with one hand while shooting the other under his crotch. He picked him up with ease and tossed him like a hay bale right into the middle of the canal.

"Dang it," Bert said, "I missed. Which one of you two clowns is next?"

The other two men had nothing to say on their own behalf and slinked off to retrieve their spokesman from the canal.

"I didn't need no help, Bert, but I thank you all the same," Joseph said.

"Yeah, I know you didn't, but there woulda been blood everywhere, probably some scalps, who needs that? Besides, I reckon that is what friends do, right?"

"Yes, friends, Bert." Joseph mulled over the thought and smiled. "This is good."

VII

The German bombardment continued day and night until we thought we would go mad. Some men sobbed. Others went numb, unseeing, unhearing. One of the explosions buried my squad in a wave of dirt and rocks. Five of us dug our way out, but we could not find the other two. We were cut off from the rear, with no communication, no rations, for three days. We could have been all alone in the world—just us and the Germans trying to kill us. We survived on a few biscuits and pieces of chocolate. Almost nothing to drink. The wounded cried for help day and night, praying for stretcher bearers to carry them away. The smell of festering wounds was terrible. The bearers, when they could get through, braved bullets from both sides and constant shelling, climbed over barbed wire, and waded through mud up to their waists to bring the wounded away. This is the "Great War." I fear it will never end.
  —Letter from a French soldier to a Marraine de Guerre ("Godmother" pen pal)

Hey, doll, how 'bout a ride!"

Clara scowled at being called "doll" and kept her eyes on the road. The car was full anyway.

"Ah, Miss Jensen, have a heart. Fred don't mean no harm," said Earl Johnson, who stood on the running board of the Tin Lizzie, clinging to the side of the car with one hand and holding his trumpet case with the other.

Bert, hanging on to the other side of the car, added in his rumbling voice, "We could squeeze on one more. No one wants to hike up that hill, and I don't see the streetcar coming."

"Oh, very well." Clara slowed down.

The men riding on the outside of the car scooted around, grumbling good-naturedly. The girls who were crammed inside giggled. Fred dashed up, grabbed Bert's offered hand, and clambered onto the wheel well, straddling the headlamp.

They reached the steep hill running along the south side of campus. "Hold on, boys!" Clara called.

She turned the car around and put it in reverse, slowly chugging her way up. On the south side of the road, the hill plunged into the Logan riverbed. Clara steered mostly by guess since she couldn't lean out far enough to see around her passengers.

They pulled up to campus without adventure. Boys shouted their thanks and jumped off even before Clara came to a stop behind the main building.

"Thanks, *doll*," Bert said, giving her a quick peck on the cheek and dashing away before she could vent her indignation on him.

The girls got out of the car with more dignity. The Tin Lizzie didn't have a driver's side door, so Clara had to wait until they'd all climbed out before she could escape the car.

She found Trudi sitting on the steps behind the main building, knitting, while a group of men practiced football on the patchy grass. The sun was warm, but the cool breeze blowing off the mountains promised an early autumn. Clara sat next to her friend and turned her face to the sunshine.

"You'll get freckles," Trudi teased.

"I already have them. They're charming," Clara said with a straight face.

Trudi laughed, her knitting needles clicking along without pause.

"What poor soul are you clothing today?" Clara asked.

"They're for *Der Deutsche Verien*."

"For the . . . ? Oh, the German-speaking club."

"We're making socks for the German Red Cross. A few people in the club served missions in Germany, and it tears them up to think about their friends in that awful fighting. And there's others like me with family in Switzerland and Germany, isolated by the war. Everything's in short supply there."

Clara nodded. "I signed up to help with the French Club's Marraine project. We're writing letters and sending care packages to the French boys who've been cut off from home by the German advances."

45

"I hope it ends soon," Trudi whispered.

They grew quiet except for the clicking of the needles and the distant "hut" of the boys on the field.

"'Lonzo says the war is none of our business," Clara said, watching her friend carefully to see how she reacted to his name. "He says it's fine to help those who are suffering, but we need to stick to our goal of peace and focus on our problems at home instead of interfering in other nations' conflics."

Trudi frowned. "That sounds like a rather selfish position. How can we ignore what's going on in the rest of the world?"

Clara gazed out over the field. *Poor Alonzo. That's not a promising answer.*

"Do you want to make some socks?" Trudi asked.

"I could make a scarf, maybe. I'm not good at socks. They always come out too small for anyone but a child."

"Children need socks too. The civilians are freezing and starving to feed and clothe the army."

Clara was quiet for a moment. "Okay, I'll try. But I'll need—"

Trudi handed her an extra set of needles and a skein of yarn.

"Thanks." Clara set about casting on the stitches for the socks. She didn't notice anyone approaching until a shadow fell across her work. She looked up with a start to find Reed grinning down at her, the blocked sunlight making a halo around his blond hair.

He probably did that on purpose.

"Good morning, ladies."

"Hello, Reed," Trudi said cheerfully.

Clara glanced away from his face and noticed the knee of his trousers. They looked like a child had sewn them, leaving them puckered and tugged at an odd angle. "Good heavens!" she exclaimed before she could catch herself.

"Oh." Reed's grin brightened. "Are you impressed with my handiwork?"

"You sewed them yourself?" Clara asked.

"Well, yes. Alonzo refused to do it, and other than my fraternity brothers, I'm all alone here in Logan."

Clara bit the inside of her cheek, torn between guilt and amusement. They really must have been his only pair of slacks.

Trudi gave Clara a pointed look.

Clara squinted up at Reed. "Did you do that just to make me feel guilty? Why didn't you use your race winnings to have them stitched?" she added darkly.

He laughed and dropped to the ground next to her. "Believe it or not, I have other expenses."

"Gambling debts?" Clara asked.

"Nah, betting on Buckskin Nelly wasn't really a gamble. She always wins." He grinned, and Clara scowled. Reed hurried on, "Sewing my trousers myself seemed the only solution if I didn't want my knee sticking out. I was hoping, though, that you might find it in your heart to forgive me? I've been incorrigible, but I have to tell you a secret: I get sort of tongue-tied talking to pretty girls."

"You're a flirt," Clara said, pulling back from his intense blue-eyed gaze.

"Sometimes. Only in fun. But I'm deadly serious now. Can we start over? Give me another chance?"

Clara glanced at Trudi, whose eyes twinkled with a teasing smile. Perhaps she had been too hard on Reed. She didn't need any entanglements—some cocky showoff always trying to tell her what to do—but she could be more friendly. She exhaled. "Oh, very well. We can start over." She glanced again at his terrible sewing job. "You might as well give me your trousers."

Trudi snorted out a laugh, and Reed's eyebrows crept up. "That's a bit forward, isn't it Miss Jensen?"

Clara's face burned red. "I *was* going to offer to fix them for you."

"And now you're not?"

"No, I'm not," Clara said. She gave him a wicked grin. "Now, I'm going to teach you to sew them yourself."

"Deal!" Reed said, extending his hand.

Clara took it, and an electric tingle raced up her fingers at his warm touch.

He pulled her closer to whisper, "I'm happy for any challenge that lets me spend more time with you."

Clara blushed again and wondered what she had just gotten herself into.

VIII

Election News

Woodrow Wilson managed to hold onto the presidency by a slim margin, riding on his promise to keep the U.S. out of the war in Europe. An interesting event occurred in the congressional elections. Miss Jeannette Rankin of Missoula, Montana, was elected as the first female representative in the U.S. Congress.

—The Logan Republican

Trudi poured the sugary, golden-brown goo from the stove onto the kitchen table. Her fingers twitched at the blistering heat. She quickly prodded the mass into a log-shaped roll and pulled it into thick ropes of candy as it cooled, keeping time with the ragtime music drifting in from the living room phonograph. She paused to swipe a lock of brunette hair from her eyes with the back of a sticky hand.

"You're going to be late." Her brother Karl poked his head into the kitchen.

Trudi glanced out the kitchen door at the pendulum clock in the living room, carved with busy milkmaids, a memento from her childhood in Switzerland. The minute hand ticked to forty-five after, and the clock chimed. She gave a start. Clara would arrive in a few minutes to take her to the football game. "I'm almost finished."

"You're doing too much," Karl washed his hands at the pump and stepped in to help stretch the candy and twist it into bite-sized pieces. "You can't save the world all by yourself."

"I just want to help. This war is a terrible thing."

"It is."

"What will happen to us if the U.S. does enter the war?" Trudi asked. "We still have family and friends over there."

"Well, President Wilson won his reelection riding on anti-war sentiments. I doubt it's something we'll have to worry about."

"Would you fight?"

Karl looked away. "Not if I could help it. But there are other ways to help the country, like your charity drives."

"I wish I could do more. The novelty of giving has worn off for most people, but there's still so much need. Over a million refugees from Belgium. And 200,000 Serbs died fleeing their own country."

"I'm proud of you for doing your part." He smiled and turned to the doorway. "Hans! Lise! Come to the kitchen!"

Footsteps echoed on the stairs.

"Karl!" Trudi said. "Let them be."

"Sometimes it's our turn to give, and sometimes it's our turn to receive."

"Hmph," Trudi said, but when their younger siblings appeared in the kitchen doorway, looking eager to get their hands messy, Trudi relented.

"Wash up," Karl told them. "We're making these for . . ."

"The Belgian Relief Fund." The icy water from the pump stung Trudi's fingers, and she scrubbed just long enough to get the sticky residue off her hands. She rushed to the living room to grab her coat, pausing to straighten her hair in the mirror.

"Trying to impress someone?" Karl teased.

Trudi laughed. "No."

"No one's caught your eye? Alonzo's going with you, isn't he?"

"Yes, and he's nice enough, but he's so quiet. Besides, you're older than me, and you've been back from your mission for a while now. We ought to be worried about marrying you off first."

"Fair enough." Karl held his hands up in surrender. "I just wondered if you had your sights set on a political career instead, now that women are being elected."

Trudi glanced at the newspaper sitting on the sofa, with its incredible announcement about the elections. Trudi's family had lived in the U.S. for almost ten years, but there were some things that still seemed as unreal as cloud castles.

"Maybe I should. Miss Rankin said that she may be the first woman in Congress, but she won't be the last." She put on her hat and gloves. "And there was that town in southern Utah—Kanab—where they elected an all-female government a few years ago. I can't imagine any of this happening back in Switzerland. Women there may never even get the vote."

He smiled at her in the mirror. "If Miss Rankin is anything like you, America is lucky to have her."

A flush brightened Trudi's face. "Well, I don't know about going into politics, but I do want to give back somehow."

Clara's horn squawked outside.

"Have fun," Karl said.

She waved goodbye and hurried out. The chilly afternoon air nipped at her cheeks. She huddled in her coat as Clara raced to campus. Trudi clutched her hands in her lap to stop herself from gripping the side of the car. Alonzo sat behind her, and she didn't want to look afraid.

"Good heavens, it's cold already this year," Clara said over the rattle of the car. "I'm going to have to put the Tin Lizzie away for the winter soon."

"It's a miserable day," Trudi said, "and I don't even like football."

"Don't say that aloud," Clara said in mock warning. "They might run you out of town. 'Lonzo doesn't like it either, and he still shows up."

Trudi nodded absently and noticed the folded newspaper sitting next to Clara on the bench seat. "You heard about the elections?"

"Yes, and it's wonderful news, but this is what you'd better be focused on now." Clara tossed the paper in Trudi's lap.

Trudi unfolded it. It was the *Student Life*, opened to the cheers the students were expected to know for the game.

The first was the school fight song:

> *Show me the Scotchman who doesn't love the thistle!*
> *Show me the Englishman who doesn't love the rose!*
> *But show me the true-hearted Aggie of Utah*
> *Who doesn't love the spot (stomp, stomp, stomp)*
> *Where the sage-brush grows!*

Not too bad. She read the next one.

> *One-a-zippa, Two-a-zippa,*
> *Three-a-zippa-zam,*

We're from the A.C.
And don't give a...
Hobble Gobble,
Wobble Gobble-Zip-Bam-Boo
A.C., A.C., A.C.U!

"Please tell me this is a joke."

"Not at all," Clara said with a laugh.

"They get worse every year."

"Maybe," Clara said with mock seriousness, "but we have to do our bit to support our men out there on the field. Especially after that loss against the University of Utah, 46 to 0!"

Trudi groaned. If she had to sit through a football game, hopefully it wouldn't be a humiliating one. Alonzo chuckled from the back seat.

They parked by the football field, and Bert and Reed waved them over to the spectator benches. Reed and Clara met with a smile on his side and a wary look on hers. The truce was still holding, but how long would it last? Trudi ended up squeezed between Alonzo and Bert on the first row overlooking the field. She braced herself for a painful game, but the A.C. scored in the first quarter.

Bert whooped and pumped his fists in the air. Trudi bounced in place as she clapped, earning an amused look from Alonzo. A chant started, and she joined in. Her voice blended with the others, her accent lost in the slightly off-key chorus. The words didn't sound as silly when everyone said them. The crowd moved together, a single organism responding to the actions on the field, its energy tingling through Trudi and making her a part of it.

In the second quarter, Montana scored.

"No, no, *nein*!" Trudi shouted, and Bert laughed heartily. "This is too tense," she muttered.

"It sure is," Bert said. "Hey, Alonzo, why aren't you out there playing? It looks like they could use you."

Alonzo shifted and looked away. "I don't like playing anymore."

"Where's your sense of loyalty to your school?"

Alonzo's eyes creased in pain. Trudi jumped in to intervene.

"Come now, Bert, aren't there more important things than football?"

"Oh, sure, plenty. But it would be awfully nice to win once in a while."

She glanced over and caught Alonzo watching her, but as soon as she met his eyes, he looked away. She noticed Clara on the other side of him. Her friend's mouth had the stubborn set it got when she was debating a point she wouldn't give up. Reed said something in a low voice. Clara folded her arms and scooted away from him, her eyes bright with anger. He smiled mischievously and whispered something in her ear. She glared at him, but a smile crept back onto her face. Trudi shook her head and grinned. Clara may have met her match.

In the third quarter, one of the Aggies got the ball and ran with it.

"Pass it, Peterson!" Bert shouted.

The Montana players closed in on Peterson. Trudi leaned forward to shout with the rest of the crowd. Peterson ran on, dodging his way across the field to score a touchdown.

"Forty yards!" Bert yelled, leaning over to shake Alonzo's shoulder. "Did you see that!"

"Sure did. I'm sitting right here," Alonzo said with a laugh.

The fourth quarter came. Trudi blew on her chilly hands and balled them into fists as the linebackers collided. Soft helmets smashed together repeatedly, the players warring over the muddy territory. The field turned into a mire, the players so soaked and dirty it was hard to tell one team from the other.

Montana kicked the ball toward the goal one last time, and their side of the field broke out into cheers.

"That didn't go through the posts!" Bert said, jumping to his feet.

Reed and Clara stood as well, along with many of the Aggies. The players on the field argued too, everyone yelling at each other and the referees. Trudi huddled back on the bench next to Alozno. His tension radiated through his rigid muscles. Trudi tried to catch his eyes, but his troubled gaze stayed fixed on his friends as they shouted down the other team.

"No!" Bert yelled. Reed booed loudly. Trudi tore her attention from Alonzo. The referee had decided in favor of Montana. A tie game. No winners, no losers. The Aggies shuffled away from their benches, shooting dark looks at the Montana fans. Reed opened his mouth as if to yell something at the other team, but Alonzo grabbed his arm and shook his head.

Earl Johnson, who'd been playing his trumpet with the band, caught up with Trudi. *"Guten abend, fraulein."*

"Grützi, Herr Johnson." She smiled. Earl's older brother had taught her family the gospel in Switzerland, and his family had officially sponsored hers when they immigrated to the U.S.

"Well, that was a disaster," Reed proclaimed. He glanced at Bert and Alonzo. "What do you say, my friends? The Bluebird?"

"Certainly, and I'd call it a celebration," Bert said. "At least we didn't lose this time. You coming too, Earl?"

"Of course. Ice cream might be warmer than this weather." He held up his trumpet. "I think the spit froze in my valves."

Trudi wrinkled her nose, and Earl gave her a teasing grin.

"You gonna drive us all, Miss Jensen?" Reed asked.

"Oh, I suppose. It'll be a cold ride."

"At least it'll be a short one."

The six of them crammed into the Model T's two bench seats. Alonzo sat in the front, so Trudi again found herself next to him. She could never tell what was going through his mind, but there was something pleasant about his warmth seeping into her arm, warding off the chill. The boys in the back seat yelped in delight when Clara took a sharp turn. It threw Trudi against Alonzo's chest, and she blushed furiously as she straightened.

Trudi's friends weren't the only ones looking to console themselves with something sweet. Disgruntled fans crowded around the marble counter and wooden tables.

They huddled together at a table with their ice creams. Trudi discreetly licked her spoon, savoring the rich vanilla flavor.

Bert gestured with his spoon at Alonzo and Reed. "The last time I ate ice cream when it was this cold was after we saw the Welsh Singers. Can you fellows believe that was a year ago? Those boys sure could sing."

Reed stared out the front window with a thoughtful expression. "A year? It feels like a long time, but not much has changed."

"It has for the people over there," Trudi said. "America's tired of the war already—or at least tired of giving to the relief efforts—and we're not even fighting in it. But it just drags on."

"That's true," Earl said. "Almost a million men have been wounded or killed just in the Battle of the Somme, and who knows when that will end?"

"Don't forget the women," Trudi said. "They're suffering on the home front, going without in order to supply the troops."

Alonzo nodded and looked like he wanted to add something, but Earl jumped in with a smile for Trudi. "You're right. I wouldn't want to forget the ladies. If you like discussing current events, you ought to come with me to the Cosmos Club next week."

Trudi hesitated, thinking of her busy schedule, but the Cosmos Club was known for its lively debates, and she hated to miss out. Besides, it was unusual for them to invite women, a rare opportunity. "That would be interesting. Thank you."

The conversation turned to bemoaning the state of the football team until they all finished their ice cream. They walked back outside, adjusting their hats and coat collars for the icy breeze. Clara gave the Tin Lizzie's crank a quick turn, but the engine stayed stubbornly silent.

"It might be too cold to start," she muttered.

Another car rattled past them. Clara glowered at it.

Reed snickered. "Say, Bert, did you hear about the girl at school who wanted to change her name?"

"No, why'd she want to change it?"

"It was Iona."

"That's not such a bad name."

"Ah, but her last name was Ford."

The men laughed, and Trudi smothered a giggle. Clara jerked at the crank, forcing the engine to sputter to life. "I'm glad you have your jokes to keep you warm on your walk home, Mr. Lewis."

"You wouldn't leave a fellow to freeze out here, would you?" Reed asked with a laugh in his eyes.

"Well, I'm not letting you back in the car. You can ride on the outside."

"You're always leaving me out in the cold," Reed lamented.

"I'm not complaining," Bert said. "Now there's more room in the car."

Reed laughed along with the others and swept them a bow from his spot on the running board. Clara smiled too as she drove back up Main Street.

The Cosmos Club gathered at the fraternity house of some of the men in the organization. Trudi met Earl on the sidewalk, and he escorted her inside. She was the only woman there. Well, Jeannette Rankin was in Congress, alone among all those men. Someone had to be the first woman to venture into new territory. Trudi stood straighter. If the men thought anything odd about her being there, they didn't show it as they welcomed her. Moses Cowley called the meeting to order.

A professor whom Trudi didn't know stood to deliver a speech about the poor preparedness of the American military. Trudi listened in alarm to the facts. Many of the men from the Utah National Guard who'd been sent to the Mexican border to stop Pancho Villa's raids didn't even know how to load or shoot their guns. They lacked the most basic military training.

Moses spoke about his experience at the military training camp, but Trudi doubted that a month of training was enough to prepare a solider for the war that was claiming millions of lives in Europe.

"If we were attacked, we couldn't defend ourselves," she said, jumping into the conversation without thinking. "We'd have to throw untrained young men into the fight. The casualty rate would be appalling."

Moses Cowley nodded. "Universal military training is the answer."

"Taking men away from the farms?" Earl asked. "Isn't it more reasonable to have a standing army of professional soldiers?"

As they debated, Trudi leaned back in her seat, lost on the edge of the conversation. They were discussing men's roles, men's lives, men's training. This was why Switzerland would never let women vote: they saw it as a privilege for those defending their country, and whatever contribution women made, it was not considered significant enough.

Trudi exchanged pleasantries with the men at the end of the meeting, but her thoughts were across the ocean with her friends and family back in Switzerland, surrounded by combatants, suffering from lack of food and clothing. And what about her mother's family in Germany? So many great and terrible things were happening in the world, and she was still sitting on the benches, unsure of her place in it all.

Reed and Clara caught up with Trudi on the way to the mandatory campus chapel meeting the next day. Trudi had stayed up late finishing her readings after going to Cosmos Club, and she wasn't feeling up to matching Reed's cheerful grin. He poked at the knitting needles sticking out of her bag and turned up the wattage of his smile.

"What do you say, Trudi?" Reed asked. "Will you make me socks for Loud Socks Day?"

"Reed!" Clara said in exasperation. She looked at Trudi. "I already told him if he wants socks, I'll teach him how to knit."

Reed made a pleading face. "I don't have the patience to sit that long."

"It's a very useful skill," Trudi said. "And I'm sure whatever you come up with will be quite spectacular."

Reed laughed.

"Besides," Clara added, "Trudi's knitting for a good cause. You wouldn't want to take away from that, would you?"

"You mean you're not making socks for yourself, with all the knitting you do?" Reed asked. "Loud Socks Day is a grand tradition. You wouldn't want to be left out of the fun."

Trudi hesitated. Everyone took part in Loud Socks Day. It was part of being an Aggie. If she knitted while she studied, she could wring a little more time out of her schedule. "Maybe I will make some for myself, but you'll have to make your own, Mr. Lewis."

He groaned good-naturedly. "Fine, but only if Clara agrees to go see a movie with me."

Clara blushed a little and feigned resignation. "Oh, very well."

Trudi went to work on her loud socks that night, making them out of spare bits of yarn in orange, green, yellow, and purple. Karl shook his head at the creation, but she enjoyed the break from thinking about the war.

When Loud Socks Day arrived, she put on her colorful workmanship and tucked her skirt up a little to show them off. She'd been up most of the night finishing them, but she was proud of the motley effect as she walked up college hill. Most of the students on campus were similarly dressed, skirts and pants hitched up enough to show off bright, mismatched socks. Reed had scrounged up some purple and orange socks, and Clara's were different sizes, one slouched down around her ankle, the other stretched tight around her calf.

Earl marched by, playing with the band, wearing wildly striped socks. Other students joined in the parade, and Trudi let them sweep her up as they snaked in front of the campus buildings. The air was cool and crisp, barely warmed by the watery autumn sunlight, and the last of the fall leaves crunched under their shoes. The whole campus had a festive feel, welcoming the upcoming holiday season. Trudi laughed and waved to friends as she marched along with the crowd.

She arrived home in a smiling mood, but the look on Karl's face instantly sobered her.

"Karl, what is it?" She asked, taking his arm.

His eyes were red-rimmed, as though he had been crying, but his voice was leaden.

"Leo Whitaker. Do you remember him?"

"I think so. He was one of your mission companions in Germany?"

"Yes, from Canada. He was killed in the Battle of the Somme. Trudi, he was killed fighting against the same people he served on his mission. We loved those people." He slammed his fist on the table and crumpled up the letter. "This isn't right."

Karl pulled away from her and retreated to his room. Trudi sat, stunned. She pulled her skirt down over her brightly patterned socks. If only she hadn't wasted her time on something silly. She could have made another pair of socks for the refugees or the soldiers.

But what good would that have done? Socks wouldn't stop bullets. Pulled candy and scavenged pennies from relief drives wouldn't end the war. Nothing she did made a bit of difference.

She buried her face in her hands and cried.

IX

The year that has elapsed since we last observed our day of thanksgiving has been rich in blessings to us as a people, but the whole face of the world has been darkened by war. In the midst of our peace and happiness, our thoughts dwell with painful disquiet upon the struggles and sufferings of the nations at war and of the peoples upon whom war has brought disaster without choice or possibility of escape on their part... Our people could in no better way show their real attitude towards the present struggle of the nations than by contributing out of their abundance to the relief of the suffering which war has brought in its train.

—President Woodrow Wilson

The chill whipped around the edges of the Model T's windscreen, shrinking Reed and Alonzo into their coats during the short drive back from Green Canyon to the Jensen's farm.

"This drive would be warmer if we had some fresh turkey piled in the back," Reed said.

"Don't worry. My mother prepared a turkey yesterday from our flock."

"You mean she lacks confidence in our manly hunting abilities?"

"Not at all." Alonzo laughed. "But she know every yahoo from miles around runs up the canyons after wild turkeys Thanksgiving morning. Probably scatters those birds all the way to Bear Lake!"

"Gee, Alonzo, have you given any thought to buying a coupe with closed-in sides?" Reed asked through numb lips. "I mean, this beats walking, but not by much."

"Sure, why not? Heck, I have my eye on a pretty sharp Cadillac, maybe a Pierce Arrow. Maybe I'll buy one of each," Alonzo said. "You remember this is Clara's car anyway, right?"

"Really?" Reed asked sarcastically. "I did wonder how she always seems to be the one driving it."

"You know, she found it in rather rough shape and sold her horse to buy it. She repaired it herself. You ought to have seen her, all greasy in those coveralls, half hanging out of that engine compartment, yelling about dang Fords."

"She's really remarkable," Reed said, as much to himself as to Alonzo.

Alonzo turned toward him stiffly. "Yes, I know, and I'm glad you see how special she is as well."

"I'd like to make a good impression today. It's just, she makes me nervous, brings out the ham in me, and I find myself annoying her pretty regularly."

The Jensen Farm came into view, and Reed recognized bare-branched apple, peach, and plum trees in the orchard as the Model T passed along the road bordering the farm. Alonzo turned into a lane through the orchard toward the two-story farmhouse.

"Home, sweet home," Alonzo announced. "Warm and comfortable, at least compared to the ride out here. I've been scraping ice off the upstairs windows in the morning, though."

"I've had to do that a time or two," Reed answered. "When the wind really blew, we'd get snow through the cracks of the windows and doors. In the summer, it was sand instead. We had to shovel it out."

He admired the farm's white clapboards and well-made picket fence. The neatness of the place stood out in the disorder of autumn. Leaves fell, but did not linger long on the ground. The kitchen garden had long since been turned over and composted to refresh the soil. Rose bushes were cut back and mulched to survive another tough winter. Everything about the place spoke of care and hard work.

Alonzo walked in first, turning his head so Clara could peck him on the cheek as she took his coat. Warmth and the scent of roasting meat and cinnamon washed over Reed. He smiled broadly at Clara and mimicked Alonzo's turned cheek. Clara took his coat but only gave him an eye roll.

"'Lonzo, please take Reed over to the fireplace to warm up. I'll tell mother you're here."

Mrs. Jensen burst through the swinging kitchen door as if everyone in the home had long since learned to stay clear of its path. She brushed flour from her hands onto her apron and kissed Alonzo on the cheek, turning toward Reed and taking both of his hands in hers. "So this is the famous Mr. Reed Lewis I've heard so much about. Welcome to our home, Mr. Lewis. Welcome."

Reed liked her immediately. She was an older, slightly more matronly version of Clara, with white streaks in her short, blond hair. Her hands, though strong and rough from work, were gentle and warm. She reminded him of his own mother.

"It's lovely to meet you, Mrs. Jensen. Thank you so much for the invitation to dine with you. I hope my reputation is a positive one in your home?"

"Oh my, yes." Mrs. Jensen laughed. "Alonzo speaks very highly of you, of course, and Clara, she talks about you almost constantly!"

"Mother!" Clara said through clenched teeth. Mrs. Jensen smiled mischievously at Reed and turned on her heels, laughing as she crashed back through the kitchen door.

Clara stood looking at the door, then toward Reed and Alonzo. Her cheeks blazed red. Reed rocked back on his heels, brushed back his jacket, and hung his thumbs in the front pockets of his vest, smiling.

"I'm . . . I'm going to help her, with the meal," Clara managed, pushing through the door just as her mother had.

"My mother," Alonzo announced, "enjoys stirring the pot now and again." Both men chuckled as they stood by the fire, the crackling of the pitch pine filling the quiet.

They all sat down for the Thanksgiving meal at the large table Reed and Alonzo carried into the living room. Mrs. Jensen insisted that Reed sit next to her. Alonzo gave the blessing, after which Reed dug into one of the finest meals he had ever had. Roast turkey, sweet and mashed potatoes, cranberry sauce, gherkins, giblet gravy, and creamed corn.

"I understand your family has a farm in Sanpete County, Reed, is that right?" Mrs. Jensen asked.

"Sure is, Ma'am. My parents established the homestead there. A lot of the ground was good for nothing but sagebrush, and it was tough work converting it for agriculture. But they worked at it and built a life there. They built a larger house later, but the one-room homestead is still there, 'up to the field,' as we say, and the newer house is 'out to the field,'"—he pointed with his fork, as if they could all see it as he pictured it—"on account of where they are on the farm."

"What crops?" Mrs. Jensen asked, scooping more mashed potatoes onto his plate and passing the gravy.

Reed drizzled the gravy over the generous helping of potatoes and passed it on to Clara, who blushed when their fingertips touched. "Well, we mostly raise cattle, but we put in hay every year for our own use and to sell. 'Course mother has a kitchen garden like yours. She puts up a whole mess of stuff to enjoy over the winter."

"How about you, what did you do on the farm?" Mrs. Jensen asked.

Reed realized she wasn't asking about the farm so much as taking the measure of him. He set down his fork.

"Well, Ma'am, we all had chores from the time we were little. I guess by twelve I could harness the team by myself, by fourteen I could plow pretty much as well as my father."

"And did you like the work? The place?"

Reed thought for a moment. "You know, one time we had a phrenologist come through town, and my father had him read my head. He said I'd be a farmer. I think he was right. When I follow a walking plow—the vibrations as it cuts the soil—there is something satisfying about it. Now sometimes, all I can think about is that this is hard work. But occasionally, there are these moments. Meadowlarks hovering over the field looking for grubs, mourning doves cooing, the larks singing, and just the sound of the horses straining in harness and the soil bubbling up on both sides of the till—I love those moments."

"What was your favorite time at the farm?" Mrs. Jensen watched him as she spread cranberry sauce on her turkey.

Reed swallowed a bite of the creamy potatoes as he considered. "Harvest. We'd work so many hours we'd sleep on hay beds under farm quilts out in the fields. When the thresher team was there, mother would cook us these great farm breakfasts. Eggs, bacon, fried potatoes, pie, even coffee sometimes." He hesitated. The church leaders hadn't forbidden coffee, but they discouraged it, and some Mormons frowned on those who had developed the habit. Well, he couldn't be anything but himself, and he loved his family; he wouldn't try to whitewash them. "Mother likes her cup of coffee now and then, though father disapproves."

Mrs. Jensen smiled and laid her hand across Reed's. "I like you, Reed. I'm going to get you some pie. It's pearmain apple from our orchard."

After she disappeared back into the kitchen, Reed asked Clara, "So, did I pass?"

"I don't know what you mean, Mr. Lewis," Clara answered.

"Why, I mean, did I pass the 'are you worthy to court my daughter' test?" Reed said, laughing.

"My mother was merely seeking to entertain an honored guest . . . of my brother's," Clara said, but her eyes twinkled at Reed.

After dessert, Clara said, "Let's sit by the fire, shall we? I believe it's time for Mr. Lewis's knitting lesson."

"Gracious, Reed," Mrs. Jensen said as she cleared plates, "you must really want company at that movie."

"Ma'am, I would knit an entire sock just for the opportunity to spend an hour with your lovely daughter watching a motion picture. Besides, I was deeply humiliated by my failure to impress at Loud Socks Day on campus yesterday. I need to make amends!"

More laughter from Mrs. Jensen as she returned to the kitchen.

"I think you've won her over, Reed," Alonzo said, putting his hand on Reed's shoulder as they walked toward the fireplace. "It's the younger blonde you've got to watch out for."

"Um, I'm right here, 'Lonzo. Perhaps you can wait until the car ride home to weigh my relative merits?" Clara said in mock anger. "Now, sit down, Mr. Lewis." She handed him the yarn, and he fumbled with the needles. Clara gave him an arch look. "We could do this with four needles, you know, but in your case, I'm glad we made it easier by half."

"Are you implying I'm half-witted, Miss Jensen?"

Clara's smile broke through her serious teacher face. "Of course not. It's just much easier at first if you knit your sock flat, then sew it up the back. Remember, the basic pattern is knit one, purl one."

Clara got Reed started on his sock, and within a half hour, he had several rather uneven rows that looked vaguely like knitting. He enjoyed the process, especially asking for help when he mixed up the order of knits and purls, and Clara's gentle hands touching his to remove the offending stitches.

"If I didn't know better, I'd suggest you're making mistakes on purpose." Clara said.

"What?" Reed said. "My dear Miss Jensen, my only objective here today is fellowship with my friends, and knit at least one sock."

"It's a bit thick in here," Alonzo complained.

"Well, I can knit and converse," Reed said. "What shall we discuss?"

"I think you should stick to knitting," Clara said.

"Let's talk about the war." Alonzo looked pointedly at Clara.

"It seems to be all we talk about these days," Clara said quickly. "Maybe we ought not to spoil this lovely holiday with you boys rehashing the same preparedness versus pacifism arguments over and over."

"Well then, perhaps you can shape the discussion by telling Reed here about your desire to get involved personally," Alonzo said, raising an eyebrow at Clara.

Clara laid her knitting on her lap and burned a stare back. "The fact that I want to help somehow, that I feel a duty to do so, hardly seems worthy of your concern."

"Yes, I have to say I think she is right," Reed offered. "There are so many opportunities to help these days. Frankly, there are far more on campus for women to participate in than there are for men. These efforts are aimed at humanitarian relief, are they not? Surely you don't object to that Alonzo?"

"She's not talking about making socks and sweaters for refugees, for heaven's sake; she wants to go to France to help in person. If she were a nurse, she'd already have gone with the Red Cross. She's always making rash decisions, jumping into things without thinking . . ." Alonzo stomped toward the front door. "I'll be back in a few minutes, I need to check on the calves."

Clara looked at the door after he closed it, her lips tight, and her face red with anger. "I'm very sorry, Reed. 'Lonzo sometimes forgets he's my brother, not my father. He had no right to violate my privacy like that."

She gave Reed a challenging stare. He just sat there with his knitting in a heap in his lap, studying the stubborn set of her soft-looking lips and the emotion brightening her eyes. She might be frustrated and a bit embarrassed, but there was a longing there too, a desire to be understood.

"Well, out with it, Reed," she said quietly. "Tell me I cannot go. That a woman's place is here, minding home and hearth."

"Clara, I don't want you to go anywhere. But, I think I know how you feel. This war, it will be our war soon. It must be. It is not enough to talk about it. Not enough to send aid to its victims. We cannot sit and watch Europe destroy itself any longer. It pulls me toward it, and I feel it in my bones. I would not presume that your feelings are any less powerful than mine."

Reed laid his hand over Clara's and squeezed gently. She squeezed back, her fingers lingering against his for a moment. They shared a shy smile, then Reed picked up his knitting, the tingle from her touch distracting him from all thoughts of knits and purls.

X

The Germans are making good on their threat of unrestricted submarine warfare. Another American ship has fallen to German torpedoes. With Germany attempting to draw Mexico into war against the United States, and rumors of German plots against President Wilson, many citizens are beginning to wonder how much longer the U.S. will endure these outrageous attacks.

—*The Logan Republican*

Clara adjusted her knit hat in the mirror, framing her face with short blonde curls. The wood-burning stove didn't quite keep the chill at bay, and drafts blew their icy breath across the wooden floor and through the windowpanes. Outside, the sunset touched the white-shrouded mountains and bathed the deep snow in a pink glow. Clara paused to stare past the curtains in wonder.

"I'm not sure you should go out." Alonzo glanced out the window with a frown creasing his forehead.

"I'll be fine. I've got my coat and two layers of wool stockings, and we'll be inside most of the time."

"How is Reed taking you to town?"

"He said it would be a surprise." A nervous thrill fluttered through her chest. They were just going to a dance with Trudi and Earl at the Church's German branch, but Reed seemed to want to make something special of the evening.

"Hmm," Alonzo said warily.

"Oh, come on, 'Lonzo. He's your friend."

"Yes."

"But?"

"I just want you to be safe."

"You're a darling." She kissed his cheek, and he rolled his eyes.

The sound of bells drifted through the windowpanes, and Clara peeked back outside. A horse-drawn sleigh pulled up in front of the house, cutting ridges into the snow. Clara covered her mouth in surprise, and the flutters in her chest multiplied. Reed raised a hand in greeting, and she waved back with a wide grin.

"Have fun, dear." Mrs. Jensen came out of the kitchen, a shawl draped over her shoulders, to give Clara a quick hug. "Be good."

"Of course." Clara took a deep breath, relishing the scent of fresh-baked bread and cinnamon that always clung to her mother.

Reed knocked on the door. Clara flung it open, and a painful wave of cold rolled through the room as he slipped inside.

"Good heavens, it's freezing," Mrs. Jensen said. "You keep her warm, young man."

"Oh, I will, ma'am," Reed said, his eyes twinkling with mischief.

Alonzo gave him a warning look.

"We'd better get going," Reed said with a bright smile at Alonzo.

Clara nodded, not trusting herself to speak without laughing. Reed offered his arm, and they opened the door once more to brave the bitter chill. Reed helped her into the sleigh and tucked a thick wool blanket around her. Then he climbed up and threw another blanket across his lap. Their breath trailed around them in wispy white clouds, and the cold bit Reed's cheeks red.

"Walk on," Reed said to the horse when he took up the reins. He shot a glance at Clara. "Warm enough?"

"Not freezing, at least. I can't remember a winter this cold."

"I heard Cache Valley had bitter winters. I thought that this was typical and I'd just been lucky the last couple of years."

"No, this is bad even for us. Everyone's already worried about having a short growing season this summer. Sometimes I'm afraid the snow will never melt and I'll never be warm again." She shivered. "So, Mr. Lewis, where did you get the sleigh?"

"I borrowed it, and it's just my first surprise for the evening. We're not going right to the dance."

"Oh, aren't we? And where do you think you're abducting me to?"

"I'm not telling."

"And if I don't like your plan?"

"You will."

She bristled at his self-assured tone. He caught her glare.

"Don't you trust me?"

She softened a little at the concern in his face. He hadn't shown himself to be inconsiderate or controlling so far, but how could she be sure? She pulled the blanket closer. "I'd better like this plan. If not, I'll steal the sleigh and leave you to walk home alone."

"Deal! I'll make sure you have a good time."

He guided the horse into Logan, the streets nearly silent, as everyone with sense stayed inside on such a cold evening. The only sound was the gentle slicing of the sleigh through the snow and the bells on the harness. It seemed like a magical world that they had all to themselves. Then, distant laughs echoed in the deserted streets. Reed pulled up to a park where a frozen pond served as a skating rink.

"You ice skate, I presume?" Reed asked.

"Of course, but I don't have any—"

Reed held up a pair of lady's ice skates.

Clara grinned. "Oh, how kind, Reed, but if I use your skates, what will you wear?"

He chuckled and pulled his own skates out. He helped Clara down. She was sorry to leave behind the warm blanket, but moving would get blood back into her tingling feet. She quickly traded her boots for the ice skates and wobbly got to her feet. Reed offered her a hand, but she found her balance and glided away. He looked disappointed until she gave him a teasing grin. He smiled back and chased after her.

Clara laughed as they whooshed over the ice, flying past children and other couples. Reed was quick, and Clara had a couple of close calls dodging him. Part of her wanted him to catch her, but part of her was scared to let him win.

Clara made a tight turn, and her skate slipped. She flailed and tumbled for the ice. Reed caught her and spun her back up onto her feet. She threw her arms around him. He held her tightly.

"Don't worry," he whispered. "I won't let you fall."

Clara almost tore away, determined to show she could stand on her own, but his embrace was warm and steady, and his look was admiring. She relaxed and took his hand, and they skated together. Reed grinned at her, and they raced around the rink, hand in hand, spinning in wild circles until Clara was dizzy.

Reed pulled her in closer, and she leaned on him for support, laughing breathlessly. She looked up to find him watching her with a quirky smile, his blue eyes intense as they met hers.

"You ever been kissed?" he asked.

Clara blushed. "Sure. There was George Hansen in third grade—"

"That must have been memorable." Reed grinned.

"It certainly was. Then there was high school."

"Oh?"

"Yeah, Ernest and Will and—"

"Okay, maybe I don't need the whole list," he grumbled.

"Jealous?" Clara asked, laughing. "I'm sure you've kissed your share of girls."

"Of course. I have to beat them away with a stick."

He leaned closer, his gaze traveling down to her lips. Clara tilted her head back to look into his eyes. The smile was still in them, and they were bright with anticipation. She suddenly felt very warm despite the chill, and a little dizzy, as though she were standing on the edge of a cliff looking over a steep fall. None of the other boys she'd let sneak kisses had made her head feel quite like that.

Reed closed his eyes and tilted his face to hers.

"Look, they're sledding," Clara blurted out.

Reed glanced up in annoyance at the kids racing down the hill, but his expression turned to interest.

"You wanna try?" Reed asked.

"Yes, but not on that hill."

"Too steep for you?" Reed asked.

"Too short." Clara pointed to a taller hill, still covered in fresh snow. "That one."

"You're on!"

Reed traded the kids a piece of hard candy from his pocket for a turn with one of the sleds. He and Clara changed out of their skates and raced up the hill, the powdery snow threatening to swallow their boots. They reached the top. The sharp drop below them made Clara's heart race with exhilaration.

Reed sat on the back of the sled, bracing it with his feet.

"Hop on." Reed's smile showed the same excitement Clara felt.

He held out his arms. She hesitated then accepted his help to settle in front of him. He wrapped his arms around her waist and held her back against his chest. She closed her eyes for a moment and savored the sense of peace, embraced in his warmth and the scent of his cologne.

"Here we go." His whisper tickled her ear, and a tingle of pleasure rushed over her.

He lifted his feet into the sled and it tipped forward, plunging down the steep hill. The cold wind whipped tears from Clara's eyes, and a thrill raced through her. Reed let out a whoop and held her tighter. They were flying together, soaring down the hill.

The sled reached the bottom and turned, careening sideways for a moment before hitting a dip and flipping over, dumping Clara and Reed to tumble into the snow. Reed still held her tight, wrapping her into his chest, so they rolled a couple of times and stopped with her head resting above his wildly pounding heart.

"You all right?" he asked.

"Yes. Let's do it again!"

He laughed. "You've gotten snow in your coat and your boots, and we ought to be getting along to the dance. People will start to miss us."

"I suppose," Clara said.

Reed helped her to her feet. When he stepped away, the cold rushed in on her. She shivered as the snow in her boots slowly melted and seeped through her wool socks.

Reed returned the sled and helped Clara into the sleigh. He wrapped her in both blankets and trotted the horse over to the Church building where the German branch was holding its dance. Clara shivered and tried to keep her teeth from chattering, but Reed noticed.

"Let's get you inside quick. Some hot cider and dancing will warm you back up."

They hurried into the building. A flood of heat and loud brass band music greeted them, along with the babble of German. Clara's shivering quickly stopped, and she was glad to shed her coat and hat.

"I hope you know how to polka," Reed shouted over the noise.

"Of course!"

"I don't speak German," Reed said more quietly, leaning down to her ear.

"Oh, they all speak English too. It's just a chance for them to be around other people who come from the same background, speak the same language."

"It must be lonesome, leaving your country behind," Reed said, in one of those flashes of seriousness that still surprised Clara. There was more to Reed than just fun. It was intriguing, and more than a little dangerous to her determination not to lose her head.

"Clara! Reed!" Trudi grabbed their hands and pulled them over to greet Earl.

Though much of the conversation around them was in German, mostly with a lilting Swiss accent, people took the time to stop and welcome Reed and Clara, using English when they looked confused by the German. The band played waltzes and polkas as well as popular tunes. Reed danced with Clara most of the night, though she took a turn doing the freshman two-step with Earl when he wasn't filling in with the band on his trumpet.

"Enjoying yourself?" Trudi asked when she caught Clara alone. "Reed looks nice tonight."

"Yes, he does," Clara said warily.

"But?"

"I like him."

Trudi linked her arm through Clara's. "And why is that a problem?"

"It scares me. I don't want to give anyone else the chance to hurt me."

Trudi's expression turned sympathetic. "He's not your father, Clara."

"I know," Clara whispered, and Reed came to lead her away.

Finally the band took a break, and some of the Swiss seized the opportunity to claim the stage and announce an impromptu yodeling contest.

Reed grimaced, and Clara hid her smile behind her hand.

"Say, Clara, this seems like a good time to get another glass of cider, don't you think?"

She nodded, laughing out loud when they escaped from the dance hall.

"Trudi should have warned us about the interlude," Reed said as the sounds of yodeling chased them down the hall.

"She probably enjoys it," Clara said. "I think she gets homesick for Switzerland. I don't blame her. I'd love to visit there someday."

"Switzerland?"

"Oh, every place. Especially Paris, once the war is over." She hesitated, then confessed, "Sometimes I feel like the mountains around this valley are a huge wall, holding me back from everything out there."

"I hope the war leaves enough of it for you to see, then," Reed said softly.

"You don't object to the idea of a young lady traveling overseas?"

"Why should I, when I'd like to go too?" He hesitated. "Maybe even with you."

She pulled away.

"What's wrong?" Reed asked.

Clara met his worried gaze. She could laugh it off and keep him at arm's length like she did with the other boys. For once, though, she didn't want to run from the edge of that cliff. She wanted to find out what happened if she jumped.

"I'm afraid," she confessed.

Reed's forehead wrinkled in confusion.

"I can't stand the thought of being controlled or locked away," she said. "Of being told nothing I do is worth anything."

Reed looked hurt. "You think I would do that?"

Clara met his eyes. "No. But after seeing the way my father acted . . ."

"Huh." Reed said, his expression softening. "So you don't want to settle down someday?"

"I do, but only if I could know that it wouldn't be like that."

"Hmm. I wish you could meet my parents, then. They're partners. They work together, and they trust each other." He smiled. "They argue like the Dickens sometimes too, because they both have strong opinions, but they're friends again when it's over. That's what I've always wanted—a woman smart and strong enough to be right by my side. One who trusts me too."

"Yes," Clara said. "I want to believe that's possible."

"Then give me more time, and I'll try to convince you."

She smiled and nodded.

Reed stroked a loose strand of blonde hair behind her ear. She took a shaky breath and looked into his eyes. He ran his fingers along her jaw. She shivered and closed her eyes as he leaned closer. His lips were soft and gentle on hers, lingering. She wrapped her arms around him, keeping him close. He kissed her again, more deeply.

The window behind her exploded in a shower of glass. Reed whirled her around, putting himself between her and the broken window. Clara clutched his arm and leaned forward to see a rock lying in the shards of glass.

"What—" she asked

Shouts came from outside.

"Stay here," Reed said, racing for the door.

Clara hurried after him, joining a group of dancers attracted by the noise. A few other young men, including Earl, rushed out with Reed, confronting a group of men with rocks and bottles of moonshine in their hands. Clara found Trudi in the watching crowd and pushed her way through to her friend.

One of the drunks threw a rock, and it caught Earl on the side of the head. Reed sprang forward and punched the drunk in the face. The drunk staggered back, and his friend swung at Reed with his bottle. Earl shouted a warning. Reed blocked the blow, and the moonshine bottle shattered on the church steps.

"Get out of here!" Reed yelled at the drunks.

"Why're you defending these Germans? Ain't you heard that they're the enemy?"

"You don't know what you're talking about," Reed said. "You're drunk. Ain't *you* heard that that'll get you arrested in Logan? Go home before we bring the police."

"If you're siding with the enemy . . ."

Reed looked at the young men at his side. He shook his head. "There's no enemy here. You don't want this kind of trouble."

One of the drunk men pulled at the other, and they stumbled off, shouting things over their shoulder that made Clara blush all over again.

Trudi hurried forward to check on Earl, who was holding a bloody handkerchief to his head.

"I'm fine," he insisted. "I'll have a goose egg in the morning, but that's all. Are *you* all right?" he asked Trudi.

"Yes," she whispered shakily. "But those men . . ."

"They're just drunk idiots looking for a fight," Clara reassured her, hoping she was right.

"Come on," Reed said, his face pale with anger. "We'd best get you ladies home. I think the fun is over."

XI

The world must be made safe for democracy. Its peace must be planted upon the tested foundations of political liberty. We have no selfish ends to serve. We desire no conquest, no dominion. We seek no indemnities for ourselves, no material compensation for the sacrifices we shall freely make. We are but one of the champions of the rights of mankind. We shall be satisfied when those rights have been made as secure as the faith and the freedom of nations can make them.
—President Woodrow Wilson

Joseph sat next to Bert on the longest bench he had ever seen, feeling swallowed up by the enormous Salt Lake Tabernacle. He was glad the crowd was quiet and subdued waiting for the start of the LDS Church's annual general conference. He wanted time to process this place.

American flags hung from the ceiling in several places, rigidly displayed as if flying in a stiff breeze across the huge domed roof. *How can that roof hold snow with no internal supports?*

The organ, front and center, was the star attraction. It looked like an altar in itself, rising toward the sky, pipes like golden upturned flutes capped with carved wood, some of them so big a man could fit inside. The choir flanked the organ, women in white on the left, men in black on the right. Joseph smiled at the men—they looked like a picture he had seen at the Washakie School of penguins standing on a big rock, looking out over Antarctic waters.

Joseph glanced at Reed and Clara, sitting with Alonzo in the row in front of him. They were unusually quiet today. He smiled to himself. He had never seen Reed and Clara together when they weren't talking intensely. *They sure spent a lot of time pretending they weren't in love yet. Glad that's over now.* He didn't know Trudi and Earl as well, but he didn't

74

detect the same chemistry between them, though they sat together and exchanged whispered comments.

Of course, Joseph knew there was more to the somber mood than just the reverence one felt in this holy place. President Wilson had asked Congress for a declaration of war on the second. Everyone expected to be at war any day. *Then what?*

Joseph glanced curiously at Moses Cowley as he sat at the far end of their group, next to Earl. A few people moving past their row stopped to greet him, some laying a hand on his shoulder sympathetically.

Bert followed Joseph's gaze and leaned closer. "His father used to be a member of the Quorum of the Twelve, but he was forced to resign in 1905 because of his strong support of polygamy. It's why Moses works so hard at everything he does. He wants to be respected, like his father."

"He wants to be a polygamist?" Joseph asked.

"No, no. He wants to be a man of conviction. His father could have kept his priesthood, even stayed in the Quorum, but he chose to follow his beliefs. I don't think Moses supports polygamy at all—but he does believe in being true to one's principles."

"Yes. See how he holds his head up? He carries his father's name with honor. I like that." Joseph said.

Bert nodded. "Say, what do you think of all . . ." but he was interrupted by the start of the conference, the choir and organist leading the singing of "Come, Come, Ye Saints." Joseph could hear his own words and those around him at first, but the choir and the organ rose in unison so powerfully they seemed to draw the sound from his lips, like he was noiselessly mimicking the verses. The organ's reverberations hit his face like waves crashing on a shore. He felt humble and overwhelmed by it all. He was glad when it was time to sit down.

Church President Joseph F. Smith opened the conference with general comments about the need to live prudently, exercising economy and industry, but soon touched on themes directly related to the coming war. LDS soldiers, he said, must not demolish or override the principles in which they believe. They were soldiers of the nation *and* of the cross, who fight to save the principles of humanity, love, and peace. Ministers of life, not death.

". . . and when they go forth," President Smith said, pausing to scan the faces in the crowd, "they may go forth in the spirit of defending the liberties of mankind rather than for the purpose of destroying the enemy."

Alonzo shifted uncomfortably in front of Joseph and bowed his head as if deep in thought. Or perhaps in prayer.

Joseph mulled over President Smith's words during the first music break. In his tribal tradition, proving oneself as a warrior was a man's deepest desire, inculcated from the time they learned to speak. Yet, after the turn of the century, there had been no more war. Confined largely to reservations, competing tribes no longer raided each other nor fought for control of hunting grounds. In Cache Valley, the land his people once called home, the white man had pushed them away completely, the last act played out in 1863 at the Massacre of Boa Ogoi, or Battle of Bear River, as the U.S. soldiers called it. Joseph saw this coming war as his way to earn the respect of his tribe, both living and dead. To take his place among warriors of the past as an equal, not a man lost among their conquerors. But how to square this with what the Church expected? Were killing and death not a part of war?

First Counselor Anthon H. Lund spoke next. He condemned blaming people for where they were born. Lund said that there are no nationalities in the Church.

"Now let us treat them not as if they were against us, but do everything to make them feel that we are all American citizens," Lund said.

Out of the corner of his eye, Joseph saw Trudi lean forward, her gaze fixed on President Lund. She nodded as he spoke.

He described the Church as one of peace. In dealing with native populations, for example, he cited Brigham Young's admonition to feed the Indians rather than to fight them. That does not mean, he said, that LDS men will not fight when they must. He said that when unruly Indians would take cattle and kill our men and women, we had to fight them.

Well, that's one side of the story. Throw us off our land, deny our right to hunt, then call the army when we resist starving to death.

Joseph was impressed by the talk by Elder David O. McKay, the man who had replaced Moses's father in the Quorum of the Twelve. McKay said that God is love. He does not choose war and pestilence: men do. We are free to choose the right, he said—or the wrong. A soldier who fights for liberty and right, to defend his home, his people, is choosing the right.

Reed nodded, and he and Clara shared a glance full of electric antic-ipation. Bert wore a thoughtful expression, and he fidgeted with the chain of the pocket watch he always carried with him.

As the talks continued into the afternoon, they focused less and less on the war, and more on traditional issues of faith and lessons that reinforced it. But as the day went on, there were increasing levels of whispered conversations, especially during breaks, on the status of the war declaration.

Moses nodded as the man behind him spoke quietly into his ear. He passed the message on to Earl and Trudi, who exchanged a concerned look. Earl leaned past her to whisper to Joseph and Bert, "It's official, men. We are at war!"

Joseph felt sorry for the last speakers of the afternoon session. Everyone shifted in their seats, some leaning forward as if trying to hurry the speakers on, clearly wanting to get outside to talk about the war, but the speeches went on as if nothing had changed. There was no formal announcement by President Smith.

Finally, they slowly filed out into the crisp spring air. The group who'd come from Logan on the train gathered in a cluster outside.

"What's next?" Bert asked the group. "A draft?"

"President Wilson said he prefers to send volunteers, so perhaps there will be no draft?" Clara said.

"Who knows?" Reed said. "The army needs to increase ten-fold, to over a million men. I doubt they'll get that many volunteers."

"What about all of you?" Bert asked the group.

"I'm needed here," Alonzo said, his stance firm, his arms folded. "This year already promises a poor harvest, and we'll need even more food now if we're sending men overseas. Besides, you all know very well my feelings on the war."

Reed cleared his throat. "My father and I have already spoken about this. He's fine on the farm with my brothers helping him." Turning toward Clara, he said, "I won't wait for a draft. Better to pick your own poison I say. Time to do our bit."

"Indeed." She looked sad for a moment, but her expression turned to annoyance. "Of course, for some of us, that bit is being stuck here, knitting and rolling bandages." She looked at Bert. "What will you do?"

"Oh, I'll serve if drafted, but I'm the only help my father has with the dairy cows right now. I suppose I belong at home. 'Course I wouldn't mind a little sojourn with Reed. I believe he'll make a fine soldier." He shrugged. "Whatever God wills, that's where I figure I'll end up. I just want to do my duty."

Clara glanced at Joseph, who wilted back a little at her intense gaze. "And you, Mr. Sorrell?"

Bert interjected. "Why Clara, Joseph isn't a citizen, so he can't be drafted."

Joseph stepped back up to the circle and raised his head. "That's true, but I'm ready to fight for my country, just like any man. I've already tried to enlist two times now, Miss Jensen. They told me no, but I'll try again now that the war is on for sure."

Clara stared at him. Tears welled in her eyes. "Mr. Sorrell, er, Joseph, if I may, I want to tell you how much I admire that sentiment." She walked over to him as she wiped away a tear and embraced him. "God bless you, Joseph. We shall surely be victorious with men like you on our side."

Clara walked back over next to Reed, taking his arm. Joseph could only mumble his thanks. He had never met anyone like Clara Jensen.

Trudi joined them with Earl, giving Clara and Joseph a curious glance. "My, there must be a good story there."

"We were all talking about the war and whether there will be a draft," Bert said. "What about you, Earl, what are your plans?"

"Gosh, I've no idea. Our band conductor did mention the other day that in the event of war, there would be a need for a good number of bandsmen to entertain the men and so forth. I'm proud to do my part, whatever it may be."

"No one asks the women, of course," Trudi said, "but I'm certain there will be plenty of war work right here at home, don't you think, Clara," she said, winking at Clara.

"Oh, yes, dear." A gleam came into Clara's eyes. "I'm sure you'll be very busy indeed. As for me though, I think I hear the guns calling. If I were trained as a nurse, I'd be over there already, but I'll find a way. Can you hear them, Reed?"

"They're practically deafening. Like the growling in my stomach. Let's find something to eat, shall we?"

Reed's tone was light, but Joseph heard the change in it. It crackled with a new kind of energy, like a thunderstorm brewing behind the mountains.

XII

September 1917
Paris Island, South Carolina

Dearest Clara,

May I begin by telling you that I am now certain that the Paris you often speak of visiting, and this place, Paris Island, have, literally, nothing in common. I will sum up my experience here so far like this: Week One: "I'm going to die." Week two: "I'm not going to die, though I wish I was." And Week Three: "I'll never die, I'm so tough." I suppose they aim to make Marines out of us or kill us, and our sergeant seems entirely indifferent either way it goes. He picks a new sap every day to pick on. Last week I had my turn when I managed to put on my campaign hat backward in my haste to join formation. I ran around the compound carrying buckets of the oyster shells with which they pave the roads until my tongue hung out. Some fun. Paris Island itself is no doubt as lovely as the eternal city. The "facilities" are built on stilts out over the water, which is an elevating experience, until high tide anyway. You said not to pick the Marine Corps just because I liked their poster best. I should have listened to you. Please write soon and tell everyone at home hello. Thank you beyond words for the photograph, Clara. I carry it with me, always.

Your Sap,
Reed

Older recruits lined both sides of the street to welcome Reed and his fellow National Naval Volunteer Marine officer candidates as they stepped off the boat at Paris Island. Although the older recruits were only a couple of weeks further on in training, these men seemed like the "old salts" Reed had heard about as they called out, "Hey, Boot! This way for silk pajamas," or, "Ice cream over here!"

The men stood in endless lines to receive their sea bags and uniforms, as well as the "782" gear they would need: belts, canteens, and other field kits. Once they stuffed it all into their sea bags, they had something heavy to carry, almost sixty pounds worth—just what their new sergeant needed as a method of introduction.

Sergeant R.E. "Bobby Lee" Griffin appeared in front of Reed's platoon like he had been there forever. He stood at a stiff parade rest, legs shoulder-width apart, arms behind his back, palms neatly overlapping, his chest stuck out like a banty rooster's. Sergeant Griffin seemed immune from the stifling South Carolina heat and humidity. He did not visibly sweat. He stood there, stiff and crisp, while the other men, particularly the non-southerners, dripped sweat and squirmed in discomfort.

"I," Griffin said, over-pronouncing it to sound like *eye*, "hate officers. Just so ya'll knows that upfront like. Now, pick up them sea bags, and put them on yer right shoulder."

The men did as instructed, but Griffin only frowned and shook his head. Thus began a demonstration of the high art and hidebound tradition of using the sea bag as a teaching tool.

"Put them back down again. Now, you boots are gonna learn to do things together, exactly like I tells you to. Do ya'll understand?"

The men did understand. Some of them nodded yes, others said "yes," out loud. Reed projected a firm, "Yes, Sir," like he had learned at summer camp the previous year.

None of these responses satisfied Sergeant Griffin. "Nope, I do not believe that you understand me a'tall, or, you would not have answered me like a bunch a disrespectful turds!"

He walked up to Reed and stomped to attention just inches from Reed's face, tapping the wide brim of his hat on Reed's forehead. "Say there, Blondie. What the heck did you just call me?"

"I didn't call you anything, Sir," Reed answered.

"There, you done it again! You will address me as SERGEANT, boot! I work for a living—don't you be calling me Sir."

"Yes, Sergeant!" Reed boomed.

"Where are you from, Boot?"

"Utah, Sergeant."

"What? Utah? You one of them poly . . . bigamist . . . you got a bunch of wives out there in Utah?" Griffin laughed like his joke was the funniest thing he had ever heard.

"No, Sergeant. I'm not married," Reed answered. "I do have a girl back home."

"Well, ain't that special. I'm surprised they could spare you one." Griffin laughed again, then stopped like he just turned off a light switch.

"Yer name John, perchance?" Griffin snickered. "Case ya get one of those letters with 'Dear John' at the top? That'd be convenient."

Training camp the previous summer had prepared Reed for Griffin's teasing. He was trying to make things stressful for Reed: push him, test him. The best response was just to stay calm. The sergeant would find some new favorite punching bag, Reed hoped. "No, Sergeant. My name is Lewis, Reed Lewis."

"Too bad. Alright there, Dear John, I'm gonna go check on chow for you boots. While I'm gone, you take charge and get these men picking up them bags like they got some discipline, understood?"

"Yes, Sergeant!" Reed yelled.

After Griffin left, Reed faced his fellow trainees. "Fellows, let's do this by the numbers. I'll call out one-two-three. On one we reach for the bag, on two we straighten back up, on three we heave the bags to our shoulders. Ready? Right shoulder, SEA BAGS! A one and two and three."

The men did their best, but many could not heave their bags up from the waist.

"Alright," Reed said, "Let's just count one-two. Bend over and grab the bag on one, hoist it all the way up on two. Ready? Right shoulder, SEA BAGS!"

Griffin came back ten minutes later and the men demonstrated they could, in fact, pick up sea bags in unison. He marched them off to chow, or as he put it, "Look at this gaggle of geese! I never seen anything so pathetic. You boots better get in step. Hup, toowp, threep, fourp. Dang it, when I count, your dad gum left heel better be hitting the ground. Do you not know your left from your right, you pot lickers? Why I'll drill the soles right offa them boots. Hup, toowp, threep, fourp . . ."

Sitting down for chow was a relief, though Reed and the others did not dare speak. Griffin sat at the cadre table, sipping coffee and eye-balling his recruits, ready to pounce. The men did share an occasional glance at each other, often with a commiserating headshake, as if to say *what have we gotten into?* Reed wolfed the meal of beans, hash, sliced onions in vinegar, and prunes. It wasn't great, but it was hearty and he was plenty hungry.

Griffin gaggled the men back from the mess hall toward their quarters, cursing a blue streak the whole time. "We ain't even turned yet! All ya gotta do is march in a straight line. You think ya'll are officer material when ya can't even count? College boys, my hind end!"

When they arrived at their hut, Griffin showed them how to stow their gear properly, neat and absolutely uniform. Sea bags under the bunks just so, tied with exactly the same knots, even how to lay the excess cord across the top of the bag in precisely the same way every time. Beds made with hospital corners and blankets so tight you could bounce a quarter off them. Every morning the men would crawl under their bunks to pull the ends of the blankets toward the center of the springs, and every morning Griffin would pull the beds apart when his quarter wouldn't bounce.

"Next time I check your rack with this quarter it better bounce so high it comes up two dimes and a nickel," Griffin yelled, grinning at his own wit.

"Boots," he snarled, "tonight the skipper is gonna come by to speak to you, pass along some of that officer wisdom we all heard tell about but ain't never seen." He laughed at his own joke again.

"Anyways," he continued, "The skipper, he ain't no ninety-day wonder like you boots trying to be. You embarrass me in front of the skipper, you ain't gonna survive Paris Island."

"Sergeant," one of the men behind Reed asked, "what's a skipper?"

"Oh, now, what we got us here, Boot? We got us an ignoramus? Tell me, did you come into the corps because of that purdy blue tunic you saw in them recruiting posters? Tell me the truth, Boot!"

"Yes, Sergeant. That's pretty much it," the man answered. The men around him laughed nervously.

"Well, at least you're an honest ignoramus, Boot! You seen one of them pretty tunics in real life?"

"No, Sergeant," the boot replied.

"Me neither, Boot. Let me know if you do. Anyway, the skipper is slang for the Commanding Officer, or CO Understand? We are in the Naval Service, so we gots all that sea stuff in our vocabu . . . how we talk."

"Yes, Sergeant. I also heard you refer to the skipper as 'Mister?'"

"Yer pushin' your luck, Boot. We call Lieutenants 'Mister' sometimes, like the Navy does with ensigns at sea. I don't know why, Boot, so don't ask."

"Aye, Sergeant," the Boot replied.

"Well then, smart aleck. You know that one already, huh? 'Cept I told you to say 'yes,' not 'aye.' Hey, Dear John—you get out them sea bags and practice following simple directions, ya hear?"

"Yes, Sergeant," Reed answered.

By the time they finished another round of sea bag tossing, it was nearing ten o'clock, and they were left alone in the wooden hut with its long rows of steel frame beds, bed rolls, and blankets, neatly folded at each head.

Still not sure if Sergeant Griffin was lurking, the men quietly went about making their beds and stowing their gear as shown. Presently, Griffin came stomping into the hut, stopped at rigid attention, and called out, "Attention on deck!"

First Lieutenant E.L. Reynolds, U.S.M.C., marched into the room, the first Marine officer Reed had ever seen. Reynolds's uniform was in perfect order. He paced the room looking the trainees over, his bearing erect, yet he seemed relaxed, confident. Disciplined, but no martinet.

"Gentlemen, I'm Lieutenant Reynolds, your commanding officer. Stand at ease. When the present war was declared, there were exactly 462 Marine officers on active duty, so we are stretched mighty thin at present, which is, of course, why all of you are here. You all took the Marine officer test in July, but until those results come out, you are here at Paris Island as privates, and we'll train you and treat you as such. Once we know who passed the examination, we will be going together for officer training at the new base at Quantico, in Virginia. In the meantime, learn everything you can from Sergeant Griffin here. Do you have any questions?"

There was a long pause as the lieutenant slowly paced in front of the men.

"No? Very well then. Carry on, Sergeant." Reynolds walked out as Griffin called the men to attention.

Reed and the other officer candidates spent eight weeks at Paris Island, the same amount of time enlisted Marines spent in training there. Individual skills like bayonet fighting, personal combat, and wall scaling followed five hours of daily drill instruction. Griffin never told them what was coming next until right before the event—another opportunity to create stress by giving them ridiculously short periods of time to scramble for the right gear and get back in formation. A ten-mile forced march with packs, bayonet fighting, drills, physical exercises, rope climbs, and swims in the surf—sometimes all in the same day—pushed them until Reed's arm muscles were a solid mass of pain. Then they topped it off with boxing or wrestling matches.

Reed collapsed at the end of each day, almost too tired to see straight, and woke each morning aching everywhere, but ready for the next challenge. The only orders that didn't bring a grin to his face were for drill or swimming, skills he'd had little use for in Utah.

Individual fighting skills were his favorite, but Griffin was there to make things harder for him and the others, always testing. He set up a boxing competition complete with brackets and clandestine betting between the trainees. Reed worked his way through the brackets with ease until his semi-final bout. Reed and his opponent stood almost still in the center of the ring, pummeling each other with no advantage being gained either direction. Reed managed to loop an uppercut under the other man's guard and caught him square in the gut, knocking the wind out of him. As the man slid to the canvas floor, Reed winked at Sergeant Griffin.

"Well, Utah, yer pretty pleased with yourself, ain't ya!" Griffin said.

"Yes, Sergeant!" Reed bellowed.

"We'll see about that. We sure will," Griffin said.

The next day, before the final bout, Griffin took Reed to the shore and had him swim and do exercises in the water for nearly an hour. By the final bout, he could barely lift his arms to defend himself and his legs felt like rubber.

Griffin stood at the center of the ring, yelling at Reed as the other trainee pummeled him. "What now, Utah? The sun ain't shinin' for you no more, is it? Are you gonna quit now, Utah, or is there more to you than being a pretty college boy? Is there?"

Reed took the pounding, striking back with uppercuts when he could draw enough breath to throw a punch. By the end of the third round, both men were exhausted, falling together in a heap in the center of the ring. Reed stood up, helped the other man up, and then stood in his corner ready to fight again.

"Aw right, Boots, that's enough," Griffin announced. "We might make Marines of you yet."

Reed enjoyed the rifle range and shooting the 1903 Springfield Rifle. The Marines called it the aught-three. It kicked like a mule, occasionally leaving a spider's web of broken blood vessels on his shoulder. But, in a competent rifleman's hands, it was deadly accurate, even at ranges out to 600 yards. Of course, at that distance, he had to rely on "butts"—fellow trainees sitting in holes below the target frames, who waved flags when he hit the target.

One day they were shooting at the 600-yard target, ten rounds per minute, or rapid fire. The shooting instructors, Marine globe and anchor insignia stuck through the crown of huge sombreros to ward off the hot sun, largely ignored him since he had been hitting the center of his target. Two of them worked on the man next to him. He seemed to be struggling with the sun and with his Springfield. Reed squeezed off his shots, rewarded by the "butt" raising a flag each time. The "butt" sometimes raised his flag twice for the same shot. This confused Reed. At the end of the ten rounds, the shooters cleared their weapons and stepped back from the firing line. The "butt" assigned to the shooter next to Reed raised a flag with a pair of women's underwear attached to them, "Maggie's Drawers," meaning he had missed the target all ten times.

Two sombreros merged over the other man's head as a stream of insults rained down concerning the validity of his parentage and questioning his manhood. *At least he gets chewed out in the shade.* Then, something occurred to Reed.

"Excuse me, Sergeant?" Reed asked.

"What, Boot? You want some attention too?" Sombrero said.

"No, Sergeant. But I think he may have been shooting at my target. The 'butt' raised his flag more than once for some of my shots."

"All right. You two Boots double time downrange and count the holes."

The two men ran to the targets. Sure enough, there were 15 holes in Reed's target, five more than he had fired.

"Thanks for getting me out of that butt chewing," the other man said.

"No worries. Besides, I'd go to war with a guy who'd shoot the German in front of me any time." They both laughed as they jogged back to the line.

The pressure of training at Paris Island sometimes had Reed waking in a panic while the others snored around him, but it didn't prepare him for Quantico. The petty tyranny of Sergeant Griffin was gone, replaced by the pressure of performing in roles associated with leading a rifle platoon, including actual enlisted Marines who had also completed eight weeks at Paris Island.

Everything was graded. Everything was a competition. Tactics classes, military topography, and classes on the techniques of trench warfare were added to the officer curriculum as well as individual fighting skills. Reed loved it. He was up for a foot race to the mess hall or a platoon-sized ten-mile road march with full kit. All he needed was a certain look from a fellow officer trainee, and they were off.

After one particular race back from the rifle range between his Second Platoon and the Marines of First Platoon, Lieutenant Reynolds pulled him aside.

"Mr. Lewis, a word please," he said, leading Reed around the corner from his platoon's hut. "Firstly, notice that I pulled you away from your men for this. An officer does not chew up a brother officer, even a trainee, in front of enlisted men. Understand?"

Reed had been laughing over his platoon's victory while trying to get his breath at the same time. He straightened at Reynold's tone. "Aye, Skipper."

"Look, I want you to harden these men, make them lean and hungry. March all day and fight all night. However, they are your men, not your playthings. Look at them right now. Many are vomiting. You ran them too hard, Lewis, too hard in this heat, and after a full day of training. For what? Your amusement? They are not here to amuse you, they are here to get ready to fight the Boche. Do I make myself clear?"

Reed looked back at his men, many of them bent over, some on their hands and knees. His stomach turned over. "Yes, Sir. Very clear. Will that be all, Sir?"

"No, Mr. Lewis, one more thing. You passed your exam for entry as a Marine officer. Learn what you can here. You're going to need it. Dismissed."

Reed walked back and stood among his ill, exhausted men. He had gotten carried away. What would his family think, or Clara? He promised himself never to put his own desires above the welfare of his men again.

Two days before his graduation in October 1917, Reed was told to report to Lieutenant Reynolds.

"Mr. Lewis, stand at ease," Reynolds began as Reed reported in. "I have your assignment here. I should tell you I recommended that you remain here and help me train the next class of officers."

Reed swallowed hard. "Sir, while I truly appreciate . . ."

"Stow it, Lewis. You think the corps cares what I think? You're going to the 4th Brigade. If the Marines get into this fight, you'll be going along. Good luck, Mr. Lewis."

"Aye, Sir," Reed said, saluting and executing an about face, trying not to smile.

After the graduation parade, Reed took the oath of office with his fellow trainees and was commissioned a Second Lieutenant, United States Marine Corps. He pinned on the gold bars of a newly minted officer and the coveted globe, anchor, and eagle collar insignia with pride. He was a Marine.

XIII

This must be the last great war.

—The A.C. Student Life

Trudi handed her cash to the clerk at Cardon's jewelry store and mumbled her thanks for the change, hoping no one heard her accent. She took her paper-wrapped package—Christmas gifts for her mother and sister—and hurried outside onto Main Street.

Shoppers crowded the sidewalk, gazing into the windows of the brick stores decorated with evergreen boughs. A placard in front of the diner announced a lunch special featuring "liberty cabbage." Sauerkraut was erased from everyone's vocabulary, along with hamburgers, now "liberty steaks." Trudi glanced away.

Across the street, the little golden dome atop the tabernacle's square tower reflected the autumn sun. The distant mountains decked with snow, and the faint scent of wood smoke beneath the stink of car exhaust, reminded Trudi for a moment of Switzerland. She experienced a strange tugging sensation, caught between two homes, longing for both and not quite belonging to either.

Trudi was meeting her family at the train station to see some of their friends off to Fort Douglas in Salt Lake City, so she ducked out of sight and arranged her bags so none of their presents showed. Once they were satisfactorily disguised, she darted out of the alcove to head for the trolley stop. She slammed right into a man on the sidewalk. Her bags spilled on the ground along with his boxed lunch.

"Oh, I'm so sorry!" she said, scrambling to pick up shirts and silk scarves. The remnants of his sandwich stuck to a wool sweater. She offered the fuzzy ham to him with an apologetic look.

The man tossed the ruined food aside. "Why are you skulking around here?"

"I'm not skulking," Trudi said. "I was just trying to avoid . . . someone."

"You sound German. Are you registered?"

Trudi flushed. Only Germans who weren't citizens had to register. Those like her mother, who had seen no reason to give up their native citizenship until it was too late. "I'm not German. I'm Swiss, and I'm a U.S. citizen." She touched the U.S. flag pin she wore on the lapel of her long coat.

"Oh, yeah? I wanna see you kiss that flag and sing the national anthem. Prove your loyalty."

Trudi stared in horror at the watching crowd. The man loomed over her, his face twisted in a threatening sneer. He was serious. Dizzy with fear and humiliation, Trudi quickly raised the cold pin to her lips and kissed it. Did they really expect her to sing? Her throat tightened.

"Leave her alone, Harrison," another man said. "She ain't your enemy. That's Trudi Kessler, and her family's lived in the Tenth Ward the last nine years."

"Oh, yeah? Well, they call that section of town Little Berlin for a reason. The papers say German spies are everywhere, poisoning our water, disrupting our factories, reporting our movements to their Kaiser."

Trudi's rescuer shook his head. "If her being well-known don't satisfy you, I saw her this morning at the Thatcher Bank buying Liberty Bonds. How many Liberty Bonds have you bought, Harrison?"

Harrison glared at them and mumbled something under his breath, storming off into the crowd. Trudi wished she could disappear too.

She looked up at her rescuer. "Thank you, Mr. . . . ?"

"Brother Burris, Miss. I know your parents. Good folks. Sorry you have to deal with bullies like him."

She shrugged. What could she say? She stuffed the rest of the now-dirty gifts into her bag and mumbled another thank you. She felt the crowd watching as she hurried to catch the trolley. The electric streetcar rattled down its tracks in the center of Main Street and came to a stop. Trudi hopped on, glad to escape the scene.

The trolley made its way down Center Street, past the Victorian mansions of Logan's elite families like the Thatchers and the Eccleses. Trudi tried to imagine what it would be like to live in such a huge house. As long as she was the one doing the cleaning, she preferred her family's little three-bedroom home. In Switzerland, they'd only had two tiny bedrooms above a small kitchen and living room. If they were still there, they'd be rationing food and surrounded by belligerent armies. Still, the incident on the street proved that the tentacles of the war were gaining a stranglehold on America too.

The trolley stopped at the train station. Trudi climbed down to find her family and the Johnsons already gathered there. Earl looked proud in his nicest suit, holding his trumpet case. He was with two other men from the city band, Claytor Preston and Guy Alexander, leaving to join the military band, and a few other Logan boys headed to Fort Douglas for training. Everyone was doing his bit.

Claytor and Guy were saying goodbye to their wives and friends. They were inseparable, playing in the city band together, married on the same day, enlisting in the military at the same time, and now going off to war together. Trudi smiled and shook her head then joined the group around Earl.

"We're going to miss you," Karl told him.

"The band won't sound nearly as good without you," Trudi added with a smile as Earl gave her a friendly hug.

Earl's father stood watching with worry lines creasing his forehead, and when it was his mother's turn to embrace him, she clung tightly to his suit as if trying to keep the memory of holding him with her. Trudi looked away from the private moment.

The whistle blew. The Logan boys hopped on the train, waving out the windows, and the crowd seeing them off waved back until they disappeared into the distance. Trudi wished she had such a clear-cut way of serving. Maybe then people like Harrison would believe that she was American too. Karl squeezed her arm, and they turned back for the trolley.

Trudi left her family at the stop nearest the A.C. The streetcar that headed up to campus wouldn't be along for a while, so she started the walk up, wishing that Clara would happen along with her car. The bells rang in the main building. Joe Havertz was still hard at work, though no one thought it was funny to call him "Kaiser" any more.

One of the other girls making the climb gave Trudi a friendly smile. At least on campus people knew who she was and didn't harass her. And today she had a Council of Defense meeting. They were organizing all the war support efforts on campus. Before the U.S. entered the war, people had been losing interest in charity drives, but now that they were preparing their own men to go overseas, there was a new frenzy of activity. And since some men like Reed had finished their semester early and left as soon as they could for training, there were more opportunities for women to step in and play a role. The Council of Defense was about half female.

The meeting itself was dull, but Trudi's mind was busy worrying over how she could do more. She was already in charge of the knitting and clothing drives, but she volunteered to help the Red Cross girls pack and mail Christmas boxes for the men in training.

The work took up so much time over the next week and half, she had to remind herself she was at college to study, and she stayed up late reading every night. When the boxes were mailed, she finally collapsed into bed for a full night's sleep, but she woke in the morning feeling restless again.

Trudi showed up the Monday morning after the Red Cross drive ready for the next council meeting and whatever new work awaited her. She was met by a room of sober, pale faces. One young woman was crying.

"What is it?" Trudi asked.

One of the men met her eyes. "There was an accident. A troop train headed east from Utah was stalled on the tracks, and another train slammed into it. A lot of the boys were hurt, and three from Logan were killed."

Trudi couldn't breathe. She caught the edge of the table.

"Who?" she asked.

"Claytor Preston, Guy Alexander, and Earl Johnson. The band was sitting in the very back of the train that got hit."

Trudi stared at him. There had to be a mistake. She'd just seen Earl off. His smile and voice were still fresh and alive in her mind. Besides, playing in the band wasn't dangerous. The danger was on the seas and in the trenches, far from home. Trudi's eyes filled with tears. She fled from the pointless Council of Defense meeting, waiting until the door closed behind her to collapse in the hall and wail out her sobs.

They held the funeral for Claytor and Guy in the Logan Tabernacle that Friday. Trudi arrived with Clara and Alonzo. Streams of black-clad mourners filled the building, cramming into the balcony and the pews beneath, until the whole building seemed to be draped in black. Flowers sent by people from all over the state provided the only color, overflowing from the front of the stand, and the red, white, and blue of the flags covering the coffins. More mourners stood out in the November chill, unable to fit inside, but waiting to join the procession after.

The choir stood to sing "America." When they reached the line, "let freedom ring," goosebumps prickled over Trudi's arms, and her eyes welled with tears.

Senator Reed Smoot stood to speak on behalf of the LDS Church. He looked over the audience, his eyes bright with unshed tears, and spoke of death and the purifying effects of sacrifice and of the honor of serving God and country. Then his gaze turned to the caskets before him. His posture was stooped, as though he carried a pressing weight on his back.

"I could not sleep last night. I saw the picture of death. I have seen it for months. I thought of the bereaved, of their sacrifice, and I thought of the dead and felt it was just the beginning of what we may expect. I have been taught that the flag represents all that is good in government, and when I voted for the declaration of war, I did it knowing what it meant to nearly every household in our country, and I prayed to God that He would pour out his blessings upon all of our armies. I now pray to the Father that He will hasten the day when this wicked conflict will cease." His voice cracked, and he wiped his eyes.

"These young men, friends and patriots in life and death, married at the same time, are on the same road to eternal life. Some are called upon to carry greater burdens than others. All these burdens placed upon us in this world will be compensated for. There will come a time when it will all be explained. My heart goes out to Sister Preston. Oh, what a strong woman she is."

Claytor's mother bowed her head, her shoulders trembling under the sympathetic gaze of the entire assembly. Next to Trudi, Clara shook with sobs. Trudi pulled her close and her own tears fell onto the wool of Clara's dress. Senator Smoot concluded his eulogy.

"The lives of these young men are worthy of emulation. They should be a lesson to all young men of this land."

Trudi couldn't help a glance over at Alonzo, whose face was stony.

"May the peace of God continue in this gathering and penetrate the hearts of those who mourn, and especially the parents of those two young men."

A violinist stood to play as the audience wiped their tears. Other speakers followed from the governor's office and the A.C., praising the exemplary character and friendship of Claytor and Guy and the sacrifice they and their families had made. Lowry Nelson from the A.C. read a poem by Rupert Brooke, a young British soldier who died in the war.

The Logan Tabernacle Choir ended the service with "The Star-Spangled Banner," sung slowly, like a dirge. After the prayer ending the service, the Logan city band played "Nearer, My God to Thee" as the mourners filed out of the building. Trudi wondered how they could manage to play through their grief, since Claytor and Guy had been among their numbers. She could hardly see past her tears to walk down the steps.

The mourners piled into cars to follow the truck bearing the caskets up to the Logan cemetery. Trudi couldn't take her eyes from the American flags hanging from the coffins. These men had done their bit. They had been willing to give whatever they had for their country, and they had given it all. The two best friends were laid side-by-side in the same cemetery lot as the sun set in a cold and nearly cloudless sky. The only sounds were the sharp report of seven rifles firing three volleys for the twenty-one gun salute.

Trudi wrapped her arms around herself and turned away. Clara and Alonzo followed, and Bert and Joseph met up with them. No one broke the silence until they'd left the cemetery.

"This is unbearable," Clara said. "I can't stand being stuck here with no way to help when good men are dying."

Bert nodded. "I'm glad Joseph and I are already drafted. I'm anxious to get out there and represent our friends. What about you, Alonzo?"

Alonzo's eyes were red-rimmed, but he just shook his head and pressed his lips together.

"Are you still eager to be gone, Mr. Sorrell?" Trudi asked.

"I always have been," he answered quietly. "This is my chance to show that I deserve to be a citizen of this country too. If I come back in a casket draped in the stars and stripes, they can't say anymore that I'm not American."

Trudi paused in surprise. How strange, that she and this Shoshone had such similar motivations. He, whose ancestors had hunted buffalo in this valley long before settlers ever reached it, and she, who could still remember the sweet smell of Swiss meadows in the summer.

Yet everything she did seemed pointless compared to the grim glory of those caskets shrouded in the flag. She had no illusions that war was grand, but if people in her country were going to suffer and die, she wanted to actually do something to help them. Something meaningful.

They always needed nurses. They paid for them to go along with the army. Trudi could take the Red Cross classes and learn enough to join. Then she could help the men, maybe save some of them.

Her determination redoubled when she went with her family to the small private funeral the Johnsons held in Wellsville, unable to bear the crowds of mourners. Mr. Johnson prayed over the gravesite then stood proud as they lowered Earl into the ground, but Mrs. Johnson wept openly. One of Earl's younger brothers held his old trumpet, playing taps with tears streaming down his face.

Earl would never play the trumpet again. Trudi remembered his lively music, the smile in his eyes when he played. Those were gone now, at least in this world. It was hard to imagine there would ever be happy music again. This was just the beginning of the war. Trudi bowed her head.

Lord, you brought my family here to this country. You saved us from being caught in this terrible war, and I am grateful, but I can't stand on the sidelines anymore. Please show me what I'm supposed to do. Show me my part.

XIV

November 1917
Greenville, Utah

The YMCA serves soldiers at home and on the front without regard to race, color, or creed. The uplifting influence of the women who work there cannot be overstated. These secretaries help to battle the temptations and homesickness that will destroy morale and lose the war for the Allies if allowed to fester. In huts in the front lines of the trenches, they offer hot drinks, conversation, and cheer, as well as reminders of the wives, mothers, and sweethearts whom the men are fighting for. They also offer care for the injured, those "walking cases" whom the Red Cross must turn away to help the more seriously wounded. Fatality among YMCA workers is as high as nine percent, but these brave women do their bit to help the boys waiting to go "over the top."

—The A.C. Student Life

Clara slammed the door to the kitchen and stomped over to the table.

"Clara!" her mother scolded.

"Well, I'm sorry, but you'd be mad too if you had to listen to what people are saying about our family."

"What are you talking about?" Her mother looked up in alarm from the soup she was stirring on the wood-burning stove.

"Alonzo!" Clara said, sitting at the table in a huff. "They're calling him a coward. I had to stop Bert from throwing one of the boys into a ditch, much as he deserved it."

"A coward?" Her mother's stirring slowed.

"Because he has an agricultural deferment from the draft. He tells everyone he doesn't want to fight."

"I don't," Alonzo said from the doorway. "This is where my responsibilities are, not fighting in a war that has nothing to do with me."

"It has to do with everyone! You can't just ignore the rest of the world."

"I'm not ignoring it. I just want no part of it. This war is nothing more than an excuse for self-serving politicians to advance their own agendas, throwing away the lives of their citizens as if they were paper dolls. What good did war ever do for the common man?"

"We're protecting ourselves—protecting democracy!"

"Democracy." Alonzo snorted derisively. "I'm surprised to hear you calling it that, when your sex can't even vote in most of the country."

"Then we'll prove we deserve it by doing our part."

"You think the government cares what you do? They don't want women in the war. They need you, and they'll use you, but they won't thank you for it."

Clara burned with anger, and with the lingering fear that Alonzo might be right.

"Clara," their mother said quietly, "don't forget that soldiers have to eat. If no one is here running the farms, the armies overseas have no chance of winning. Everyone has a part to play."

"We can manage without Alonzo. The Kesslers always work for us in the summer, and the government is sending younger boys to help out on the farms." Clara shot Alonzo a challenging glare.

He just shrugged one shoulder. "I'm staying here."

"Then I'm not!" Clara shouted. "I'm going!"

"You can't fight," Alonzo said.

"No, but there's plenty I can do. I speak French. I can join the Navy and work in the office or learn to operate a telephone."

"You're not a clerical worker any more than you're a nurse."

"Then I'll join the YMCA. They've been talking about it on campus. They need women to help run the canteens on the front lines." The idea warmed Clara, starting in her chest and spreading down to her fingertips with a tingle of excitement. That was the answer. "I can go overseas and do my part," she said more quietly, but with more conviction.

Her mother dropped her spoon. "Clara! Not on the front lines. That's dangerous. Help at the training centers, if you must, but don't go over there."

"I've heard they're restricting the women going overseas," Alonzo said quickly.

Clara smiled. "That's only women who have family members in the military. If my brother would fight, then I would have to stay home, but if he won't go, then I can. I'll go to Paris." Let Alonzo hide at home where it was safe. She would find her place in the heat of the action.

"It's expensive," Alonzo said. "They don't pay volunteers. You have to make your own way."

"I'll sell the Tin Lizzie," Clara said, her heart twisting a little at the thought. "I have my college money saved up. It will be enough."

"You're giving up college?" her mother said, tears in her eyes. "Oh, Clara, you worked so hard."

"And I can work hard again. I'm not giving up on college, but this is an opportunity to be part of something bigger—an opportunity I'll never have again. I'm not going to miss it." She hurried past Alonzo to hug her mother. "It's not as if I'll be fighting. And I won't be alone. Reed and a bunch of the boys from home will be there too. I'll be helping them."

Alonzo's eyes creased in worry. "War is a terrible thing, Clara."

"Then I have a responsibility to ease the burden for my brave friends who are going to fight. You can't talk me out of it, and you can't stop me from going."

"I know," Alonzo said quietly.

Clara drove her Model T up to campus for the last time before she sold it. The cold canyon wind whipped leaves down the road, and she looked out over the last of the fall colors in the valley, already feeling the tug of nostalgia. It was quickly replaced by excitement at her decision. She would be in France by Christmas.

She just had to convince the university president, E.G. Peterson, and his committee to approve her absence so she could return to school after the war. She would go even if they didn't, but she still wanted to finish college when everything was back to normal again. Either way, this was her chance to finally be in the heart of things, free from the wall of mountains hedging her in. She wasn't going to miss it for anything.

She found the room in the main building where the committee waited for her. All men. Of course it would be, especially since she was studying general science instead of home economics, but it suddenly struck her as one of the those injustices Alonzo had alluded to. Reed had no trouble getting his early withdrawal from campus approved, but he was a man going to officer training. Clara tried to stand as straight as a soldier in uniform as she approached the committee.

"Miss Jensen," President Peterson said, "I understand you want to leave school?"

"Temporarily, Sir, to do my part in the war."

"Are you a nurse or a telephone operator?"

"No, Sir. I plan to join the YMCA and go overseas to work in the canteens, helping to cheer the men serving our country."

The men on the committee shifted. President Peterson raised an eyebrow. "Not the safest choice of places to volunteer, and you may find it puts you in situations that don't fit your sense of propriety."

"Propriety, Sir?" Clara asked. "It's a war. Men are suffering and dying. I can think of nothing more proper than helping them. I'm a farm girl from Utah. I grew up working alongside men. I assure you I'm capable of doing so without encountering anything to blush about."

President Peterson smiled a little. "We could use women like you here. With so many men gone, there's plenty of work for young ladies, helping with the Red Cross or even at the YMCA huts. You'd be able to continue your education and develop more skills to serve your family in the future. We need people to defend the hearth as well as the front. If the farms suffer, so will the armies. Indiscriminate volunteering helps no one."

"My brother is staying to run the farm. He's quite capable. And my choice isn't indiscriminate. I speak French, and I work hard. I believe I can do the most good over there."

President Peterson sighed. "Give us a few minutes, Miss Jensen."

She nodded curtly and marched out of the room. They shut the door behind her, and she paced the hall, wondering what they were saying. Would they really refuse her request because she was a woman? Would she miss out on her hard-earned chance to go to college? Well, going to France would be a different kind of education, and if that was all she was allowed, she would make the most of it.

The door swung open. She gave a start and wiped her hands discreetly on her skirt. President Peterson motioned her inside. She stood at attention in front of the committee.

"Miss Jensen," President Peterson said, his voice sounding weary. "I believe it's important for young men and women to finish their educations before rushing off to war. It will make them better prepared now and for the future."

He paused and Clara took a slow breath, meeting his eyes. He looked away.

"However, I will not stand in the way of a person who feels compelled to sacrifice for their country. The committee approves your absence, and if you need a letter of introduction, I will write you one."

"Thank you, Sir," Clara said with a wide grin.

She turned on her heel and hurried out of the room, wanting to whoop out loud. She was going to France!

XV

December 1917
Camp Lewis, Washington

Dear Uncle,

I am safe at Camp Lewis after a long trip on the train with my buddy Bert. I like army life so far. Some guys kick about it, but I know it must be hard so we can make them Dutchmen pay when we get to the big fight. Old Bert likes it too. He likes his chow, and we don't have to dig around for something to eat—they feed us three squares a day. 'Course he wasn't liking it so much this morning. We was crawling under barbed wire and he got wound up in it pretty good. Had to cut him out of it. Ha ha.

I'm still sore they drafted me after turning me down for enlistment twice, but I guess it don't matter much anymore. We're all here together in the 91st "Wild West" Division. Uncle, you ain't never seen such a mix of men. The lowest hobo to men with college educations. Not too many Indians, so I guess I stand out some, though there's a Japanese fellow from Brigham City named Kuramoto. Nobody called me "Chief" or anything so I ain't punched anybody in the nose. Ol' Bert gives 'em a look if they give me a hard time even though I can take care of myself. And Uncle, I remember what you said. I know who I represent and I aim to prove myself every day.

I'd better end this letter pretty quick. We are all sharing this ink bottle while we write in our laps. Nobody wants to spill any 'cause we don't want to scrub this dang wood floor again. Say hello to everyone in Washakie, won't you? Take care of Buckskin Nelly.

Don't breed her yet—I aim to make some more money with that mare when I get home; she's still the fastest thing around.

Your Loving Nephew,
Joseph Sorrell, Private, U.S.A.

As the Oregon Short Line train pulled into the main station in Logan, Joseph had a bird's eye view of Bert's send-off from his window seat. He had boarded in Brigham City earlier that morning. He was tempted to jump off and say goodbye to his Logan friends, but watching the tearful crowd gathered around Bert, he decided to leave the moment to him. Joseph took out the little parfleche pouch his uncle had given him—the rawhide painted with blue, red, and yellow triangles—and felt the small reminders of home tucked inside.

He recognized Alonzo, Clara, and Trudi in Bert's large contingent of family and friends. Bert didn't say anything; he just bear-hugged every single person right up off the ground. All the women carried baskets of food and treats for him, and his huge hugs were a mash of arms, baskets, kisses, and tears.

He climbed up on the train, struggling with his single suitcase and armload of baskets. Joseph noticed Clara didn't give him hers. She followed him onto the train and to their seats. She laid the basket next to Joseph, leaned down, and kissed him on the cheek. "May the Lord keep you and protect you," she said, her eyes welling with tears. "You too Bert, you big bear." Bert crushed her with with another hug and walked her to the train's steps. As always, Clara's kindness left Joseph speechless. He did enjoy the strange looks he got from other passengers who saw the pretty blonde girl kiss him.

The men were quiet for a while, though Bert took gleeful inventory of their baskets. As they neared Preston, Idaho, Joseph nodded toward the Bear River, the site where his people were massacred by U.S. troops. "You ever been down there, where Beaver Creek meets the river?"

"Sure." Bert squinted out the window. "My father and I went fishing there many times. Lots of good holes for trout, plus they lay up right where the creek empties into the Bear."

"I guess that's why my people camped there. The fish, rabbits, probably deer in that sage over there. Maybe elk. They could get fresh water too, even in winter."

"Not much protection from the elements," Bert said. "It must have been bone cold when the wind kicked up."

"Maybe. But they had no place else to go. They were pushed out of the rest of the Cache Valley. This must have seemed like their last chance."

Bert nodded.

"It is strange, Bert. For me. Here," Joseph said, his voice too low for the other passengers to overhear. "The massacre was only fifty-four years ago. My uncle brought me here so I would remember. His father died here, so did many of his family. My family. How they hated the *Toquashes*. Now I am one. Strange."

"It's what you chose. You're not a citizen, yet you accepted the draft notice, even though it's probably illegal," Bert said. "Your place is here and now, not in the past. We're going 'over there' to fight together, right?"

Joseph smiled. "The last thing my uncle said to me was, 'You have good medicine for them. You kill them Dutchmen and then you come home.' I guess that's his blessing. It is enough."

Bert looked at him. "You know we're not fighting the Dutch right?"

Joseph laughed. "It's just how my people refer to them. I don't know why. 'Course we ain't actually fighting any Huns either."

Bert chuckled. He watched out the window, turning his pocket watch over and over in his hand. Joseph remembered what Bert had said about it, wondering if he was as brave as those who'd come before. Well, now they were going to find out.

Camp Lewis was a sprawling military training center spread around the American Lake among the evergreens, with snow-capped Mount Tacoma looming in the background. It was the greenest place Bert and Joseph had ever seen, so unlike the open dry grassland and sagebrush of home. There were mountains here too, but they seemed further away, except for the striking dome of Tacoma.

The men quickly settled into the routine of training: several hours a day of drill along with physical exercise, basic personal combat techniques, bayonet fighting, and training with chemical warfare gas masks. They also received corny lectures on the moral dangers of military life. Bert was an old hand at it after his time at the preparedness camp.

"I'm surprised you didn't train to be an officer like Reed," Joseph said after Bert helped some of the men get their masks on right.

Bert shrugged. "Reed's the type that has to be doing. He wants to be out there leading the charge. Me, I just want to do my best at whatever task the Lord puts in front of me."

"Well, I'm glad for your company, anyway," Joseph said.

They had their evenings free for writing letters and so forth. Bert and Joseph found their way into more than a few card games.

When they weren't busy training, their drill instructor found plenty of details for them.

Joseph and Bert scrubbed the wood floor with soapy water and brushes. "My knees are killing me," Bert complained, "I think I've scrubbed more floors here than my mother did in her whole lifetime."

Joseph laughed. "Yes, but tell me, why do we have to polish the stoves every day? They're designed to be dirty ain't they?"

"Heck, I don't know. Why are those boys whitewashing the rocks along the path to the headquarters? Tell ya the truth, I'm wondering if the action overseas will all be finished and we'll still be here scrubbing floors and painting rocks."

"Me too. If I go home after this without proving . . . I just don't know what I'd do. We got to get over there, Bert!"

One night the men were tasked to go on a night maneuver exercise to find and rescue comrades in a trench a mile from camp while wearing their gas masks. They were split into two-man scout teams. Bert and Joseph went out together.

Many of the teams headed off on what looked like well-used paths or game trails into the forest. Their lack of experience navigating at night and the limiting effect of the gas masks on their breathing and peripheral vision soon took its toll, as many quickly got lost themselves without locating the people they were supposed to rescue. Others who stayed on the well-used paths were caught by the instructor cadre waiting in ambushes and made to do rigorous exercises as punishment for their lack of imagination.

Joseph and Bert drew a small map of what they knew of the search area, dividing it into sectors they could search by making loops from one central point, like the petals of a flower. They started on the petal at ninety degrees from their starting point, working loops in a counter-clockwise pattern. They stayed off the trails to avoid ambushes, working carefully through the thick pines.

They both paused when they heard voices in front of them.

"We're just going in circles! I seen that same stump three times," a soldier whispered.

"Well, if you're so dang smart, you take the lead," another answered.

Joseph and Bert crept up beside the pair without being seen. Bert called, "Boo," and the lost men about jumped out of their boots.

"Guess you're our prisoners now," Bert whispered with a grin.

The men grumbled and fell in behind Joseph. They stumbled on another pair of lost soldiers and added them to their growing flock.

Bert spotted the trench they were looking for on their third loop. Joseph gathered the evacuees while Bert organized the other rescuers into a patrol formation for the return trip to camp.

"Which way is it?" one of the men asked when Bert told him to take lead and move out. Bert made a chopping signal with his hand indicating the direction. He turned toward Joseph without saying anything and raised his eyebrows, as if to say, *city boys*.

As they reentered the camp, a group of the instructor cadre stood watching, gathered around the company commander, a captain. The captain walked over to the men and demanded, "Who's in charge here?"

Bert looked at Joseph, who shrugged. "I guess I am, Sir," Bert said. "Me and Private Sorrell here."

"I see," the captain said. "You know, Private, not many teams even find the trench line, much less get their people back here. You did that, plus I figure you found a couple lost patrols as well?"

"We did, Sir. Yes, Sir." Bert replied.

"Very good, Private. Very good indeed." He studied Joseph. "Say, you there, you an Indian?"

"Yes, Sir." Joseph replied warily.

"Well, don't that figure. You Puyallup Indian?"

"No, Sir. Northern Shoshone. I'm from Washakie in Utah."

"I'll be danged," the captain said. "Utah. First one I've met. You one of those Mormon Indians?"

"Yes, Sir. Latter-day Saints."

"Uh-huh. Well, I'm marking your training records, and the big guy there, what's your name, private?"

"Lyman, Sir. Bert Lyman."

"Lyman and Sorrell. Marking you down as scouts. Damn dangerous work. You boys up for it?"

"Yes, Sir!" both men yelled.

Walking back to their hut, Joseph asked Bert, "What does a scout do?"

"Heck, I figured you knew. I suppose we get to find the Huns so we can commence to killing them."

"That's fine by me, then." Joseph replied.

"Me too. I can't wait 'till we get over there, do our bit."

Two weeks later, Joseph and Bert boarded their troop train east, ready to go to overseas with the rest of the Wild West Division.

XVI

Dearest Mother,

I wish you could see New York City! It's too amazing to describe, so I'm sending this postcard. Getting ready for the sailing. I'm with the other YMCA girls, in good company and good spirits. Tensions are high, but I'm excited, ready to do my bit.

With all my love,
Clara

Clara stepped off the train onto the platform in Grand Central Station and let the crowds sweep her up the stairs to the main concourse. She had thought the tabernacle and temple in Salt Lake City were the grandest buildings she could imagine, but the massive granite terminal soaring overhead seemed large enough to qualify as its own city. Signs pointed to a ladies waiting room, where maids waited to attend female passengers, as well as shoeshine booths—segregated by sex—and barbers speaking a babble of languages.

After five days of traveling, Clara still felt the gentle rock of the train as she swayed across the concourse, trying to get her bearings. People pushed past, hurrying to their destinations. Soldiers in uniform marched by, shoulders back and eyes forward, reminding her that she wasn't there for sight-seeing. She held her bag tighter and took stock of her situation. She needed to find the local YMCA headquarters.

She approached a uniformed attendant and asked for directions in her boldest tone. He pointed her down the street. She nodded her thanks and headed out of the building. Cars careened down the wide streets, dodging electric streetcars and the occasional horse-drawn carriage. Newsboys hawked their papers, and food vendors filled the crowded streets with the scents of sizzling meat. Chicago had seemed impossibly crowded when Clara stopped there to change trains, but it was nothing compared to the man-made canyons of New York City. She joined the rush of people hurrying down the sidewalks, threading her way past fancy hotels.

The cold wind blasted down the streets, taking Clara's breath away. Her wool coat was warm enough for Logan's mountain winters; it should have been warm enough for New York City. Yet the cold here was different, damp. It sank through the wool and into her arms. She touched the eagle, globe, and anchor pin Reed had sent her, which she wore on her lapel. Home was far behind her, and her journey wasn't over yet. She wrapped her scarf more tightly and searched the street numbers until she found the YMCA.

She presented herself to the woman at the front desk, along with the letters of recommendation she'd gathered before leaving and proof that she had the money she needed to support herself in an American Express account, ready to be wired to Paris.

"All the way from Utah?" The frazzled-looking woman behind the desk scrutinized her after glancing over her letters of introduction. "Well, our next group of girls will sail in about a week. You'll have to hurry to get your passport by then, and you need to go through a basic orientation before we ship out."

The woman gave her instructions on where to go to get her passport, where to lodge, and how to buy her tickets for the ship. Clara checked into the YMCA building where the other girls were staying and started on her long to-do list.

The first step was getting her passport. She once again presented all of her papers, this time to an unsmiling man behind a small desk.

"Any family serving overseas?" He fixed his gaze on the Marine pin on her lapel. "Brothers or husband? We don't want any distractions for our boys."

"No, Sir." No need to mention Reed. She wasn't going to distract him. She was going to do her bit for her country.

He studied her, and she met his stare without flinching. "Hmm. It's a dangerous trip, you know, and we can't make any guarantees about your safety."

"It's a war," Clara said. "I wouldn't expect you to."

She filled out a pile of paperwork and left it with the man, who promised the passport would be ready in a few days. Already exhausted, she headed back to the YMCA building. She found her new roommates gossiping over tea.

"You must be the new girl," said a plump girl with dark, shiny curls. "Would you like some tea?"

"Thank you, but no. And, yes, I'm new. I'm Clara."

"I'm Lily." She pointed to a quiet, mousy girl. "That's Maud. Are you going to France too?"

"Yes," Clara said. "Both of you are going?"

"Yep," Lily said. "Where are you from?"

"Utah."

"Where's that?"

"The West, between Nevada and Colorado."

"I thought it was all outlaws and cowboys out there."

Clara laughed. "We have some of those. My family are farmers, though, and I was at the agricultural college before this."

"Have you got a sweetheart?" Lily asked.

Clara flushed, and Lily grinned. "It's alright, Maud and I have beaux going over there too. Is yours Army or Navy? No, wait, I bet he's an aviator!"

"He's a Marine," Clara said.

The others girls giggled and went on to tell more about themselves. They were both city girls from around New York.

"I wish I was trained as a nurse so I could really help the boys," Lily said.

"Not me," Maud said. "I don't want to see people die. I'd rather save souls than bleeding bodies."

"I have a friend who joined the Navy, and she's in Washington DC," Lily said. "She drills like the men and gets a sharp-looking uniform. They make the nurses dress almost like nuns, though. Don't want the boys thinking impure thoughts."

"I doubt they would be when they're barely hanging onto life," Maud said.

Lily turned back to Clara. "We should be getting some sleep. We'll have training tomorrow, and then you can come with us to see a play."

"A play?" Clara had enjoyed the productions at the A.C. and at the Thatcher Opera House on Main Street before the building burned down. She'd never imagined seeing a play in New York City. It seemed unreal.

"Unless you have some religious objection," Lily added.

"Not at all."

The next morning, they went to the training for YMCA "secretaries," where a tall, angular woman lectured them about their duties and behavior.

"You may hear and see things that aren't fit for young ladies, being around men from different backgrounds than you're used to, and in stressful circumstances. You'll have to put aside any tendencies you have to be shocked and do what you can for the welfare of the men. There will be no fraternization, though." She gave them a steely-eyed look of warning. "You're to think of the men in a brotherly, Christlike light and nothing else or we'll send you home on the next ship."

Lily, sitting next to Clara, gave her a wink at that, but Maud leaned forward intently, drinking in the instructions. Clara folded her hands in her lap and tried to focus, but she was glad when the lecture was over and they could get ready for the play. When the other girls pulled out their evening gowns, though, Clara realized she would look like a hick even in her best Sunday dress.

Maud sized Clara up and said, "You probably didn't think to pack a gown. I have an extra one you can borrow."

Clara smiled her gratitude for the tactful rescue. They went to the Winter Garden Theater to see a musical, *Doing Our Bit*. Clara tapped her foot along with the ragtime music, but she felt an odd disconnect, knowing that she'd be going over there soon, and it would be nothing like the upbeat play, filled with love songs and dance numbers.

Afterward, she let the other girls talk her into going window-shopping at the most expensive shops. Broadway and Times Square shimmered with electric signs, and all the store windows glittered with gold and silver Christmas decorations. They made Clara homesick for a moment, but with so many of her friends already gone for training, it had seemed wrong to wait. She saw a stunning blue dress, and imagined wearing it for Reed, maybe to go dancing. When they said the girls were not to fraternize, did that mean she wouldn't have a chance to spend any time with Reed? She hoped they would find each other in France, but she wouldn't risk being sent home in shame.

Clara picked up her passport after a few more searching questions from the clerk, and a few days later, she went with the other girls to board the steamer that would take them to France. Clara paused in horror to stare at the monstrosity in front of her. The steamer was painted in blocky patterns of black, gray, and white. The broad stripes and geometric shapes met at impossible angles, like a floating crazy quilt. It stung her eyes to look at it for long.

"What happened to the ship?" she asked Lily.

"It's called dazzle. It's supposed to confuse the Germans if their submarines spot us."

Clara stared a moment longer, almost queasy from trying to focus on the ship. It wouldn't do to get seasick before she was even on board.

The other passengers were somber as they climbed the gangplank. Maud and Lily embraced family members who had come to see them off, but it was a quiet, almost sad farewell, with none of the fanfare or cheering Clara had imagined.

Crates of food and medical supplies went into the ship's hold. Clara wondered if any of them had come from Logan. Suddenly she wished there was some friendly face there for her. But there was no one to say goodbye, and there would be no one to greet her. Even if Reed had received her letter, he had more important things to do than hang around the harbor. She just had to hope their paths crossed in France. She touched his pin again as a tugboat prepared to pull the ship from the harbor.

They set off without much ado. Of course, they had to draw as little attention as possible. The girls were all quiet as they slid through the dark waters, past the Statue of Liberty, strong and proud with her torch stretched high.

"Just think," Lily whispered, "That's the last American girl the soldiers leaving for France will see." She smiled. "Except for us."

"It will remind them of what they're fighting for," Maud said reverently, "and so will we."

The statue had been the first sight of America for European immigrants like Trudi, and now it was the last for those going back over there. Clara studied Liberty's face. She looked stern, determined, and, Clara thought, a little sad. It was asking a lot, to expect girls of flesh and blood to take the place of such a symbol. She remembered her debate with Reed about treating women as people and not symbols and smiled sadly.

The statue had been a gift from the French. Clara wondered what they had been thinking of when they gave Liberty such a sober face.

Once out to sea, their ship joined a convoy escorted by destroyers. Some of the other ships were painted a dull gray, but most shared the eccentric striping of her own steamer.

The passengers were allowed to stow their bags in their shared rooms, but then they had to return to the deck to practice the abandon ship formation. Clara prayed they'd never actually use it.

"Always keep your life preserver close," the captain instructed. "Wear it at all times when you're on deck. I recommend staying away from the railings. The convoy won't stop if someone goes overboard. When you get sea sick, try not to go feeding the fishes, and if you throw garbage over, I'll confine you to your berth for the rest of the trip. We don't want to leave a trail for Herr Boche to follow."

A few of the girls giggled nervously at his instructions. Clara glanced up at smoke trailing from the ship's funnels. If a German submarine got close enough, their convoy would be easy to spot. The crazy quilt camouflage might confuse a person taking aim at them, but it wouldn't slow a lucky torpedo. Icy cold wind bit Clara's cheeks and burrowed into her coat. She had no illusions about how long anyone would live in that wintery water. The *Titanic* disaster five years before was still fresh in her imagination. She hoped there were enough lifeboats.

At night the windows were papered over and the lights had to be kept out. They sailed in darkness except for the sickly glow of a few weak electric bulbs in the ship's interior. Clara, unable to sleep with the strange rocking of the boat and slap of the ocean against the sides of the ship, put on her life preserver and snuck out onto the deck. The cold, salty air stung her nose.

She glanced up and caught her breath. She had thought she could see all the stars in Logan, and she had missed their familiar presence in New York, where the electric signs had washed the night sky a uniform gray. Nothing had prepared her for the sight of the stars over the ocean. The Milky Way draped across the black dome like a diamond necklace against a black velvet dress. Their beauty was cold, though. They watched wars and suffering with the same indifference that they saw kindness and joy. Usually the stars made Clara think of God's hand guiding all things, but now their distance and eternal stillness left an uneasy feeling deep in her stomach.

The ship pitched, and Clara caught herself against the wall, breaking the spell. She made her way back to her cabin and finally let the ship's rocking lull her to sleep.

The next morning, she was jolted awake by a lurch that nearly sent her tumbling to the floor. A boom echoed through the ship. She grabbed her life preserver and rushed out with the other girls. Her hands trembled so hard it took three tries to fasten the buckles. The floor bucked under her feet, and she slammed against the wall. Were they under attack? Was the ship sinking? Wouldn't there be some kind of alarm, or was it too late?

On the deck, they found the crew running about, hurrying, but not panicked. The sea rolled in great, gray waves, pounding the side of the ship.

"What's happening?" Clara shouted over the noise.

"Storm! Return to your cabins!" The sailor shouted.

Clara risked a quick glance at the low, gray clouds, the same hard, steely color as the relentless waves, and she rushed back to her room. The booming continued, an endless roar that tightened Clara's nerves until her shoulders were a mass of knotted muscles. The other girls tried to talk, but it was hard to hear, and the conversation trailed off into nervous listening. Clara read, but her book couldn't distract her from the sound or the horrible motion. A pit formed in her stomach, a queasy, greasy feeling that reeled and sloshed until she gagged. Soon she was hunched over a bowl, heaving up her dinner from the night before. She groaned and crawled back to her bed, praying the ground would hold still, and afraid it never would.

The storm roared on for days. All of the passengers were sick, struggling just to keep down water. The sour stench of vomit and sick bodies was trapped in the cabins along with the girls. Clara was convinced the ocean wouldn't quit until it swallowed the ship in those ceaseless, icy waves. The storm would save the German submarines the trouble of destroying them.

Clara woke one morning to find the ship rocking gently again, and her stomach calm enough to grumble at its emptiness. She crawled out of bed and almost whooped with joy when the floor didn't pitch her back down. The girls in her room dressed quickly and hurried to the mess hall. Other passengers gathered around the tables, scarfing down fruit and toast as they laughed at the pure joy of being healthy and whole and exchanged stories about the storm. They greeted Clara and her bunkmates with bright waves and hellos, as if they were all old friends after surviving their ordeal.

Clara ventured out again that night to see the stars, only too happy to trade the stale scent of her cabin for the cold, salty ocean air. This time, the moon hung low in the sky, casting a silver light down to frolic over the gentle waves.

A huddle of tense sailors wandered into view. Clara stepped back, and one of them jerked around to stare at her. He closed the distance between them in two strides. His wide hand slapped over her mouth before she could scream for help, and he pushed her back against the wall. She gave a muffled shout and tried to squirm away, but he whispered in her ear.

"Not a sound! One of the destroyers spotted a submarine out there."

Clara went still and nodded. He released her, and she scanned the horizon. She thought she saw an odd, blocky shape on the horizon, but the waves shifted and she couldn't be sure. She—everyone on the ship—had to hope their ship was just as hard to see, and she was grateful for the blacked-out windows. How strange, to see her first glance of the enemy over there, so close, so silent, engaged in a war of stealth and blackness instead of booming guns and flashes of fire.

Clara snuck back to her bed and spent the night listening, praying for no break in the quiet slosh of the ocean against the side of the ship, that no glint of moonlight would betray them.

They next day, the passengers were quiet. Word had spread about the sighting of "Herr Boche." Many waited on the decks, naturally falling into the abandon ship formation. The wakes of the ships in the convoy meandered like rivers as the ships wove a zigzag course across the water to confuse any submarines in the area.

A distant explosion boomed across the water. Clara and the other passengers rushed to the railing. The roar of guns made Clara's hair stand on end. There was really a submarine out there. One of the destroyers turned away from the convoy.

"They're following the wake left by the submarine's torpedo," one of the sailors explained to the girls. "That gets 'em close to the submarines, and they drop pressure mines. We'll pick up speed and show 'em a clean pair of heels, don't you worry."

Clara held her breath, but the torpedo must have passed their convoy by. The dazzle had worked. They left the submarine behind, but the tension lingered, hushing conversation and dulling appetites.

"We've crossed into French waters," the captain told them a few evenings later. "Everyone will sleep on deck tonight, fully clothed and wearing their life preservers. German subs patrol these waters heavily, so we have to be ready to evacuate the ship at a moment's notice."

The girls huddled together that night, shivering under their blankets. Clara hardly slept at all, wondering at every sound if the Germans were prowling closer.

Dawn washed the ocean with cold, gray light, and Clara made out the vague outline of land in the distance. A loud hum sounded over the other noises of the ship. What Clara took for birds in the distance grew larger.

"French airplanes!" one of the sailors shouted. "They're escorting us to shore."

The planes buzzed just overhead, and the pilots leaned over to wave at the ships. The biplanes looked fragile as they sailed above, their wings painted with concentric red, white, and blue circles for the allied forces.

One of the airplanes circled around to fly with them, gliding along over the ship like a kite.

"*Bonjour, mes amis!*" the pilot called, blowing a kiss to the girls.

The girls giggled in amazement and waved back.

"Sammies?" Maud asked, misunderstanding the French words for "my friends."

"That's just what they call American soldiers," the sailor explained.

Clara shook her head but didn't correct them. "*Vive la France!*" she yelled to the pilot, who tipped his wing in acknowledgment.

Eight days after leaving New York, the ship docked in France. Clara had trouble adjusting to the dry land, and she stayed close to her friends from the YMCA, hardly taking in the foreign accents and grim faces of a country three years into a bloody conflict. American soldiers were everywhere, unloading boats and moving cargo. They were almost all black men. The only white soldiers in sight were the officers overseeing the work. It gave her a chill, as if she were seeing into a past world of plantations and slaves.

Some of the French men whistled and made crude comments to the girls.

"What did that mean?" Maud asked.

Clara shrugged. She remembered what the YMCA woman had said about putting aside notions of propriety.

When they boarded the train to Paris, Clara was grateful for its reassuring sway, and she finally took a moment to look out the window at the verdant green fields and forests rolling past them. Her stomach fluttered uncomfortably, not so different from her earlier seasickness, and she took a long breath. She was in France, speeding into the heart of the war.

XVII

Dear Trudi,

Here I am in Paris at last, though it is not exactly as I dreamed it would be. I'm staying in a hotel with other YMCA workers near the Champs-Élysees, walking distance to the Eiffel Tower, the Louvre, and so many amazing cathedrals with their Gothic spires, but I haven't done any sight-seeing. During the day I am too busy, and at night they keep the city as dark as Logan. I did pass by Notre Dame, and was shocked and disappointed. All the beautiful stained glass windows are gone. Someone told me they took the glass out to protect it from the Germans.

The streets and buildings are crowded with refugees—mostly Belgian. The horrors they have been through are beyond anything I can imagine. The German soldiers burned a path through Belgium, even reducing libraries filled with ancient books to ash. They butchered town leaders and priests then rounded up civilians—men, women, and children—and shot them at random. Systematic terror. So much for German progress.

I know you sometimes think the work you do doesn't matter, but I can tell you how important it is after seeing these poor people. They have nothing left and nowhere to go. It is winter and freezing, but some don't even have coats or shoes. The children are the most heartbreaking. I cannot write of how pitiful it is, but please believe that the things you do matter more than you can imagine to people who you'll never meet, even if those things seem small. As for me, well, it is not only the refugees who are hungry and cold, though the YMCA keeps us supplied as best as they can, and I'm as well as can be expected. Tell everyone not to worry.

I'm looking forward to making a cozy Christmas for these children. I don't see much of the soldiers. American soldiers aren't allowed in Paris for fear the pretty French women will distract them from their duties. Reed had better not be distracted, wherever he is. I have to ring off now.

Yours,
Clara

The sound of bugles startled Clara from a light sleep. In the dark, her roommates stirred awake, some swinging their feet out of bed and grabbing their coats.

"What's that?" Clara asked. "What's going on?"

"It's the *Garde a vous,*" one of the girls said, "the warning call to attention. It means we might be under attack. We have to go down to the cellar."

Clara fumbled for her coat. Lily, who slept in the bed next to hers, took her arm, and they followed the other girls down to the shelter. In the dark of the cellar they met Maud and a handful of other YMCA workers—both men and women—and some of the refugees sheltered in their building.

"What do you suppose it is?" a small, dark-haired girl asked.

"Probably someone thought they spotted a zeppelin," one of the male YMCA supervisors said. "It will turn out to be a false alarm."

"How long do you think it will last this time?" another girl asked, lighting a cigarette.

The man shrugged. "I wish they'd have the courtesy to bomb us during the day."

They all grew quiet and listened to a round of explosions in the distance.

"Anti-aircraft artillery," the man said.

Clara clutched her coat tighter. "Do they shoot if there's nothing there?"

"Sometimes," the girl with the cigarette said, but she sounded more nervous now, and the others shifted closer together.

"What kind of cowards attack a city full of refugees? Full of women and children?" Clara asked.

"Barbarians," the smoker said. "I hate them."

A wail sounded outside, growing louder then speeding past them into the distance.

"Fire trucks," someone whispered in the dark.

Clara peeked out the window into the blackness of the streets. A horse-drawn wagon raced by. Sparks flew from the horses' shod hooves as they hit the stone. A searchlight passed overhead, brushing against the patchy clouds and flashing across the top of the Eiffel Tower before plunging the City of Light back into darkness.

They listened and waited, the only light the tip of a cigarette drawing strange orange patterns against the black. Finally, the bugles sounded the all clear.

With a great deal of mumbling, everyone returned upstairs. Clara huddled in her bed, still wearing her coat, but stayed awake long after the other girls' even breathing told her they had all drifted off.

She climbed out of bed, retrieved a stack of newspapers from her bureau, and snuck out into the hallway. Using a little pair of scissors, she cut snowflakes from the folded sheets of grim news. She had little time for the project during the day, but she wanted to do something to make Christmas cheerful for the refugee children.

All the time she worked, she imagined the huge shape of a zeppelin blotting out the moon and stars, keeping Paris in darkness forever.

The next morning, the news was that the zeppelins had come to the outskirts of Paris, but turned back when the French airplanes took to the air.

"They want Paris, but they can't quite reach it," said Maud as she helped Clara prepare breakfast. "They'll go to London instead. Those zeppelins have killed hundreds of people over there."

Clara imagined a zeppelin drifting over Cache Valley, dropping bombs on the A.C., the temple, her family's farm. As much as she couldn't sleep the night before, what must it be like to live in a place where the fear was constant, not just for yourself, but for your loved ones too?

Thank you, Lord, that it has not reached us in America. Please let us stop it here.

Clara went upstairs to serve the refugees. She saw the extra strain in their faces. Of course, they knew better than anyone what it would mean if the Germans captured Paris. Last time the Germans came close, America had flown a neutral flag over the great museums and monuments of the city to protect them in the name of all humanity. Now, though, the Americans were Germany's enemy, and the only way to save the ancient city was to stop the offensive.

The refugees accepted their bowls of porridge without meeting Clara's eyes, and their shoulders were hunched as they walked slowly to their seats. The children did not laugh or play, but stared at their food with solemn, adult eyes.

One man had a dog with him. The creature's ribs stood out against its patchy fur. Like the man, it kept its head low, but it stayed close to his side and wagged its tail, giving him a hopeful, almost worshipful look when he paused to pat its head. They were not supposed to supply food for the refugees' animals—there was little enough for the people—but Clara pretended not to see when he let the dog lick the remnants from his bowl. When the man walked past her, Clara stepped in front of him and pressed a bit of dried meat into his hands. He looked at her—met her eyes for the first time, and his own filled with tears. She hurried back to her work.

As they were cleaning up breakfast, one of the secretaries called Clara in to meet with the supervisor. Clara dried her hands and straightened her dress, wondering if she was in trouble for the man with the dog. She couldn't bring herself to regret it.

She stood outside the supervisor's office, unable to avoid eavesdropping on the loud conversation going on behind the door.

"There are Negro soldiers working the docks, and now they're sending them out to the front—doing the dirty work the white boys don't want to do—but there won't ever be Negro soldiers in Paris. Y'all won't let them come into the city, and you won't let us leave it. We want to be serving with our own men."

"The docks and the front are too dangerous. The work you're doing here is helping all the men."

"Those boys need to see a friendly face. They need to talk to someone from home, someone who understands. It's dangerous everywhere, and I'd rather be out there."

"I'm sorry. Request denied."

The door burst open, and a tall, imposing black woman stormed into the hall. She gave Clara a quick glance and swept past her. The man in the room mumbled something. Clara waited for a few long breaths before knocking on the open door.

"Come in!"

"Sir, Clara Jensen. You asked to see me."

"Yes, Miss Jensen. I'm reassigning you. We need more people helping at the canteens behind the front lines, caring for the walking wounded."

Clara thought of the decorations she had been making, her plans for Christmas with the refugees. Well, she was here to do her bit. "Yes, Sir."

He nodded, looking relieved, perhaps, that she didn't argue. "We're sending a truck out in the morning. Be ready to go."

She nodded and left to pack her things.

XVIII

Dearest Reed,

I hope you are well. With Christmas coming, I certainly miss you and everyone from home, but if I had to choose a place for my exile, I don't think I could have done better. I'll be spending my holidays in a French resort. I've never seen a place so opulent, everything in gold trim and velvet. There's enough space for everyone to have their own room, but they don't like to leave us girls alone, so I have a roommate, Lily Crane, from New York, who I met on the trip over.

Don't worry that I'm enjoying myself too much. This is one of the stations for the boys recovering from injuries, waiting to be fit enough to go back over the top. We make them food and serve hot drinks, and we try to keep them entertained, playing checkers and chess, even teaching a few of them to read. Yes, we've done some dancing, but trust that I'm only thinking of you. Many of the men like to talk about their sweethearts or wives back home. I'm glad to think that wherever you're stationed, you'll have similar comforts. I can tell some of these boys have had a hard time. My thoughts and prayers are with you.

Yours truly,
Clara

Have you seen Sanders?" Lily asked.

Clara sighed. "No. Do we need to look for him again?"

"I'm afraid so."

They put on their coats and headed outside. They knew which direction to go. There was a local tavern that made a brisk trade selling alcohol to the soldiers.

They found Sanders in the street, staggering a little and leaning on the arm of a woman whose drunken sway and heavy makeup suggested loose morals. Despite the warnings of their officers and doctors, and the disciplinary action taken if the constant health inspections turned up signs of venereal disease, some of the American boys kept chasing the local ladies.

"Private Sanders," Lily said, putting her hands on her hips.

"Ah, Miss Crane," he said plaintively. "I'm just having a drink."

"You've had enough. You're coming back with us now."

He grumbled but complied, leaning on Clara and Lily. He reeked of alcohol, but Clara didn't pull away. This was exactly what they had been warned about and trained for. When they got him back to the resort, he slumped down in a chair, burying his face in his hands. He sat like that as Lily hurried to get him a cup of coffee. He roused at the scent and rubbed his shaved head.

"No more for me. I just want to sleep it off."

"Are you feeling well enough now?" Lily asked.

He looked her in the face. "Miss Crane, I'm never going to be 'well' again. But if you won't let me drown it out in drink, then you might as well let me sleep. I'm one of the lucky ones—no nightmares. The only bad thing is waking up and knowing where I still am."

With that, he pushed himself up unsteadily and staggered off to his room.

Most of the men had gone to sleep, so Clara and Lily cleaned up and went to bed as well. Clara kept herself busy planning a homey Christmas for their boys. They decorated the resort with paper strings and made paper ornaments for the lop-sided pine tree some of the men had cut down. Clara hoped the children back in Paris were having a good holiday. She placed care boxes for the men under the tree. Some of them may have been packed by Trudi, or maybe her latest efforts were going to the refugee children instead. Of course, Clara didn't forget that the food she was cooking and eating could have been grown on her own farm. It was strange to think of the things that connected her to home during Christmas—not the usual traditions, but more important ties of hope and survival.

On Christmas morning they had canned ham and hot chocolate. Most of the men were in a jolly mood, opening letters from home or from kind strangers and finding the small treasures in the care boxes, like socks, cigarettes, and squares of chocolate. One young man wept openly as he pulled some hand-knitted gloves on.

"It's what Mother would have given me," he said.

A few of the men turned very quiet after opening their gifts. As the others gathered around the piano to sing Christmas carols, Clara tried to encourage the stragglers to join them.

"Do you like to sing, Captain Garrett?" she asked one young officer.

"Not very much, Miss."

"You could just listen. It might help you forget for a while. Do you think, out there on the front, that they're having another Christmas truce like in 1914? Maybe the Germans and Americans are playing football right now."

He looked up, his gaze hard. "I hope not. I don't think we can waste a single day playing games. We have to destroy the Boche."

Clara recoiled from the bitterness in his voice. "But on Christmas—"

"You think that will stop them? Nothing stops the war. The commanders were angry about the truce. They forbade it. Well, they got what they wanted. No more peace."

He got up and stormed out of the room. Clara sat in shock.

One of the girls who'd been in France longer came to sit beside her. "You can't play ball with a man one day then shoot him the next and still stay sane. At first these men didn't want to fight, but now many of them do. Not for their country or for any vague concept like glory, but because they're starting to forget how to do anything else."

Clara knew the war was hard on men, that they suffered from nightmares and memories they couldn't escape. But she'd never seen such raw hatred before. As the men sang about peace on earth, she wondered how that would ever be possible when war bred such bitterness and left it festering in men, even when they left the front, so they could find no joy in a day of peace.

XIX

January 1918
Brest, France

The deadliest weapon in the world is a Marine and his rifle.
—General John J. Pershing,
Commander of the American Expeditionary Force

Reed stood on the wharf with his new company commander, Captain George Hamilton, as his Marines pulled stevedore duty yet again, unloading ships laden with the material of war.

"Sir, why are we still here? It's been two months of this. We came all this way to pull guard duty and unload ships?"

Hamilton, his hands clasped loosely behind his back, turned partially toward Reed. "Because Pershing hates our guts, that's why."

"I don't understand, Sir. We came to help, to fight. Why would General Pershing not want to use us?" Reed asked.

"Oh, ye young and innocent one." Hamilton chuckled. Though only two years older than Reed, he was a "real" Marine officer. "Pershing, and the U.S. Army, for that matter, did not, do not, and will not want the Marines in this fight. They aim to do all the fighting and to take all the credit for it. The corps talked the politicians in Washington into forcing us on Pershing whether he wanted us or not."

"So that's why we are assigned under the 2nd Division, and our commanding officer is an army general?" Reed asked.

"Exactly, Lieutenant. Never happened before in the history of the corps, and I'll wager it won't happen again. But, here we are. Carrying supplies and yellin', 'Halt! Who goes there?'"

"All I know is I just want to get to the action before it's all over," Reed said.

"You and the rest of the U.S.M.C. I reckon you'll get your chance, Lieutenant."

XX

Dearest Clara,

To answer the obvious, yes, I do know where I am in France, so you need not needle me on that one thank you very much! If I did show my location, all you would see is a thick black line courtesy of the censor who will read this letter before you.

I am quite well. We have begun training in earnest to join the fight, finally. The men and I are desperate to do our bit, end this war, and go home. So we train hard, choke down yet another tin of canned Willy, hug ourselves to try to stay warm, and run through trench lines like trained mice, trying not to impale each other with our bayonets.

Please tell me where you are and your plans, if you can. I know something is always cooking in your mind, and you are no doubt wanting to "see the elephant," just like us boys. Trust that I won't try to talk you out of it, but I'll sure try like the dickens to see you here in France.

During quiet moments, the first thing in my mind's eye is home, and you, always you.

Happy Valentines Day,
Reed

Although they were not yet in action, Reed relished the training he and his men underwent at Naix-les-forges with the French Alpine Chasseurs, the famous "Blue Devils." Nearly halfway between the Marne and Meuse Rivers, the area certainly looked like the war zone it was. While Reed and his men had practiced some trench warfare back at Quantico, these French soldiers had been fighting and surviving in trenches for three years. They taught the men the principles behind how the trenches were dug, for instance, why they tended to zigzag across the land. If the enemy captured part of the line during a general attack or raid, the zigzag pattern prevented rifle fire down the length of the line. They also taught the men how to reinforce the sides to prevent collapse, and how to construct dugouts and bunkers to help protect against artillery.

After the class, Hamilton walked his platoon leaders through the training trenches to show them some finer points. Reed blew on his hands down in the trench, noticing how much colder it was than on the surface.

"First, note that this trench is ten feet deep," Hamilton began, "that's standard depth. Then, every few feet there are these firing steps that allow the riflemen to shoot through the loopholes cut into the parapet. I can't emphasize enough, gentlemen, that you cannot, under any circumstances, stick your head over that parapet. You're gonna want to so you can see what's going on. You might get away with it once, but by the second time, a German sniper is going to shoot you right in the head. Use mirrors and trench periscopes. Understand?"

There were earnest head nods from all the platoon leaders.

"Now," Hamilton continued, "there is only one trench line here, for training, but in the real line, there will be three or four lines of these trenches. The first line is the 'fire' line, for obvious reasons. The second is the support line. The third is for the reserve. I'll rotate your platoons between trench lines on a schedule so your men get what passes for rest here."

"How do we get between the trench lines?" asked another platoon leader.

"There are communication trenches dug perpendicular to the main lines, both between lines and to the rear," Hamilton explained. "That's where your ammo and other supplies will be brought up."

"Sir, what do we do when it thaws? The mud and everything," Reed asked.

"Good question. Soldiers have actually become so stuck in trench mud that they drowned. Many more were evacuated for what they are calling 'trench foot.' Men have lost their feet because of it. Rotting skin, infection, it's just awful. Ya gotta do bucket brigades and get the water out as much as possible. Ya gotta find ways to keep your men's feet dry."

The next morning, Reed and the other platoon leaders went with Captain Hamilton to learn how to move under a rolling artillery barrage. Fortunately, the French captain teaching the class spoke nearly flawless English.

"First, you prepare in the trenches to conduct *l'attaque*, yes? You queue up at the trench ladders, ready to move. We fire artillery along a line in front of you as close as we can, one salvo, then you go over the top and move forward. Then, we fire at the farthest point we can at the rear of the enemy positions. This traps them in place. We fire again, forward of your new line, and you move again. So we roll, yes? Everyone understand?"

"How many casualties result from friendly fire?" Captain Hamilton asked.

"Ah, yes. When the English started this technique, they expected ten percent friendly casualties. But we are much better now at coordinating, yes? As well, these are French crews on French guns, so maybe better than our English friends."

Reed and the other platoon leaders looked at each other with raised eyebrows. *Ten percent? Couple rounds of that we'll be out of the fight!*

"Wouldn't it be better just to hit the Germans with a massive barrage right on their line, Sir?" Reed asked.

"I wish it were that simple, *mes ami*. We have been trying that for three years now. The Germans dig like moles on their main line. Massed artillery is no fun for them, but they always survive, like rats. They have bunkers ten to twelve meters deep. We found some with toilets and electricity, even wallpaper on the walls. No, we must draw them out to receive the infantry attack, then hit them while they are above ground— make them move."

On the walk back from the training, Reed asked Captain Hamilton, "Sir, are we going to have French artillery in support or the 2nd Division's?"

"Why do you ask, Mr. Lewis?"

"Well, seems like it would be easier coordinating fire with American artillerymen, that's all."

"True, but on the other hand, those boys ain't ever fired a shot in anger, much less a rolling barrage. You wanna let them practice on you?

I vote for French artillery, but I don't guess my vote will count much. Anyhow, for now, focus on getting your boys ready to move."

"Where we headed, Sir?"

"You keep this quiet until we move out. We're gonna get into the fight, Mr. Lewis. We leave in the morning. Verdun."

"About dang time, Sir! We'll be ready." Reed said, his steps light.

"Oh, and Mr. Lewis. I left a little surprise for you back at your platoon," Hamilton half-smiled. "Hope you like it."

Reed half walked, half ran back to his men. He found his "surprise" in the person of his new platoon sergeant, Gunnery Sergeant Allen, who called the men to attention as Reed approached.

"Good afternoon, Lieutenant." Allen saluted. "Gunnery Sergeant Allen, reporting for duty, Sir."

Reed had heard of Allen, a living legend in the corps, but he had never seen him in person. Allen was a thirty-year Marine. Lean, hard, and leather-faced, Allen had been shot in the jaw in the Battle of Guantanamo Bay during the Spanish-American War, and the resulting injury left him with a permanent hole in his right cheek, which whistled when he talked and foamed when he was angry. And he was angry a great deal.

"I'm Lieutenant Reed Lewis, pleased to meet you." Reed stuck out his hand awkwardly, not sure what else do to.

Allen took Reed's hand in a firm grip. Reed felt like Allen was taking his measure so he gripped back just as firmly.

"You have a given name, Sergeant?" Reed asked.

"Only the one the corps issued me, Sir, Gunnery Sergeant." His lip turned up in a faint hint of a grin.

"Fair enough, Sergeant," Reed said, flashing a smile. "Get the men ready, we move out in the morning."

"Very good, Sir." Allen saluted Reed again, executed a facing movement toward the men, and began barking orders. Marines scurried everywhere at once, packing their gear and tents. *I could get used to having him around.*

"Sergeant," Reed called out after Allen.

"Yes, Sir?"

"Aren't you going to ask where we're heading?"

"No, Sir. I reckon if you wanted me know that, you'd a told me already. We gonna kill some Boche?"

"Yes, Sergeant. I expect so."

"Good enough for me, Mr. Lewis."

XXI

March 1918
Verdun, France

Diary of Reed Lewis, March 14, 1918

Trucked with the men to the city of Verdun, then marched in with full packs to the front, I'd guess 10 miles or more. Boys were in fine fettle, shouting "Oui, oui," at the French—the only words they know. Pretended not to notice when they ran into shops to buy bread or potatoes and vin rouge as we passed through villages. War has not dampened their "taste for the creature." Our food is bad, and the boys are always hungry. Farmers sowing and reaping right near the front lines as if nothing is going on. Surreal. Fruits and flowers don't know of war. Everyone has gas masks, even the women. Horses have them! Verdun has been in the heat of the fight almost since the war started. Passed through the little village of Fleury, right near the front. French guide says it changed hands sixteen times during the battle in 1916. There is nothing left of it. Hearthstones scattered like the families that lived there. Our guide said the village died for France. We approached the trenches and I felt like we were sneaking up on some terrible thing, a place where life stops. Not a blade of grass, not one intact tree, rivers of rusted barbed wire. Graves marked Soldat Francais on bare wood crosses. No man's land.

Reed stood just behind Captain Hamilton as they watched the French *Poilus* slowly file out of the trench below. No hint of blue on their uniforms; the men were gray from head to foot. The only color Reed could see was the flash of their eyes when they looked up as they passed. Few of them did that much.

"They don't look happy to see us, or even to be leaving," Reed whispered.

"They expected to die here, or in an attack over the top," Hamilton said. "'Course there hasn't been much of that since the revolt last year," he whispered. "I think they're just numb."

"Were these men part of the revolt, Sir? Did they refuse to fight?"

"Keep your voice low. They don't talk about it. Anyway, it doesn't matter. The whole French army was affected by it. They didn't refuse to fight; they just wanted a stop to useless attacks."

"Well, Sir, I don't expect our Marines will refuse to attack," Reed said.

"We just got here, Mr. Lewis." Captain Hamilton nodded to the *Poilus* filing out. "That's the last of them. Get your men squared away. Stand-to at 1700 hours tonight."

"Aye, Sir," Reed said. He led his men into the trench, spacing them as he'd seen the French do. He called up to Hamilton. "Sir, these trenches are only about eight feet deep. I thought they were supposed to be ten?"

"They probably were ten feet deep two years ago," Hamilton replied.

"Should we start digging them out?"

"Nope. Better to build up, unless you want to see what's buried beneath your feet."

"Aye, Sir," Reed said, his stomach churning as he walked on the uneven trench floor.

Reed and Sergeant Allen checked that the men had stowed their gear. They ate an early supper of punk—dry bread with the texture of rotten wood—and a stew of water, potatoes, meat, and—Allen said— dirt, washed down with cold coffee.

At stand-to, every man stood at the parapet with rifle at the ready, a routine they would repeat at dusk and dawn every day, the most likely time the enemy would attack.

After stand-to, Reed noticed that Allen was gathering his gear. "Where are you going, Sergeant?"

"Inspection, Sir. Gotta check every man, every rifle."

"I'm coming along. You can show me how."

"Aye, Sir."

It was different in some ways than an inspection in barracks. Sergeant Allen had them field strip their weapons, checking for dirt and rust. He made each man take off his boots and Allen checked to see if their socks were dry by squeezing their feet. The Marines down the line saw this and began unraveling the hated leggings before Allen got there.

"See that, Sir?" Allen gestured with his head. "We ain't even done the whole line and they're already learning the routine. We're going to build habits in them like this, Sir. Clean, dry socks and uniforms. Personal hygiene, too. Remember to check the action on their bolts, make sure it's smooth—well oiled."

Allen carried a little rack he had made for drying socks to show the men so they could make their own to stake out next to the fires they were allowed to build during daylight hours.

He talked to the men the whole time he was inspecting, so practiced it reminded Reed of how his mother chatted while knitting. Allen used the opportunity to get to know each man, where he was from, how well he knew his duties, and how he was doing physically.

After they finished with the last man, Reed said, "Sergeant, I'd like to continue coming with you on these inspections if you don't mind."

Allen turned to look at him. "Officers don't usually do that, Sir." Then he pondered for a moment. "But you're most welcome, Lieutenant, any time."

Reed knew it was not his job to inspect to the level Allen intended, but he also knew he could find himself without an experienced Non-Commissioned Officer, or NCO, like Sergeant Allen. He wanted to know every detail.

The men spent the first night improving their dugouts, using blankets to chemical proof the entrances so gas would not gather inside when the men took shelter during an artillery barrage. They also began filling bags with dirt so they could deepen the trench by stacking them several deep and wide on both sides of the trench. Reed was glad for the annoying officer's bamboo cane he had to carry—it was the only way he could feel his way in the dark as he checked on the construction. It also seemed to scare off the rats, which was far better than feeling them brushing over his boots and squealing as he walked in the dark.

The line at Verdun was quiet, but that only meant the Germans were not launching a major offensive. It did not mean they had forgotten about the Frenchmen, and now the Americans, facing them.

The vague rumble of artillery had vibrated under Reed's feet ever since they approached the front, but at 0200, the rumble grew to a roar and rounds began landing in their sector of the front. A loud whistling sound split the air before a tremendous explosion about 100 yards to their front blew a rain of dirt down on them.

"Under cover!" Reed yelled, and Allen ran down the line repeating it. "Under cover! Get in the dugouts now!"

Reed and Allen dived into their dugout, dropped the new curtain, and waited. Rounds impacted sporadically, each one shaking the ground, knocking dirt between the shelter's supporting logs, making Reed wonder if it would collapse on them. Each one that landed within a football field of them batted them around the dugout like marbles in a can. Reed grimaced at each screaming whistle—they all sounded like they were going to land right on him.

Allen's raspy voice pierced the dark. "Lieutenant. Just in case you was wondering, them shells, if you can hear 'em, ya probably ain't gonna die. See, they say them rounds travel faster than sound. So the one that gets you, you ain't gonna hear it."

Reed sat with his legs pulled into his chest, shaking. "That's a big relief, Sergeant," he said, sarcastically. " I feel ever so much better now."

As more dirt fell on them between the logs, Allen laughed. "Always a pleasure, Sir."

The darkness grew quiet. After a minute or two, Reed said. "Let's get the men to stand-to, Sergeant, be ready for an attack."

"Aye aye, Sir," Allen said. "They ain't coming though, that's just harassing fire."

"You mean a barrage is worse than that?"

"Oh, yes, Sir. You see all them shell holes when we came in, like they was almost touching each other? That's what a barrage looks like."

Reed stood, his legs wobbly. "Very well. Let's go to stand-to anyway."

This exhausting routine continued, working at night, resting in the daytime when possible, stand-to, and crappy chow. Then the rain came, bringing with it relentless cold in the damp trenches.

"Lieutenant, put your socks out to dry on my rack. The men watch you, Sir. Ya gotta set the example. Plus, you ain't immune from this weather just because you're an officer," Allen growled.

Reed felt anything but immune. He couldn't remember the last time his feet and hands were warm. Unwrapping his mud-encrusted leggings in order to change his socks covered his hands in cold sludge. One more layer of grime and another round of trying to warm his hands enough to be able to write or clean his pistol. More often than not, his cold, numb hands dropped weapons parts into the mud at his feet, and he had to fish them out and clean them off with even colder hands.

Utah was plenty cold, especially on the range, but here, this wet cold, it permeated everything and everyone.

Allen worked like a madman to keep the men as dry as possible, organizing details to bucket the new mud out of the trenches and to dry socks by the gross. Despite his efforts, the Marines soon looked very much like the *Poilus* they had replaced, their green uniforms no longer distinguishable from Army gray or French blue.

After two weeks, boredom and misery were the order of the day. The artillery came as it did every night, sporadically at first, but then before dawn one day it increased like a soft rain turning to a downpour after thunder.

Reed assumed his normal sitting position, legs pulled in tight, head on his knees, but soon found himself on his back, on his side, face down, thrown about like a rag doll. Dirt from close rounds dropped into the trenches like crashing waves, covering the men, dirt stacking like snow-drifts against their shelter covers. He could no longer hear whistles at all, just one, continuous roar, blotting out everything else. He could not hear, could not speak, could not think.

Sergeant Allen's rough hands turned him over. "Sir," he screamed in his ear, "you wounded?"

"I don't know. I don't think . . . We have to . . ." Reed stammered.

"We gotta stand-to, Sir. Those Boche are coming for sure this time."

Reed got to his knees, trying to breathe. *Come on, Reed. These men depend on you. Allen can get up. I will too!* "Call stand-to. I'll go left, you go right, get the men on the line."

"Aye, Sir," Allen called out, already halfway out of the dugout. He stumbled down the line while Reed turned the other way, on his feet now, unsteady, he began dragging dazed Marines from their dugouts and up onto their firing platforms. "Stand-to, Marines, stand-to. Time to kill those Boche!"

He met Allen back at the center. Allen was looking over the parapet, calling out firing orders to the men. "We got movement to our front. You pick your targets, squeeze that trigger nice and easy."

"Sergeant! You gotta use a mirror or periscope, your gonna get picked off!" Reed called.

"Aye, Sir, 'cept I can't find a dang thing. Everything's buried," Allen replied, then more quietly, "Sir, we lost four men down the south end of the trench. Round landed right in it."

Before he could answer, Captain Hamilton came running up from the support trench, suffering from the effects of the bombardment, rocking back and forth like he was on a ship as soon as he stopped.

"Phone line is down. I called for flares to your front. Be ready. I don't think this is a probe, Lewis. Get your periscope up and see what you can when the flares come up."

"Aye, Sir," Reed said as Hamilton ran back to his position. Reed sprinted to the dugout and retrieved the spare periscope he had stashed there. He got up on the platform next to Allen and scanned the front as the flares started bursting overhead to cast a pale intermittent light on the battlefield. As he scanned across the entanglements with the little frame of the periscope, it was like looking at a forest through a peephole. There were moving figures in the barbed wire, dozens, no hundreds of them, stacking up at the wire as their forward elements tried to cut their way through.

"Platoon!" Reed screamed. "At 100 yards, enemy in the wire, rapid fire, fire at will!"

Almost simultaneously, the Marines poured rifle fire into the Germans approaching the wire entanglements. At only 100 yards, the weak light didn't matter. Each 30-06 slug found targets in the dark shapes they had crossed an ocean to fight.

Reed turned to his runner. "Go find the Captain. Tell him we have a battalion-sized attack to our immediate front. Need more flares, and artillery beyond our wire at target reference points one through four. Go!"

Allen called down from the platform, "Sir, still coming. Dropping like flies, but it's a big attack. They ain't stoppin'."

"Ammo bearers, plenty of rounds to each rifleman; we need steady fire!" Reed yelled as he climbed up. No need to remind either man that looking over the top could be fatal; bullets plowed into the parapet like punches to a pillow, others whizzed over the top, shredding the air.

Reed looked down the line. The men were working the actions on their rifles with precision, each jolted back by the powerful recoil of their aught-threes.

As the French guns behind them opened up, Reed watched the artillery blast apart the formations heading toward the wire. Whole groups of them disappeared. The fire was directed on target reference points the Marines had picked in advance, so the French knew exactly where to put the rounds. It looked devastating through the periscope, but Reed could see Germans had made it inside the wire, safe from the French guns. Many of them had gone to ground, still moving toward the Marine line.

"They're gonna be on us soon," he whispered to Allen.

"We best fix bayonets, Sir."

Reed looked at Allen and nodded.

Allen turned toward the line and bellowed in an unearthly way, "Fix! Bayonets!"

The men reacted instinctively, hours of practice back at Paris Island paying off, snatching their bayonets from nearby sandbags they had stuck them in and affixing them to the front of their aught-threes. Their firing barely paused. The Germans were close enough that the Marines were dropping them as fast as they could work the actions on their weapons. But they kept coming.

When the German infantry got within range, they threw the grenades the men called potato mashers. Those that rose to their knees to throw were almost always cut down, but others lobbed them from the prone position. Most of them landed in front of the trench to little effect, but every one that did land in the trench killed or wounded several of Reed's men, thinning his line.

Reed looked over to the extreme right since there was a flare floating over. The Germans were nearly at the trench on that end. One of them carried a large tank on his back and some kind of nozzle instead of a rifle. *Flame thrower!*

"Right side of the line! Shift your fire to the far right!" Reed jumped off the platform and ran down the right side, calling to the rifleman posted there, "You see that Boche with the tank on his back? Concentrate fire on that tank!"

The men shifted their weight to the left to be able to fire down the line to the right. Multiple rounds knocked the flamethrower carrier to his knees, then exploded his tank in a huge fireball. Still the Germans came on.

Captain Hamilton sprinted up again. "Lewis! Fall back! Get your men to the second trench line now. I'm calling artillery on this position!"

Reed shouted, "Every other man from the right, secondary line, MOVE!"

Just like they had rehearsed in one of Sergeant Allen's many "routines," half the men fell back, the other half stayed on the wall to cover them so the Germans would stay down.

As the last of the first wave disappeared into the communication trench, Reed called out, "Marines, fall back, secondary trench, MOVE!" The second group sprinted for the communication trench like their hair was on fire, closely followed by Allen and finally Reed. French rounds pounded their former trench line with seconds of their movement. Unencumbered by the need to avoid friendly troops, the French artillery butchered the remaining Germans, as they had done since 1914.

After spending the rest of the night at stand-to in the support trench, Reed and his men were ordered to the rear for refit, rest, and replacements. They needed it. Reed had lost nearly a third of his platoon in the fight.

He sat up against a tree stump, staring at nothing, still in his filthy uniform, too exhausted, too depressed to sleep. Captain Hamilton approached Reed and he started to get up, but the Captain waved him still.

"You need to get cleaned up, Mr. Lewis. Get a fresh uniform. The men need to see you back on your feet, just like they need to be."

"Aye, Sir." Reed said flatly. "The ones still alive, anyway."

Hamilton looked at him thoughtfully. "You need to know how well you and your platoon did last night. You fought bravely and well. That's all the corps or anyone can ask."

"So many men, Sir. We have to bury them today. I have to bury them today."

"This is what war is, Lieutenant, plain and simple. You see this battlefield? During three hundred and three days of battle here, there have been more than a million casualties. Your story repeated thousands of times. We came here to end this, but we aren't special. It's gonna cost us. Like it did last night. So you pick yourself up, clean up so you look like a Marine officer again, then you bury those boys with the best dignity you can muster."

"Aye, Skipper," Reed said.

"I'm gonna need you again, Lewis. You're a fine leader."

Reed let the compliment slide off him. "Skipper? Those Germans, are they all like that? They just wouldn't be beat."

"Ah, no. They were *Sturmtruppen*, elite soldiers. The British call them the Hindenburg Circus. They get into trench lines with pistols, knives, flamethrowers, grenades—then they raise Cain. You did well to slow them down."

Reed stood with Sergeant Allen, both freshly attired in U.S. Army issue uniforms, one more way General Pershing had to tell them they weren't welcome. Their Marine collar insignia and helmets were the only thing distinguishing them as Marines.

One thing there was plenty of was plain pine coffins, and they watched as the men loaded the dead, or at least those they had been able to recover, into carts for the trip to the improvised cemetery.

They could only muster up one American flag, so they moved it to each coffin as it was carried forward in its turn.

Once all the men were laid to rest, the chaplain gave a brief service, the platoon fired seven rifles in three volleys, the company bugler played taps, and the men were covered up, their graves marked with crosses the men made from wood pried off a nearby barn.

Reed gathered his men.

"Marines, the chaplain said these men gave their lives for their country, for this cause. I don't know about that. What I do know is that they died for you and me, their comrades in arms. We faced a test together, and we persevered. You fought with honor, like the Marines you are and the Marines who came before you." Reed hesitated. "I don't know what role God plays in this war, but I believe he has plans for each and every one of us. All we can do is give our best and do our duty for our nation and for our friends. Fall out." *The men needed my reassurance. I hope it's true. I hope God even remembers us trapped here in this nightmare.*

Reed, Allen, and their men returned to the trenches for three more weeks, though they never faced a German attack of that magnitude again.

Captain Hamilton addressed Reed and his fellow platoon leaders. "Gentlemen, we have received orders to move to Chaumont en Vixen, for open warfare training. I believe we're going to need it. General Pershing believes the only way to win this war is by attacking, not dying in some trench. I'll reckon we'll be testing that theory soon enough."

Reed winced inwardly, but he kept his shoulders square. Open warfare would mean even more casualties, but they weren't making any headway in the trenches, and neither had the French and British for the last four years. This was why they were here, to bring the war to an end, and he would play his part. It wasn't just about making the people at home proud. His men relied on him too, a weight as constant as the never-ending rumble of the guns.

 XXII

March 1918
Somewhere in France

The newly formed Bolshevik government of Russia has signed a treaty with Germany and the Central Powers, ending Russia's role in the Allied forces and freeing Germany to concentrate the full force of its military might on the Western Front. The spirit of America is not shaken by this news. The American people hope the Russians may find their own route to democracy, and are proud that America has stepped in at this crucial moment to show the world that right is more powerful than might.

—The Stars and Stripes (Paris, France)

Clara's shift in the YMCA canteen was almost over. She'd been transferred to a "hut" closer to the front, where she served coffee and donuts, helped illiterate soldiers write letters, and loaned out books to those who could read. The latest rush was over, and the last group of soldiers filed outside. Only one man still sat at the counter, tracing abstract patterns with his finger.

"Hot chocolate or coffee?" Clara asked.

The soldier didn't look up. She watched him quietly. Her YMCA training had prepared her for the men who swore regularly, lost their tempers at the smallest provocations—real or imagined—or seemed to always be in pursuit of girls or alcohol. What she could not have imagined were the other men. Those like the one in front of her, who reacted to stress, fatigue, and loss, not by flailing out at the world, but by curling into themselves, suffering somewhere in the dark depths of their minds. It was a little different for each of them, but she had learned to wait.

The man finally glanced up.

"Hot chocolate or coffee?" she asked again, keeping her smile.

"Umm." He stopped his movement, staring at the counter then back at her. There was something in his eyes. Something lost. It was almost childlike, but the pain there was nothing like most children knew, even the refugees. "Hot chocolate or coffee," he repeated.

He looked at her again, imploringly. She poured the hot chocolate. "This is a special treat, isn't it? Nothing tastes better on a cold day. They say this winter was unusually hard for France, but it's almost spring. Where I'm from, in Utah, the winters last so long I sometimes wonder if they'll ever end, but the snow always melts eventually."

The soldier watched her carefully as she rambled, as if absorbing every word. Then he relaxed and took the cup, wrapping both hands around it and letting the steam drift around his face for several moments before closing his eyes and raising it to his lips.

Adelaide, the canteen worker sharing Clara's shift, scowled at the soldier. As Clara untied her apron, Adelaide whispered to her.

"I can't stand the ones like that."

Clara glanced back at him. "I know. It's heartbreaking."

"Heartbreaking? It makes me furious. Trying to get out of work or get attention by acting strange. I can't abide it."

"You think he's pretending?" Clara kept her voice low.

"Oh, maybe not consciously. But he must be weak to act so . . . broken."

Clara stared at Adelaide, then back at the soldier. Perhaps a part of him was broken, but she wondered if it was because he had tried too long to be strong. She had been watching these men for several months now, and they acted tough, especially when they were flirting with the girls, but underneath it all, they just seemed young. It was a heavy burden, going out there to face injury and death, and it left marks.

She remembered what it had been like when she had to face her father every day. He'd never caused her any serious physical injury, but his cold anger and harsh words still stung. She hadn't been able to run away, any more than these men could. But she had tried to escape anyway. She still wasn't sure if she had spent her life running toward something or away from it, but she always kept moving because holding still meant facing that terrible voice in the back of her mind, asking her why she couldn't be better and stronger. These soldiers weren't much different. They were asked to be impossibly strong, but the human mind could only bear so much torment before it found a way to flee.

"I don't think it's about strength," she whispered, more to herself than to Adelaide. Or maybe she was talking to the soldier, who'd spilled a drop of the hot chocolate and was now painting figures on the counter with it. "I think it's about surviving what no one was meant to survive."

Adelaide wiped up the counter, clearing away the soldier's chocolate sketches. He jumped when her rag swept by him. Clara squeezed his shoulder as she walked past, glad to see that Maud was one of the girls coming to replace them. Maud's quiet gentleness relaxed everyone around her, even the most wounded spirits. Clara never knew how to help such men, and she felt awkward and useless in their presence.

The cold outside hit her in the face and took her breath away. She pulled up the collar of her coat and pressed into the wind, glad for the flimsy shelter of the YMCA huts. The one behind her truly lived up to its name. It was hardly more than a tin shack. This close to the front, many of the soldiers came in grim-faced, with only a chance for a short break at the rear before they were called forward again. Clara was glad for the chance to provide them some small comforts, but she wished every day that there was something more she could do.

She shook her head. Maybe her motivations weren't so altruistic. The soldier back at the hut reminded her that she wasn't as suited to this work as someone like Maud. Maybe she was just running again—running away from anything that held her back or made her feel worthless, running toward the challenges that let her prove that she was competent.

She walked toward the YMCA tents. An ambulance sat next to one of them. Clara jogged over. A middle-aged woman in a fashionable blue dress stood by the vehicle, dangling a long cigarette holder, while a man in a black suit bent over to stare hopelessly at the engine.

"What's happened?" Clara asked.

The woman just wrinkled her forehead in confusion. Clara tried again in French.

"The engine died," the man replied in French. "I think it is too cold. We just acquired this ambulance, and I am afraid it might not have been a good deal."

Clara looked at the ambulance more closely. It was a Ford. She smiled sadly, remembering the evening at the Bluebird with Trudi and the boys. "I have started a Ford when it was colder than this." She replied, grateful for her French classes. "May I look?"

The man gave a careless wave.

Clara took off her gloves to examine the engine. "Here is the problem. The spark plugs need to be cleaned."

She blew warm air over her hands and flexed her cold fingers, then found a wrench in the cab to unscrew the spark plugs and wipe off the carbon build-up with the corner of her handkerchief. She replaced them and checked the oil, water, and coils for good measure. The timing adjustments on the steering wheel were a little off, so she leaned in to adjust them and went around to jerk the crank. The engine jumped to life.

"Well done!" The woman said in French. She gestured at the ambulance with her cigarette holder. "Can you also drive?"

"Yes, of course," Clara said.

"You are American? A YMCA secretary?"

"Yes, Ma'am."

"And you like this work?"

"Yes, but . . ."

The woman motioned her on, flicking ashes on the ground.

"I like being able to help the men. I often wish I could be more involved."

"You must be adventurous, to come all this way. And the danger does not bother you?"

"No, Ma'am. I mean to say, I did not come here for the danger, but I do not mind it."

The woman smiled. "The YMCA will be angry if I steal their girls, but did you know there is a desperate need for ambulance drivers? The Germans are launching a massive movement against the Western Front. Many men are wounded every day."

Clara nodded. Reed was out there, "somewhere in France," as the saying went. "Ambulance drivers?"

"Women as well as men. Some objected to the idea of letting women drive, but when the need is great, we show them what we are capable of, do we not, Mademoiselle?"

Clara grinned. "Yes, Ma'am, we do."

"And you would like to drive one of these ambulances?"

She glanced at the vehicle, a new excitement stirring in her chest. This was a job tailored to fit her. It might be just another reckless race to the next challenge, but how could she say no? "I would."

"We are a private ambulance company, all volunteer. You would have to pay your own room and board, and for your own gas. It is not much more, I think, than it costs you to be with the YMCA, though."

"I believe I could do that."

"You have medical training?"

"No more than the basics the YMCA taught us," Clara admitted, and the warm new glow of excitement dimmed as quickly as it had grown.

"Unfortunate, but we can still use you. The need is desperate."

"I would be honored to help," Clara said.

"It is messy work. You see some things here that are unpleasant, but driving an ambulance, you will be dealing with the injured. The dying. The sights and smells are disturbing—too much for some people."

"I am from a farm, Ma'am. I have seen unpleasant things, and they do not frighten me."

The women nodded and tossed her spent cigarette to the ground, crushing it under her boot heel. "Then we would be happy to have you. I am Madame Guillot. What is your name?"

"Clara Jensen."

"Jensen," the woman said, struggling over the unfamiliar sounds. "Welcome, Miss Jensen. I like to send my girls out in twos. It keeps them a bit safer, and if one is hurt, the other can still drive. Do you know any other girls who drive?"

Clara remembered Lily talking about learning to drive from her brothers. "Yes, I do."

"You will get in touch with her, ask her to join you in Paris?"

"Yes, Ma'am," Clara said.

Clara returned to Paris, her single suitcase, now rather worn and battered, clutched in her hand. She found her way to the modest Left Bank boarding house recommended by Madam Guillot. The tiny old woman who ran it tottered ahead to show her to the room she would be sharing with Lily, then gave her a nearly toothless grin along with a pat on the arm and left her alone. The threadbare sheets and ivory curtains were worn to holes in some places, and the little round table in the corner wobbled when Clara set her suitcase on it, but everything was polished clean. It would do.

Parisians hurried by on the tree-lined avenue below, mixed in with soldiers. Here and there, some of the stately trees had been chopped down for firewood, leaving an empty spot in their neat ranks, like soldiers picked off by gunfire. Clara's stomach flip-flopped, and she turned her gaze to the riverfront in the distance. A few couples strolled along the banks of the Seine or sat at sidewalk cafes, temporarily forgetting the war in the romantic pink haze of springtime Paris. There were no Americans, though—at least among the soldiers. How lonely and odd, to be so close to her friends—to Reed—and never be able to see them.

Most of Clara's driving duties would involve moving soldiers from one hospital to another. It wasn't usually dangerous or interesting work, but Madame Guillot warned her that when the fighting was hot, they would go in closer to the front. She might see her friends. Of course, in those circumstances, she wouldn't want to. She would be able to help, though. She would be moving again. Running away from something, or toward it? She let the curtain fall on the street scene below.

That night, as Clara was drifting off, the air raid alert shrieked in the darkness. She sat up with a groan. This part of city life, she could do without. All the residents of the house funneled down the staircase together to the cellar.

They sat in awkward silence for a moment. There was a distinct crack outside, something Clara had never heard before in the air raid warnings.

"A zeppelin?" she asked.

The others gave her a look that made her feel terribly ignorant.

"Mademoiselle, that is a shell from Big Bertha," one of the men said.

"What?" Clara asked.

"The Germans' Paris Gun."

Clara clutched her coat tighter over her nightgown. "The Germans are close enough to fire on Paris?" She hadn't known the situation was so dire.

"They are 120 kilometers away."

"They're . . ." Clara did a quick translation in her head. That was 75 miles, about the distance from Salt Lake City to Logan. "How is that possible?"

They all just shook their heads. Clara sat in the darkness, listening to the crash of shells from a gun so far away it would take her two or three hours to drive to it. She wanted to get closer to the front, but it seemed the front was coming to them. Paris was undefended, though, full of refugees. Reed, Bert, and Joseph were somewhere out there, pushing against the German tide. If they failed, it wouldn't matter whether Clara was driving an ambulance. The Germans and their guns would storm through Paris, and nothing would stop them from being another Belgium. And what then? Perhaps Britain would fall, and maybe even America.

XXIII

Are you "doing your bit?" Are you enlisted in the Armed Forces or working on a farm or in a factory to provide for the boys going "Over There?" Have you Hooverized your meals by giving up wheat, butter, sugar, and meat to save these essential foods for shipping overseas? Have you bought your Liberty Bonds and Thrift Stamps? Before we reach the end of this war, every man, woman, and child will have to make personal sacrifices.

—The A.C. Student Life

The rattle of guns echoed over campus. Trudi clutched her books tighter, then forced herself to relax. The R.O.T.C. was holding a mock battle north of the school, just outside the cemetery. Trudi shivered at the thought. Had they chosen that place on purpose, to remind the boys what was at stake?

She made her way to the gym, where the girls' regular physical education class had been canceled indefinitely in favor of female military drills. Not with guns, of course. Trudi had seen the pictures of earlier generations of A.C. women drilling with their uniforms and rifles. That tradition had faded away, but now the school paper encouraged the girls to prepare to go with the Red Cross, or to form a "Legion of Death" in America if the Germans invaded. Another volley of gunshots reverberated off the buildings, and Trudi flinched. Hopefully the need would never come.

As she practiced marching in the gym with the other female students, she mulled over the rest of the paper's words. It reminded the girls that they would likely marry returned soldiers—if the war continued on much longer, America would sacrifice an entire generation to the trenches, as the European nations had—and drilling would teach the girls strict, silent obedience.

The sentiment chilled Trudi. Not that she expected to be a rebellious wife, but there was something unsettling about the idea of becoming nothing but a silent, obedient shadow. Some days she already felt like her attempts to be a model citizen—to fit in—were erasing her.

Still, she kept her shoulders back and marched, reaching for the energy to move precisely despite her exhaustion.

"Excellent work, Miss Kessler," their instructor called over the drum setting the cadence. "Everyone pay attention and try to follow her lead. Miss Kessler is perfectly in step."

Trudi smiled, but her happiness at the compliment felt pale and watery. The idea that clung to her was the idea that she was being prepared to be a soldier's wife. Perfectly in step. Would the war last long enough for her to marry and send a husband off to war? Would he return hating the Germans, hating her native tongue? That could mean always hiding a part of herself. Strict, silent obedience.

She had little time to worry about it. Her time outside of class was engulfed with planning the Win the War Day celebrations on April 6th, the one-year anniversary of the U.S. entering the war. No matter how hard she worked, there were always stacks of projects vying for her attention. The campus buzzed over the news that the army had chosen the A.C. to host a training detachment of draftees from outside the state who needed to learn more mechanical skills. More soldiers. Would there be any room left for the students?

On her way back from another planning meeting, she paused to look at the Service Flag. Over a background of crimson and white stripes, three hundred and fifty stars represented the students from the A.C. already enlisted. She picked out the two she had sewn on for Reed and Bert. Clara didn't have a star on the flag. Neither did Joseph. Her friends were the reason Trudi was doing all of this, though. That, and to prove she that she was as American as the rest of them.

Main Street was so crowded for the Win the War Day parade, Trudi had to wriggle her way through mobs of people in hats and long coats to find a place to stand. Everyone in the valley seemed to either be in the parade or watching it. Trudi stood at attention during the flag ceremony and sang the national anthem with more enthusiasm than she felt. Volunteer spies for the American Protective League could be watching her, gauging her loyalty. Mobs across the country were attacking German speakers who didn't act "American" enough, tarring and feathering them. The only way to avoid being suspected as a spy was to be more patriotic than any native citizen. She barely paid attention to the parade promoting war gardens and Liberty Bonds, though. All the activities had become a blur.

The next week, she was back at another Council of Defense meeting, planning another clothing drive. Between her classes and her Red Cross training, she still found time to knit, and to promote the Liberty Bond drives, and to cook meatless, wheatless, sugarless meals with her mother. Women's War Work Week was coming up in April, and there would be extra things to do: drives to collect quarters, empty lots to hoe and plant with war gardens, letters to write to soldiers. Like the war, the work never ended.

Trudi picked up her pen and started a letter while the men talked about the success of Win the War Week and criticized those who hadn't attended.

Dear Clara,

I hope this letter finds you well. We haven't heard anything from you for a while, but I know the mail can be slow. I hope you're getting our letters and know we're thinking of you and keeping you in our prayers. Everyone here is fine. I had a quick note from Bert. He can't say where he is, but it sounds like he and Joseph are in good spirits and anxious to go over the top. I'm glad to know that you, at least, are safe and far from the fighting.

Trudi tapped her pen quietly on the table, not sure what else to say. She ached to talk with Clara in person, to feel like she had a friend for whom she didn't have to put on a face, but she didn't want to make Clara feel homesick or guilty for leaving. At the end of the meeting, she packed the letter away unfinished and wove her way across campus, past boys with uniforms and rifles.

"Trudi!"

She turned. Alonzo waved as he made his way through the crowd. He looked stiff and uncomfortable in his khaki uniform, but his grin brightened his face when he caught up with her. She returned a weary smile.

"How are you, Alonzo?"

He shrugged. "Well enough. I had another letter from Clara. It looks like she sent it last month, but it just got here. I thought you'd like to see it."

"Oh, thank you! Is it good news?"

He held out the folded paper, his expression serious. Her mouth felt dry as she took it and scanned the lines.

"She's driving ambulances? Isn't that dangerous?"

He nodded.

"Oh, Clara," Trudi said, handing the letter back. "She'll be all right, won't she?"

"I hope so." He met her gaze. "And how are you?"

"I'm holding up. Doing my bit."

"That's what we're all supposed to say, but how are you really?"

Sometimes Trudi forgot how long Alonzo had known her, and how observant he could be. She lowered her voice. "I'm feeling dispossessed."

Alonzo didn't say anything, just looked curious.

She went on, "There are soldiers everywhere. I know they're the same college boys who are usually here, but with their uniforms on . . ."

She paused and glanced at his khaki uniform shirt.

He nodded. "It's different, when you put it on. They're not just clothes. You're wearing a new role, a new face. There's an authority that comes with it. Some people forget there's a responsibility too."

"You hate the uniform," Trudi said.

He looked down. "No, I hate that I *like* the uniform. I hate that strangers look at me with more respect just for wearing it."

"You don't think we should respect our soldiers?"

"Of course I do. They're making terrible sacrifices, even if they don't realize it yet." He tugged at the pressed collar of his shirt. "I just . . ."

He trailed off with a frown and looked down. Trudi put a hand on his arm. "What is it?"

He looked up, and the vulnerability in his eyes shocked Trudi. He cleared his throat. "I just wish people could respect me when I'm not wearing it too."

Trudi winced inwardly. Of course he must know people were calling him a coward. People ostracized him, even at church. She wondered herself about his reluctance to fight. His agricultural deferment was legitimate, but he made no secret of the fact that he didn't want to go over there. He only went to drill practice because it was mandatory if he wanted to stay in school.

"I'm sorry," was all Trudi could find to say.

He nodded, and they stood in silence for a moment. The bells struck three o'clock. Alonzo frowned and looked at his watch. "Joe Havertz is ringing the wrong time."

Trudi laughed. "You forgot to set your watch ahead for daylight savings."

He grimaced. "I don't understand why the government now feels the need to tell us how to set the clocks."

"It saves fuel," Trudi said.

"It's a nuisance, and no one told the cows about it."

Trudi chuckled.

"Are you planning on going to the production of *The Importance of Being Earnest*?" Alonzo asked. "They're donating the proceeds to the Red Cross."

"Oh, I suppose I am." Another good cause. Normally Trudi would enjoy a play, but now it was just a patriotic requirement.

"We could go together," he said. "I mean, I could give you a ride. I don't have the Model T, of course, but I've got the buggy, and the weather's nice."

Trudi studied him. Was he asking her on a date? He hadn't said so specifically, so there didn't seem to be any commitment required. "Thank you. I appreciate that."

He smiled and relaxed a little. "I'll see you then."

It wasn't a real date, Trudi told herself, but she still spent a little extra time in her room getting ready. She looked pale, and her fingers trembled a little as she curled her brown hair. She wasn't getting enough sleep, but she didn't want people to notice. She was just doing her bit like everyone else.

She walked softly down the stairs to find Karl deep in conversation with another young man from the Tenth Ward. Soft whispers in German drifted through the room. Their father had warned them not to speak it anymore, even at home, though their mother still struggled with English. German was *verboten*.

The other young man glanced at Trudi with a guilty start, and Karl broke off. His brow furrowed. "I thought you were going to the play."

"I am. Alonzo Jensen is giving me a ride."

Karl nodded distractedly and handed something to the other young man, who slipped it into his pocket. Trudi frowned. It wasn't like Karl to miss the chance to tease her.

A knock sounded on the door, and Trudi hurried to meet Alonzo, leaving Karl to his mysterious friend. Alonzo helped her into his buggy. He'd brushed it clean, but it still carried the faint, comforting scent of hay.

"Is something wrong?" Alonzo asked.

"Oh, no, I'm fine," Trudi said, plastering on a smile.

He nodded but didn't look convinced. When they took their seats for the play, she sat stiffly, embarrassed when her leg accidentally brushed his. The curtain went up, and she settled back as the witty dialogue drew her into the story of romantic pursuits and mistaken identities. Alonzo's deep chuckle sounded along with her laughter at times, and they exchanged amused looks over the antics on stage. She let her arm rest against his, and a warm, comfortable feeling spread through her chest. It surprised her, how pleasant it was to share a moment of unguarded emotion with someone. When had hiding her thoughts and feelings become a habit?

She felt deflated after the final rounds of applause faded, not ready to step back into the work-a-day world.

"Do you want to go to the Bluebird?" Alonzo asked. "My treat."

Then this was a date? She hesitated.

"Think of it as an order from Clara," Alonzo said. "She told me to make sure you didn't work too hard."

"Oh, well I suppose I dare not refuse then." Trudi chided herself for being a bit disappointed that Alonzo wasn't asking for himself. He was handsome, in his sturdy way, but she'd known him since she was in braids.

Alonzo drove them down to the Bluebird. Trudi whispered her order to Alonzo, not wanting the crowd to hear her accent. The newspapers had been running a series of articles reminding people not to "fear the hyphens." The German-Americans. The Swiss-Americans. As long as they did their part, they were still Americans too; as long as they bought Liberty Bonds, didn't vote for socialists, and didn't say anything in defense of the country of their birth. If you did everything right, you could rise above the hyphen, but no one forgot it. It was a little pointing finger, always aimed at you.

"You enjoyed the play," Alonzo said, stirring the caramel into his ice cream.

Trudi nodded, poking at her own dish and forcing herself to take a bite. It was creamy and sweet—such a change from the meals they'd been eating at home. "Oh, I'd forgotten how good dessert could taste."

"You've been strictly no sugar?"

Trudi nodded, and her lips curled in a smile. "Saving everything to send overseas to the soldiers. We made my little brother a wheatless, butterless, sugarless birthday cake. My mother tried to use oatmeal and juice from some of the sugar beets we grew in our garden. It was . . ." she searched for the right word and made a face. "Awful."

Alonzo laughed. "It will make a good story someday."

"Yes. I hope Hans thinks so. He was very brave trying to eat it, but he looked like he wanted to cry." Trudi laughed again, a cleansing defiance of the constant stress.

"It's good to see you smile," Alonzo said.

She nodded. "Everything has been so serious lately."

"The war," Alonzo said.

"Well, yes, and . . ."

He watched her with silent sympathy in his eyes. She lowered her voice. "I'm tired of people thinking I might be a spy. It's silly, isn't it? Why would anyone care what's happening in Logan?"

"Hmm. It might not be so far-fetched that Germany would want to know what's happening here. We're training a lot of soldiers."

"Oh, I hadn't considered that." Trudi forced herself to take another bite of ice cream. Could there be spies around them after all? Would she be able to recognize them? She sighed. "I feel like I'm condemned just because of my heritage. It's a part of who I am, and I don't want to be ashamed of it, but I feel like I'm supposed to be."

"You feel guilty."

She nodded, surprised at how easily Alonzo understood. It was different for him. He fit here, a successful farmer with pioneer blood.

"You shouldn't," he said. "You're doing so much. Maybe too much. Sacrificing yourself for the war effort."

"Other people are sacrificing their lives."

"I know. No one should be forced to do it, though. Especially for a government that persecuted them for their beliefs not so long ago."

Trudi shrugged. He could afford to defy the system. If she did, she wasn't just a coward or a traitor. She was a war enemy. Fort Douglas, in Salt Lake City, was already full of German-Americans suspected of sympathy for the Kaiser, detained indefinitely. And in Illinois, a mob had lynched a German-born man, despite the fact that he was a citizen who had tried to join the U.S. Navy.

A thin layer of frost formed on the inside of Trudi's glass bowl. She swirled her spoon, mixing the dark brown of the chocolate with the vanilla to make a muddied color.

Alonzo cleared his throat. "I heard they're offering aviation classes at the A.C. now. For once, I'm glad Clara's not here."

Trudi smiled in spite of her gloomy thoughts. "Yes, can you imagine how she'd try to storm her way in?"

He smiled. "And Reed would have taken the classes. Clara's head would have exploded, she'd have been so jealous."

"Do you suppose it would have been safer for him?"

"Being a pilot?" Alonzo shook his head and pushed his empty glass away. "Not many of them will come home. It's all random, though. Did you hear about George Cook?"

Trudi nodded and slid her half-full glass away. "I read about it in the school paper. He was so excited to go to aviation training. And then to die of pneumonia. Had he been sick?"

"I don't know. They're not saying much about it."

It hung over them—the darkness of the war, the worry for their friends. Trudi searched desperately for something to talk about that didn't have the specter of suffering and death hovering behind it, but there was nothing. She rubbed her arms, and a cough caught in her throat.

Alonzo gave her a heavy-hearted look. "I should get you home."

Trudi sat at her desk at home, trying to finish her letter to Clara. She considered telling her about going out with Alonzo the previous weekend, but something made her hesitate. The words on the paper blurred, and she rubbed her tired eyes, willing away the dull ache building behind them.

Someone knocked at her bedroom door.

"Yes?" she asked.

Karl opened the door and stepped in. His face was pale, but his eyes were hard. She stood. "What is it?"

"You haven't heard?"

She shook her head.

"They've banned the teaching of German throughout the state."

"What?"

"The government has banned our language. They're afraid it will make people feel sympathy for the enemy. We can't have that, can we? We wouldn't want anyone to remember that they're people too, out there on the other side of the front." The muscles in his neck were strained, his hands curled into fists. "We came here to be free, and . . ."

Trudi sat slowly, supporting herself on the edge of the desk. "Other states have done so as well," she said quietly.

"That's not all. The Church is closing the German-speaking branch."

"The Church?" Trudi's stomach knotted. "But . . ." She took a deep breath, willing herself not to cry. "Then it must be right," she said in resignation. "They're probably trying to protect us from becoming a target for anti-German protests."

Karl shook his head and stormed out of the room. He slammed the door, and Trudi flinched. Hands trembling, she picked up her pen and stared at her letter to Clara.

Oh, Clara, Utah has banned the teaching of German. I suppose they are afraid it might weaken our resolve to fight. The Church has also closed the German-speaking branch. Maybe it's for our safety. I don't know. It's the right thing to do, of course, but I will miss the regular meetings with my friends.

The sour feeling in her stomach roiled. She tightened her grip on her pen.

I'm not okay, Clara. It hurts that even God seems to frown on my language. The German-speaking club on campus was already gone. German is nothing to celebrate anymore. It's treason. It's sin. I'm tired of hiding. I'm tired of trying. I'm just tired. I hate this. I hate it. I hate it.

The frustrated words glared at her, accusatory in their honesty. She tore the paper and rushed downstairs to fling the pieces into the wood-burning stove in the living room. They quickly dissolved into ash. Gone. Safe.

Trudi screamed into one of the pillows on the sofa and kept her face buried in the scent of home as she curled into a ball to cry. Her sobs turned into wracking coughs. A scratching closeness choked her, and she gasped for breath. She clutched the sofa, hands trembling.

Slow down. Breathe.

She took a long breath through her nose. Her throat itched and a cough welled in her chest, but she forced herself to stay calm and draw in a steady stream of air. She cleared her throat and wiped the tears from her cheeks, chiding herself for working herself into a fit.

A gentle knock sounded on the front door. Trudi straightened her blouse and wiped her face again before rising to answer it.

Alonzo stood on the threshold, his expression somber. He took in her disheveled appearance and whispered, "You've heard the news?"

"News?" She clutched the door, swaying. Her mind jumped to her darkest fears. "Not Clara?"

He grabbed her arm. "Not Clara. I meant about the ban on German."

"Oh." She leaned into his strong grip, and new tears welled in her eyes. "Yes, I heard."

"I was angry when I heard about it at the feed store. I thought you would be upset."

"I . . . I am. I mean, I was. It hurts, but if the Church leaders are supporting it, it must be right." She swayed again, and he tightened his grip on her.

He led her to the sofa, his forehead creased. "You don't think even church leaders can sometimes get caught up in the spirit of the moment?

I don't mean about big things—the things they preach at conference. They have the mantle of authority, and I defer to that. But underneath that mantle, they're still people."

"You think so?"

"Of course."

Tears dampened her cheeks, and she trembled, trying to keep her feelings under control. Her own body, her own emotions rebelled against her.

"Trudi?"

"I don't know what to think. We have to obey. It's the only way to stay safe, isn't it?"

"I wish it worked that way." Alonzo stared out the window, his eyes sad. "If always obeying meant nothing bad happened to us, though, I suppose there'd be no challenge and no growth in doing the right thing."

"Oh." Her teeth chattered, and chills raced through her core.

"Are you all right?"

"I don't know what's wrong with me. I feel cold." She stood to get closer to the fire, and her legs buckled.

Alonzo caught her as she crumpled to the floor. "You're burning up! How long have you been sick?"

"I don't know. I've been tired for so long. I just need to rest." She tried to stand, but her knees felt like pudding. She relented and leaned into Alonzo's arm.

"You're working yourself to death," he said.

Her chills multiplied, sending tremors down her limbs. "I'm so cold."

He shucked off his coat and wrapped it around her, then turned his head to call up the stairs. Trudi relaxed into his chest, tears of exhaustion and frustration seeping into his pressed, white shirt. Her mother and Karl ran into the room, but she was hardly aware of what they said. She only knew that she was soon in her bed, and that the warm smell of Alonzo lingered close by, making her feel safe, until someone gently removed his jacket from her shoulders.

Trudi was sick in bed for two weeks. Two weeks missing classes and meetings and drives of every description. When she was well enough to sit up, she started knitting again, though her mother frowned over her insistence on staying busy.

"You are sick, *Liebchen*. You should rest. Why not read a book?"

"All my favorite ones are in German," Trudi said.

Her sister slept in the parlor while she was ill, but her siblings visited her room, and she helped the younger ones with their homework. They laughed and talked, carefree, living in a world foreign to Trudi despite sharing the same home and blood. Of course, they'd been younger when the family immigrated. They spoke English without an accent, and they probably didn't remember much about Switzerland. Their Teutonic heritage was already behind them, of little concern in their day-to-day American lives.

The family doctor came by to check on Trudi.

"You're looking much better," he said. "You can start getting up more, but don't overtax your strength. With influenza, it can cause a relapse."

"Influenza? That's what I had?"

"Yes. I've seen several cases lately. Smallpox is going around too. I think some of the new boys coming to the A.C. for military training brought it here with them. You get so many young people living in close quarters and then traveling from place to place and it's an ideal breeding ground for disease."

"Is it that dangerous?"

He shrugged. "Nothing to worry yourself about much. Smallpox is a concern, but it's clearing up, and this strain of the flu doesn't seem to be very dangerous."

"It can cause pneumonia, though, can't it?" Trudi remembered George Cook. If soldiers were getting the flu, could that be what caused his death?

"Usually only in the very young, the very old, and those who are already weakened. You healthy young people have nothing to fear. Just don't run yourself ragged, Miss Kessler."

She nodded, and he left. Karl watched from the doorway, his arms folded.

"Doctor's orders," he said. "You have to slow down. Maybe I should have Alonzo Jensen keep an eye on you." He smiled a little.

Trudi's cheeks warmed. She didn't want Alonzo looking after her. Did she? She remembered the warm safety of his arms. "I'll find work that doesn't tire me out."

"You're not going to stop?"

"How can I?" She gave him an imploring look. "My friends are out there suffering to keep us safe."

XXIV

June 1, 1918
Belleau Wood, France

Diary of Lieutenant Reed Lewis, May 31, 1918

Arrived at our assembly area and dug in. Cap'n says we'll attack some woods in the morning. Should be lightly held. Called Bois de Belleau. These woods are on the road to Paris, to Clara. We must take them, stop the Boche. Ready to do my bit. All of us are. I catch the men stealing glances at me, to see if I'm scared. They don't look at Sergeant Allen like that. They know he isn't scared, he loves this. Hope they won't wonder about me after tomorrow.

Reed stood facing his platoon, rigid at attention, the curve of his officer's bamboo cane pinned at his hip, the tip touching his right collarbone like a saber. He stood composed, his back to the Germans waiting to kill him.

The men fell into formation quickly, the rows dressed under the cold eyes of Gunnery Sergeant Allen. If they were to die, they'd do so in straight lines. They faced Reed, their aught-threes at shoulder arms, rigid, waiting for the call.

Sergeant Allen took his position, gave Reed a slight nod, and Reed executed his best about face, toward the wheat field, just 600 yards to the edge of Belleau Wood, and the Boche.

It was as if he were completely alone. Desperate to see his fellow officers on his left or right, he uncaged his eyes without moving his head but could see no one in his peripheral vision, no comrade with whom to march forward. *An officer leads from the front.*

He slid his left hand along his trouser seam up to his chest to grip the whistle lanyard, then the whistle itself, hoping he could blow it when the time came. He knew the other men were terrified too, he could hear soft prayers behind him. Not the words, but the rhythms, the meter.

The march from the assembly area had surely not helped their morale. It seemed like every human being capable of travel was heading the other direction. Everyone except the U.S. Marines. The French villagers even drove their goats and sheep away, trying to keep them from the Boche.

The French *Poilus* trudged by with the civilians, their blue uniforms dirtied to gray, their faces worn and lifeless. Few looked up. The German surprise attack with twenty-nine divisions across the Chemin des Dames plains broke the linear French defense, deployed without depth or reserve formations. Field Marshall Petain likened the French divisions he sent to plug the gap "like dropping water on a hot stove." Mass burials in hastily constructed field cemeteries along the route to the front provided stark testament to the price the *Poilus* had paid.

Reed and the Marines of the 4th Brigade had been rushed to the front in camions, much like Paris taxis had rushed their *Poilus* forward when the Boche threatened Paris in 1914. And like 1914, if the Germans took Chateau-Thierry and the Marne River Valley, the road to Paris was open.

Images of retreating French soldiers filed past again in Reed's mind, utter exhaustion on their faces after five days of fighting retreat. Those few that spoke said things like *La guerre est finie* or *Beaucoup d'allemands*. Reed remembered enough French from his classes to understand. "The war is finished." "So many Germans." G*ood thing the boys don't speak French.*

Sergeant Allen marched up alongside him, stopping just behind his left shoulder and stomped to attention. Reed jumped involuntarily, still a little intimidated by his Gunnery Sergeant.

"Mr. Lewis," Allen addressed Reed.

"Yes, Sergeant," Reed answered, without turning his head.

"Are you ready to go forward, Mr. Lewis?"

Reed turned his head, "I am, Sergeant."

"I've been watching you, Sir. I believe the men will follow you across this field. But if they don't, they'll get this here bayonet right in the rear."

"Fair enough, Sergeant. Say, we're already in range from the edge of those woods. Why don't the Germans fire?"

"Well, Sir, I reckon they're disciplined soldiers. They're waiting until we commit, 'til we get well into that wheat, then they open up with them Maxim machine guns, and put some artillery to our rear. They ain't lookin' to scatter us, Sir, they aim to kill us."

"Well, that makes us even," Reed replied, clenching his teeth.

"Aye, Sir. Lord willing, I'll see you in them woods shortly." Allen stomped back to the formation, standing even with the first rank of men.

Alone again, Reed looked toward the edge of Belleau Wood, an area just one mile long and varying from 400 yards to one half mile wide, elevated above the surrounding wheat fields, the trees in full leaf with deep undergrowth. He could just discern the outlines of German soldiers moving about at the wood's edge, getting ready to defend against the American attack. He closed his eyes for a moment. *Heavenly Father, if you're listening, I don't know what to ask . . . just please don't let me fail.*

Captain Hamilton marched confidently to the front of the assembled platoons, ahead of where Reed stood. Reed felt better at the sight of Hamilton, a man he admired and respected. Not one for convention, Hamilton carried an aught-three with bayonet fixed, just like the men. He raised it up over his head, bayonet pointing toward the wood, blew his whistle, and stepped off toward the Germans.

Reed raised his cane straight in the air while he blew his whistle, then swept it down, pointing at the wood, and stepped forward with his men, line abreast, ready to fight in the open formation style Pershing insisted on for his Americans.

There was silence at first. The only sounds Reed heard were his own breathing and the crunching of wheat under hundreds of feet. But then all the sounds of movement vanished, erased by the competing staccato of dozens of Maxims, all firing in bursts, raking the wheat field with grazing fire a meter off the ground. Reed could look to his left and right now, but he quickly locked his eyes forward, lest the carnage overwhelm him. Men fell in sheets, dropping like scythed wheat. Entire first ranks disappeared, dropped into the tall blades, then entire platoons, whole waves of the attack destroyed.

Reed kept moving, stiff, waiting for the stream of lead he could feel all around him to cut him down. He heard an occasional epithet from Sergeant Allen, telling the men to close up; to get up; to keep moving. It was all Reed could do to keep standing, to move forward, to fight the overwhelming urge to go to ground. His men needed him to lead.

Then came the artillery. Like Allen predicted, the Germans began to fire heavy rounds back toward the Marines' assembly area, trapping them in the kill zone, then shorter-range trench mortars to disrupt the Marine formations.

Shrill sounds of incoming artillery ripped the air, each one sounding like it would land on the Marines—the inexperienced Marines as yet unable to tell whether a round was going to land near them. Men simply disappeared in the middle of an explosion, or emerged from a cloud of smoke and dust, armless, staggering. Pieces of flesh and body parts landed among untouched parts of the formation, unnerving the Marines. Reed gritted his teeth. Onward toward the Boche.

The air soon filled with smoke and dust and the smell of cordite. The earth seemed to rise and fall like it was breathing in short, ragged breaths, spewing dirt that hit Reed like a slap, undermining his footing. He hit the ground hard on his knees, unaware his legs were bent, slamming down hard, biting his tongue, then face down, the wide brim of his helmet shoved forward over his face.

A strong hand grabbed the back of his tunic and lifted him partially up. "Mr. Lewis, you ain't dead yet! Did you think you'd live forever? Let's go, Sir!" Allen said as he helped Reed to his feet.

"Which way, which way are the Germans?" Reed stammered.

"That way. Follow the sound of the Maxims. Here take this." Allen jammed an aught-three into his hands. "Ya can't bayonet no Boche with that bamboo stick."

The advance finally stalled in the tall wheat, along a ditch filled with cold water and reeds. The first assault waves had melted. Captain Hamilton was alive, as was Reed, but the other nine officers were dead or wounded in the two companies lined up in the area where Reed stood.

Though pinned down by Maxims, the Marines were far from helpless. While their own machine gun companies were not yet in place, the emphasis on marksmanship in all phases of training began to pay dividends as they picked off Germans who showed themselves. Reed fired his own gun automatically. The Germans wouldn't have faced accurate rifle fire like this in some time, and must have been surprised to be hit by aught-three fire, as a German soldier would simply drop, mortally wounded, without hearing the sound of the rifle.

The Marines began to rush individual German machine gun positions, in small group attacks, which often came down to one remaining Marine attacking three German gun crew members with his aught-three, his bayonet, his fists, whatever it took.

Reed lay at the edge of the ditch, Allen close to him on the right. "What are your orders, Sir?" Allen hissed.

"Sergeant, I count two machine gun positions to our front. Take three men and assault the position on the left, I'll do the same for the one on the right."

Allen nodded, clapped Reed on the back, and was off without a word. Reed tapped the three Marines closest to him and yelled, "Follow me. We're taking that gun at our twelve o'clock." He stood up and sprinted toward the Maxim, not looking back to see if the men would follow.

The machine gun positions were sited with care by the Germans, who by this point in the war had mastered the art of interlocking and mutually supporting fire. This meant that every position was covered to its front by a position to its right or left, and quite possibly by both. Reed knew attacking two at once gave the Marines an advantage, because it would take extreme discipline from the defenders to keep their focus off their own plight and on that of the neighbor for whom they were responsible.

Reed ran right at the parapet in the center of the machine gun pit, hoping the gap it created to the Maxim crew's front would protect him. It did, but two of the Marines with him went wide of the parapet, right into the Maxim's field of fire. Both were cut down within a few steps. Reed kept running, pushing the rifle out in front just like in training, ready to thrust it into a dummy, ready to hammer its sandbag head with the butt of his aught-three.

His vision narrowed, he could see only the parapet, and the bursts of fire coming from both sides of it. His breathing was hard and short, a series of gasps for air as he sprinted forward, his remaining Marine at his side, shoulder to shoulder, charging. Both men instinctively fired as they reached the elevation necessary to fire over the parapet, almost over the top of the position, right into the three-man crew. Both Marines stumbled into the hole, bayonets thrusted forward, stabbing whatever they came in contact with. Apparently, the Germans had not seen them coming behind the parapet, so their personal weapons were still stacked. It was over quickly.

They stayed in the hole amongst the dead Germans, weapons over the edge toward the wood in case the Germans counterattacked. Reed fought for air, tried to broaden his field of vision, decide what to do next. Along with the fear, though, he felt something else, a rise in his pulse not caused by the exertion. An odd feeling he couldn't place, yet somehow familiar.

Reed looked to his left amid loud shouts, to see that Sergeant Allen and his three Marines had taken their position as well. Allen had a wild look in his eyes, and Reed could see his old wound frothing away from fifty yards. Exhilaration. The Sergeant was in his element. So was Reed. He fought the urge to laugh out loud. *How—this can't be right. All this death, the screams, the fear, yet I want to laugh. Why?*

"Well, dang, Mr. Lewis, let's take us some more!" Allen screamed. He dragged the Marines with him out of the German pit and stepped forward. A hail of Maxim fire swept the four Marines back like a push broom into the position they had just taken. Sergeant Allen was gone. Reed stared at the space the men had occupied. He felt the strength ebb from his body as he wondered how he could possibly do this without Sergeant Allen at his side.

Rounds raked Reed's position as well, but he and his remaining Marine were still below the lip of the pit as the bullets danced over their heads. The Germans had more than mutual support. The machine gun positions were deployed with depth as well, which meant the Marines would take a position, just to have the Germans open fire from one placed further back, but only after they waited until the fight for the first position was over.

The Marines barely held a foothold at the edge of Belleau Wood at the close of the first day. The Germans wanted it back.

XXV

Dear Alonzo,

I'm sorry my handwriting is shaky. I'm writing this on my lap as I sit beside the road in my ambulance with Lily. We're not doing anything too risky—just transporting refugees displaced by the latest German offensive.
It's hard work some days, but I'm doing my part for these brave men. I haven't seen anyone we know yet—there are so many people here I could hardly imagine!—and given the circumstances where I usually see the young men, I am glad none of them are familiar faces. I feel I'm in the center of the whole world and all the action taking place in it. It's something I'm sure I'll never forget and that I wouldn't miss for anything.
I know I said some pretty sharp things to you when we parted, but I am glad you aren't here. Don't fret for me, though; I'm not in any great danger. I miss you all and hope you are well. You're in my prayers. I have to ring off now.

Love,
Clara

The thick tide of refugees flowed past Clara's ambulance like storm water down an irrigation ditch. Somewhere, not far behind them, the Germans rolled forward with ruthless efficiency. Few young men trudged past. They stayed behind to fight or had already been captured or killed. Some of the women and old men carried guns, clutched like holy tokens to ward off the invading hordes. The fortunate ones had horse-drawn wagons loaded with their belongings, and others had smaller carts pulled by goats or dogs. A few pushed handcarts. Handcarts. Like the pioneers. Clara shook her head. The worst off had nothing except maybe a small sack with a few items rescued from the Germans.

A little boy stopped to stare up at the ambulance, his eyes wide. Clara smiled at him. None of the refugees paid him any attention. None stopped to look or call for him.

"Where is your family?" Clara asked.

His forehead wrinkled.

She repeated the question in French.

He shook his head. "*Je ne sais pas,*" he whispered. He didn't know.

Clara motioned him into the back of the ambulance, where a few other women and children sat: those who were too old, ill, or injured to go further on foot.

The crowd continued its shuffling march. A young mother stumbled along with three small children. One wore a bloodstained bandage wrapped around her head. Clara gently pulled them aside. The mother wept as Clara helped her into the back. With the ambulance full, Clara cranked up the engine and climbed into the passenger side. Lily carefully steered them into the unending flow of people moving toward Paris.

"Well, you wanted to be a part of things," Clara mumbled to herself.

"What?" Lily asked.

Clara smiled and shook her head. "Nothing."

As the rest of the refugees flowed on toward Paris, Lily turned the ambulance aside, past withered fields, to the tree-shaded drive of a grand, old chateau. Some philanthropic Frenchman had loaned it to the Red Cross as a hospital for women and children. Lily parked, and they hopped out to open the back, helping the huddle of refugees out. The women blinked at the sunlight and those with children pulled them closer as they studied the chateau with dazed expressions.

Red Cross workers greeted the refugees, asking for names, making lists. If the refugees had family members living outside the war zone or in other refugee centers, the Red Cross searchers would help them reunite. Clara took the boy's small, clammy hand and guided him inside with the others.

Cots lined the drawing rooms and dining room, even the grand salon, where just a few years ago the *haut monde* had danced and flirted.

The windows stood open to the breeze from the fields, and Red Cross nurses hurried bedpans and dirty linens outside for cleaning, but the stench of illness and sweating bodies clung to the rooms.

Clara passed the boy off to a smiling worker in a Red Cross uniform.

"*Tu es sain et sauf,*" the woman told the boy. You are safe.

"For how long?" Clara asked one of the other workers. "If the Germans keep pushing forward at this rate, we'll have to evacuate the entire hospital in a couple of days."

"Have you not heard?" the girl asked. "Your U.S. Marines have brought them to a stop!"

"The Marines!" Reed's cocky smile flashed in Clara's mind.

"Yes. In fact, they need ambulances at Belleau Wood. The casualties have been high."

The blood drained from Clara's face. She dashed for her ambulance.

"Clara?" Lily asked as she rushed past.

Clara's fingers shook as she shoved the key into the ignition. She jumped out to crank the engine, but it didn't turn over.

"No!" Clara slammed her palm against the bumper. "Useless Ford. Dear Father in Heaven, please let it start!"

She tried again. Nothing. She jerked the crank another half turn. The engine backfired, snapping the crank around hard into her forearm. She fell back in the dirt, cradling her stinging wrist. Bruised, not broken. As the pain eased, she kicked the bumper several times, wearing out her frustration.

There were no mechanics at the chateau. Her countrymen needed her help. She had to fix this. Clara stood and dusted herself off, reinserted the key, and adjusted the timing and throttle.

"Please!" she whispered.

"Clara?" Lily stared at her in concern. "You hurt your arm?"

Clara nodded.

"Let me," Lily said. She turned the crank, and the engine grumbled to life.

Clara exhaled in the relief. *Thank you, thank you, thank you.*

"What are you doing?" Lily asked.

"I know we're supposed to be moving refugees, but it's the Marines. Reed . . ."

Lily nodded. "We'll go. You drive."

"Thank you," Clara whispered.

"We're in this together," Lily said with a smile.

Clara blinked back tears as she climbed into the driver's seat and adjusted her goggles. She raced over the rutted roads, gritting her teeth against the jarring. She slowed as she passed the refugees. A few looked hopefully at the ambulance. She steeled herself and did not meet their eyes, maneuvering through them and onward toward Belleau Wood.

Distant booms of artillery rattled the windows of the ambulance and echoed in her chest. She pulled over at the casualty clearing station near the end of the road, letting the engine idle.

A nurse glanced up at them, and Clara saw the momentary surprise when the women took in Clara and Lily's feminine uniforms.

"Are you here to move the serious cases?" the nurse asked.

Clara hesitated. Taking those in need of extra care to a field hospital took her farther from the action. Farther from Reed.

Another ambulance driver loitering with the nurse glanced over Clara's vehicle and gestured at it with his cup of coffee.

"Those Ford ambulances are the only ones with a high enough ground clearance to navigate the fields. They should go forward to the dressing stations."

The nurse frowned. "But, they—"

"We're going," Clara said, mentally apologizing to her ambulance for berating it.

She eased out into fields trampled to bare dirt by the passage of troops. The ambulance rocked and dipped over the uneven ground, nothing like driving a horse and plow through the fields at home. More like trying to keep a boat steady on choppy waters. The thunder of the artillery rang in her ears. She tightened her grip on the metal steering wheel.

She spotted a gaggle of nurses gathered around a dressing station and steered toward them. Some men were working to excavate a dugout, but for now the dressing station was in a tent. Clara climbed down unsteadily, half expecting the ground to rock under her feet from the booms resounding through the trees.

"Thank goodness you're here!" one of the nurses called, hurrying to greet the girls.

"Has the fighting been bad?" Clara asked in a low voice.

The nurse nodded. "Entire companies wiped out. Most of the officers are dead."

"What about—" Clara choked on the words. "What about the Fourth Marines?"

"I don't know. They were all hit hard."

Lily squeezed Clara's arm. Clara followed the nurse in a daze, everything around her muffled and far away. They walked past rows of dead and wounded men lined up on the field. Clara forced herself to examine each face. Many of the men were missing arms and legs. Some had parts of their jaws blown away, and they looked around with frightened, unfocused eyes. A few screamed or called for their mothers. Black clouds of flies buzzed around oozing wounds.

Clara stopped. Shut her eyes. Took a long, slow breath, fighting waves of nausea. She gagged on the reek of blood and sweat-soaked wool and unwashed bodies.

In the distance, the artillery boomed again and again, punctuated by the rattle of machine guns. The almost-rhythmic pounding reminded Clara of the steady beat of the steam engine in the thresher on the farm. These men were caught in a great machine, pounding incessantly, pounding out broken bodies instead of oats and straw.

"Miss?" the nurse asked. Her voice was gentle.

Clara slowly opened her eyes, met the girl's sympathetic gaze, and nodded once.

"How many stretchers can you fit in your ambulance?" the girl asked.

"Three."

"We'll bring you a few of the stretcher cases then."

A line of orderlies carrying stretchers wound their way forward like mourners at a funeral parade. Clara moved automatically, aware that she, too, was part of the great machine of the war, just a gear in its workings.

She and Lily opened the back doors of the ambulance as the solemn parade of men approached and offered up their gruesome cargo. Two orderlies hefted an injured Marine into the ambulance. They'd thrown a blanket over him, but it caught and pulled back enough for Clara to see his bare leg, crossed with a line of bloody wounds like large, clumsy stitches.

"Machine gun fire," one of the nurses whispered. "He may lose the leg, but he'll probably survive, thanks to you girls and your ambulance."

Clara took another deep breath and glanced at the young man's face. Not Reed. She sagged a little. Of course, if Reed was hurt, he might be in some other dressing station, waiting for some other ambulance driver.

"Please keep him safe."

She wasn't sure if the prayer was directed at God or the other ambulance drivers. Maybe both.

She pulled herself into the driver's seat and steered away from the battle. The ambulance bounced over the field, and the men in the back cried out from time to time. Clara winced at each bump. She alternated between driving faster, pushing to get back to the main roads quickly, and slowing down, hoping to ease the painful jolting as the men whimpered and groaned.

Finally, they reached the field hospital. Clara watched the orderlies unload the men and then sat silently, her mind numb as she rested her forehead on the warm steering wheel.

"Clara," Lily said quietly.

They had to go back. They had to do it again. Mechanically, Clara shifted the ambulance and headed back to the field. Again and again, they shuttled mutilated men to the hospital, heard the boom of those terrible guns, and checked the faces of the injured. They only stopped when they ran low on fuel and had to turn back.

Clara reported to the main office of the ambulance service as sunset painted the sky a bloody red. A British officer supervised the work. He shot her an appraising glance.

"There's a dance tonight for the servicemen. Get changed and you can catch the truck going to Paris."

"A dance?" She glanced down at her uniform splattered with dark stains. Reed and the other Marines were still out there in Belleau Wood, standing alone against the crushing force of the German army. If he was even alive. "You expect me to dance?"

"Of course. What, do you have a beau? Don't worry. We're not trying to set up any romance. Just keeping up the soldiers' morale. That's why you're here, after all."

"Oh, is it?" she asked, her voice shaking a little. "Forgive me. I was under the impression I was here to help the wounded."

"War is a terrible burden for these men. You're here to help them in any way you can."

Clara squeezed her eyes shut, picturing the maimed men lying in fields. Then the hollow expressions of the refugees returned to haunt her, of the mothers and nurses trying to pretend, for the children, that their world wasn't crumbling behind them with every step.

"War is a burden for everyone, Sir. I am here to drive ambulances. I am tired. I have my countrymen's blood on my clothes. I am going to my room to clean up, and then I'm going to sleep. If you want to entertain the men, you can put on a dress. Sir."

She turned on her heel and marched to her room, stripped off her uniform, scrubbed her face and hands until they were raw, then collapsed on her bed, too tired to cry.

XXVI

Who said I was dead? Send me the mortars and a thousand hand grenades.

—*Captain George W. Hamilton*

Reed and his men hunkered down in the positions formerly held by the Germans at the edge of Belleau Wood, straining to see through thick undergrowth in creeping darkness, expecting a German counterattack.

Captain Hamilton came diving into Reed's position, landing on top of him like he was a mattress, then rolling off Reed and onto his back. Rounds zipped over them, snapping the few remaining twigs from their limbs, pounding tree trunks like lead fists.

"Very good to see you intact, Mr. Lewis," Hamilton said, between deep breaths. "I'll need you again in the morning."

"Aye, Skipper," Reed replied.

Pointing toward the thick underbrush, Hamilton continued, "There is a hill, directly ahead, about 150 meters. Hill 142 on the map. German Maxims and snipers giving it to us good from up there."

"We are to take the hill, Sir?" Reed said.

"We are indeed, Mr. Lewis. But we're going to do it differently than earlier today. When we kick off, divide your men into small groups and attack individual Maxim crews and sniper teams. Sneak up on them, get their flanks. Kill them. Got it?"

"Got it, Sir. Sir, the men could use some hot chow and coffee."

Hamilton turned his head. "So could I. Doing what I can. We attack at 0400. Carry on, Mr. Lewis."

"Aye, Skipper."

Hamilton winked at him, took a deep breath and heaved himself out of the hole for the sprint to the next platoon. Reed counted as

Hamilton sprinted. His training had taught him how long Hamilton could run before an enemy rifleman got a good enough bead to drop him. *One, two, three, I'm up, I'm seen, I'm down! Get down, Skipper!* Hamilton plunged into the next shell crater, bullets creasing the dirt. *Bravest of the Brave, they call him.*

No whistle or cane this time. Reed trotted along the line of his men. They lay prone, clustered in the dark in groups of three and four. He kicked the soles of their boots, sending them into the undergrowth. They could do no reconnaissance, so they had to find the German positions before the Germans found them—or face an ambush.

Not sure what else to do as his last team left, Reed grabbed an aught-three and joined them, crawling forward into the wood.

Agonizing. Desperate to hear signs of Germans, Reed crawled forward over the debris. Each crackle of snapping twigs sounded like trees being shattered in the early morning stillness. He stopped, listened, waited for an explosion of Maxim fire, and then moved forward again, crunching along, trying to control his breathing, his fear.

They found the main German line dug in at the base of Hill 142. Reed could see it because of infantrymen moving behind the machine gun positions. He pulled out the bayonet he had shoved into his belt so he could crawl with the aught-three, tapping the feet of the two closest Marines with it. They fixed their bayonets, moved into a crouch and waited for Reed's command. He indicated the Maxim position on the far left of the German line, at least the part he could see, in hopes they could take that one and then move along the German flank to catch the others unprepared.

Rapid fire to his left told him time was up. Maxims and other German small arms cracked all along the German line. Marine teams returned fire with aught-threes, and now, for the first time, with French Chauchat automatic rifles and Hotchkiss machine guns, which supplied the Marines with the ability to conduct suppressive fire of their own during an attack.

"Now!" Reed yelled.

The three men sprinted for the Maxim at a dead run, without pausing to fire. The position was firing, but the gunners had found targets to their extreme right, causing them to miss the Marines running directly at them. They tried to turn the gun at the last second, but it grounded on its left limiting stake, short of the line Reed and his men attacked along. Reed reached the position first. He plunged his bayonet into the helpless gunner's chest. The other two dispatched the assistant gunners who were climbing out of the rear of the fighting position with bayonets through the back.

All three stood for a second looking at each other, gasping. Reed made a chopping hand signal to indicate the next position along the line. Both Marines nodded, and they moved off again at a run.

Reed and his men fought all along the German line like this, one position after another, until all the machine guns were silent.

The Marines lay prone at the base of the hill, looking up, the steep slope pockmarked with German infantry fighting positions and still thick with the trees and shrubs that survived the preparatory bombardment. Reed placed his men along the base then found Captain Hamilton on the line. Reed dropped next to him with a thud.

Hamilton turned toward him, his face streaked with dirt, sweat, and speckled blood. "Well, Mr. Lewis, you keep turning up like a bad penny. Good to see you."

"Yes, Sir. Bad penny, Sir! What are your orders, Skipper?"

"It seems you and I are the only officers left out of two companies. We're low on ammunition; out of grenades; out of water, and the Boche will counterattack any time. So, we are going to take this hill, get the high ground, and then hold it as ordered, before it gets any dag gum hotter. Clear, Bad Penny?"

"Aye, Skipper. We'll be ready," Reed replied.

"Fifteen minutes," Hamilton said, turning his eyes toward the hill.

Reed readied his men, and then took a knee, staring up at the German positions among the trees. A fleeting thought of racing Clara up the snowy hill with that ramshackle sled—*oh to be cold for a moment.* His entire uniform was soaked with sweat, the green wool picked up dirt and debris until it turned gray. Rivulets of sweat carved eddies into the caked dirt on his face. His eyes burned and his mouth was bone dry. His tunic suffocated him. And yet, the hill remained.

He looked at his watch, then down the line at Hamilton, also on one knee, his aught-three held low, whistle at the ready. Reed readied his own whistle, then echoed Hamilton's signal to attack. He let go of the lanyard to grip his rifle with both hands, and pumped his legs furiously up the hill.

For once the Maxims failed to help the Germans. Sited for suppressive fire in the flat areas approaching the hill, they could not depress enough to fire down the hill directly. Still, the Germans were formidable, with rifle pits and grenades to defend the slopes.

Reed and his men pounded uphill, pumping their heavy aught-threes back and forth like pistons, powering their legs to climb higher. The Germans rained grenades on them, to good effect, but Reed saw the man on his right pick up a live grenade and throw it back at the Germans, taking advantage of its delayed fuse. Marines across the line followed suit, and they steadily worked up the hill, isolating then killing the Germans in each line of positions.

Reed climbed and fought, climbed and fought, without pause, without rest. Adapting a pace he could maintain, he and his men began leapfrogging from one position to the next by having some Marines suppress the German rifleman while others maneuvered to their flank and took the position with cold steel.

The assault lasted thirty minutes. Marine survivors flopped, exhausted, into a loose defensive ring along the military crest of the hill. Many gray and gray-looking uniforms dotted the slope below, their bodies a gruesome record of individual courage and combat, German and American, united in death.

The Marines had taken part of Belleau Wood.

The airplane looked like a large dragonfly from a distance as it skirted the edge of the wood. Its drone drifted over the otherwise silent battlefield, circling them. It kept its distance. The men, exhausted, still turned to look; for many it was the first airplane they had ever seen in flight.

It was no novelty for Captain Hamilton. "Lewis, get your men in those German positions, get them as deep as possible—that's a German artillery spotter for sure; we're about to get it."

"Aye, Skipper," Lewis yelled as he struggled to his feet. Hamilton ran off to warn the men on the other side of the crest.

"Marines! Get into the German holes, hunker down in them now!" Reed screamed, jumping in the nearest one himself.

They didn't have long to wait. The Boche did not need coordinates from the spotter to begin firing. They had already plotted target reference points for the whole hill. They just needed the spotter to confirm the hill was in fact in American hands before they began firing.

It was a box-shaped barrage. The artillerymen drew a box over the rough dimensions of the hill, and then fired rounds in a pattern to hit everything in it.

The first rounds hit along the base of the hill, then crept up, like a god of thunder taking pounding steps, shaking the hill at its base, then beating it to dust as it climbed to the Marines on top.

Reed looked down from the edge of his position. The hill seemed to be disappearing below him, enormous clouds of dust spewed like a volcano erupting from the bottom out. There were more men than holes. Reed saw some of the Marines fighting over a small depression, frantic to get low, away from the terror of the explosions. One Marine bayoneted another, then dragged him from his hole, only to be obliterated himself by the artillery as it crept closer. Reed shrank down in horror, covering his eyes—*no more, for heaven's sake. Please, Lord, help us.*

There was no distinction between explosions. It was a continuous roar, so loud Reed could no longer think, so dense was the displaced soil and dust he could no longer see, so acrid was the smoke he could no longer breathe—choking, spitting, screaming, the explosions directly over his head now, in the trees.

Something hit his arm, multiple punches at once. A wetness spread down his sleeve, trickling onto the bare skin of his hand and wrist.

Soil around him churned like a giant sod plow ripping through it, mixing him within it, slamming him back to earth and burying him. *Must get up, must breathe. Lord, I need your strength.*

Reed compressed his arms, palms facing what he hoped was down. He pushed up as hard as he could, until his face was above the now still surface. He lay like that, gasping in the smoldering air, unable to emerge further. Dirt slid back toward his nose and mouth. His Marines pulled him free and rested him along the parapet of his position.

"Marine, we need to dress those wounds," someone said.

He could see the men but could not differentiate one from another. The only distinguishing features were the eyes and the teeth, shining brightly in a new world of blackness, everything and everyone scorched or blasted the color of dirt and soot.

Many could not hear, their expressions when speaking overemphasized pronunciation as if trying to speak to a lip reader. The corpsman that dressed the shrapnel wounds on Reed's arm talked to him as he walked him down the hill to be evacuated, but Reed could not hear him. The corpsman was gesturing toward something at the bottom of the hill. Reed focused, following the man's finger. Then he saw it.

Yellowish clouds rolled slowly around the hill from both directions, staying low along the base, distinct from the smoke the high explosive artillery rounds had caused, cutting off their route to the rear. Reed tried to reason it out: *The gas is settling low, it's why we can see it at the bottom of the hill, but, it must have been fired . . .*

"Gas! Gas! Gas!" Reed screamed, reaching for his own gas mask, pointing at the medic to don his as well. *That gas could have been mixed in with the rounds fired higher up the hill. We could have already breathed it, had it cling to our skin.* Meanwhile, the mustard gas at the bottom of the hill gathered in density, like a moat of death, preventing their escape.

The French suppressed the German artillery with counter-battery fire, but the men nonetheless spent two more days on the hill among the dead and dying, defending a now treeless, lifeless dirt pile, living like rats, running from hole to hole, dodging snipers.

At night, they stood watch, bleary eyed, bayonets fixed, as the Germans fired flares all around them to make them think they were surrounded.

Reed managed to stagger from position to position, tell the men they would be okay, while he privately pulled up his jacket sleeves looking for blisters and took deep breaths to see if his lungs were burning yet. His wounded arm hurt badly, and needles stabbed him every time he moved it. He did his duty.

Finally, the gas cleared enough to pass, and Hamilton ordered them down the hill. As they passed the Marines relieving them on the third day, Reed saw his men hold their heads as high as they could as they staggered along, grouping together in a rough formation. They were not beaten. They had not given ground. They would march out like Marines.

XXVII

Some rest. Two days at this aid station while they pluck pieces of French oak out of my arm. Doc says they'll leave some of them, come up like crops in the spring. Funny guy, that doc. No hot meals here, so the men have not eaten a real meal in eight days. Even when they did, all they got was monkey meat anyway. Sent out dog robbers to look for food in the town gardens before I left for the aid station. Doc says I can return to duty tomorrow. Can't say I'm excited about the prospect. Funny thing about combat—you don't get less afraid with experience, you get more. I flinch at shell sounds, even distant ones. Medical folks ask me if I'm Okay, why am I breathing so hard. I tell 'em I'm fine. I'm a Marine officer. But inside, when I feel the ground shake, I think I'm being buried again, suffocated. I need to write Clara, but I don't even know if she is still in Paris. What the heck would I say? "Other than a few shrapnel wounds and a bout of cowardice, dear, I'm just dandy"? I hope she is not seeing this, this horror, but I fear she is. I hope she is stronger than I am.

Reed trudged back toward his unit with only his helmet, rifle, and gas mask, as familiar now as living friends. The ruins housing the aid station looked vaguely like a French village, but any signs of color and life were long gone, the flower gardens and the scent of fresh bread replaced by burned-out houses and a sour stench lingering after the rain.

He passed a large tent serving as the post office, and he paused. It was stuffed with packages and boxes of letters for men at the front. So many letters would go unanswered—so many packages unopened—forever. *Got to write Clara, tell her . . .*

As he walked into camp, he had to ask where his company was. He scanned the faces but recognized few men. His old platoon was led by a young sergeant, in the corps less time than Reed had been. All of Reed's platoon leaders were NCOs now; there were no more officers left to assign to platoon level.

Captain Hamilton spotted Reed and walked over to him. "How's the arm?"

"Sore, Skipper, but still attached."

"It's good to see you, Reed. It really is," Hamilton said. "You're officially the company commander now. I'm your battalion CO Come over and meet your fellow company commanders. We have some coffee."

Reed followed Hamilton to a small campfire, where the two new officers sat.

"This here is Lieutenant Heiser, and this is Lieutenant Edgar Allen Poe, Jr.," Hamilton said, winking.

Reed looked at Poe quizzically.

Poe smiled. "It surprises everyone. No, I'm not the son of *that* Poe. He died in 1849. My father was a distant cousin named for him, and he passed along the curse of confusion to me. And no, I have no designs on a literary career."

Reed returned Poe's smile. "Thanks for laying all that out for me. I was actually wondering where I could find a cup for some of that coffee." Both men laughed.

After they had chatted for a while, Hamilton stood. "Gents, hate to break up the party, but we need to get ready for the morning. I'd prefer to have more time and more training before we hit the Boche again, but the woods still need to be cleared. Let's get to it." Hamilton strode off toward his headquarters.

Reed stood up to leave, but Lieutenant Heiser touched his arm. "Mr. Lewis, we'd like to know—can you tell us what it's like?"

Reed stared at Heiser for a long moment. "No. No, I can't describe it. You just have to make yourself stand there in front of the men and make them believe they can do it. The urge to run or curl up like a baby is so strong you have to fight it every minute. They can't see you falter. It's . . . it's okay if you're afraid. The only men who aren't afraid are probably already dead."

XXVIII

Dearest Clara,

I hope this post finds you well and safe. I have had several days rest and feel quite well, though visions of your mother's Thanksgiving feast dance before my eyes on occasion. I carry those little memories around with me like a locket I can open when I need a boost. A soaking wet sled ride on a cold night, a stolen kiss after a party, the touch of your hand while I pretended to forget how to knit. These locket memories keep me going.

I know the style of the day is to be oblique and coy in letters, but I feel like I must tell you what is in my heart. If nothing else, our experiences in France must surely teach us that life is fleeting and that we must live it fully while we can.

To that end, I tell you now and forever that I am in love with you. You may have guessed this from my many clumsy attempts at courtship, but from the day I saw you stand up and hold your own at that debate, I was enthralled. Whatever providence intends for us in this great struggle for freedom, I wanted to be sure you knew my heart.

Yours,
Reed

It was eerily similar to the first time he stood facing his men outside Belleau Wood, and no less uncomfortable. He led three platoons now, and three young men faced him, each tasked with the leadership role Reed himself filled just a week earlier.

His legs felt like he was walking waist deep in the surf back at Paris Island. The familiar, and now closer, thud of artillery rounds caused him to stiffen his muscles to resist the urge to flinch. And the Maxims. He could hear the horrible "chug chug" sound they made, imagining men dropping from streams of bullets they could not see. He drew deep breaths and prayed for calm. *Can't let the men see my fear.*

Captain Hamilton took his place with the battalion staff. He looked calm and composed. Reed wondered how he did it.

Turning around to look at his men, Reed saw they looked ready, determined, their bayonets fixed, rifles at port arms. He scanned for Sergeant Allen's face, forgetting for a second that he was gone. Many of the men were replacements, with names and faces Reed did not know.

Reed raised his rifle high over his head at Hamilton's signal and the Marines were off once again, in near-perfect skirmish lines marching toward the Boche. Hamilton had told them that this section of the wood was lightly held, but he also warned them there had been no reconnaissance to confirm this.

Maxim fire soon beat the overgrown field like a hailstorm. Any grass over a meter high was chopped off. The Marine attack faltered as officers fell, replaced by sergeants, who were replaced by corporals, then by privates, as the Marines surged forward and the Germans fought in place. The advance finally stopped short of the wood line, and Hamilton ordered the men to the ground as they stacked up against an imaginary line like waves on a jetty. The German fire slackened, lacking targets.

"Bad Penny!" Hamilton called out.

"Here, Skipper!" Reed yelled.

"Where are you? I can't see you. Maybe you should stand up so I can," Hamilton called.

Reed watched Maxim rounds continue to clip the grass above his head. "Maybe you should stand up, Skipper, so you could see me!" Reed answered. Many of the men within hearing distance laughed, probably exactly as Hamilton had intended.

"Listen, Reed. I want you to work your men up in small teams, get us a foothold in that wood line like we did last time, then provide some cover fire while we get the rest of the battalion up."

"Aye, Skipper."

This time Reed did not move up with the teams, but moved across his platoons to make sure they stayed relatively in line as they approached the edge of the woods, crawling. He had a front row seat to the incredible bravery of the Marines as they rushed one gun after another. He saw one Marine take out a Maxim crew by himself with his rifle and bayonet, grabbing the barrel of the gun with his hand and overturning it as a round from the gun blew his hand off. He recognized the Marine as he moved past Reed to the rear for aid. He was from Reed's original platoon: Private Joseph M. Baker.

Reed shucked off his fear like a wet blanket. Rage replaced it, and a determination to get his men forward into the wood. He ran back and forth along the front line of his troops, grabbing men and urging them forward, dragging a few.

He found Captain Hamilton once the line was secured inside the wood. "Sir, looks like it wasn't all that lightly held after all."

"Nope. Frankly, I don't even know if we can hold what we've taken so far. I estimate we lost almost fifty percent. If they counterattack—all bets are off."

"Skipper, you see that knoll right there? Think we ought to put some men on it? If the Boche get guns on that, they could pin us down while their infantry counterattacks."

"Yes. Good call. About ten men should do it. And remember, you are the company commander now; YOU don't take them out there."

"Aye, Skipper," Reed answered. "Ah, Sir, how about Heiser and Poe, they okay?"

Hamilton looked at him, then turned his eyes toward the front. "No. Heiser got decapitated by Maxim fire. Poe is wounded, out of the fight. Just you and me again, Bad Penny."

"Aye, Skipper," Reed answered, his voice flat. There was not even time for mourning any more. Reed felt numb as he returned to his men to get them ready to hold the position all night.

Shortly before dawn, Reed got a message from Hamilton: "Get your men off that knoll. Division is going to hammer the Germans in one hour and that knoll is the forward edge of the barrage."

No time to delegate this. Reed grabbed two Marines, and the three of them sprinted toward the knoll under the cover of fading darkness. The barrage started just as they arrived.

"Get your gear, follow us!" Reed screamed. Rounds impacted around them. Nausea and disorientation swarmed Reed's senses as they had during the barrage on Hill 142 and back at Verdun. He gritted his teeth and ran toward the Marine lines with his men, all of whom made it back safely. They lay on the ground gasping for breath as the full weight of the barrage fell on the German lines.

When the artillery ceased fire, Reed stood up to check his line for the coming attack. He didn't hear the report of the sniper's rifle. A blow pounded his chest like a sledgehammer. It turned him almost completely around, the woods spinning in his mind like a top, then down to the earth, then nothingness.

XXIX

June 1918
Near Paris, France

The door that nobody else will go in at, seems always to open for me.

—*Clara Barton*

Clara stumbled into headquarters as the sun rose. She and Lily had spent the night driving through black fields, headlights off, shuttling wounded men around shell holes and barbed wire.

"Coffee?" one of the other ambulance drivers asked as they walked past the dining room.

Lily shook her head. "All I want is sleep."

Clara glanced at herself in the mirror. Her eyes were the only part of her not splattered with mud. Her goggles had left a negative image on her face, so she looked like a raccoon in reverse. She laughed. "I think I want a bath first. Soak off the filth."

Lily nodded.

"Oh, Miss Jensen," the other girl said. "Mail came for you just after you went out."

Clara took the two envelopes. The first one, dirt-smudged, was from Reed. She smiled and held it close, looking forward to reading it after her nap. Then she saw that the second letter was from the Red Cross—the kind of message that no one wanted to receive. Her heart went cold as she tore it open.

"What is it?" Lily asked, taking Clara's arm.

Clara scanned the lines, tears clouding her vision. "It's Reed."

188

XXX

My stretcher is one scarlet stain, And as I tries to scrape it clean, I tell you what — I'm sick of pain, For all I've heard, for all I've seen; Around me is the hellish night, And as the war's red rim I trace, I wonder if in Heaven's height Our God don't turn away his face.

—*Tommy Crawford, 15th Durham Light Infantry*

Reed felt like he was floating as his eyes opened. The shattered stalks of the wheat field surrounding Belleau Wood brushed alongside him as he moved, but something was clearing a path ahead of him. He tried to raise his head, but searing pain made him see stars and his head slammed back down.

"You're gonna be okay, Sir" the stretcher bearer at his head said. The stretcher bounced hard as the bearers struggled over uneven ground, wincing as stray bullets whizzed by them.

Reed could barely speak. His mouth was parched. Thirsty. "What happened? Where are you taking me?"

"You got shot, Sir. We're taking you to the field aid station. They'll take you to a field hospital. I think you need surgery."

"Is it bad?"

"You lost a lot of blood, Sir. But the bullet went clean through and your lung didn't collapse. We got you bandaged up pretty good."

"How do you know that my lung wasn't hit?"

"We wouldn't be talking like this if it was, Sir. Now you just rest. We have a mile or so to go before the aid station."

Reed tried to relax but he had to grip the sides of the stretcher to keep from sliding around as the bearers carried him. He turned his head to the side to see a little. They passed through a road intersection turned into a quagmire by recent rain and the heavy vehicles and carts transiting it. The bearers grunted and drew ragged breaths as they slogged through the mud. Reed saw them step on corpses to get better traction through the muck, and he turned his head to the sky so as not to watch. *There is no end to the horrors of this war.*

The bearers placed Reed carefully down in the triage area outside the aid station, flopping down next to him to catch their breaths.

"Lieutenant, what happens next is a doctor or nurse is going to triage you, that is, decide where you go. My guess is you'll go right to the field hospital. We gotta go, Sir. Lots more men to tote back here. Good luck to you." The bearers stood to leave.

"Privates," Reed said. "Thank you. You guys are heroes in my book."

"*Semper Fi*, Sir," one of the bearers replied. And they were off to help others.

Because he had a chest wound, Reed was categorized as "severe but survivable," and the doctor ordered him to be evacuated by ambulance to a field hospital. As the orderlies carried him to the waiting vehicle, Reed saw that the drivers were both women. He desperately wanted one of them to be Clara, but at the same time he was terrified to have her see him like this.

Clara wasn't there. He wanted to ask if the girls knew her, but they were occupied cramming the ambulance with wounded, too busy for conversation. Along with Reed, there was one other stretcher patient, and four ambulatory patients with wounds serious enough to warrant evacuation.

A surgeon examined Reed in the field hospital later that day. "Well, Lieutenant," the doctor said, "you were pretty lucky, I'd say. You did lose some blood but not enough to require a transfusion. The bullet seems to have missed any vital arteries and it certainly missed your lung. However, it may well have clipped your clavicle. If so, there may be bone fragments that we need to get out. In any case, we need to do surgery as soon as possible to excise the wound."

"What does that mean, to excise the wound?" Reed asked.

"We have to remove any dead tissue, and anything that may have got into the wound, such as bullet fragments, pieces of your clothing, and any other battlefield debris. The object is healthy, bleeding tissue to avoid gangrene or tetanus."

The doctor came to examine Reed again the day after his surgery. "How are you feeling, Lieutenant?"

"It's sore, Sir. That's for sure."

"Let's have a look." The doctor removed the dressing from Reed's chest, revealing an open wound almost three inches long. "It looks good so far. There is a smaller incision in your back—that is probably the source of a most of your discomfort since you're laying on it. The surgery went well, but we did have to make fairly wide margins to get all the bone fragments out. The impact broke your clavicle, so you will have a lengthy recovery."

June 20, 1918
Field Hospital Near the Front

Dearest Clara,

I'm told you received the Red Cross message that I have been wounded. Sorry for the unfamiliar handwriting. My right arm is in a sling so I asked one of the Red Cross ladies here to write for me. They tell me I am recovering well, but that it will be at least two months before I'm fit enough to return to duty. I feel strange about this. I feel guilty, mostly, like I've let my men down by not being with them. But at the same time, having been in three fights, I don't relish the prospect of more. The bravado of training camps back in the U.S.—"to get at them Huns," and such—doesn't last long once one has done so for real.

I had a letter from Ol' Bert telling me that he and Joseph are now in the French countryside training after months of waiting in the states and in England. He says they are anxious to get at the Boche. I hope they never see action.

Clara, I had not been to an aid station or field hospital before I was wounded myself. I thought of you in these places and it made me shudder. It was as if the stretcher bearers collected all the evidence of suffering and death on the line and dumped it in one place, leaving you and the medical people to sort it out.

Stretchers out in the open everywhere. White linen bandages on arms, faces, and legs—everywhere a bullet could strike or a shell fragment could slice. Men's faces and uniforms grimy beyond color, making the linen stand out in contrast.

And I could hear men wailing, calling for their mothers. I'd heard these sounds on the line, but this was condensed, packed men all racked with pain, some waiting for death.

They cry for Heavenly Father's help, though all this is the work of man, not God. I used to doubt when people spoke of God directing their lives—to wonder if He was really that aware of us. Now, I feel his hand in my survival, but I don't know why I'm still here when so many good men are not.

I don't know how you do this, Clara. No one expected you to come here and some insisted you shouldn't. You could have done your bit handing out cocoa at the train depot in Logan, but you chose this, maybe the toughest place on earth to serve. Maybe you're the strongest woman on earth. You're certainly the strongest woman I know.

Let's dream of a better place and time, and a future of peace together.

Yours,
Reed

XXXI

*We are happy to see that the suspicion which originally cre-
ated barriers between the citizens of Logan and the boys from
Wyoming stationed here for the U.A.C. Training Detachment
are finally starting to come down. Though fear of the negative
influence of the soldiers initially created a desire to ostracize
them, the citizens of Logan and of the A.C. are remembering
their duty and reaching out to these boys who are doing their
bit. Just as we hope the sons of Logan are finding a warm
welcome wherever they are training, we ought to offer the
same to these sons of Wyoming. In that spirit, we remind the
women on campus that it is not improper for them to dine
in the canteen along with the soldiers. This Saturday there
will be a dance for the soldiers, and students are encouraged
to attend, especially the females, who should remember their
duty to make the soldiers feel at home and help them forget the
war for a few hours.*

—The A.C. Student Life

Trudi sat in the Council of Defense meeting, her mind on the latest letters from "Over There." Bert was excited to be getting into the fighting soon. Reed had been wounded. Clara sounded optimistic that he would recover, but some of the overseas letters went past censors. Trudi wasn't sure what to believe anymore.

"Will you be able to help with the dance?" one of the other students asked Trudi.

"Of course," she answered automatically, wondering what she'd just volunteered for. She tried to focus on what the others were saying.

"They're asking us to make the soldiers feel at home while they're here training. Each ward's Relief Society has been assigned to bake for the boys, and families will be asked to invite them over for dinners, but they need some social interaction too. We're to make them feel a part of the community while they're here."

Trudi pressed her lips together. Some of the soldiers had already gotten in trouble for finding liquor in spite of the city's prohibition laws and starting a fight downtown. As they dragged one of the soldiers away, he'd complained loudly about the lack of fun and female companionship in Logan. Trudi wasn't sure they were going to integrate very well.

The committee assigned Trudi to be in charge of the drinks. She quickly settled on lemonade and decided to station someone nearby to keep a discreet eye on the pitchers and make sure no one tried to liven them up. If soldiers were going to invade her community, they would have to learn to adjust.

Outside, she had to thread her way past soldiers in uniform and the young men working on the construction of the new buildings to house them. All non-war related construction had ground to a halt, so Trudi had to admire President Peterson's cleverness in using the demand for soldier training to help the college grow. They were adding new classes too: military tactics, military French, aeronautics, surveying, and motor repair. All for the men. All for the soldiers. For the women, there were the Red Cross nursing classes, teaching them to care for the boys when they were ill or injured. Everyone was constantly reminded of their roles. Trudi just wished hers didn't squeeze her like a straightjacket.

Trudi glanced up and saw Alonzo moving through the press toward her. At the sight of his familiar face, she smiled in spite of her worries. He stood out from the throng, the only man not in uniform. One of the soldiers shoved him with his shoulder as he passed. Alonzo's football days served him well. The blow hardly phased him, but Trudi saw the anger flash in his eyes. His expression softened when he reached Trudi. He pulled her aside, out of the river of people.

"Were you headed over for lunch?" he asked.

"I don't know. I don't like eating with all the soldiers."

"If you come with me, they'll give you a wide berth," he said.

She smiled. "You'll protect me?"

He leaned closer with a grin. "You'll protect me. They won't try to pick a fight with a lady present."

She laughed, surprised he was able to make jokes about his awkward situation. "I guess I can't refuse, then."

"Tell me, are you looking forward to the dance?" he asked, escorting her toward the canteen.

"I don't know. I'm a bit nervous, hosting all those soldiers from out of state."

"Want to make a good impression?"

"More worried about the impression they're going to make on us," she mumbled.

He tilted his head. "How so?"

"They're, you know . . ."

"Outsiders?" he asked in a low voice, holding the door open for her.

Trudi paused at the threshold. Wasn't that her problem? That she felt like an outsider? It wasn't the same, was it?

"That's not exactly what I meant," she said slowly. "But I remember how everyone treated Mormons in Switzerland. Utah was supposed to be our refuge. What do we do when we lose that?"

The quiet murmur of conversation and clink of silverware on plates filled the canteen.

"Maybe we can help them understand that we're not that different," Alonzo said, then smiled slyly. "Last time I checked, we don't have horns."

Trudi laughed. She'd been shocked to learn anyone was naive enough to believe that rumor about Mormons. "Don't you?" she asked. "They gave me mine the day I was baptized."

He chuckled.

"Thank you for the advice," she said. "I'll try not to worry so much."

Despite Trudi's resolve not to worry, she did warn the girls who would be serving the drinks at the dance to keep on eye on anyone trying to add anything to them. She told herself that Mormon boys had been known to pull that prank too, so she wasn't being prejudiced.

Trudi spent extra time getting ready on Saturday. As she secured one of her brunette curls with a bobby pin, she wondered if Alonzo would be there. Probably not. He wouldn't want to spend any more time around the soldiers than necessary. Trudi straightened the long, airy layers of her pastel pink dress and headed out early enough to help with the final preparations.

"Going out?" Karl asked.

"There's a dance tonight. For the soldiers."

"Oh."

His cold response surprised Trudi, but he headed upstairs before she could question him about it.

The gym looked like an accident in a flag factory. Bunting draped across the wall, hung from the ceiling, and even festooned the chairs and tables. Any empty spaces were swathed in flags of various sizes. The explosion of red, white, and blue clashed with the girls' pastel dresses.

As the soldiers trickled into the room, Trudi forced her shoulders to relax. Some of the young men had a cocky strut or condescending expression, but most looked excited or nervous—just boys going to a dance. The band played a two-step, and the locals and soldiers mingled. The only hitches Trudi noticed were the young men who were slow to pick up on some of the dance steps that were popular at the A.C.

One young soldier stood against the wall like he was at attention, his back ramrod straight and his eyes fixed forward. Trudi walked up to him and smiled.

"How are you enjoying the dance?" she asked in her best American accent.

"Very well, thank you, Miss." He still didn't make eye contact. Maybe he'd never been to a dance before.

"My name's Trudi Kessler."

"Private Matthew Spencer, Miss."

"Do you dance, Private Spencer?"

He looked at her with wide eyes then scanned the room as if seeking an exit. "Not well, Miss."

"Would you like me to teach you?" she asked.

His Adam's apple bobbed. "I don't think so. Your people have been very kind, but, it's just that . . . I've got a girl back home."

"Oh, I see." Trudi said, smiling at the image of this young man shyly wooing his sweetheart. "She'd think you unfaithful if you danced?"

His Adam's apple jumped more rapidly. "I don't want to be disrespectful, Miss, but there are certain aspects of your lifestyle which I'm just . . . just not comfortable with."

Trudi racked her brain, trying to decide what aspect of clean-living Logan could be offensive to him. Her eyes brightened with understanding. "Oh, you don't think we're polygamists, do you? That's been over for decades, and most Mormons didn't practice it anyway."

"It's not that. It's . . . Really, I think it's indecent of you to make me explain it."

"I'm so thoroughly confused, I think it's indecent of you not to."

He turned his gaze to her imploringly. "It's the . . ." he dropped his voice. "The free love, Miss."

"The what?" Trudi's voice came out louder than she intended.

His face reddened. "You know, the free love. The . . . immorality. It's just not right."

Trudi stared at the terrified young man with new understanding, and she burst out laughing, leaning against the wall as tears rolled down her cheeks.

Private Spencer reddened further and, if possible, stood even straighter. "You may think me prudish, but—"

Trudi waved her hand. "Not at all. I admire your courage in standing up for your principles. Who told you our terrible secret?"

He looked offended by her light tone. "All the boys are talking about it. Some of them couldn't be happier to be assigned to Utah, but the rest of us . . ."

"Are rightly horrified," Trudi said, sobering as she realized what a problem this might cause. "I'm afraid your more amorous comrades are going to be disappointed. We don't believe in free love. In fact, we're probably at least as 'prudish' as you are."

"Really?" he asked, looking both relieved and skeptical.

"Really. You know we don't even allow drinking."

"I did think that was an odd contradiction. I have to admit I'm relieved. You folks seemed so kind, I hated to think there might be something awful behind it. Some ladies brought me and the other boys a whole pie each." He looked a bit embarrassed. "I ate mine all in one sitting. It was as good as one of Mama's."

Trudi smiled at him. "I hope you find Utah more enjoyable now that you know the truth. You'd be doing me—and all the young ladies— a favor if you squelched those rumors anytime you hear them. We don't want any unfortunate misunderstandings."

"Of course, Miss Kessler."

Trudi scanned the room, looking for signs of trouble. Here and there she spotted a stormy expression that made her wonder if there had been a "misunderstanding," but overall the crowd seemed to be enjoying themselves. Still, she circulated to check on the refreshments and drop a warning word in a few people's ears.

A hand on her arm stopped her. She looked up to see Alonzo looking sharp in his best suit. Some of the soldiers gave him hostile glares. He wasn't the only local boy to have shown up, but he was the only one who'd refused to wear his uniform. The only other men in suits were the chaperones.

"Are you enjoying yourself?" he asked.

"I . . . I suppose I am," Trudi said. She hesitated, then told him about her conversation with Private Spencer.

Alonzo chuckled. "And he was terrified of you, of course. A pretty Mormon woman, and him thinking that."

Trudi blushed at his off-handed compliment.

"Have you danced?" Alonzo asked.

"Not after Private Spencer's refusal."

"Come on, you need to enjoy yourself a little. We don't want you working yourself sick again."

Trudi hesitated then took Alonzo's hand. "Thank you."

His strong fingers wrapped around hers, and he led her to the floor. She noticed a few more glares shot in his direction, but he ignored them and led her through a two-step. She relaxed in his easy company. He didn't ask her to talk or entertain him; he just seemed happy to be holding her in his comfortable grip. It was a moment of peace in the frenzy of activity.

The rest of the dance went as smoothly as could be expected. People commented on the tastefulness of the decor, which made Trudi snicker to herself, and no one tried to spike the lemonade. Trudi waltzed and two-stepped around the floor with some of the soldiers, but when Karl asked her whom she had danced with, the only person she could remember was Alonzo.

"We have been assigned to host some soldiers for dinner tonight," Trudi's mother announced the next week at breakfast.

"Excuse me," Karl said, setting down his napkin and leaving the room.

Trudi and her mother exchanged concerned glances.

"Do you think they'll wear their uniforms?" Hans asked, his eyes bright.

"Probably, dear." Trudi forced a smile. "Are you excited to see them?"

"Yes! I want to wear a uniform someday too."

Trudi's heart caught at the thought of baby-faced Hans sent off to war. Yet in Britain, boys as young as thirteen and fourteen fought with the army and navy: an entire generation sacrificed to the hungry trenches. "I'm afraid the fighting will probably be over before you're old enough."

"Oh." He frowned and kicked his feet absent-mindedly under the table.

"What are we going to make?" Trudi asked.

"What about potatoes with a cheese sauce? Very Swiss. We would be contradicting our war efforts to serve them meat and bread, *ja*?" Her mother smiled, and Trudi sensed a hint of defiance in her tone. So, her compliant mother was feeling a little rebellious? Giving up her language obviously hurt, and being forced to register was a slap in the face.

"At least we have the vegetables from our garden to make it a meal," Trudi said.

"What about dessert?" Hans asked eagerly.

"Pick some gooseberries," Trudi told him. "We'll do something with them."

As soon as she got home from classes later that afternoon, she put on her apron and went to work alongside her mother. She plucked the stems and flower ends from the gooseberries Hans had picked until her fingers were sore, then used honey and oats to make a sort of cobbler. A little tart, but it would satisfy Hans's sweet tooth.

When the soldiers arrived, Trudi grinned to see Private Spencer standing shyly in the living room. She greeted him and his companion warmly, and they gathered around the table. They must have noticed her parents' heavy accents, but said nothing about it, and acted perfectly at ease talking with her father about their hometowns.

"Where's Karl?" Trudi asked.

"He had to work late at the canning factory," her mother said quietly.

Hans looked up in confusion. "But his shift is always over by dinner."

"We all have to do our bit," Trudi said quickly, but she felt a stab of uneasiness.

The dinner went off without a hitch, everyone respectful and on good terms. Her father asked one of the soldiers to say grace, and the boy's prayer for the health and peace of their homes and the soldiers overseas sounded so familiar, Trudi wouldn't have known he was from anywhere but Utah. Not so different, as Alonzo said.

That night, though, Karl still hadn't come home. Trudi lay awake in the room she shared with her sister, listening. Well after the family had gone to bed, the back door creaked open. Trudi whisked off her covers and snuck to the hall. Two voices spoke downstairs. One of them was Karl's, and they both used German.

The uneasiness in her chest grew, a heavy weight over her heart. She tiptoed back into her room. When Karl's footsteps padded down the hall, she peeked out and saw him slip into his room with a box under one arm. Frowning to herself, she lay down, but it was deep in the night before she was able to sleep.

Trudi was late getting up the next morning. She'd slept through her first class, and she had to rush to be ready in time for Red Cross training. Someone knocked on the door just as she was gathering her books. No one else was around, so she answered it.

"*Guten tag,*" the young man at the door said.

"Hello," Trudi replied cautiously.

"Christian!" Karl said, intercepting the young man and steering him away from Trudi. He whispered, "*Sei ruhig.*" Be quiet.

Trudi watched them walk into the parlor, their heads bent in whispered conversation. Christian passed a package to Karl. Trudi hurried outside to catch the streetcar to campus. What was Karl doing?

As she sat through her classes, she couldn't focus on the lessons. Karl was an adult. He didn't need his sister spying on him. But the thought of spying made Trudi cold to her core. Would Karl betray his own country? Did he even think of the U.S. as his home? Would he lie to everyone—to her?

Alonzo caught up with Trudi as she wandered across campus, dodging groups of boys in uniform.

"Trudi? Are you ill?"

"Oh, I suppose I am a little."

"Would you like me to take you home?"

"No!" Then she would have to face Karl. Alonzo looked alarmed, so she softly said, "I mean, no thank you."

"Trudi?"

She met his worried gaze. "Alonzo, can I . . ." She stopped. What was she going to do? Tell Karl's secrets to Alonzo? No. She couldn't betray her brother. But what if he was betraying all of them? What if he was doing something that might hurt her family? Or Clara and the boys overseas? "Can I ask you something, Alonzo?"

"Anything," he said.

"You don't like the war. But you wouldn't do anything to harm your country?"

"Of course not. I don't want to see people hurt."

She nodded. "What if you were in a situation where one person you cared about was doing something that might endanger another, but the only way to stop that person would hurt him?"

Alonzo studied her curiously, but instead of pressing her for more, he looked away at the distant mountains. "I think I would look at the kind of hurt that would come to people and decide, in the long run, which decision would cause the least pain."

Trudi mulled that over. She didn't want to see anything happen to Karl, but if he was involved in some conspiracy that could hurt not only their friends and family but him as well, she would have to find out what he was doing.

"Thank you," she said, squeezing Alonzo's arm.

"Of course," he said, bemused. "You know if you're ever in trouble, you can come to me, right?"

"I know, Alonzo." That knowledge reminded her she wasn't entirely alone and warmed her, making her feel brave enough to do what she had to.

Trudi went home early again that day, sneaking in through the front door. Her mother was humming in the kitchen, but otherwise the house was quiet. Trudi hurried up the steps, skipping over the one that squeaked, and tiptoed to Hans and Karl's room.

The box and package were nowhere to be seen. She checked under the bed and in the drawers. Maybe he'd passed them on to someone else. She looked in the closet. One of the boards in the floor didn't lie flat. With shaking hands, Trudi knelt and ran her hands over the raised edge. The tip of her fingernails fit into the crack, and she pried the board up.

There, in the dark space under the floor, huddled several small boxes. Trudi sat back. This was her last chance to choose ignorance. But she wasn't ignorant, really. She could never be, now that she knew the boxes were there. She pulled one out and carefully lifted the lid, her stomach clenched into sickened knots.

The box was full of yarn. She lifted it out and ran her fingers through the warm threads. Wool. It had become almost as precious as wheat and sugar, illegal to sell or send overseas, except to soldiers. She put the box back. What was he doing? Smuggling it? Selling it on the black market? But why?

There was only one way she would ever find out. Karl would be angry, but she couldn't imagine that he would do anything to hurt her. She cornered him alone after supper.

"Karl, I saw what's in the boxes."

His eyes narrowed. "You've been snooping?"

"Why are you doing it, Karl? Are you selling it to someone? Are you stealing it?"

"You could really suspect me of such things?"

Trudi looked down. Did she?

"Little sister, I haven't stolen anything, and I'm not making any money."

"Then what are you doing?"

He sat next to her on the sofa. "I'm sending these things to my friends in Germany. The people I served while I was on my mission."

Trudi paled. "Karl! You could go to jail for treason! And if people found out . . ." There hadn't been any tarring and feathering in Utah—maybe the people remembered well enough when it had been their own grandparents who suffered at the hands of mobs—but that didn't mean it couldn't happen.

"I know," Karl said. "I debated with myself over it. But how can I ignore the sufferings of people I love?"

"You're aiding the enemy."

"They're not my enemy. The German leaders are despots, forcing their people to fight, deluding them with talk of cultural supremacy. And some of the people are fools for believing it. But most of the Germans are just as much victims as the French, Belgians, and Serbs. Their own government is starving them, freezing them. Taking everything for the war effort. Do you really think withholding aid from the common people is going to weaken the German government's resolve to fight?"

"Maybe not," Trudi admitted. "But it's illegal—it's wrong!"

"I don't know. I suppose there might always be a right and a wrong answer to everything, but we can't always see what it is. I'm just doing the best I can, Trudi, and I can only see darkly. I understand why you work like you do, even when it nearly kills you. I hope you can understand why I can't see my friends suffering without trying to help."

Karl left her alone with her confused thoughts. Seeing darkly. The scriptures said something about that. She flipped through the family Bible to find 1 Corinthians 13 and read the passage about seeing "through a glass darkly." They all saw everything imperfectly. Alonzo had said that even the prophet and apostles were only human beneath their mantle of authority. How could anyone do the right thing?

Trudi kept reading. The rest of the chapter was about love. *Charity never faileth.* Without charity—love—they were nothing. That was Karl's motivation. Could Trudi say as much? She was motivated by guilt and duty more than anything else.

What would Alonzo tell her? Trudi couldn't ask for his advice, not when he would have to report Karl or keep his smuggling a secret. Alonzo had said he would do whatever caused the least damage. The scriptures seemed to say that love needed to guide us when everything else was unclear. She loved Karl, and he loved the people he was helping. Trudi gently placed the Bible back on the table. She would say nothing. Yet it gnawed at her, like glass in her stomach. She wanted everything to be cut and dried, but the longer this war went on, the more everything turned to confusion.

XXXII

September 12, 1918
St. Mihiel, France

Dear Uncle,

We are to begin our first offensive against them Dutch tomorrow. I'm excited after all these months of training and waiting. Me and Bert are to scout, which suits me fine—anything to get out of these dang wet woods. I thought you would like to know we went fishing—but not how we do at home. Bert found a box of potato mashers so we tossed a few of them in a hole near the bend in a creek and lo and behold our breakfast floated right up to the top. Fried 'em up with the can of grease we tote with us. Let me tell you, it was fine, especially after eating the hardtack and dried carrots the army thinks is food these days. We see strange things every day and that ain't the half of it. I saw a tree with a dud artillery round stuck in it. There was a bottle of French wine sitting on the end of it! Plus I got a haircut sitting on a barber's chair made out of a tipped-over tombstone. Made my hair stand on end. Ha ha.

Me and Bert went to the "Y" to get some writing paper and cocoa the other day. There was some Negroes in there and some of the fellows kicked about it. It don't bother me and Bert, though. We figure if they're good enough to fight, they're good enough for some cocoa too. Them fellows mighta kicked about me too except I'm covered with enough mud to pass for a regular doughboy.

After all I seen so far, I must say the fate of the horses is the worst, Uncle. So many dead and maimed just lying there rotting, some still in harnesses. The horses pulling wagons and caissons, well, they work them right to death. Such a shame. You can see they was some fine animals at some point. The cavalry horses *fare better, 'til they attack them Dutch, then they all gonna die. Never seen such waste and hope never to again.*

I thank you for your letter! I'm sure the folks at home are behind us like you say, though they are a long way behind us, and probably happy to stay that way. My best to everyone in Washakie.

Your Nephew,
Joseph Sorrell, Pvt., U.S.A., 1/362 Infantry, France

Though their sergeant had warned them to expect a great artillery barrage to their front, Joseph and Bert huddled close to a large diameter tree, covering their ears and trembling.

Bert shouted over the incredible din, "Sergeant said there are a thousand guns firing at the Boche—it sounds like ten thousand. Why aren't they firing back?"

"'Cause I heard the Captain say we caught the whole dang German army on the move. Their artillery too. They ain't set up to fire back," Joseph yelled, even though Bert was only a foot away.

Every pause in the roar of field guns was filled by the whine of allied aircraft coming low over the woods, heading toward the German lines. Joseph caught glimpses of hundreds of red, white, and blue wingtips buzzing past. He tried to count, but the roar rattled his concentration. He thought of lying on his back in a field of winter wheat during a cold Utah winter, watching geese fly overhead, too high to shoot at but low enough to quicken his pulse.

Since the advance was a general one, there was little need for scouts at this point. Bert and Joseph reported to the Stokes Mortar Platoon for temporary duty as ammunition bearers.

The platoon sergeant told the boys his name but Joseph couldn't hear it. The sergeant grabbed them both behind the head and pulled them close. "Listen. Your job is simple. You go back to the ammunition dump, about five hundred yards toward the rear, and you carry up those mortar rounds as fast as you can. You're here because my other bearers are all dead—so if I was you, I'd move fast. Got it?"

"Yes, Sergeant," both men answered. Joseph looked at Bert and nodded to the rear. They ran.

They returned with a load of mortar rounds just as the platoon began firing as a battery. The sergeant saw them watching and called them over, grabbing their heads again so they could hear him.

"Each of them guns is firing eight rounds. By the time the first round impacts, the other seven will already be in the air. We fire, then move closer. Pound the Boche lines as we go. We're killing a buncha them today. Now get your rears back to the ammo dump."

The boys made fifteen trips back and forth that day. Between the heavy load on the return trips and the mud and rain, Joseph was exhausted. Mud clung to his leggings up to his knees, weighing on him like lead. Sweat turned cold when he stopped, adding to the aching chill. He was relieved when their regular platoon sergeant came to claim them as dusk settled.

"Men, the CO wants scouts out tonight in case the Germans counterattack. You two get some chow, then meet me at the company headquarters for orders at 2400 hours."

Joseph looked at Bert as they hurried back to their gear in the forest. "I don't know about you, but I feel like I was rode hard and put up wet already. This ain't gonna be a fun night."

"No. About like the time you rode up on that gelding trying to look all fresh back at the fair, huh?" Bert laughed.

"Nah, I don't feel half that good," Joseph said, grinning.

"Now, here's your mission, boys," the Sergeant said. "You're to find and fix the first line of enemy trenches. They've fallen back, but we don't know how far. This is important, see? If we don't know where they are, then all the artillery fire in the world in the morning isn't gonna help much. Understand?"

Before they moved out, Bert and Joseph checked all their personal gear for noise. They filled their canteens to the top so they wouldn't slosh. They stuffed spare socks into their ammunition pouches so the rounds wouldn't clink together. Both men tore off small strips of cloth from an old shirt they found and tied them over the swivels of their rifle slings so they didn't squeak. Both men jumped up and down to verify with the other that they were quiet. Finally, Joseph applied shoe black to his face.

"Why you putting that on?" Bert asked. "You already look pretty dark to me."

"Big medicine. War paint! Besides, the idea is not to darken the face, but to keep the light of flares from reflecting off of it. When being chased by the bear, one need not outrun the bear, just his pale, shiny white partner," Joseph said with mock solemnity.

Bert chuckled. "Gimme that shoe black."

The two men moved through the woods with silence and stealth, as they had each done many times growing up hunting in the mountains of Utah. Here the game could shoot back, though. They stepped carefully over branches and twigs. They moved along the edges of clearings, never crossing them directly, and never close to the edge of the forest. They did not use trails, not even game trails, for fear of ambush or anti-personnel traps.

Joseph and Bert both counted their paces, knowing that their "pace count" would tell them how far they had traveled along their assigned route. They counted off 100-yard increments by sliding knots along a piece of string, one knot for every increment.

They came to a huge meadow covered in deep, untended grass and huddled up to decide what to do.

"This meadow wraps around this edge of the forest. I can't see the end of it. I think we should pass through it," Joseph said.

"OK, but let's get low, stay below the top of the grass," Bert replied.

The meadow was eerily quiet as they moved; the only sound was the gentle swish of the grass as they pushed through it. Both men froze. Whispers. They slowly went to ground, Joseph pointing his weapon forward, Bert covering their rear. The whispers increased. They were all around them. Speech, but the words—German!

Joseph heard Bert quietly slide his bayonet out of its scabbard, then the metallic noise as he seated it on his aught-three. He slid back toward Bert until they were touching back-to-back while he fixed his own bayonet.

The grass rustled nearby, the sound of one person moving. The whispers ceased. Then a voice called out in broken English. "'Ello, Americans? 'Ello. Surrender please?"

"The heck we will," Bert mumbled, just loud enough for Joseph to hear. He got into a crouch, rifle at the ready. Joseph followed suit. Had they stumbled into German lines? At least they would take some of the Boche with them. A warrior's death.

"'Ello. Ah, we, we surrender, *ja*?" The voice called.

"What did he say?" Joseph whispered.

"I think they want to surrender to us?" Bert said.

"Maybe they don't know it's just us." Joseph said.

"Only one way to find out. Let's stand up. Heavenly Father is watching over us."

Bert and Joseph rose, rifle butts tight into their shoulders, eyes scanning through their iron rifle sights. Joseph's finger eased over the trigger guard and gently caressed the trigger, ready to squeeze off a round. A lone German soldier stood ten yards away. He looked to Joseph like an officer, though he'd never seen one before. The German had an erect bearing and wore a field cap with a visor rather than the metal German army helmet. He stood calmly, even though Bert and Joseph were aiming their rifles at him.

"Good day, Americans. My men and I wish to surrender to you. *Und*, we have some French people." The officer put his hands in the air slowly.

"Have your troops stand," Bert called out, slowly and deliberately.

"Of course," the officer replied. He came to attention and called out "*Kompanie, achtung!*" Thirty more soldiers popped to rigid attention all around them, followed by what looked to Joseph like a hundred civilian men. Joseph's heart raced as he pivoted around, not sure which direction to point his rifle. After another command, the German soldiers simply dropped their weapons and raised their hands. The civilians just stood, looking at the Germans, then the Americans, confusion clear on their faces.

"Who are these people?" Bert asked the officer, nodding toward the civilians.

"They are workers. French workers. We were to take them to the train so they work a labor camp in Germany."

"And why did you surrender?"

"Because, I see what comes. We lose more every day. Too much, *ja*? I, we, do not want to die for nothing. We wish to go home."

"Well, not today," Bert said. "Tell me, where are your front lines?"

The German looked at him in confusion and did not answer.

"You know what I'm asking, don't pretend you don't. You tell me where your lines are or we ain't going anywhere." Bert said.

The German hung his head. "Very well. You see that hill to the southwest, *ja*? Take my field glasses and look. You see soldiers clearing the trees for artillery?"

Bert took the field glasses. "Yes, I see them. That's the German line?"

"*Ja, Das ist,*" the German replied. "May we go now?"

"Let's march them all back," Joseph said. "You take the front, I'll take the rear."

All the way back to base camp, Bert kept turning around to look for Joseph at the end of the snaking line, Joseph nodding at him each time, assuring him they were all still there. Doughboys stopped in their tracks as they passed through American lines, but Joseph and Bert didn't pause until they got to their unit.

Bert stopped outside headquarters at Rembercourt and gathered the prisoners in formation. The Frenchmen were allowed to sit down.

"Joseph, run inside the HQ and tell them what we got. I'll watch these boys," Bert said.

Inside headquarters, Joseph rocked slightly on his heels while waiting for the platoon sergeant. He casually scanned the other soldiers bustling around the tent, trying and mostly failing to stay out of each other's way. A jolt ran down his back at the sight of the man sitting at the field telephone. Another Indian! The soldier glanced up and met his surprised gaze with a nod. Joseph scooted closer.

"Where are you from?" Joseph asked.

"Oklahoma. Choctaw tribe. You?"

"Utah. I'm Shoshone."

Before Joseph could say more, someone handed the Choctaw soldier a message. He scanned it and picked up the phone. After a moment, the "Hello Girls" at the switchboard in Chaumont connected him, and he spoke quickly in a language Joseph didn't recognize.

Before Joseph could puzzle out what the Choctaw solider was doing, the platoon sergeant appeared.

"What is it, Private?"

"We have a surprise for you outside." Joseph grinned and led him out of the tent.

"Dang, you two!" the platoon sergeant bellowed as he came up beside Bert and Joseph. and slapped them both on the backs. "Did you find the German lines?"

"Not directly, Sergeant," Joseph answered. "These here Dutch was all laid out in a grass field and we walked right into the middle of them. But the German lines are only four hundred meters further east, least according to that German officer. We figure bringing these boys in was the best play."

"You got that right. You boys go find a rack somewhere in town there. Move up to us with the supply train tonight."

"Thanks, Sergeant!" Joseph grinned.

The two of them half trotted away before the sergeant changed his mind. Once they were clear of the headquarters area, Joseph swatted Bert's arm to get his attention.

"Ya know what? There was an Indian in that HQ building, talking on the wireless."

"Oh, yeah?"

"Yeah. The strange thing was, he was talking Choctaw. It made no sense to me. The only person who would understand him would be another Choctaw." Joseph stopped and laughed. "So them Dutch won't understand it neither, if they intercept it."

Bert nodded. "Like a code. I'll be danged. They found a way to keep the Boche from listening in on our messages."

Joseph trotted along with Bert, smiling at the thought of all those confused Germans scratching their heads over the Choctaw language. That meant American battle plans were safe. Joseph wondered how many Americans lives the Choctaw language was saving—his own included, maybe—and how much faster the war would end because of them. Let anyone try to say Indians didn't deserve to be American citizens now!

After some searching, they found a decent shed they could sleep dry in. Bert pulled out his fake "officer quarters only" sign and hung it on the door. It always came in handy to keep sergeants from taking their quarters for themselves. After twenty-four hours of constant movement, they slept pretty well indeed.

XXXIII

September 26, 1918
Argonne Forest, France

During our march forward we had passed column after column of troops of other divisions and interminable truck trains had rumbled all night through every billeting town that we occupied. And now, hidden in the Foret de Hesse, we began to be surrounded by an ever-thickening concentration of artillery, long-range rifles, stumpy howitzers, battery after battery of smaller guns. They came in night after night, and by daybreak each new increment had melted out of sight in the woods and high roadside hedges, or had disappeared under camouflage in the open. It seemed as if all the guns in France were gathered together in the crowded forest."
—The Story of the 91st Division (1919)

Two weeks later, Bert and Joseph waited for the start of the great American Meuse-Argonne offensive. Sleepless in their dugouts on the reverse slope of a hill, Joseph and Bert listened to the all-night artillery duel preceding the million-man attack they were to take part in the following morning.

"All these men, all the big guns, them trucks and wagons. This has to work, right, Bert?"

"It sure looks like it. But we ain't the first ones to think that in this war."

"It's the waiting I hate the most. Wish we could just get on with it," Joseph said.

"We oughta get some rest, but danged if I'm not wound up like a watch spring," Bert said. "You'd think that twenty-mile forced march would do the trick, but all I got is sore feet."

"Yeah, me too. Going out first to cut the wire ain't gonna be fun."

Bert put his hand on Joseph's shoulder. "Listen. Tomorrow, if I don't make it, there's a letter to my folks in my breast pocket. I also have my pocket watch. I'd like you to have it. I don't have a brother, and, well, you're the closest thing I got."

Joseph looked Bert in the eye. "You're about the best friend a man could have. It don't matter to you we come from different people; it never did. I have a letter too, and this pouch I wear. There's not much in it, just some old arrowheads my uncle found around his place and a few stones from home. But it's been good medicine for me so far. You take it, Bert, if things don't work out when we go over the top."

Bert nodded, tears welling up. "That's enough of that stuff. It's almost dawn. Let's heat us up some bully beef. I even have a bit of chocolate to go with it—I traded our cigarette rations for it. This way we can kill Fritz on a full stomach."

As jump-off time approached, Bert and Joseph fixed their bayonets and waited, rifles in one hand, wire cutters in the other.

"Bert, you think we ought to pray?"

"I think the Lord's watching over us, but, yeah, we don't want to forget Him when we need Him the most."

Bert and Joseph knelt, still clutching their guns.

Bert bowed his head. "Heavenly Father, please bless us as we go forward today. We pray that we will be able to do our duty. That we represent our faith, our families, our nation, with dignity and honor. Father, please bless us and all the men of the 362nd. Amen."

"You think them Dutch are praying too?" Joseph whispered.

"I would be if I was them. But that don't make them right."

"I guess not," Joseph answered. "Just seems like we ask a lot of the Lord sometimes. Bunch of scared boys who just want to go home."

"We're all in His hands now," Bert said.

Joseph glanced down the line and saw officers begin to move up with their men. Almost time. He tried to calm his breathing, but it came in ever-shorter bursts, like he was already running. His hands grew slick with sweat against the cold steel.

When the massive assault kicked off, Bert and Joseph ran hard over the crest of the hill, then down toward the German lines. Stretching as far as Joseph could see, thousands of American men moved down the slope, led by wire cutting teams to breach the German barbed wire, almost every man shouting the division motto "Powder River!" at the top of their lungs. Joseph tried to yell too but could not project anything but hollow sounds. His legs pumped furiously to keep up with Bert. He felt like he was running through tall grass rather than over hard, bare ground.

Both men reached the wire at the same time. Joseph looked over the wire for a split second, shocked that the Germans were not firing at them. They furiously clipped and pulled away the wire to make lanes for their regiment to run through.

A smoke screen fired from American lines helped cover their advance, but it made it hard to see the ground. Bert fell into a nasty tangle of barbed wire and was soon stuck, wire ripping his uniform in several places.

Joseph cut him out of it. "Man, why am I always pulling you out of barbed wire?"

Bert sprang to his feet and moved to the next obstacle. "It's a great mystery of life. Like why the Germans aren't shooting at us."

"That one's easier. Our artillery flattened them," Joseph said.

They moved forward for an hour and a half before making contact with living Boche. The first lines of German trenches looked like piles of freshly turned earth.

"Look at that poor horse," Bert said. The dead horse had been lifted into the air by an artillery shell, landing in the branches of a large tree, suspended there as if it were running at full gallop. Joseph looked away.

They kept moving as the doughboys took out isolated German machine gun nests and snipers one by one, and the line of Americans advanced steadily. Bert and Joseph passed many of these positions. Small heaps of dead, bleeding German bodies marked their path.

The advance finally stopped at the town of Epinonville. Artillery rounds landed among the men. Joseph was prone on the ground, wondering which way to go.

"Those rounds are coming from behind us. Friendly fire!" Bert said.

Joseph looked up to see the regiment's commanding officer, Colonel John Henry "Gatling Gun" Parker stride into view, his six-foot-three frame erect, smoke billowing from his pipe, his cane whipping about like a willow.

Among the cries of "first aid!" from artillery wounds, Parker's voice boomed over the whole area. "You boys better get up and move. The fighting ain't done. You've got to get ahead of this artillery. You'll take that dang town over there and you'll take it right now!"

Individual men stood, then small groups, then Joseph and Bert were on their feet and moving, along with the whole regiment, despite the continuing friendly fire to rush toward the town.

German machine gunners and snipers held the town in force, and it took house-to-house fighting to clear them out.

Joseph and Bert's platoon sergeant grabbed them and yelled out orders over the crack of bullets. "You two are to scout that high ground to the east, find us a safe place to dig in for the night."

The two men rushed from house to house working their way to the edge of town, hugging walls with their shoulders and peering around corners to pick their next stop.

"Bert, let's go for that well."

They sprinted to take cover behind the well's thick stone wall, crouching to make themselves small while gasping for air. A single round ricocheted off the top of the stone, inches from Bert's head.

"Gotta move! Head for that outhouse," Bert said.

They worked their way beyond the last structures in the village, crawling through an orchard and into the hills beyond.

"Let's get up on that ridgeline, see what's beyond it," Joseph said.

"Okay. Head up that draw right there, the one with the trees. Good cover."

The draw was steep, but they were safe from fire from the town so they could make the ascent without crouching. They crawled when they neared the top of the ridgeline and stopped at the top to use their binoculars to see what was beyond it.

"That's a town. See that smoke? Chimneys," Joseph said.

"Right. Let's get back and report."

By the time they returned from the scouting mission, the town was eerily quiet. The buildings were mostly intact, but windowless and pockmarked, devoid of life.

They reported to their company CO. "Sir," Bert said, "we recommend digging in along the near side of that ridgeline there to the east. It'll give us protection from small arms and some from artillery too. We glassed over that top edge and you can see pretty much to Gesnes from there."

"Very good men. You can get back to your platoon. Dismissed."

The position turned out to be a good one. The Germans couldn't hit them with direct fire, and the fact they were largely out of the German's sight made artillery spotting difficult for the Germans as well. They fired nonetheless.

"I reckon this will be another night without sleep," Bert said. He was shivering. Joseph's teeth chattered. Mud had penetrated his uniform and undergarments so they stuck to him when he moved.

"Maybe so, but the CO said Gesnes is the third German line, the Kriemhilde line, he called it. We break that line tomorrow and them Dutch are finished here."

The Germans fired a lengthy barrage in their direction, many of them overshooting the American line. Joseph noticed a distinctive whobble whistling sound in several of the inbound shells.

"That's gas. GAS! Masks!" Bert screamed down the line.

Bert and Joseph hunkered down and waited. They couldn't see any evidence of gas, but it was pitch dark by then.

"I smell that garlic smell," Bert shouted through his mask. "Do you smell it?"

Joseph shook his head.

Every time they drifted off to sleep and leaned their heads against the sloped ground, the air seal on their mask would release, waking them with a blast of cold air against their skin. Bert didn't take his off when the "all clear" was given.

"Joseph, I still smell that garlic smell, don't take off that mask."

Joseph looked at Bert, blinked his eyes, and shook his head.

"What is it?" Bert asked.

"There, there's a two-inch tear in your carrying bag. Let me see your mask."

Bert held his head up while Joseph checked him over. He stopped when he lifted Bert's chin. "You've got a tear, right under your chin. Maybe the barbed wire cut it. We need to get you to the aid station right now."

"Oh, no. I didn't come all this way to get on some sick book," Bert said, ripping off his mask. "I'm okay. Let's get ready, cause I'm going in this attack."

Joseph nodded, knowing that arguing with Bert was useless.

The men stepped off together once again for the attack on Gesnes. This time the Germans concentrated heavy fire on them at the outset, and continued clear across the open ground. Joseph couldn't see the town now. Artillery rounds lifted sheets of dirt into the air, and acrid smoke hung in the air when the dirt fell back to Earth. Maxims chugged from the Boche lines, their staccato faint, far away at first. But the bullets they fired were not faint, ripping the air all around them, whispering death.

Shoulder to shoulder, the Americans ran across the open ground, screaming, "Powder River, let 'er buck," or whatever else came to mind, even as men dropped from being hit.

Joseph felt outside himself, as if he was watching this crazed man sprint toward his death and he could not stop him.

Joseph screamed, "Bear River!" which Bert immediately copied. They ran until they could not breathe, then walked fast, panting, until they could run again, constantly looking left and right to stay even with the other men of the platoon.

They dropped on the new line established beyond the last set of German trenches. The 362nd Infantry—Utah, Colorado, Oregon, Idaho, and Washington boys all, had broken the German Kriemhilde line. Bert and Joseph, like the rest of the men, were too exhausted to celebrate, but they looked at each other and smiled as they lay beyond the German's last line.

As they dug in for the night, Bert started to cough. Lightly at first, then more urgently.

Joseph put his hand on Bert's arm, stopping him from digging. "Sit down and rest. I'll finish the hole."

"Joseph, I think it's time I went to the aid station. My eyes are burning something awful."

Joseph nodded. He walked with Bert to the aid station, and waited with him until an ambulance could evacuate him to the rear.

"My friend, I'm sorry," Bert said. "I don't think I'll be able to see this thing through with you."

Joseph had to force himself to speak. Tears ran down his face and his chest heaved. "You just get well fast. I'll go and kill the rest of them Dutch. Here, you take my pouch." He pressed the brightly painted little parfleche bag into Bert's palm, closed his hand with his own, and squeezed it. "It's for a warrior. Powder River, Bert!" Joseph smiled weakly.

"Bear River!" Bert grinned. The ambulance closed its door and drove away.

XXXIV

October 6, 1918
Argonne Forest, France

Telegram to the Jensens from Clara:

IN A HOSPITAL NEAR THE FRONT *STOP* NOT
IN GRAVE DANGER BUT UNABLE TO WRITE *STOP*
DON'T WORRY BUT PLEASE PRAY FOR ME *STOP*

The boom of artillery drowned out the grumble of the ambulance engine. The guns were American. Clara couldn't name all the weapons used by the troops, but each country's artillery sounded different. They had their own accents. Soon, the deep voices of the American guns were met by the reply of the German ones. This massive allied offensive churned out hundreds of broken, shell-shocked men, but General Pershing seemed determined to overwhelm the Germans no matter the cost.

"Do you hear them at night?" Lily called over the noise.

"Hear what?" Clara asked.

"The guns. The screams. Do you hear them at night, when we're away from the front?"

Clara nodded, keeping her eyes on the muddy track that passed for a road in the woods. The ground sloped away from them, giving them glimpses over the forest. The fighting here was fresh. The trees hadn't yet been blown to splinters, though many had lost branches. Some had shell holes blasted through them, like little windows onto the Western Front.

Clara followed the chatter of gunfire toward the battle. The back lines had hardly even had time to set up here, but there was supposed to be a dressing station nearby. With the growing ranks of wounded soldiers, every available ambulance rode to the front, returning overcrowded from each trip. Last time, Clara and Lily had crammed two wounded men into the front seat with them. Bloody fingerprints still marked the dashboard.

"Have you heard anything new about the battalion behind enemy lines?" Clara asked.

"Not yet. They've been sending airplanes to drop food to them." Lily lowered her voice. "The battalion sent a message by pigeon. The American artillery had the wrong coordinates and were shelling the battalion. Can you imagine, killed by your own men?"

"It must be terrible," Clara said. "It happens too often. But in their circumstances . . ." The battalion had pushed through the German line as ordered, but the units on their flanks had not followed suit. Now they were cut off, and the Americans couldn't reach them through the gunfire and barbed wire. It didn't bode well for the American offensive. If they couldn't rescue one lost battalion, how were they going to break the German lines? The war might drag on until both sides ran out of people able to hold a gun.

"What's that?" Lily grasped Clara's arm.

Clara looked where she pointed. Something moved in the trees below the trail. It couldn't be an animal. There weren't any left alive.

"Drive faster!" Lily said.

Clara hesitated. "What if it's someone who needs help? We have to stop."

"If it's a German who's broken through . . ."

"Then we'll take him prisoner," Clara said, though they had little chance of doing so unless the man was badly wounded.

She slowed the ambulance to a stop. Staying low, she followed Lily out the passenger's side and watched from behind the vehicle's protective bulk.

A soldier in an American uniform stumbled out of the trees. He collapsed, screaming and clawing at his bloodstained shirt. Clara rushed forward and slid down the steep embankment beside the road.

"Watch out for barbed wire!" Lily shouted.

The ground at the bottom was muddy, but Clara slogged forward. The man writhed on the ground, crying out incoherently.

Clara gently grabbed his shoulder. "Where are you hurt?" Blood splattered his shirt and soaked the leg of his uniform, but the wound didn't look serious enough to cause such distress. Perhaps he had seen a friend die and lost his mind.

"Gas," he hissed. "Someone stole my mask."

Clara yanked her hand away and fumbled for her own mask. A smell clung to the man, something more than unwashed body and damp wool. "Mustard gas?"

The man nodded, his bloodshot eyes wide with terror.

She lifted her mask then paused. The longer one was exposed to mustard gas, the greater the damage, and it lingered in low places like this ravine. The soldier had been crawling through it. She gritted her teeth and put the mask on him, despite his half-hearted refusal.

"We have to move," Clara shouted. "Can you walk?"

He groaned and pushed himself up, then stumbled to his hands and knees in the mud. Clara couldn't leave him like this. They had to escape the silent toxin creeping through the woods.

"Lily! Get the stretcher and put on gloves! He's been gassed!" She turned back to the soldier, stopping herself from touching his contaminated uniform again. If the gas had soaked into the fabric, it could be enough to poison her too. "Don't give up. Move! You have to get to higher ground!"

He whimpered but struggled to his hands and knees, crawling through the mud to the slope. He stopped and hung his head at the sight of the steep incline. Lily was dragging the stretcher out of the ambulance. Every moment was killing the man, and possibly Clara too. She grimaced and caught his arm, tugging him up.

"Clara, no!" Lily screamed.

Clara counted the seconds of exposure.

One.

Two.

Three.

Four.

They reached the top of the embankment, and Clara dropped the man's arm, letting him sag onto the stretcher. Lily stared at Clara in horror.

Clara held her hands out, resisting the urge to cover her face. She was contaminated. How long until the horrible blisters formed on her skin? Until she was screaming in agony?

"Let's get him in the ambulance," Clara said. "I can lift the other end of the stretcher." It wouldn't be long until she couldn't do anything at all. Best to be useful while she could. They gently slid the soldier into the ambulance.

"You'll have to drive," Clara said, her voice leaden.

Lily slammed the ambulance door and hurried to the driver's side. Clara trudged to the passenger side. She opened the door with her elbow and sat, keeping her hands carefully laced in her lap. A count of four, plus touching the soldier's uniform, and whatever gas was in the air at the bottom of the hill. How much damage had she done? She stared at her fingers for a moment. Normal. They looked normal. There was no sign that she was poisoned.

Lily careened over the rough ground. Their patient cried out in protest, but Lily pressed her lips together and kept driving. When she reached the main road, she slid the ambulance into high and shot forward. Clara tasted the dust and the musty scent of the forest. For a moment, she imagined she was in Logan again, racing to the college. Two years ago. The world wasn't the same place it had been two years ago. Not only did she know it better, but it had changed as she watched, something of innocence dying in everyone around her as the machines of war pounded on.

Lily raced straight to the field hospital. When she arrived, an orderly waved her to a stop. Clara nearly fell out of the cab. The orderly reached to help her, but she jerked away from his touch.

"Mustard gas!" she said. "The man in the back was hit hard. I touched him . . ."

The man nodded in understanding, pity flashing in his eyes. Clara bit her lip and refused to cry. The orderly called over help to get the gassed man out of the ambulance. Clara felt like she was watching from a great distance.

"Will he live?"

"He might," the orderly said. "It depends on how much he inhaled. We'll know in a few days."

Clara hadn't realized she'd spoken aloud. She glanced down at her hands then held them out in a gesture almost like a prayer. The man gave her a sympathetic look.

"Come inside and we'll do what we can for you. You're not likely to die if you didn't inhale it."

"I don't know for sure."

"Did you smell it?"

Clara nodded. "But just on his clothes, I think. When . . . when will I know?"

"Soon," the man said. "We'll know everything . . ."

"In a few days," Clara said quietly. She looked down at her hands again. Red spots were forming on her fingers.

The blisters remained confined to Clara's hands and arms, but the pain burned through her nerves. It was all she could do not to scream. Many of those around her, more badly injured, knew no restraint, and shrieked through the night. The gas survivors each lay in their own individual tents inside the hospital. Their nurses couldn't touch them. They could only do small things to relieve their suffering while they waited to see if they would live or die.

When one of the doctors poked a head in to check on Clara's progress, she asked about the man she'd brought in.

"Your mask probably saved him. He's blind, but I think he'll live. At the moment, he doesn't want to, but that may change once he adjusts."

Clara blinked back tears.

"Do you regret it?" the doctor asked.

She looked up quickly. "No, Sir. I do not."

He regarded her for a moment then gave her nod. There seemed to be a weight of approval behind the small gesture.

Clara laid back and stared at the ceiling. She would have scars. Her hands would recover, but she would carry the marks of her decision for the rest of her life. She could not regret it. For once, she hadn't been acting thoughtlessly. It wasn't that she'd considered her options or the consequences before she darted out to save the man, but she hadn't done it out of selfish recklessness. When she started driving the ambulance, she'd already made her decision to do whatever she could to save the boys in uniform. She had done her bit.

She looked again at the open sores on her arms. Her mother would be horrified. Many of the people back home would be. But Reed? Reed would understand.

When a nurse came to check on her, Clara pressed for news of anything outside the white walls of her sheet tent.

"I'm not used to being out of the action," Clara said with a sheepish grin. "And, I have friends out there. I want to know what's happening."

The nurse glanced around and lowered her voice to a gossipy whisper. "There's a new sickness going through the troops."

"I've heard about the Spanish influenza." The flu had slowed down boys on both sides of the trenches.

"If this is the flu, it's the worst one anyone's seen. Some people say it's the Black Plague. It starts with fevers and aches, and it can turn into pneumonia, but it makes people cough up blood, and bleed from their nose and even their ears. They turn so blue from lack of oxygen we can't tell if they're Negro or white."

Clara stared in disbelief. "How have I not heard of this?"

"They're trying to keep it quiet. They don't want to affect morale. It's spreading, though, here and on the home front."

"That's terrible." Clara was still skeptical, but she didn't want to drive away the chatty nurse. "What else have you heard?"

The nurse looked thoughtful, then her face brightened. "You heard about the lost battalion?"

Clara nodded.

"They rescued them—the ones that survived, anyway—as part of a big push. Most of the men in the battalion were injured, and they were all starving. The food the airplanes dropped never got to them. But they held off the Germans in spite of it, and now we have a victory."

Clara sank back into her cot. They'd rescued their lost men, brought them back into the fold. It wasn't much, but it was a step forward, and that was how this war was fought, and how it would have to be won: Blood and agony and countless lives sacrificed for a few precious yards at a time.

XXXV

October 1918
Logan, Utah

Influenza Epidemic

Alarming reports are reaching us of a new type of influenza affecting our troops. The sudden and mysterious appearance of this disease leads us to wonder if it was introduced by German spies to hamper our war efforts, which it will certainly do if it continues to spread. Citizens can avoid falling victim by getting plenty of fresh air and sunshine, and staying in good physical condition. Don't let illness slow the war work!
—The Logan Republican

Trudi watched out the window of the home economics building as the boys practiced drills on the quad—not just the regular soldiers in the training detachment, but also the Student Army Training Corps, which gave more boys the chance to get practical training for military jobs like blacksmithing and engineering while staying in college. The women were now confined to one building to make room for all the soldiers.

At least the Red Cross classes continued. The army had already drained away so many doctors and nurses, and they were desperate for more. Soon, Trudi would be able to go overseas as a nurse. Newspapers reported that some of the enemy states had made overtures toward peace, but President Wilson had firmly rejected these. An odd move for a man who claimed he did not want war, but battle frenzy seemed to take hold of everyone. Trudi clung to a selfish hope that it would last a bit longer too. Like the boys drilling below, she needed the chance to prove herself before it ended.

"Did you go to general conference last weekend?" one of the other girls asked.

Trudi pulled away from the window. "No, I had too much work to do." She still felt guilty about the decision. She'd sent her siblings on without her. Her priorities might not be what they should.

"They say Spanish influenza broke out in Salt Lake City, at Fort Douglas."

"It's here?" Trudi asked, goose bumps prickling her arms. She'd heard rumors about Philadelphia and New York City. The cities shut down. The mass graves.

"The newspaper reported that it was easily contained. The victims have already been quarantined. Nothing to be alarmed about."

Trudi nodded, but she had trouble focusing for the rest of the day, an uneasiness that she couldn't shake settling heavily over her shoulders. People from all over Utah had gathered in Salt Lake City while the flu lurked nearby. But the newspapers said they were safe. Surely there would be some warning if the disease had spread.

She was home in time to help her mother set the table, and they all sat down for supper. During the prayer, Hans coughed. Each rough bark made Trudi jump, and she watched him carefully during dinner. He sniffled occasionally, but ate with a hearty appetite. Trudi relaxed. Everyone had colds this time of year. It was nothing to worry about.

Karl stood suddenly.

"Karl?" their mother asked, her voice sharp with concern.

He looked over everyone at the table, his face pale, then collapsed to the floor.

Trudi shoved her chair back and ran to her brother's side. "He has a fever. Help me move him!"

Her father and Hans lifted Karl and carried him to the boys' room.

"Everyone else stay out," Trudi ordered. "But don't leave the house. We need to be quarantined."

"Trudi? What is it?" her father asked.

"Influenza," Trudi whispered.

Trudi hardly left Karl's side for the next week. Her younger brothers and sisters developed coughs and mild fevers, but none of them needed more than a day or two in bed. Trudi didn't get sick. She prayed in gratitude for the influenza she had caught in the spring, since it let her tend to Karl while her mother and father cared for the younger children. She only took occasional breaks to grab a nap while one of her parents took a turn watching. Her father called for the doctor, but his wife told them he was too sick to get out of bed. The disease was everywhere.

Trudi read newspaper reports about the flu until they came apart at the creases. Those who collapsed suddenly were in the most danger. Trudi kept the light burning next to Karl, checking the color on his fingers and lips frequently. His breathing was labored, and he coughed up blood, but the dreaded blue—signs that his lungs were failing—still hadn't materialized. He opened his eyes occasionally, but did not focus on anything in the room.

Trudi changed his sheets often, instructing her mother to burn the ones stained by blood. She kept the window open so clean air could whisk the infection out of the room. The days and nights blurred together into a nightmare of fevers and racking coughs.

"Trudi?"

She started from a shallow sleep, hardly recognizing the weak, scratchy voice.

"Karl? Are you awake? Do you understand me?"

"*Ja*. I'm so thirsty."

Hands shaking from excitement and exhaustion, Trudi helped him drink.

"What happened?" he asked.

"Influenza. You've been very ill."

"The others?"

"They're recovering. You were the worst."

He nodded and closed his eyes. Trudi tiptoed downstairs to tell her parents. Her mother burst into tears.

"I will watch him now. You rest."

Trudi nodded and went into her room, falling into a deep, blissful sleep. She awoke the next day and hurried to check on Karl. He was still pale, but sitting up in bed to sip broth.

"That's good," Trudi said. "Don't overtax your strength, but sit up and move around as much as possible. Get fresh air, but keep yourself isolated from anything that might make you sick again."

"Yes, Fraulein Doctor," Karl said with a weak smile. "I'm very glad you took those Red Cross classes."

"So am I!" Trudi said. "In fact, I think I should see who else needs my help."

"You'll have no shortage of people asking for it." Her father showed her the paper. The flu had crippled Cache Valley. The headlines promised it was contained, but announced that all public gatherings had been shut down, and anyone going out was required to wear masks. There were several funerals mentioned in the local news. The college had also been infected. All those boys in close quarters.

"I need to go," Trudi said. "They'll want every pair of hands they can get."

Her father nodded. "We'll be all right here."

Trudi made a mask out of gauze and hurried outside. The streets were quiet. Eerie. Maybe the newspapers were overly optimistic about the short duration of the sickness.

She found the way to campus blocked by military guards, also wearing masks.

"I'm here to help," Trudi said. "I'm training with the Red Cross as a nurse."

One of the men went for a doctor, who inspected Trudi, asked her questions about her earlier sickness, and finally admitted her. They had turned one wing of the main building into an infirmary. Hundreds of young men lay on cots, overworked nurses hurrying between them.

"I'm glad you're here," the doctor said. "So many nurses have already left the country, and most of the ones who stayed are caring for their families. We have the girls from the home economics department cooking for us, but we need more people to care for the sick men."

He gave her some instructions, all of which matched what she already knew, and left her to wash up, put on a nurse's uniform, and get to work.

Most of the boys didn't seem as ill as she had feared—few were as bad as Karl had been, or like what the newspapers on the East Coast had described. Perhaps the virus was burning itself out as it spread. Still, sick, frightened boys and exhausted doctors and nurses crammed the rooms of the main building. Trudi took temperatures, changed sheets, and wiped sweat and vomit from young men's faces.

She was surprised to see Alonzo helping one of the doctors move cots out into the hallway, making room for more sick soldiers.

"Alonzo!" she called when he took a break. "What are you doing here?"

"They needed able-bodied men to help. Since there aren't many left on campus, I offered."

"Oh. That was good of you. Have you had the flu too, then?"

"No, but I suppose I'll either get it or I won't. I might as well be doing something useful."

He nodded farewell and carried off an empty stretcher. She admired his easy, confident stride until the crowd swallowed him. How had she thought he was selfish? He didn't want to fight, yet he was risking himself to help the soldiers who made his life difficult.

Some of the sick recovered enough to be released, but more kept coming in to take their places. Trudi greeted a young man who slumped down on his cot.

"What's your name?" she asked.

"Private White, Miss."

"I'm Miss Kessler."

He nodded. "I think we met at a dance last month. I suppose I won't be making a good impression on you today."

"You just focus on getting better. That will impress me." She looked at his color and his temperature, both good. "You'll be dancing again in no time."

Alonzo and another man carried a stretcher into the room, shifting the sick soldier onto one of the cots they'd just set up.

"He collapsed suddenly," Alonzo told Trudi and the doctor.

The young man had blood running from his nose. His lips were already a dark blue.

The doctor's face took on a resigned look. "Make him as comfortable as you can," he said to Trudi with a meaningful look.

She nodded. They would do what they could, but there would likely be a mother or sweetheart somewhere getting a telegram soon. Would they blame the war for his death? He had given his life trying to serve his country, even if he never left Utah.

She checked on the young man as often as she could. The blue slowly spread over his skin, and blood ran from his ears. He died later that afternoon. He'd never woken.

Alonzo returned with the stretcher to help carry the body to the morgue. He shifted the sheet-wrapped body, but a hacking cough doubled him over.

"Alonzo?" Trudi asked.

He glanced up. He was flushed, and sweat beaded his forehead.

"Good heavens, you're sick!" Trudi touched his forehead. It was burning hot. "Put that stretcher down." She called over to one of the other nurses. "I need a cot!"

Alonzo looked like he wanted to protest, but he was ushered away by the other nurse before he had the chance. Trudi moved to follow, but the doctor called her. She had duties.

She watched Alonzo's cot throughout the night. She couldn't get close enough to see how he was doing. If he was bleeding. If he was turning blue. What would she tell Clara? Her heart twisted. She was worried about Clara, but it was herself she was terrified for. Alonzo was always there. He always had been. She'd come to rely on him. She couldn't imagine him not being there. She hadn't realized it until she thought of him being gone.

"Go check on him," one of the other nurses whispered to her. "I'll switch spots with you for a while."

"What?" Trudi asked.

"You're going to hurt your neck, always straining to watch him. You might as well go see how he's doing . . . in case."

Trudi flushed to know she'd been so obvious, but she hurried to Alonzo's side. His temperature was very high, and his lips had a blue tint. Trudi dropped by his bed and took his hand. He didn't respond, all awareness lost in the fever.

"Can you hear me, Alonzo? I'm here. You have to get better. Clara will be furious if you don't." She squeezed his hand. "And, I think my heart will break. Don't leave us. We need you."

His eyes moved beneath their lids, but he didn't show any other response, only trembled from the fever.

Trudi leaned close to his ear. "Please."

She reluctantly placed his hand back on his chest and went to the other nurse. "Let me know if there's a change . . . either way."

The nurse nodded and gave her a sympathetic pat on the arm.

Trudi finished her shift and looked for reasons to linger.

"You need to get some rest," the doctor told her.

"Yes, Sir, but—"

"That's an order," the doctor said gently.

Trudi nodded and trudged away, finding a place to sleep in a classroom with the other off-duty nurses.

She awoke to grab a quick bite to eat, then hurried back to the makeshift infirmary. Another young man lay in Alonzo's cot. The world dropped out from under Trudi. She grabbed the doorframe for support.

"No!" She choked back a sob. "Nurse! What happened to the man in that cot? Alonzo Jensen."

"I don't know. I just got here."

Trudi scurried through the aisles of cots, scanning each face. Had they moved him? Had he died? Who would know? She spotted the doctor. Deep circles hung under his eyes.

"Sir, did anyone die this morning?"

"This morning? No, thank heavens."

Trudi almost sagged against him in relief. "My friend Alonzo Jensen was in here. I can't find him."

"I had him moved to the recovery area. We're keeping this section for the most serious cases." He glanced at his watch. "You have a few minutes before you're needed back here."

"Thank you!" Trudi rushed in the direction he indicated.

There was Alonzo, his head propped up with pillows. His bloodshot eyes widened when he saw Trudi. She dropped down beside his cot and threw her arms around him.

"I'm so glad to see you recovering. When I found someone else in your cot . . . oh, Alonzo, I couldn't bear it."

He tilted her face up to look into his eyes. "Trudi?"

Her face burned when she realized everyone in the ward had gone very quiet to watch their little drama.

"I couldn't lose you," she whispered.

"I'm not going anywhere," he whispered back then cleared his throat. "Maybe we should talk about this later?"

She laughed and nodded, and a few of the nearby men chuckled or whistled as she hurried back out to care for the soldiers.

XXXVI

Dear Uncle,

I'm writing this sitting in a hole I just dug in a turnip field so please forgive my shaky writing. At least it was easy digging. The soil is good here, but it amazes me they got a crop in since there has been fighting here for four years now. I have all the turnips I could ever eat but that ain't saying much. I've seen some war, but this place tops it all. Miles and miles of turned earth and shell holes. Bits of uniforms sticking out of the ground, pieces of equipment blowed to bits scattered like kindling. Tanks crushed flat by artillery. The towns we seen, well, they are just gone, just piles and piles of bricks, along with some pieces of walls sticking up. You remember that old cabin we found up in the Wellsvilles, with just the hearth and some foundation stones left? Whole dang towns here look like that. They fought three big battles near here at Ypres. No, I don't know how to say it, Uncle. Maybe like EERPS? I'd ask some of the local people but I ain't seen many. They're hiding out in cellars and such. Not a bad idea given what's coming in the morning.

Uncle, my friend Bert, I told you about him before. Well, he got gassed in our last fight so he's in the hospital. I feel like I lost my right arm. I turn to look for him every time we set off on a march. I sure do miss him, and I reckon I will sorely miss him tomorrow when we step off for this fight. Please pray he comes through okay and that he gets home safe. A little prayer for yours truly would be appreciated as well.

Took an Iron Cross off a dead German officer back at Gesnes. I took it as counting coup. I don't know for sure I killed him, 'cause

me and Bert both shot at him, but I figure if my brother warrior
killed him, it's pretty much the same deal.
Tell me in your next letter how that mare is doing. Say hello to
everyone and send my love.

Your Nephew,
Joseph

Joseph returned to the line after escorting Bert to the aid station, hoping he could visit him in a few days.

He sought out his platoon sergeant two days later. "Say, Sergeant, I was wondering if I could get a pass to visit Bert, er, Private Lyman at the field hospital."

The sergeant sighed and tightened his lips. "Sorry, private. We only have 75 of the original 200 men in the company left. CO ain't gonna sign any passes."

The next morning they marched to Cheppy Woods to rest. The tired, sick men flopped wherever they were when a halt was called. The ones with dysentery curled up on the ground, holding their stomachs and groaning that they would prefer bullet wounds.

Joseph polished off his meal, his first "hot" in days, then looked around, still hungry. He watched another private staring at his full plate. "Ya gonna eat that or what? It's getting cold."

The other private looked squeamish and pale. He handed Joseph his plate. "Nah, you take it, Sorrell. I don't have any appetite. When I do eat . . ." He nodded toward the field sanitation trench.

After only twenty-four hours rest, the men of the 362nd were assigned to the 1st Infantry Division, then a few days later, the 32nd, each assignment accompanied by long marches and bad food.

Finally, Joseph and the rest of the men were put aboard a train for a thirty-six hour ride to Belgium, to help the French face the Germans in Flanders.

The preparatory artillery began at "zero hour," 0530. Fired by French guns, it was a creeping barrage. As Joseph moved forward, he could see its path marked by lines of geysers of soft dirt and turnips. *It's raining turnips!*

This fighting was different. The men fought from hedge to hedge, and then in small villages from house to house. Joseph and his platoon mates soon learned how to attack hedgerows by suppressing the defenders with covering fire while part of the team maneuvered to the rear of the hedgerow to take the Germans from behind.

In the villages, they had to dodge snipers and machine gunners while they fought room to room with bayonets and grenades. Joseph found two dead German officers in one upstairs bedroom.

"Sergeant," Joseph called out, "Come see this."

"What do you make of this, Sergeant?" Joseph asked.

"Looks to me like they were killed by their own men," the sergeant said.

"Why would they do that?"

"Beats me, private. But it tells me the Boche are about done. Let's move on."

XXXVII

November 11, 1918
Meuse-Argonne, France

"The eleventh hour of the eleventh day of the eleventh month . . ."

Reed had returned to the 4th Brigade at the end of October, just in time to participate in the immense Meuse-Argonne Offensive. He didn't recognize any of the men in his unit. Everyone he knew had been wounded or killed and replaced by fresh recruits. Bert had been writing to him, and he guessed from the little Bert was able to say that his friend was somewhere nearby. It was strange to think they were fighting together in a way. Clara wasn't far behind the lines either, but he never saw either of them.

On November 1st, the brigade advanced thirty kilometers under the cover of heavy artillery fire. The Marines took the heights beyond the Meuse River. Reed stood before his men again and again, as he had at Belleau Wood, but he avoided looking at their faces. They always looked hopeful when he did, as if he could protect them, get them through this. He knew he could do no such thing.

As they awaited further orders, Reed crouched in the middle of a ring of newly arrived officers, pointing out terrain features and likely tactics they would use to move the company forward when it came time to advance on the Rhine. He had built a scale model "sand table" of the terrain in the dirt.

"The important thing is be able to see this terrain in your head in three dimensions, so that when you cross it, you know where danger areas are, as well as avenues of approach into enemy ground that shield you from direct fire."

Reed stopped and stood up as Captain Hamilton approached. Hamilton practically skipped over to them with a huge grin on his face.

"Gentlemen. It's over. The armistice is signed. As of 1100 hours this morning, we are at a cease fire."

"Class dismissed!" Reed yelled, and all the men clapped each other on the backs and ran around giddy with delight.

"Go tell your men, platoon leaders," Hamilton said, laughing.

There was no need, though. It spread like wildfire among the men. "Hip hip hooray" and other yells sounded like echoes all over the line. In the distance, though, all was silent. No more guns. No more artillery. Peace.

Reed was quiet.

"What's on your mind there, Bad Penny?" Hamilton asked.

"Don't know, Sir. To tell you the truth, I didn't expect to survive this, so I don't know what happens next."

"In the short term, I expect we'll still march to the Rhine, only the Boche won't be trying to kill us. Then, occupation duty I suppose."

"Yes, Sir. But I was talking about after that," Reed said.

"After that? You've got a girl you love, a place to go home to, and a life to build. That's as good as it gets, Bad Penny."

November 11, 1918
A field hospital behind the Meuse-Argonne lines

Dearest Reed,

I have found Bert in the hospital. He is slowly recovering from the immediate effects of the gas, but he still struggles to breathe. The doctors are afraid that pneumonia has set in. I am doing what I can for him. It is not much. He is in God's hands, and though I still know that God is over all, it is hard to feel it in this place.

My hands have healed, but the hospital is in such desperate need of nurses, even without training, that I stayed to help. The flu is moving through the troops, as you must know, and through the hospitals too. It is a scene out of hell and makes me wonder if this is how the world is to end. We have all four horsemen of the apocalypse now: War, Famine, Pestilence, and, of course, Death.

It surrounds me, the stink of it, the terrible sounds. I feel our entire generation must be dying here, in spirit if not in body. What is to become of us all?

I am sorry to write you such depressing letters, but I know you'll understand. Indeed, I think you're the only person who will. How can we ever tell the people at home what we have seen? They will not want to know, and we will not want to speak of it.

Yours truly,
Clara

Clara moved between the beds of the wounded men in the predawn light, offering water and words of reassurance. She avoided the area reserved for flu victims. Nurses, draped in masks and robes until they looked like ghosts, moved silently through the white sheets of the quarantine tents.

The bodies of victims piled up outside. Clara avoided looking at them, but they were always there, on the edge of her awareness. The illness killed more than the war now, on both sides of the trenches. Yet President Wilson kept sending more boys. Boys already infected with influenza, or who caught it on the ship. They came here only to die and be heaped in mass graves. It was a game of percentages. The government was so determined to refill the failing lines that they did not care if one in ten were cast aside like the blood-soaked linens of the influenza victims. It sickened Clara as much as any of the carnage she had seen on the battlefield.

She paused by Bert's cot. He was still sleeping, though his forehead creased deeply at some fitful dream. It didn't help that, on waking, the nightmares continued, especially in this place. Through her mask, Clara caught the stench of dying flesh and sick, sour bodies.

One of the men in the ward had lost most of his face to shrapnel. Even sleeping he wore a painted tin mask. It gave him something close to the appearance of a whole man when he was awake—people might stare, but they would not recoil in horror at the sight of one who appeared to be a walking corpse. In sleep, however, it gave his face the strange stillness of death, and every time Clara passed, she bent to be sure he was still breathing.

A young man stirred as Clara walked by and stretched out a hand for her. She stopped and knelt by him. The bandage around his chest did not stop the blood and pus seeping into his sheet. His face was pale and sweaty, waxy with approaching death. His eyes were frightened. Clara took his hand.

"Miss, will you help me?" he asked in a raspy voice.

"Of course. What do you need?"

"I need to write a letter. Or two. Can I write two?"

"Yes, I'll write as many letters as you need. Just a moment."

Clara found pen and paper and hurried back to the young man. His eyes were closed, and his breathing shallow.

"Sir?"

He opened his eyes blearily.

"What's your name?" she asked.

"Ira Jensen," he whispered.

Clara gave a start at hearing her own last name. She said a silent prayer of thanks once again that Alonzo was safe at home. "Ira, who do you need to write to?"

"My mother. And Bella. She's my . . . I was going to marry her. I would have married her." He squeezed his eyes shut, and Clara could only guess at the vision of shattered happiness floating through his mind.

"We'll write to both of them. What are their names and addresses?"

She wrote as he dictated in his weak voice. Kansas. They were farm people too, then. Not so different from the Jensens of Utah.

"What do you want me to say?" Clara asked softly.

Tears slid down his cheek. "I don't know. I can't tell them everything. I don't want to. I just . . . I just want them to know that I love them. And I want Bella to know . . ." his chin quivered and the tears flowed more freely. "We had so many dreams," he said in a choked voice. "I want her to be happy. Can you help me find a way to say goodbye? I'm scared, and I don't know how to say it."

Clara's eyes blurred with tears. "Ira, I've never been good at goodbyes, but we'll figure it out together."

He nodded, and Clara chose careful, loving words to tell the grieving mother and sweetheart that Ira thought of them at the last.

My dearest Bella,

When this letter reaches you, I will have been called home to God. My only regret is that I'll never hold you again. I am proud to have sacrificed like so many others so that the world could know that might does not make right. Please find a way to be happy again. Keep living for me, and for yourself.

Clara hesitated, then added one more comforting lie.

Don't fear for me. I did not suffer.

Ira nodded as she read the words back to him.

"Do you need anything else?"

"I don't suppose . . . would you be able to find out about my horse?"

"Your horse?"

"I was in the cavalry," he said. "After I was shot . . . I probably don't want to know. They're man's best friend, you know. Duke carried me through everything, just because I asked him to. It couldn't have made any sense to him. He trusted me. I guess I'll see him again soon." He shivered and looked at Clara, his eyes full of pain and fear. "Will you stay with me? I'm afraid. I don't want to be alone."

Clara blinked away warm tears that slid down her cheeks to soak her mask. She took his hand again. "I'll stay as long as you need me. You won't have to be alone."

"It won't be long," he whispered.

Those were his last words. He closed his eyes, and his breathing grew more labored and shallow, his face an unearthly gray. The lines in his forehead eased as he slipped from consciousness, though his grip on Clara's hand didn't slacken until he exhaled his last raspy breath. Clara waited a long moment to see if he would draw another, then slipped her hand free and sobbed over the dead boy's chest. An orderly came by and gently pulled Clara back.

"What are you doing?" she asked.

"We need the bed," the man mumbled, not meeting her eyes.

Clara watched mutely as they took Ira to rest until Judgment Day in soil far from Kansas. She hurried away before she had to see the new occupant of the bed. Ira's letters were still clutched in her hand, so she wandered over to post them. While she was in the office, a wild cheer went up outside. She and the other nurses hurried out.

"What is it?" the nurse next to her shouted.

"They signed an armistice!" someone called. "The war is over!"

The shouting and cheering rolled around Clara in waves, but she felt numb, apart from the happy crowd. Armistice. The war was over. No winner. No loser. Just an admission that it was time to quit. But they were quitting too late. Too late for Ira Jensen and his Bella in Kansas.

Clara drifted back inside and found Bert's bed. She laid her fingers on his forehead. Hot.

He stirred at her touch. "What's that racket?"

"The war is over."

He shifted. Turned to see her better. "Did we win?"

"They signed an armistice. I think that means . . ."

"No one wins." He laughed a little, but it came out as a wheeze, and he coughed.

Clara grasped his hand. His fingertips had a bluish cast.

"We just need to get you better, and you can go home," she said quietly.

He shook his head. "Not going home."

"Oh, Bert," Clara burst out. "Don't give up. Please don't."

"Can't fight God's will."

"Nothing about this is God's will! He couldn't possibly want all this."

"Don't think He did." Bert closed his eyes for a moment. "He let us choose."

"You didn't have a choice. You were drafted. Most of these men were drafted. Our leaders dragged us into this war, and it only happened because the other governments—the Germans!—were proud and greedy."

"We chose how we would fight. What kind of men we would be." He squeezed her hand. "Don't hate, Clara."

She pressed her lips together. "I can't help it, Bert." She lowered her voice. "I'm angry at God too. I thought He watched over people who tried to do the right thing, but I just feel powerless—helpless—when I see all the injustices around us. It's so wasteful. So empty and pointless."

Bert coughed. "My mother said, 'There's not a reason for everything, but God can make reason out of anything.'" He drew breath to say more, but his face contorted in pain.

"Shh," Clara said. They were both quiet for a moment, surrounded by distant sounds of celebration and Bert's wheezing.

Clara breathed along with Bert, as if she could somehow lend strength to his failing lungs. She would make her peace with God, but how could she not hate? She hated the war. She hated the smell of blood and rotting skin. She hated watching the light die in men's eyes.

"You should rest," she whispered around the lump in her throat.

"Soon enough," he whispered. He fumbled for Joseph's parfleche bag, still resting on his chest. "Bury me with this, if I don't make it. A little piece of Utah. A reminder of a friend."

"Of course," Clara said. "But please keep fighting."

"The war is over." He smiled a little. His lips were blue. "Maybe, though . . ."

"Yes?" Clara asked.

"A priesthood blessing."

Clara glanced around the hospital. All the time she'd been in France, she hadn't met one other Mormon. "I don't like to leave you."

"I'll hang on."

He closed his eyes, his chest rising in rattling breaths. Clara hurried away. How was she supposed to find a man who held the priesthood in all this?

Heavenly Father, please . . .

She stepped outside. Nurses, doctors, and orderlies who weren't on duty gathered in small groups to celebrate.

"Is anyone here LDS?" Clara asked again and again. She received only blank stares.

"Are any of you Mormon?" she tried.

"Nah, my name's Jerry." An orderly pointed. "I think Norman went that way."

She rolled her eyes and marched up to another group of doctors. They all had cigarettes and glasses of wine, except one.

Clara paused. Was it possible? She approached the man.

"Excuse me, Sir?" she asked.

He glanced at her nurse's uniform and gave her an annoyed look. "I went off duty an hour ago."

Clara shrank back. Just because he didn't smoke or drink, it didn't mean he was Mormon. But she'd come this far. "I was wondering if you happened to be LDS."

"I am," he said, with a wary glance at the other doctors.

"There's a young soldier in the hospital from Logan, Utah. He would like a priesthood blessing."

A couple of the other men looked skeptical and shook their heads.

The doctor's expression softened. "Of course."

As they walked together, he cleared his throat. "I'm sorry for snapping at you. I guess, out here, I've become used to being a doctor first and a priesthood holder second, but that's not how it's meant to be."

"I think all of our nerves are worn thin," Clara said.

They reached Bert's bed. The doctor looked grave as he touched Bert's shoulder, rousing him.

"I'm Tom Moulton, from Salt Lake City. This young lady said you wanted a blessing?"

"Yes, Sir. Albert Christian Lyman."

Tom Moulton put his hands on Bert's head.

"What are they doing?" asked a dark-haired nurse who came up behind Clara.

"It's . . . a blessing, kind of a special prayer for healing."

"Huh," the nurse said, folding her arms and watching with narrow eyes.

Dr. Moulton bowed his head and called upon the name of God.

Clara watched Bert's face, uncertain what to hope for. She believed in miracles, in theory, but she had never seen the type she read about in the scriptures or pioneer stories. She thought about Trudi, who had trained to be a nurse on the front and ended up helping soldiers in Utah. And Reed, whose injury kept him out of the worst of the fighting, maybe kept him alive. Perhaps God worked in quieter ways. But what about Bert? He had always been everyone's friend. She focused on the words of the blessing.

"Albert, you are a beloved son of God and have served Him well during your sojourn on earth. He is pleased with the life you have lived and the love you have shown to others. You have touched the lives of many, and your positive influence and example will be your legacy on the earth to future generations."

When he said amen, the nurse wiped her eyes. "That was real nice," she said quietly. "We could use more of that around here."

Clara nodded, blinking away tears. A peaceful feeling came over her, and with it, the knowledge that Bert wouldn't be going home.

November 11, 1918
Logan, Utah

The influenza ran its course through the A.C., and slowly they reached the balance, where more men were released than admitted, and the cots began to empty. Only six young men had died. Few compared to other places, but there would be six mothers in mourning. Six tables with an empty chair at every meal.

The newspapers announced the armistice in November. Trudi cheered with the rest of them, then went right back to work.

Private White looked down when she told him the news.

"You're sorry?" she asked.

"I never got to prove myself. I spent the war in a hospital."

"At least you won that fight," she said.

"And now I have to go home. I wanted to learn more, finish my education. I'm not sure I'll get another chance, and it would have made such a difference."

Trudi nodded. So many boys had been willing to sacrifice for the opportunity to advance their studies, knowing it could change everything for themselves and their families. Her parents had worked hard to make sure their children got an education. It was part of the promise of America.

"You'll find a way," she said. "You've proved you're a fighter. A survivor."

He smiled uncertainly, a boy still in his own eyes.

Alonzo was slowly recovering his strength, but he still leaned on Trudi's arm as he took his daily walk in the fresh November afternoons.

"It's strange that I've known you for so long, but I feel like I never really *knew* you until recently," Trudi said.

He smiled. "I always knew you."

"You're obviously much wiser than I," she said with a teasing grin. "It seems like you used to be more outgoing, though. I remember playing when we were younger, and then you sort of closed off. It was about the time—"

"Of the football game where I hurt George Nielsen."

"I'd nearly forgotten that. You broke his collarbone. But it was an accident."

"No, it wasn't." Alonzo slowed his pace. "I lost my temper. I hurt him on purpose. It scared me. It was like something my father would do, and I swore I would never, ever hurt anyone again."

Trudi squeezed his hand. Even dead, Clara and Alonzo's father cast a long shadow over their lives.

"That's why you didn't want to go to war."

"It's part of it. I don't think the government has the right to force people to fight. What if they're like me, and it brings out something dark in them? Even our pacifist president got bloodthirsty after he joined the war. It's wrong to demand that of people."

"I used to think we just had to obey," Trudi said. "That was our duty. But I can see now it's not that simple."

"Are you planning to go into politics and fix all our problems?"

She smiled and shook her head. "No, I've lost all such grand notions. I think I want to teach. Education will fix more problems than politicians—help overcome the ignorance that leads to prejudice and inequality."

"I think that's a good plan." He hesitated. "Do you think you could teach and still be a farmer's wife?"

She looked up quickly, and he gave her a shy smile. She grinned. "I think if the opportunity presented itself, I could find a way to do both."

Alonzo drew her closer and placed a gentle kiss on her forehead. She closed her eyes with a happy sigh. He kissed her lips, warm and lingering, then pulled her into his chest. She sank into him, trying to hold onto the perfect moment. It couldn't last, though. She raised her head.

"What's wrong?" Alonzo asked. "If I shouldn't have kissed you—"

"It's not that. You should have. I mean, you should again." She bit her tongue to keep from saying anything else silly, but Alonzo's mouth twitched with a smile. Trudi met his eyes. "It's just . . . I'm worried about the future, for all of us. Like, my brother, Karl. He's not ill anymore, but he doesn't seem quite himself."

Alonzo drew her arm through his and continued their walk. "I've seen it in some of the men here too. They've lost their vibrancy.

"I asked the doctor about it. He said the illness may have affected Karl's mind. He doesn't know if he'll ever be quite the same."

Alonzo looked down at her sadly and pulled her into another embrace. She leaned against his chest, grateful for his strong arms and steady heartbeat.

"Did you hear that Joseph F. Smith is dying?" she asked into his shirt.

"What?"

"It's pneumonia. At least he got to see the end of the war. They say there's not going to be a public funeral. Too much risk of influenza. He was the last prophet to have met Joseph Smith. It's like we've lost a link to the past." She hesitated. "Nothing's ever going to be the same, is it?"

In answer, he just held her tighter, and she tried to lose her fears in the warmth of his comfort.

November 11, 1918
The Western Front

Joseph and the 362nd pushed with the rest of the 91st Division more than 60 kilometers northwest, all the way to the Schedlt River. They only stopped there because the Germans had destroyed all the bridges across.

The division was planning an assault across the Schedlt using bridges built by the engineers when word of the armistice came. The men took in the news quietly, stoically, as they took almost everything in those days of war.

Their fast march had outpaced the mail by several days. A few days after the peace, the mail clerk handed Joseph a letter and he sat right down, eager to read it.

Dear Joseph,

I am so sorry to tell you in this way, but I feel I must let you know that our friend Bert passed this morning. I was with him to the end and I hope I was of some comfort to him. We spoke of our many fond memories of home, at the college, and of course laughed at my racetrack antics. He spoke of you with the utmost respect, Joseph, as one speaks of a dear brother and friend. He asked me to tell you that he was honored to serve with you—a true Shoshone warrior. He also entrusted me with his pocket watch, and I promised to give it to you in person. I pray that is soon—when we are both home together.

Bert is buried in the new American Cemetery at Romagne-Sous-Montfaucon. He sensed the end was near and he asked to be buried with the talisman you gave him. I saw to it personally. He considered wearing the pouch you gave him a great honor, better than any medal.

I have written Bert's family to express my sympathy, though of course they have been notified by official means as well. I know they will take his loss hard, as will we all. We have all sacrificed. We have all lost. I have not met anyone who chose to fight in this cause whom I admire more than you, Joseph, nor anyone who has sacrificed more. May Heavenly Father keep you safe, and may the full blessings of liberty and freedom follow you the rest of your days.

God Bless You,
Clara Jensen

Joseph pulled his knees to his chest and tucked his head down, and he sobbed. Hard, painful, racking sobs. All the suffering and death he had seen, all the carnage and destruction, not even the horrors inflicted on beloved horses, had made him shed a tear. He had become numb to it all. But Bert . . . Bert was not of this place, he was of home, his world before all of this. Bert had broken through into the in-between place where Joseph dwelled and befriended him out of choice, out of kindness, not because of circumstance or convenience. Joseph had never had a friend like Bert, and he knew in his heart he never would again.

XXXVIII

December 1918
New York City

Dear Mother,

I am coming home. I may reach you before this letter does. There is still much work in France among the soldiers and refugees, but the influenza outbreak appears to be weakening, so more nurses were available to treat the wounded. I felt like an unneeded extra appendage. I'm looking forward to seeing you all, and returning to my work on the farm and my studies. Trudi wrote that the school was closed because of the epidemic, but I hope that will be over soon and that all of you will stay well.

With all my love,
Clara

The streets of New York were nearly empty. A few people with gauze masks hurried by, but there was nothing like the bustle of life that had greeted Clara last time she passed through. Many of the stores were closed, and the clerks in the open businesses watched nervously, as though dreading a potential customer. For a moment, Clara imagined herself in a war-ravaged village, and she squeezed her eyes shut. Under her own mask, her warm breath tickled her face, a contrast to the cold air.

The wind swept past, rattling through newspapers proclaiming the influenza epidemic over, claiming there was nothing to fear. Yet on a nearly empty streetcar, a sign announced, "Spitting causes death."

Logan wouldn't be this bad, Clara reassured herself. There were fewer people, and in less crowded conditions. Still, she hurried to the train station. Was it just a year ago she had come here and thought it such an adventure?

Clara bought her tickets and found a bench to wait. Grand Central Station felt hollow, cavernous, and subdued. People sat at cautious distances from one another, and the shoeshine stalls were empty.

A woman settled on the other end of Clara's bench. Even with her mask on, she looked stylish in her wool suit trimmed with silk braid, cut to show off a clean, white blouse. Her polish made Clara aware of her own drab cotton dress, a dingy gray button-up. There had been nowhere in France to buy anything new, and Clara had packed away her uniform and left most of her work-worn dresses behind for the refugees.

The woman smiled at her. "Just back from overseas?"

Clara glanced down at herself in dismay. Her clothes must be worse than she thought. "You can tell?"

"We've seen quite a few of you coming this way lately. You all have the same look in your eyes," the woman added gently. "You've seen things that make what we've gone through seem like a holiday, I think."

"It couldn't have been easy here," Clara said quickly.

"No, it's been terrible. Were you a nurse?"

"Ambulance driver."

The woman nodded. "If you'd come through here two months ago, that might have been enough to get you practically kidnapped. All the doctors and nurses were gone, and almost everyone had a family member sick. Some of these poor people had their whole family in one room, and they were all sick—too weak to care for each other. One family member would die, and they'd have to leave them lying with the others, sometimes for days."

Clara felt like she might throw up into her mask. "I'm sorry. I wish I could have helped."

The woman glanced at her. "And you mean that. It's always the women you can count on. You know, the men hold the power, run their corrupt government. Tammany Hall!" the woman said it like a curse. "They appoint their friends to run the health department—men who aren't even real doctors. They don't bother closing the theaters or saloons. Then, when the city shuts down, the women's volunteer organizations are the only ones left to help—the ones they thought were just a quaint way for rich women to put on a patriotic front. They don't want to admit how much they rely on us."

Clara nodded. It had been that way on the front, too. The French gave medals to women who drove ambulances and worked in hospitals, but the Americans pretended they weren't there.

"Where are you from?" the woman asked.

"Utah," Clara said.

"Utah," the woman said slowly, as though she were testing the taste of the word. "Do women have the vote there?"

"Yes, we've had it for a long time."

"Here in New York, we just got it last year. It's one victory at a time, moving the front lines one foot closer with each battle. The war may be over, but our fight isn't."

"No, I suppose it's not," Clara said, wondering again what waited for her in Logan.

Clara watched the familiar scenery whip by outside the train: Ogden, Brigham City, the Wellsville Mountains dusted with the first snows of the season. It looked the same, if not smaller than she remembered. As much as she hoped to find everything safe, it seemed impossible to find it untouched.

The train pulled into Logan station. A few people in flu masks stood on the platform. Clara was out of her seat and rushing forward before she had time to think.

"Mother! 'Lonzo! Trudi!" She threw herself into their arms, slowly registering the fact that Trudi and Alonzo had been holding hands.

She pulled back to grin at them. "When did this happen? Neither of you mentioned it in your letters."

Alonzo took Trudi's hand again. Trudi laughed, her eyes bright above her mask.

"It sort of happened slowly," she said. "And you know how quiet 'Lonzo is about things. We thought we'd tell you when you got back."

Alonzo held up Trudi's hand, and Clara saw the little diamond sparkling in its band. Clara whooped and hugged both of them again while their mother smiled with glowing contentment.

"I'm so happy for both of you. When?"

Trudi and Alonzo shared a glance.

"We were thinking of waiting until all of our friends were home," Trudi said.

"All the ones who are coming home," Alonzo added softly.

Clara nodded and embraced him again. "Oh, 'Lonzo. I'm so sorry about Bert."

"I'm glad he had a friend with him." Alonzo hugged her more tightly.

Clara's mother took her arm and gazed fondly at her as they waited for the streetcar. Clara basked in the familiar comfort of family.

"Are you still writing to Reed?" Trudi asked.

"Yes. Our boys aren't coming home right away, though. A lot of them have gone to Germany. I'm . . . anxious to see him again."

Her mother squeezed her arm. "He's a good young man, all the way through."

Clara met her mother's eyes and saw understanding. A lot had changed, and Reed certainly would have as well. Hopefully the bedrock that made him who he was hadn't been damaged by the artillery shells and horrors of death.

"You're back in time for the parade," Trudi said.

"Parade?"

"For the S.A.T.C. boys. Now that the war's over, they're going home. They've been doing drills and inspections in masks—I wouldn't be surprised if that's how the parade is too. Most people think the precautions are silly."

Clara remembered New York City. "It's not silly. I'm so glad you weren't hit as hard as the East."

Trudi nodded. "Well, they're insisting on the parade, and it'll make the boys feel like they did something. I'm glad they don't have to fight, but I'm sorry they have to leave the college. It was a great chance for them."

Clara nodded.

Trudi glanced at her. "The instructors are staying on, though. There are lots of new classes for the returning students, as soon as they can start regular school again. They say the A.C. has perhaps the best auto mechanics program in the West."

"Really?" Clara perked up.

"Careful," Alonzo said. "They may resist letting women in."

"We'll see," Clara said.

A few days after Clara had settled back into her home, she made the hike up College Hill, wearing one of the nicer dresses she'd left behind. It hung a little loosely on her, but with her mother making all of her favorite pies and dishes, it wouldn't take long for her to fill it out again. College Hill was as steep as she remembered it, but the hike didn't seem as long. She went to President Peterson's office and waited until his secretary admitted her.

"How can I help you, Miss Jensen?" President Peterson asked.

"I'm trying to register for a class and having some difficulty."

"Which class is that?"

"Auto mechanics."

He set down his papers. "Auto mechanics. Why do you want to take that?" He smiled a little. "Are you planning on opening an auto shop?"

"No, but it would be helpful on my family's farm. When I marry, it would be valuable to my husband too. I believe I could take the more advanced classes. I drove an ambulance in France, and I had to do my own repairs."

"Miss Jensen, the war is over. It's time for all of us to return to normal. There are boys—returning soldiers who served their country—who need those classes to find work and support their families. We have new classes available for women now too. Business classes. You can learn to manage a hotel or cafeteria."

"I did that in France too, Sir," Clara said through clenched teeth. "What about a college? Or a city?"

"What?"

"Do you have any classes for women on how to manage a college, or a city?"

"No," he said.

"Then I suppose I'll have to learn it on my own. Good day, Sir."

Clara walked out of the room. It took all of her self-control not to slam the door behind her.

Whatever she was going to do, she would learn to do it on her own. She knew she could. France had taught her she could handle things far beyond her imagining. It was part of a legacy she understood better now. Her ancestors had walked across the plains, burying loved ones along the way, to find freedom and a better life. Her mother had cheerfully raised her children on a farm with a critical, unsupportive husband. The women of Utah were strong.

Like the ladies in Kanab who'd formed the first all-female town council a few years before. The mayor had been elected under an assumed name because she was a polygamous wife who'd spent years on the underground hiding from federal officials so her husband wouldn't go to jail. She'd learned to be tough, to take care of herself, and to cooperate. The men in the town thought it was a good joke, but the women did not. They'd run the town—improved it—while giving birth to children, serving in the Church, and caring for their homes and families. If they could use their experiences to make a difference, so could she.

Clara paced the school grounds, past new buildings under construction. Peterson had gotten what he wanted out of the war—he had helped the college grow—and now he wanted to put everything back into the neat order he envisioned for it. Clara knew, though, that the world wasn't tidy. She'd seen its ugly underbelly, and she wouldn't ignore it, even if everyone was determined to stand in her way.

"Excuse me, are you Miss Jensen?"

She whirled to face a man she didn't recognize. "Yes?"

"I thought so. I heard you wanted to take my class."

"Your class?"

"Auto mechanics."

She studied him warily. He was dressed in a suit, but there were oil stains on his fingers. "How did you hear that?"

"President Peterson told me."

Clara straightened. Was he here to lecture her too? "I do want to take it, but apparently it's not open to women."

"Do you need credit for it, or do you just want to learn?"

Clara considered the question. "The credit would be nice, but I really just want to learn. I only have experience with Model Ts, and the steam engine on my family's farm. I'd like to learn more."

"President Peterson thought you'd feel that way. I can let you sit in on the class. You wouldn't be enrolled, but you'd learn everything the boys would."

"Really?" Clara's dark mood lightened a little. "May I ask why?"

"I like to see students—any students—who take an enthusiasm for the subject. And, my boy fought in the war. I know you were over there helping them. Officially, they may want to forget it, but some of us remember."

Clara's eyes filled with tears. "Thank you, Sir."

He nodded and studied her. "People are scared of change, Miss Jensen. They want to think they can control things, but they can't, and changes are coming at us fast. God may have a hand in human affairs, but all we can control is ourselves—how we react to things."

Clara nodded. Things had already been changing—for her, for Utah, for the world. The war was a crucible, bringing it all to a boil, showing them what was worthwhile and what was dross, if they cared to look. "I think I understand."

He smiled. "I'll see you in class."

XXXIX

Every good citizen makes his country's honor his own, and cherishes it not only as precious but as sacred. He is willing to risk his life in its defense and its conscious that he gains protection while he gives it.

—Andrew Jackson

Joseph spent the next six weeks touring Belgium via hobnail boots, greeted in each town by flowers and cries of "Vive Les Americans" as they marched along. A pretty Belgian girl kissed his cheek and pressed a loaf of bread in his arms. *Ol' Bert would've loved this.* His eyes teared up, though he managed a sad smile for the girl.

They finally received orders to report to their designated port in France, then sat there for weeks waiting for orders to ship home. They sailed on the 2nd of April 1919.

Their ship steamed into New York harbor on the 14th of April. Joseph stood with his fellow soldiers on the rail, taking in the view of the city. There were no cheers from the men. Joseph could feel the emotion around him, but the men seemed lost in thought.

One soldier commented, "There she is boys, the AEF's best girl," pointing to the Statue of Liberty.

"Man, ain't she a sight for sore eyes. That's freedom boys. We are coming to freedom just like our ancestors did."

Joseph smiled at that one, in spite of his somber mood.

The Utah and Wyoming soldiers of the 362nd were sent to Fort D.A. Russell in Wyoming to be demobilized out of the army, which mostly involved documenting their service and their health, and providing onward transportation.

It felt wrong there, lonely, without Bert. Joseph couldn't help noticing the biggest difference between himself and the other men: they were coming home, having served their country. He was coming home, still not a citizen of the country he had served.

He asked one of the sergeants out-processing him if there had been any provisions made for citizenship applications for returning Indian veterans. The answer was no.

Joseph finally boarded a train for home. He arrived in Brigham City on April 30th. He had sent a telegram to his uncle, so he hoped he and his aunt would be there to take him home. They were, along with more than a hundred members of his tribe from Washakie. It was quite a sight. Joseph didn't know whether to be happy or horrified. He straightened his uniform as best he could, carefully donned his wedge-shaped field cap, and stepped off the train.

Among the crowd of conservatively dressed Utahns, Shoshone dancers in traditional costume sang, beat drums, and danced to welcome their returning warrior. He got so many handshakes, slaps on the back, and kisses and hugs that he felt like he had been mugged or dragged behind a horse.

Amid all the chaos, his uncle put both hands on his face and pulled him in until they were eye to eye. "I'm sorry your folks could not be here, Joseph, but know how proud they are of what you have become. You honor your people, Nephew, so today we honor you."

Joseph nodded with tears streaming down his face. He'd represented his people, his friends, and his country to the best of his ability. It was all he ever wanted to do.

XL

Dearest Clara,

We finally got word today that we are to head home at last. We have marched from town to town for weeks now, one German village after another, all across the Rhineland. East, west, than back again. Showing the flag, I guess. We are as confused as the German villagers we meet, though they have been surprisingly kind. They seem relieved it is finally over. In my down time, I've learned to darn socks. The German children all gather to watch the strange American soldier who knits. They'll probably tell stories about me to their children and grandchildren someday.

I can't wait to see you, though I must admit I'm as nervous as a cat on a hot stove. I think of you and home every minute, dreams that sometimes seem so very far away, so unattainable. To know I'll be in that dream soon, living it, is overwhelming. And wonderful. I will see you soon.

Yours,
Reed

Clara jumped down from the trolley at the train station. Her heart beat an erratic pattern, and sweat made her gloves stick to her scarred hands. Alonzo helped Trudi down after her, and they followed Clara with their arms linked. A crowd milled around the train platform. A few people still wore masks, but for most the terror of the influenza had passed.

"Are you sure about this, Clara?" Trudi asked quietly. "I know you've been writing to each other, but a lot can change in two years."

"I'm sure," Clara said. She clutched Reed's last letter to her chest.

She knew even better than Trudi how much things could change. The mountains around them, once so confining, now provided a close comfort, keeping the violence and horror of the war at bay.

A young man and a girl about her age stood next to her. The girl clutched the man's arm, her face lit with excitement. The young man kept his straight posture, his soldier's training showing through his civilian clothing.

The girl noticed Clara's gaze and smiled. "Who are you waiting for?"

"A . . . friend," Clara said. "What about you?"

"Our brother." The girl bounced on her toes a little as she spoke. "We'll finally have our family together again. Everything will be back to normal."

The young man's jaw tightened, and he gave his sister a worried look. When she glanced at him, he smiled, but his eyes remained sad.

Clara looked away. She had seen that same sorrow in too many young men's eyes. The mountains couldn't keep out everything. The soldiers coming home carried the battle with them. Even the ones with visible scars were expected to show off their medals and then pack them away. As if they didn't still have nightmares filled with shrieking, sobbing men and the never-ending voices of the guns.

Clara wondered how everyone else missed seeing their burdens. Maybe they just didn't want to. Most of the soldiers bore it in silence. Others, though, carried a spark of anger that flashed to life at times, frightening Clara. She had to see Reed, look in his eyes, and then she would know if he was still *her* Reed.

The train's whistle announced its approach. The crowd leaned forward as if pulled by a single string, their faces lined with an anxious hope and excitement.

The train doors opened. Passengers disembarked, and the crowd erupted in gasps, laughter, and tears. Clara realized she was holding her breath and forced herself to exhale slowly.

A young man limped past her, a crutch under his arm. Clara recognized his gait from the hospital. He had an artificial leg, though his pants hid the prosthetic. Still, the crowd shifted away from him, leaving him alone as he worked his way across the platform. Clara met his eyes and smiled, and he returned a wary nod. A woman who must have been his mother rushed forward to embrace him, and he closed his eyes. A look of peace settled on his features, momentarily erasing the pain creasing his forehead.

Clara looked back at the train just as Reed stepped off. She recognized his figure immediately, though he was, if anything, more fit and lean.

"Reed!" she called, but her voice caught in her throat, drowned by the happy cries around her.

He scanned the crowd, and Clara stepped back, her heart beating fast. Reed's cockiness had been replaced by calm self-assurance. His face was no longer smiling, but weary and a little sad. Something else too. Hopeful and nervous.

"Reed!" Clara made her voice louder that time, and his head snapped in her direction.

His gaze found hers, and he pushed his way forward, his face lighting up with a grin. It wasn't the same flirtatious smile he had always worn, but something warmer and deeper.

When he reached her, they stood staring at each other for a moment—two people in a swirling, chattering crowd with the train rumbling impatiently behind them—and they could have been alone. Silent understanding passed between them, a kinship born of suffering.

Reed folded her into his arms, held her tightly for a moment, breathed, "Clara" into her ear. Then he bent her back and kissed her fiercely, as if he were trying to sweep them back two years to before everything happened. She kissed him in return, clutching him close, showing him she was still there.

XLI

Dear Clara,

How I miss you and the other YMCA girls. Home doesn't seem like home anymore, and I wish I could talk to someone who understood.

My fiancé, Billy, has been missing since the Argonne-Meuse. I keep hoping one day we'll get a letter from him in some hospital in England. Or even better, see him walking up the street, whistling like he always did. Every day that passes, though, a little more of my hope dies. At this point, I would even appreciate bad news of him. Anything but not knowing.

My mother and sisters have talked to me about dating again, but I never will. Billy didn't want to marry me before he left because he didn't want to leave me a war widow, but in my heart, I already am. I plan to devote my life to nursing. With every person I care for, I'll imagine I'm helping my Billy. I'm going to a rally tonight to tell my story. I hope I can convince people that America should never go to war again.

Please don't neglect to write to me. The things we saw will always haunt me, but the burden is less oppressive when there's someone to share it with.

Your friend,
Lily

Clara crossed Main Street in Logan at 200 North to meet Reed in front of Logan Garage and Supply. He was nowhere to be seen. The parade was supposed to start in an hour and they had both promised to take part. People were already setting out chairs to hold spots along the route. There were American flags and bunting on the buildings and the streetlights. She could just make out the lead floats, and it looked like Americana was the main feature of those as well. A half hour passed, still no sign of Reed. She decided to go to her assigned float for the parade.

As she walked past the lead floats, she cringed at some of them. There was a giant box-shaped representation of a battlefield complete with trenches on both ends, doughboys, and fake, pointy-hatted German soldiers to face them over the no-man's land in the middle.

She could not decide what her assigned float was supposed to represent, other than an attempt to completely cover the Ford truck laboring underneath. A huge flag covered the cab. Clara wondered if there were eyeholes in it for the poor driver.

The back of the float was a nicely scalloped white canopy, with red roses along the seams and more roses in large bouquets at every corner. One of the soldiers standing alongside helped her up, and she sat on a white muslin-covered box for her ride down Main Street. *Well, at least it's a pleasant place to sit.*

The float leading the parade was even more confusing than hers: some poor girl painted completely green in a lady liberty costume, holding up the eternal flame for the whole route with no obvious signs of support. Standing next to her were what looked like Roman legionnaires, complete with swords and helmets.

Clara wore her battered but clean and pressed olive drab ambulance driver's uniform with her Sam Browne belt and matching hat. She left off the goggles—no mud or driving rain on this gorgeous day. Reed's Marine Corps insignia was on her lapel, as always. The gold paint had long since worn off from her rubbing it.

The sight of all the soldiers and sailors, safe at home, filled Clara with a warm sense of peace. Some of the men wore the uniforms they had worn home, others civilian suits with ribbons denoting their service. Clara even saw a Marine serving as part of the color guard, and she knew Reed would laugh to see the blue tunic. *Where was he?*

The parade began, moving slowly south down Main Street. The marching band played patriotic songs and the crowd waved at Clara and she waved back, but she doubted more than a few of them knew why the heck she was riding on a float. It was still nice, if just to see the crowd save its loudest applause for the loose formations of returning veterans, all mixed together with different uniforms, headgear, and civilian attire. It seemed right to Clara, that these men who were in the midst of transitioning back to civilian life were honored in this way. She could testify to how much they deserved this recognition.

As her float passed Logan Garage, she spotted Alonzo and Trudi standing on the curb with her mother, applauding and shouting her name. Trudi carried a lovely bouquet of flowers and she ran up to the float and handed them up to Clara, blowing her a kiss. "We haven't seen Reed yet, where is he?"

"I don't know. We were supposed to meet here before the parade and he stood me up," Clara said. "I'm going to find him after and let him have it good."

"Sure you will," Trudi laughed as she walked along. "He'll just flash that grin and you'll melt like ice cream on a July sidewalk! We'll see you two later."

After the parade, Clara bypassed the celebrations on the tabernacle grounds and walked all the way to Reed's fraternity, missing her Tin Lizzie more than ever. She found Reed sitting on the floor of his living room, staring out the window. He wore his best green service uniform, his Croix de Guerre and Silver Star medals for heroism neatly in place on his tunic.

When he saw her, he scrambled to get up, but Clara put her hand on his shoulder. "No, I want to sit with you." She eased herself down on the hard floor next to him. The look of pain on his face made her forget all about being stood up.

"I'm very sorry. It was rude and thoughtless. I should have told you yesterday," Reed said, his head drooping, refusing to look Clara in the eyes.

"Tell me what?"

"That I just couldn't march in that parade. I thought I could make myself do it. I put all this back on." He gestured at his uniform. "I meant to be there for you. I'm so sorry."

"There's no need for that. But I want to know what's really troubling you. You deserve the recognition, just like the rest of the boys."

Reed closed his eyes. "No, I don't. All those people along the route, many are someone's parents. Maybe they lost a son. I lined up whole bunches of their sons and led them into a meat grinder. They all died, Clara. They all died, then the corps gave me more, and I got half of them killed as well. If I hadn't been shot, I would've gotten the rest of them pinked too. I'm dang fine at doing that."

"But, you had no choice. You did your duty. You know those men followed you for a reason, right? They respected you. You had a job to do, and you all did it!"

"I doubt that would satisfy any mother whose son got cut in half by a Maxim. She might wonder why I get to be here with my shiny medals, and her son is rotting in some mass grave at Belleau Wood. I wonder about that myself, about twenty-three hours a day. Last night I dreamt I was in the parade, and the parents of all my men were there, staring at me in contempt. My parents were there too. They tell me they're proud, but in my dream, they saw that I'm a failure, a fraud. They were so disappointed. And you looked at me like . . ."

"Oh, Reed. I would never . . ." Clara's heart ached at the misery clouding his expression. She gently took his hand and rubbed his calloused fingers. "I never led anyone. I was only responsible for myself. But I saw the war in all its horror, over and over. You're asking a lot of yourself to take the blame for war being what it is, not to mention questioning the Lord's will in your own life. Perhaps the question in your mind shouldn't be, 'why was I spared?' but rather, 'what is my purpose now?' Maybe answering the second question will help you cope with the first. We've seen some terrible things, but God doesn't want us to stay unhappy."

Reed's face relaxed a little, and he laid his hand over hers. "I hope you're right. For now, it's enough to be here with you, sitting on this old oak floor. If I have you, anything else is possible."

"I'd prefer a nice sofa, but you, I'll keep." Clara smiled.

Reed tightened his grip on her hand. "Do you mean that, Clara?"

"Of course."

He studied her for several moments, his expression somber. "Would you . . . do you think you'd want to stay with me forever? I know I'm not who I was when we first met, but . . . I think you're right about God's hand in our lives, and I believe I met you—fell in love with you—for a reason. Whatever my purpose is now, I'd like you to be there with me."

For just a moment, the old desire to flee fluttered in Clara's chest, but it melted away at the thought of a future side-by-side with Reed.

After everything they'd faced, they were ready for whatever challenges came their way. "There's nowhere else I want to be."

Reed smiled in relief and leaned in to steal a kiss.

XLII

BE IT ENACTED . . . that every American Indian who served in the Military or Naval Establishments of the United States during the war against the Imperial German Government, and who has received or who shall hereafter receive an honorable discharge, if not now a citizen and if he so desires, shall, on proof of such discharge and after proper identification before a court of competent jurisdiction, and without other examination except as prescribed by said court, be granted full citizenship with all the privileges pertaining thereto, without in any manner impairing or otherwise affecting the property rights, individuals or tribal, of any such Indian or his interest in tribal or other Indian property.
—1919 American Indian Citizenship Act

Joseph Sorrell stood on the steps of the courthouse with his aunt and uncle by his side, watching as his Logan friends pulled up to the curb. He wore his uniform for this one last time, proud of its somewhat faded color, the hard roads he had traveled in it, the pine tree patch of the Wild West Division still on his shoulder.

It was a lovely spring morning. Sunshine kissed the beautiful courthouse building all the way up the bell tower, as if highlighting the importance of the day. Spring. Time for things to begin anew after long, hard dormancy. Fitting.

He smiled to see Clara Lewis driving, Reed sitting sheepishly to her right. She'd asked for a car to fix up instead of a fancy wedding ring, and she'd had it running in time for their honeymoon. Trudi and Alonzo sat in the rear seat, huddling closer together than the balmy weather probably required. A second car pulled in behind Clara. Bert's parents, Mr. and Mrs. Lyman.

The Logan group walked up the steps and stopped in front of Joseph on the landing. Everyone looked a little awkward until Clara stepped forward with a big smile and hugged Joseph, then his aunt and uncle in turn.

Reed shook Joseph's hand. "Well, I think Clara's glad to see you! So am I, my friend."

"Thank you for coming. It means a great deal to me." He turned toward Bert's parents. "Mr. and Mrs. Lyman, I'm so happy to see you here. Welcome."

Mrs. Lyman hugged Joseph for a long time. She stepped back, still holding him by the arms. "Bert wouldn't have missed this, Joseph, nor would we."

"He's with us, always," Joseph said, touching his breast pocket where he carried Bert's pocket watch. "Let's go inside. The judge is waiting for us."

They filed into the judge's chambers and stood by Joseph's side as he raised his hand to take the oath as a citizen of the United States of America.

The judge began, "Mr. Joseph Sorrell. By an act of the Congress of the United States, dated November 6, 1919, Indians who served in the last war are granted the right to petition for United States citizenship. Having duly filed said petition, it is my honor to administer the oath of citizenship to you today."

The judge offered Joseph a sheet of paper from which to read, but there was no need. He knew it by heart. He promised to support and defend the Constitution. He promised to take up arms in defense of his nation when required. He certified he took the oath freely and without reservation. All these things he believed in his heart. All these things he had lived.

After hearty handshakes and hugs all around, the group gathered on the courthouse lawn for a picnic. Clara, Trudi, and Mrs. Lyman laid out the baskets and served the food while the men tossed blankets down to sit on the still-damp ground.

"Joseph, what will you do now? What are your plans?" Reed asked.

"Well, I expect I'll keep farming with Uncle. All I dreamed about over there was living this life again. Funny how much I missed all the chores! I wondered a couple times this winter if I was off my knocker when I wanted to be back here so bad," Joseph chuckled. "I'm also gonna work up another string of race horses. Already got Buckskin Nelly with foal so that's a good start."

"You're not gonna race that mare anymore?"

"Nah. She's almost seven now. Probably better as a brood mare."

"That's too bad. Missed some of her prime while you were gone."

Joseph nodded. "Yes, but some of my people who served lost far more than that. They came back and found their families had to sell off their land, their livestock too. They didn't have much to begin with, now they have nothing. I'm lucky Uncle was able to keep the farm without me."

"That just seems so wrong," Reed said. "At least Congress saw fit to recognize your service and grant citizenship. That's a start."

Clara sat down on the blanket, lowering herself carefully, and Reed paused to help her settle comfortably beside him.

He continued, "Of course, now you'll have the dang politicians courting your vote every election. Bandwagons and empty promises, oh boy!"

Clara shot Reed a sharp look.

"What did I say?" Reed complained, "I already meekly submitted when you wanted to drive Lizzie."

"Reed, Utah hasn't granted Indians the right to vote," Clara said.

"How is that possible? Don't citizens get the right to vote?"

Joseph spoke up. "Not in Utah. States have the power to decide who can vote. They see us as not being residents of the state since we have our own nation."

Reed shook his head. "So you can fight for your country, maybe die for it, but not decide who represents you in its government? The wrongs just pile up, and you can't shovel to the bottom of it."

"Yes, we still have some fighting to do," Clara said. Based on the steely look in her eyes, Joseph pitied whichever politician she decided was her enemy.

He changed the subject. "What's next for you and Clara?"

Reed and Clara shared sly smiles.

"I saw that look. What news in the Lewis family?"

Clara demurred. "I don't know what you mean, Mr. Sorrell. Of course, we have 'Lonzo and Trudi's wedding to plan for this summer. We're both busy with college and establishing our little home together."

Joseph laughed. "That's not it, is it, Mrs. Lewis?"

Clara smiled. "This is your special day, Joseph. We didn't want to intrude with any Lewis family news."

"I saw how carefully you sat down. Either you fell off a horse, or . . ."

"Very well. We're expecting a baby around mid-September," Clara said.

"That's wonderful," Joseph cried. "I was thinking about spring as you pulled up. New beginnings, how life goes on after a hard winter. My life lies before me, as does yours. Many blessings to you both."

Reed nodded and stood to face everyone. "I spoke to Mr. and Mrs. Lyman about this earlier, but I wanted you to know, especially you Joseph, that we have picked a name for this child, if it's a boy."

"What's the name?" Joseph asked.

"Bert Lyman Lewis."

"A good name," Joseph said, tears in his eyes. "A warrior's name."

Discussion Questions

1. Why do you think young men and women like Reed, Bert, and Clara, who had the rare opportunity to go to college in 1917, would give up so much to serve in Europe?

2. Alonzo hated conflict and felt that the American government was not justified in entering the war. When do you believe your country should become involved in fighting overseas? Are there times it should not? Should citizens be allowed to decide if they're willing to fight, or do they have the obligation to adhere to their government's decision?

3. What do you think about how German-speakers like Trudi were treated during the war? What about the native peoples like Joseph and the Shoshone? How would such treatment make you feel about your citizenship? How would it change life in your home town?

4. During World War I, there was little understanding of post-traumatic stress disorder. How did this increase the challenges faced by veterans returning from the war? Why might society have been slow to recognize these challenges?

5. How did their participation in the war efforts affect the individual characters? How do you think the war affected society as a whole?

Historical Notes

November 1915, Logan, Utah

The *A.C. Student Life*, the *Logan Republican*, and *The Stars and Stripes* featured in this novel are all real newspapers, but they are used fictitiously here. The articles in the novel, though based on real sentiments of the time, are, for the most part, not exact quotes from the papers.

The Gwent Royal Welsh Singers toured the United States multiple times. They were highly popular, almost the Beetles of their time. Originally a choir numbering more than 20, they split up into smaller groups to tour. The group that performed in Logan and Salt Lake City was originally seven members, three of whom drowned in the sinking of the *Lusitania*. They were described in period newspapers as a quartet.

The Bluebird in Logan opened in 1914 and was a popular ice cream parlor among college students. In 1923, it moved to its present location, and it is the now the oldest restaurant in Logan.

Football was huge at the A.C., though the team did not always live up to expectations. Descriptions of the action in Student Life *took on a martial feel as war approached.*

Courtesy of USU Special Collections and Archives

June 1916, Logan, Utah

Military Summer Camp at Monterey, California in 1915 and 1916 was part of the Preparedness Movement, or Plattsburg Movement, an effort led by Theodore Roosevelt and General Leonard Wood to prepare the U.S. for "armed neutrality." Captain George C. Marshall was the commanding officer at Monterey in 1916. He went on to become the Chief of Staff of the U.S. Army during World War II, and later Secretary of State and Secretary of Defense.

Moses Foss Cowley was an accomplished student at the U.A.C. He was a "big man" on campus. Little is known about his life after college. He served in World War I as an army officer, serving until at least 1922 as a captain. He died in Salt Lake City in 1929. He was the son of Matthias F. Cowley, one of the Twelve Apostles of the LDS Church. The elder Cowley was excommunicated from the Church due to his continuing support of plural marriage, though he later rejoined the LDS Church. Moses's half-brother Samuel P. Cowley also graduated from the Utah Agricultural College. He became an FBI Special Agent. He partnered with Melvin Purvis to catch John Dillinger. He was killed in a gunfight with George "Baby Face" Nelson in 1934.

Baseball, usually written as two words in those days, was still a young sport in 1916. It was very popular in Cache Valley, where nearly every town hosted a team. A baseball game on a Saturday afternoon was so important that some farmers suspended the harvest so they could attend. The Washakie Shoshone fielded a team for many years.

Aggie Baseball Team, Circa 1916.

Courtesy of USU Special Collections and Archives

September 1916, Logan, Utah

Model "T" Fords of the type driven by Clara did indeed perform better uphill when driven in reverse. This was because the carburetor was fed fuel by gravity, not by a fuel pump. It would often come to a complete stop when driving up a steep hill.

Der Deutsche Verein, or German-speaking Club, met regularly on campus and seemed to have wide support. It disappeared during the war without explanation, though it's not hard to understand why.

Debate was a big deal on campus. Students competed in various oratorical contents, which received extensive coverage in *Student Life*, the campus newspaper. They also competed in various debates representing their class or clubs. The college formed teams to compete with the other Utah universities and with colleges in the region. Like Clara, a few women stepped into what had been a male-dominated arena, competing individually to join the college team.

Joseph "Kaiser" Havertz was a custodian on the U.A.C. campus. A Mormon convert, he immigrated to Cache Valley in the 1890s with his family from Cologne, Germany. He was highly popular with the students, and they often wrote snippets about him for the school paper. They said he was so good at ringing the college's bell that he could play "Deutschland Uber-Alles" on it. They also described his skills as a baseball umpire, a story we used in our fictitious game. The stories they told about him seemed to have been in good fun and based on their affection for him. But as time passed, and anti-German sentiment soared in the last years of the war, Havertz complained about being called "Kaiser." He considered himself a loyal American who bought Liberty Bonds. At home, he forbade the speaking of German. This would have been hard on Mrs. Havertz, as she did not speak English well and did not work outside the home. Joseph's son graduated from the college and became a career U.S. Army Officer. His son, Dr. David S. Havertz, is an Emeritus Professor of Zoology at Weber State University. Dr. Havertz also served his country in the U.S. Air Force.

Buckskin Nelly was a real Shoshone racehorse. She won many races and no doubt surprised those who bet against her. Horse racing was a much more popular sport during the early part of the twentieth century, and while betting on races was illegal in Utah, friendly wagers no doubt changed hands as spectators were caught up in the excitement of the sport.

The Washakie Shoshone are a branch of the Shoshone whose leader joined the LDS Church following the Bear River Massacre. They helped build the LDS temple in Logan and settled on church allotments in Washakie, Utah, rather than join other Shoshone on the Fort Hall reservation in Idaho.

October 1916, Logan, Utah

The Marraine de Guerre program was an effort to provide comfort to French troops cut off from home because of how the Western Front developed. Pen pals in the U.S sent letters of encouragement and small comfort packages to help cheer the *Poilus*, as the French soldiers were known.

Boche, Hun, Fritz, Heine, Krauts. In every war, the sides think of derogatory names by which to refer to the other side. The Germans seemed to generate a record number of nicknames. Joseph refers to them as "Dutchmen," though of course he would have known they were not Dutch. The term Dutch was commonly used in the U.S. to refer to German-speaking peoples generally. For example, we still say "Pennsylvania Dutch," even though most of those immigrants were actually German. It was not used as a derogatory term until the period this novel is set in.

November 1916, Logan, Utah

Jeannette Rankin of Montana was the first woman elected to the U.S. Congress. She was a pacifist, and she voted against entering both World War I and World War II. She was proud to be the only woman to vote on the Nineteenth Amendment, giving all women the right to vote in 1919. Kanab, Utah, is the first known U.S. municipality to have an all-female city government. Switzerland did not give all women the right to vote until 1971.

Loud Socks Day was an annual celebration held on campus at the end of November. We haven't been able to find its origins or when the tradition stopped, though it seems to have happened during the war years, which ended an upbeat era for the U.S. as well as the rest of the nation and the world.

About 200 LDS missionaries were serving in the Swiss and German Mission (headquartered in Switzerland) at the beginning of World War I. They had been expelled from Germany on several occasions, and Church members and missionaries there were frequently arrested and persecuted. The missionaries were evacuated at the onset of the war, but the mission was never officially closed, and many of the local Church branches continued functioning during the war despite ongoing harassment. After the Armistice, the LDS Church provided food and supplies to starving German civilians and reestablished missionary work in 1921 to a more religiously tolerant population (at least in regards to Mormonism). The first LDS temple outside of North America was the Bern Switzerland Temple, dedicated in 1955.

Thanksgiving 1916, Greenville, Utah

The town once known as Greenville, Utah, in Cache Valley is now called North Logan.

Though the LDS Church's health code, known as the Word of Wisdom, dates back to the early days of the Church, it was considered a suggestion rather than a commandment until after World War I, so some Mormons in good standing still drank coffee, tea, or alcohol, or smoked. Still, many Mormons who fought in World War I were glad not to have a nicotine habit, as they could trade their cigarette rations for other necessities.

March 1917, Logan, Utah

Logan had a large population of German speakers, mainly from Switzerland, but also from Germany. Most of these had come to the United States as Mormon converts, and settled in Logan near the missionaries who taught them about the Church and sponsored their immigration. The Tenth Ward section of northeast Logan was known for many years as "Little Berlin." Originally, the LDS Church sponsored a German-speaking branch in Logan, but it was quietly shut down during World War I.

September 1917, Paris Island, South Carolina

Parris Island, South Carolina is a primary basic training site for U.S. Marines. It was spelled with one "R" until the 1920s. The land had belonged to a man named Parris, and evidently the name change was just a spelling correction, not some statement against our great friends in France.

Soldiers in World War I certainly received "Dear John" letters. Perhaps the most famous of these was Ernest Hemingway; he was snubbed by a nurse he had fallen for while he was recuperating from his wounds. The expression "Dear John" was probably not in common usage at the time as far as we can tell, though we could not find a period-appropriate term.

November 1917, Logan, Utah

Guy Alexander and Claytor Preston were indeed victims of the tragic train accident described in the narrative. They were among the first Utah soldiers killed as a result of the war. This incident really brought the war "home" to Utah in a shocking, visceral way. The Logan Tabernacle was packed beyond capacity for their funeral and the people lined the streets for their funeral procession. There was a third Utah victim of the train crash and, like the fictional Earl Johnson, he had a separate, probably private, funeral.

Some Native Americans who were denied U.S. citizenship were drafted in the U.S. Army, despite the promise of the government that noncitizens would not be drafted. The Shoshone and Goshute of Idaho and Utah protested at being asked to register for the draft and fight for a government that treated them as second class, at best. Many were arrested and forced to register. On the other hand, many Native Americans saw serving in the war as a way to prove themselves and their loyalty. Members of the Choctaw tribe acted as "code talkers" for the U.S. in World War I, paving the way for the more famous Navajo code talkers of World War II.

December 1917, Camp Lewis

Moichi Kuramoto probably never would have crossed paths with Joseph and Bert since he was drafted after they were, but his story shows how minority groups experienced the war differently. He was born in Hawaii to Japanese parents, but was drafted from Perry, Box Elder Country, Utah, according to his draft registration card. He doesn't seem to have gone overseas during the war, serving instead as a private in a Depot Brigade in New York, which helped to train and equip troops going "Over There." The 1920 U.S. Census shows that he survived the influenza epidemic that ravaged the East Coast training camps, and was married and farming in Payson, Utah. Again following him through census records, he and his large family moved to California during the Great Depression, and were still living there in 1940. He died in California in April 1941, early enough to miss Pearl Harbor, but his wife, Ichiyo, and his Utah- and California-born children were imprisoned in Rohwer War Relocation Camp in Arkansas. At about the time his family was sent to live behind barbed wire as potential enemy aliens, his military veteran headstone was delivered to the Lodi Cemetery in California where he was buried. His wife and children returned to California after World War II.

December 1917, New York City, New York

Pilots in slow moving airplanes of the day could have been heard as they passed by, particularly over water, which reflects sound well.

December 1917, Paris, France

Despite the rampant prejudice and violence they faced in the U.S., over 200,000 African American men served overseas in the U.S. armed forces in World War I—the only American ethnic group to serve in segregated units during World War I. Only a handful of African American women are known to have been allowed to go overseas, all with the YMCA, though others may have "passed" as white to help the troops. The African American YMCA women had to fight against prejudice and bureaucracy to finally be allowed to serve with the African American troops. In reality, the first African American YMCA worker didn't arrive in Paris until early 1918, a little after the scene we included in the story, but it is otherwise an accurate representation of the experience of those pioneering women.

A German Zeppelin like the one Clara heard in Paris.

Courtesy of USU Special Collections and Archives

January 1918, Brest, France

Captain George Wallis Hamilton was a real Marine officer, the "Bravest of the Brave." He fought in every battle the U.S. Marines participated in during the war, serving both as a company, then as a battalion commander. He was awarded two Distinguished Service Crosses, the Navy Cross, and four Silver Stars. He was nominated for the Medal of Honor, and would almost certainly have received it, had General Pershing's staff not resisted recognition of Marines. He survived the war without a scratch. He became a Marine Aviator. During an annual demonstration of how the Marines would fight the Battle of Gettysburg with modern tactics and equipment in 1922, he crashed his aircraft on the battlefield and died in a place so many other Americans gave their lives for their country.

March 1918, Verdun, France

The Battle of Verdun took place in 1916. When Reed and Hamilton fight there, it is after they occupied the same trench lines, nearly two years later.

March 1918, Somewhere in France

Post Traumatic Stress Disorder, or shell shock, was not well understood during World War I, and those who suffered from it were often stigmatized and denied combat benefits and medical help for fear it would encourage their behavior.

Women performed many important jobs for the military during World War I. Nurses are probably the best known, but women also worked in YMCA huts with refugees and soldiers, operated telephones, did clerical work, and drove ambulances, earning medals for heroism and sometimes being killed in the line of duty. Despite this, even those women who worked directly for the military and not for private companies were not treated as veterans in the U.S. or recognized for their service until many years after the war. Clara's experience is loosely based on a real Utah woman, Maud Fitch. Maud went overseas to be an ambulance driver, but because of the disorganization she encountered, she ended up working several jobs in addition to driving wounded men from the front, and she received the French Croix de Guerre for her bravery. Her wartime letters are housed in the State Archives of Utah.

June 1918, Belleau Wood, France

The Marines were rushed to Belleau Wood in Camions, or buses, due to the crises caused by the huge German offensive across the Marne. The French had rushed some of the brave *Poilus* there in 1914 via taxis to face the first German attempt on Paris.

Private Joseph M. Baker was one of so many Marine heroes at Belleau Wood. Private Baker took out a machine gun position by himself, earning the Distinguished Service Cross, and later the Navy Cross.

A field funeral in France, much like that described following Reed's experience at Belleau Wood.

Courtesy of USU Special Collections and Archives

July 1918, Logan, Utah

Nels Anderson, an LDS serviceman who kept a rare (and forbidden, for enlisted men) diary of his experiences in World War I, commented on his surprise and amusement on finding that many other soldiers thought Mormons practiced "free love." He corrected the false notion, but encountered many other misconceptions about his beliefs during his service overseas.

Though Britain had a legal minimum age of eighteen to serve in the armed forces, it was easy for tall young men to lie about their age. Since recruiting officers were paid for every man they enlisted, and the army badly needed soldiers, they were motivated to look the other way. Sidney Lewis was the youngest soldier to fight with the British Army at age twelve. He fought in the Battle of the Somme at age thirteen, until his mother proved his age by showing his birth certificate and he was sent home. As many as one in three British sailors were between the ages of fourteen and seventeen.

October 1918, Logan, Utah

Influenza, or the Spanish flu, was a devastating worldwide pandemic brought on by the conditions of war, with people traveling back and forth in unsanitary conditions. It was called the Spanish influenza because Spain, which was not participating in the war, was one of the few countries to allow newspapers to print factual accounts of the spread of the disease. It appears to have actually originated in the United States. The first round of the disease in the spring of 1918 was relatively mild, but the flu that struck during the fall of 1918 crippled troops on both sides of the front and on the home front. Unlike most variations of the flu, it was often young men and women in the prime of life who were struck by the influenza of 1918, often falling victims to the overreactions of their own immune systems. Victims in major U.S. cities were sometimes buried in mass graves, and entire cities were shut down. The war effort was affected as well, though the government continued to send sick men to the front.

Soldiers in training being fed on campus at the A.C. The Spanish flu crept through their ranks and the A.C. doubled as a military training center and hospital.

Courtesy of USU Special Collections and Archives

Nurses meeting returning soldiers at the Logan Train Depot in 1919. Note they were still wearing masks even though the threat of Spanish flu had largely passed.

Courtesy of USU Special Collections and Archives

November 11, 1918,
A field hospital behind the Meuse-Argonne lines

Though we often think of "Man's Best Friend" as referring to dogs, the cavalry sometimes used the term for horses instead. A horse barn (later known as the Art Barn) was built on the A.C. campus in 1919 to replace the older barn torn down to construct barracks for soldiers in training (now classrooms surrounding the quad), and it bore an inscription over the door, "Man's Best Friend," framed by horseshoes. The exact inspiration for the quote is unknown, and the university demolished the historic building in 2015, but it may have owed its origins to cavalry training in fields such as blacksmithing on campus.

A horse blown into a tree by artillery in France. Nels Anderson described a scene like this in his memoir. One of the many horrors of war.

Courtesy of USU Special Collections and Archives

283

For Further Reading

Barry, John M. *The Great Influenza*. New York City: Penguin House, 2009.

Britten, Thomas A. *American Indians in World War I: At War and At Home*. University of New Mexico Press, 1998.

Clark, George B. *Devil Dogs: Fighting Marines of World War I*. Presidio Press, 1999.

Gavin, Lettie. *American Women in World War I: They Also Served*. University Press of Colorado, 2006.

Johnson, Thomas M. *The Lost Battalion*. Bison Books, 2000.

Krause, Susan Applegate, *North American Indians in the Great War*. University of Nebraska Press, 2007.

Kreitzer, Matthew E. "NW Shoshone Sports of the Washakie Colony of Northern Utah," 1903–1929, in *Sport in a Global Society*, C. Richard Kind, ed., Rutledge, 2008.

Meldrum, T. Ben, *A History of the 362nd Infantry*. A.L. Scoville, 1920.

Nelson, Lowry. *In the Direction of his Dreams: Memoirs*. Philosophical Library, 1985.

Powell, Allan Kent, ed. *Nels Anderson's World War I Diary*. Salt Lake City: University of Utah Press, 2013.

Tuchman, Barbara. *The Guns of August: The Outbreak of World War I*. Random House reprint, 1994.

Acknowledgments

We'd like to thank the entire staff at Utah State University's Special Collections and Archives, especially Bob Parsons, Dan Davis, and Randy Williams. Their research assistance and advice were invaluable as we parsed through the primary source material in their care. We are also grateful to the staff at the Utah State Archives for making Maud Fitch's letters available to us, and the American West Heritage Center archives for their materials on social and cultural history in Cache Valley.

We were very fortunate to have some highly qualified early readers whose advice and encouragement were absolutely critical. Among them are: Dr. Tammy M. Proctor, Department Head of History at USU; Anne Stark, Lecturer in Creative Writing at USU and fellow novelist; great friends Paul and Catherine Ermer, whose support means so much; faithful beta reader Sherrie Lynn Clarke; fellow WWI novelist A.L. Sowards; the members of UPSSEFW; and the Cache Valley Chapter of the League of Utah Writers, whose thorough critiques of every chapter of this book improved it immensely, and whose consistent support will not soon be forgotten.

Special thanks to Dr. David S. Havertz, for taking the time to talk with us about his grandfather, Joseph Havertz. It was so great to be able to tell Joseph's story. Also to Janean, Diane, and the rest of the Huppi family for their insights into Logan's Little Berlin and Swiss immigration to Cache Valley, to Chris and Chrissa Rogers and Nicole Fuerst for language advice, and to Bob and Virginia Harris for letting us climb all over their Ford Model T and for Bob's great stories of motoring in Cache Valley.

Thanks to Emma Parker, Emily Chambers, Michelle May, Jessica Romwell and the entire team at Cedar Fort Press. What a great experience working with you on this book!

Last, but never least, thanks to our families for your patience, encouragement, critiques, and support. We could not do this without you.

E.B. Wheeler

E.B. Wheeler attended Brigham Young University, majoring in history with an English minor, and earned graduate degrees in history and landscape architecture from Utah State University. *No Peace with the Dawn* is her third novel. She's the award-winning author of *The Haunting of Springett Hall* and *Born to Treason*, as well as several short stories, magazine articles, and scripts for educational software programs. In addition to writing, she consults about historic preservation and teaches Utah history at USU. She lives in the mountains of Utah with her family.

Scan to visit

ebwheeler.com

Jeffery Bateman

Jeff served in the U.S. Air Force for 32 years, retiring as a colonel in 2010. He holds an MA in history from Utah State University and an MS in strategic studies from U.S. Army War College. Following his military career, Jeff worked as a civilian historian at the Air Force Research Laboratory and the Air Force Flight Test Center. His work as an historian has been published in several peer-reviewed journals and other platforms, including the *Utah Historical Quarterly*, Airpower History, and the U.S. Army War College Press. Jeff currently teaches Utah history, American military history, and U.S. Institutions at Utah State University. An award-winning member of the League of Utah Writers, Jeff is the author of *On the Death Beat*, forthcoming in 2017, Grey Gecko Press, and coauthor of *No Peace with the Dawn*, Cedar Fort Publishing. Jeff lives on a mini-farm in Hyde Park, where horses, gardening, and playing the bass fill the time he isn't writing or teaching.

Scan to visit

jsbateman.com